THE NEW YORK DETECTIVE

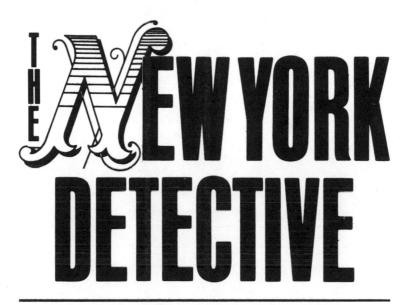

THE NEW YORK DETECTIVE

WILLIAM MARSHALL

THE MYSTERIOUS PRESS

New York • London
Tokyo • Sweden • Milan

Copyright © 1989 by William Marshall

The Mysterious Press, 129 West 56th Street, New York, N.Y. 10019

Printed in the United States of America
First Printing: December 1989
10 9 8 7 6 5 4 3 2 1

Library of Congress Cataloging-in-Publication Data

Marshall, William Leonard, 1944–
    The New York detective / William Marshall.
        p.   cm.
    ISBN 0–89296–366–2
    I. Title.
PR9619.3.M275N49   1989
823—dc20

89–42605
CIP

This is for Bill Malloy

1

He could see next week's edition of the *National Police Gazette* now. *Saturday, May 26, 1883:*

FAUCET FIEND STRIKES AGAIN!
UNPLUGGED TO PENURY!
Flush Gent Flushed to Fiscal Fix
Are Our New York Detectives All Fools?
Third Awful Incident in a Month!

In the great marble and tile cathedral de piss in Niblo's Garden Theatre under the rear of the Metropolitan Hotel on the corner of Broadway and Prince Street, the caped and top-hatted Master Criminal, piston pumping his shoulders and nodding, said, "Yes! Yes!" Grover, The Master Criminal, said, "Hee, hee, hee—*yes!*"

Except for one single closed cubicle, the place was empty, an ode to decorum and stained glass and gently burbling water and perfumed vinaigrettes and the toilet architectural genius of the firm of J. L. Mott Iron Works, Premier Plumbing and Inside Sanitary Ware Makers, 86, 88 and 90 Beekman Street, New York.

He carried a long ebony cane with a figured pewter top. He touched it gently to his top hat and set the rim back on his head and gazed at the pure beauty of the place in the glow of the four Edison Lights on the ceiling.

He sighed with pleasure.

It was Mott's Doric line, all the pull-down out-of-sight Discretional urinals on the far tiled wall a line of molded petals hand painted with daisies and roses and asters, all the water closets in all (all but one) of the half-open cubicles dolphins supporting on their golden backs gleaming white porcelain "Unique" front-outlet, side-flushing toilet bowls hand worked and molded to be great ivory sea-conch shells.

He unscrewed the head of his cane and withdrew from it a tightly rolled square of paper, a short thin steel rod, two lengths of twine, and a tiny brass valve with a hexagonal thread exactly thirty-three and one-half sixty-fourths of an inch wide engraved with an arrow and the word *Turn* on it.

Putting the valve gently to his lips he blew through the intake and nothing happened and he nodded. Against the right-hand wall, not hidden but there to admire, was Mott's pipe plumbing: a symphony of parallel brass tubes and valves and cocks and junctions carrying water to all the cisterns in all the cubicles with not even the faintest whisper of an air bubble or even one single drip.

Beautiful. He had heard they had landed the contract to replumb the Sistine Chapel in Rome—it did not surprise him in the least. Mott's was heavenly. The Master Criminal unrolled his paper and stuck it on the inside of the gray-tinted glass entrance door to the place.

Out of Order. For a moment, as he tied the entrance door closed with the first length of twine, in the sweet perfume of the place, he almost felt guilty. The Master Criminal said to himself in a harsh whisper, "Grover, pull yourself together . . . !"

He took his pocket watch out from his fob pocket and consulted it. 10:40 P.M. Upstairs, onstage, the third act would be about halfway through—the good part with the girl in the pink tights— and unless he got the victim in the closed cubicle in the next fifteen minutes he was not going to get a victim at all. It was his artistic nature: he could not look at a Mott's toilet without his heart lightening and all his evil impulses flowing away in a rush with their patent perfume.

"Grover, harden your heart."

He hardened his heart. He got down quickly on his hands and knees and peered in under the closed cubicle door from across the room to check that the gent with the carpetbag was still in there.

He was. He saw his shining black boots and the creased legs of his pants as he sat in there through eternity, his digestion all shot from a life of profit, theater-going and carrying around carpetbags of money.

He got up and, like a hangman moving at lightning speed, spun the second length of twine about the brass knob on the cubicle door and made it fast with a wonderful knot to the hinge on the next cubicle.

10:42. Ducking down a little, his cape flying behind him, he took six quick strides across the tiled floor and was at the wall where the brass pipes were, unscrewing the nut for the pipe to the closed cubicle before he had even stopped moving.

Motts did that to you—they made you feel like a gazelle.

In the great, yellow-lit, gently burbling, sweet-smelling rapture to human requisite, Grover took off his top hat, removed from inside it a spherical copper hemisphere with a threaded socket for his brass valve, and, gently humming to himself, happy, began unscrewing a tiny inspection nut of exactly thirty-three and one-half sixty-fourths of an inch with the fitted end of his cane, slowly, carefully, a single half turn at a time from the brass low-pressure water pipe to the closed, silent, busy cubicle.

> "Sold into Slavery"
> Scene Twelve
> **IN THE HEATHEN SAVAGE'S LAIR**
> Innocence Cruelly Defiled
> Hood's Tooth Powder Whitens the Teeth

Onstage—in one of the last heart-fluttering moments of Professor C. K. Quarternight's Great Wild West Round-up and Educational Entertainment, as the orchestra-pit violinists stopped sawing, the piano and organ players stopped playing and pumping, the cymbal and bell players stopped crashing and tinging, in the flickering, tallow lamp–lit great buffalo-hide lodge of the odious Red Man, the odious, half-naked, grinning Red Man carrying his tomahawk and his knife came in.

"Mother—!" Cowering in the far corner of the vile habitation, Sweet Mary Hampton lifted her eyes to Heaven.

In the audience, somewhere in the breathless hush, a woman stifled a sob.

"Mother, I come soon to meet you in the soft clasp of Jesus—"

A man in the audience, a manly man, gritted his teeth to hold in a strangled cry.

The Red Man—his name was Despoiler of Women—struck a pose and cackled.

Sweet Mary, in the white dress of her innocence, fell to her knees to clasp her hands together in prayer. What soul could resist her pure pleas?

The vile Red Man could. The vile Red Man, naked to the waist, thumping his bare chest—another woman in the audience, perhaps a young girl of delicate sensibility or vivid imagination said, *"Ohh!"* —brute that he was, said, *"Ugghh!"*

"We will gather at the river . . ." She had a voice like a bell.

In the packed, two-thousand-seat-audience, someone—someone else, someone of good heart, said—*"Ooohh . . ."*

Grover had his threaded brass valve fitted to the brass pipe. He had his copper air hemisphere fitted to the valve. He had his hand on the lever that opened the copper air hemisphere fitted to the valve threaded to the pipe. He was a man of brutish feelings.

Grover said, "Heh, heh, heh . . . !" He looked quickly at his pocket watch. Upstairs, upstairs onstage, now . . .

Upstairs, onstage, Sweet Mary drew from her bosom a knife. It was the small pocketknife her late father, a miner, a forty-niner, had carried for his nightly homely pipe of tobacco before the terrible accident that had made her an orphan. In the orchestra pit, the lead violinist drew a single chord.

"I am alone with no one to defend me!" Mary Hampton, drawing back the family blade in both hands to reach Paradise in a single thrust to her bosom, said, "All my hopes for a long life and happy family unfulfilled!"

She keened as the grinning fiend, raising his tomahawk, advanced toward her, "Alone on the prairie! Lost on the brink of ruination!" Sweet, innocent, pure Mary Hampton, her cheeks running with tears—not a dry eye in the house—seeking Jesus in the blackness of night, cried out, "Oh, my poor parents!" She grasped the knife: "I do this for my honor!"

She drew back the knife.

She looked once at the simpering red brute.

He had no pity.

She drew back the knife.

At the copper hemisphere fitted to the valve threaded to the pipe, Grover turned the lever. He had no pity.

* * *

The Indian said, "UGGG!" A voice from the audience, quickly hushed, said, "*Swine!*" The Indian with a single swipe of his hatchet knocked the aging pipe reamer of her father's friendly corncob from her hands. The Indian said, "Ha, ha, ha!"

The Indian, making Indian noises, the grunts and growls that in his loutish race passed for civilized conversation, said, "Burb, burb, *burb!*"

There were people sobbing openly in the first three rows of the stalls. In the balcony, men clenched their hands into fists and felt for their revolvers.

"*Blurk!!*" It was the brass water pipe. Hit by fifty atmospheres of pressure from the copper hemisphere, it leaped from the wall, expanded, started to fracture, and then, as the pressure caught the water flowing through it, turned into a hose, a gun barrel, a crossbow.

"*BLURK!*"

The water, gallons of it, under a terrible sudden pressure, went through the pipe in a solid mass toward the cistern above the closed cubicle like a terrible, unstoppable, swift spear.

It hit the cistern inlet valve like a steam train hitting a sheet of window glass, demolishing it. It filled the cistern in a thrice and exploded down onto the plunger apparatus as if it were not there. It filled all the pipes in the twinkling of an eye. It laughed at Mott's careful industry. It overflowed the cistern like Niagara. It rushed down the front outlet and formed a giant airlock in the S bend. It blocked the side outlets in a terrible cascade. It drowned the golden dolphin holding the conch-shell bowl. It belched, it blurked—it BLURKED! It struck the air pocket in the S bend and started, in a rush, to come back up again.

The Master Criminal, howling with joy, shrieked at the top of his voice, "You! You in there with the carpetbag! Now! This instant! Divest—*or drown!*"

Sweet Mary's last moment was upon her. In the wings, the lighting manager took his unlit cigar from his mouth and said, nodding to his assistant, "Get ready for the thunder and lightning, Herbie.

Thunder first." He leaned a little forward and, holding the cigar between his fingers, hooked his thumbs into the pockets of his waistcoat and watched the action.

"Sir, oh, sir, have you no nobility in your Race? Have the pity of a swift death upon a poor, motherless girl!" In his filthy lair, the savage beast advanced toward an unarmed, defenseless female, making animal noises. In the theater, men, women and children were howling with emotion. Sweet Mary, praying to the odious scum, to the heartless heathen—*to the ravager!*—begged, "Have you never held your own helpless women to your breast and felt the Christian virtue of protection that any true man feels?"

Little Mary cried out in floods of tears, *"Oh, is there no one to save me now?"*

No one was going to save Moneybags now. In the toilets, Grover shrieked above the rising cataract, "Drown like a rat! The Flood is coming!" He turned the lever a fraction to increase the pressure—

BLURK!!! It came, the final deluge. In the S bend, the pressure reached critical point, and, an instant before everything Mott's had ever built turned to dust and debris, the ocean itself exploded out of the S bend in a single, bone-crushing, drowning fountain of foam.

"Throw out your carpetbag or suffer the consequences!"

The figured plaster, all cherubs and maidens, on the ceiling, turned to mush and French chalk and came down in a rain of splitting laths and falling nails.

"No one? Is there no one at all?"

The hide of the lodge suddenly split in the single slashing of a razor-sharp knife.

Nothing. Not a sound.

In the toilets, crouched at the hemisphere, dancing to keep dry, Grover yelled, "Whoever you are—throw your money out!" Shouting above the commotion, Grover called for the last time, "You! You!"

"Who? Who?" Perhaps it was Father saved miraculously from the mine.

The Indian brute raised his hatchet.

"Who? A savior? Is it—?"

You could tell that Red Coward was afraid. His eyes rolled back. You could see him cringe in fear. You could tell.

"Is it—?"

Two shining black boots without feet in them came floating out from under the cubicle door.

"*Who . . . ?*"

"*You—*" It was a manly voice. It was the voice of a man who had held helpless women to his breast and felt the Christian virtue of protection that any true man felt. Oh, you could tell. Every man, woman and child in the audience could tell.

"You . . . evil . . . *CUR!*"

In through the slash in the tent, his jaw set and his gaze steady, his twin golden long-barreled ivory-handled Single-Action Army .45 revolvers in his hands, his buckskins and boots all glittering with medals and Mexican silver, stepped Salvation.

They were two left shoes. Behind them floated out trousers with no legs in them and a flat, wet carpetbag with no money in it. Behind them, three cubicles down the line, slowly, swinging outwards, one of the half-open mahogany doors began to move.

He loved thunder, did young Herbie. He rubbed his hands together in anticipation. Picking up the great sheet of iron to make thunder, Herbie, sucking in his breath and pushing out his manly eighteen-year-old skinny chest, prepared to make thunder.

Hearts fluttered. The manly voice said—

The voice said, "Professor C. K. Quarternight. The Western Long-Eye, Spirit Tumbleweed of the Prairie, Undisputed Champion Shot of the World, Hero to All Christian Children and Stiffener of the Resolve of Men—at your service, miss."

They went mad. They cheered and screamed and applauded and dabbed at their tears, and womenfolk pressed hard against the biceps of their husbands. Boys gritted their teeth. Young girls, laced too tightly in their first corsets, went white for lack of breath.

His manly voice said to the Indian, "You . . . you *stain!*"

There was a roll of thunder. The Avenger came toward the Indian like a lion.

He came out like a bat nailed to the back of the mahogany door.

Grover's heart fluttered. The manly voice said—

The manly voice shouted above the deluge, "I gave you a chance. Any fool could have seen that they were two left feet!" The manly voice, coming from a small, black-suited, bowler-hatted, grinning man balancing on two footholds on the trim at the bottom of the door and seemingly nailed by the shirt collar to a coat hook at the top, a Colt Lightning in one hand and a glittering polished copper badge in the other, said, "City Detective Virgil J. Tillman—and you, sir, *are under arrest!*"

He thought he would throw his vicious tomahawk into the chest of The Western Long-Eye and Spirit Tumbleweed of the Prairie. Ho, ho, ho. He thought wrong. With two shots The Undisputed Champion Shot of the World split his little axe to matchwood. The Hero to All Christian Children, with a contemptuous toss of his head, said, "Now, before a man, you become a mere jest!"

City Detective Virgil Tillman thought he would step down from his foothold on the trim of the bottom of the door and grasp Grover by the scruff of the cape and manacle him for delivery to the Tombs.

He thought wrong. He couldn't get his collar off the hook.

The Master Criminal said, "Ha-*HA!*" He went for the door, reaching out to undo the knots that held it.

Someone in the audience yelled, "Shoot the savage!"

Sweet Mary, her hands to her white breast, said in a gasp, "Oh, sir!"

City Detective Tillman yelled, "Stop where you are or I'll shoot!" He was twisting, trying to get loose, swinging like a bag of laundry in the wind, ducking the fountain of water as the hemisphere of pressure, giving of its last, sprayed water from Mott's dolphin bowl like a volcano.

He was at the knots. Grover, working the twine, glancing back over his shoulder at the twisted bat, yelled, "You can't shoot an unarmed man!"

He couldn't. Quarternight—a moment before Herbie, getting carried away, gave a roll of thunder that verged on the Biblical—said in his firm, strong, calm voice, "I cannot shoot an unarmed man however little he deserves mercy." If only all men were like him.

Thunder. It drowned out what she said.

Mary gasped, "His tribe will hear the shots and be upon us!"

"My faithful steed Liberty is tethered not twenty feet from here in a secret place. Liberty will carry us away." In the audience, their respiratory systems laced to extinction, young girls gave up and swooned in their seats. "Liberty at least will carry one of us away." No need to ask who.

In the audience, a woman shrieked, *"No! Don't die, Professor!"*

"Lightning, Herbie!" In the wings, the stage manager yelled, "Herbie! They're stoking like hell in the generator furnace room—let go the electric lightning!"

He was pinned to the door. In the toilets, Tillman ordered Grover, *"Don't touch that door!"*

Grover yelled, "I sentence you—to swing!" Grover yelled back from the door, "You tricked me! What you did wasn't fair! What you did was a *trick!*"

There was a ripping sound. It was his collar. He came off the hook like a tree falling and went face down into the seething water on the floor. Tillman yelled—

Herbie hit the switch. It lit up the stage in a bolt of lightning of cataclysmic proportions. It illuminated the savage, as Quarternight, gathering Sweet Mary up in his arms, knocked the cowering coward craven cur savage senseless with one blow from the butt of one of his shining revolvers of righteousness. It dimmed, turned to white heat all the lamps in the corridor outside the toilet door as Grover got out, and then it blasted them all into darkness. It sent an electric tingle up the necks of all the panting women in the first three rows of the audience. It was a wonder of modern mechanics.

"Thunder!"

Herbie gave them thunder.

"Hooves!"

He had his coconuts ready. Herbie gave 'em hooves.

"Ride!"

In the darkness, pursued by screaming Indians, the Savior of Women and Helpless Children and the Helpless Woman he had saved, rode.

He ran. The cop was right behind him and in the darkness, Grover, losing his top hat, dispensing with his cape as he went to speed his feet, ran. Everything was dark. He was running down dark corridors, feeling the walls, pushing at locked doors and, panting, trying to get his breath, he ran.

"Speaking tubes!" The coconut hooves were galloping, galloping.

Herbie, bending down—working in pitch darkness—grasped a lever with his teeth and jerked open the mouthpiece to all the brass speaking tubes and converted brass ear-trumpets throughout all the theater.

The hooves became not the hooves of Liberty, but of Pegasus. They thundered.

"Hang on for your life, dear woman! We must ride up this hill at night! Hope for lightning to illuminate our way!" You could hear those heartless red fiends a-yelling and a-whooping just behind them.

On the great craggy mountains of the West, Professor C. K. Quarternight commanded, "Liberty—for the sake of this pure young woman, be surefooted this night!"

In the corridor, City Detective Virgil J. Tillman yelled, "You goddamned son of a bitch, wherever you are, *Halt!*"

He made it to a door that opened. The cop was right behind him. He had a horse. He had had a horse hidden somewhere. The cop had a horse and he was riding Grover down on his horse. The sounds were getting louder, louder. It was a huge horse. There was an iron stairway just inside the door and Grover, clutching out in the darkness for the handrail, took the steps two at a time. He was running up, getting higher. The hooves were getting louder. The cop just didn't stop. Grover said in a gasp, "Oh, my God, oh, my God . . ."

The hooves stooped. There was a terrible shriek of blood lust.

Grover said, "Oh, my God, oh, my God . . ." He shouldn't have laughed at him. There was a twang. It wasn't a bullet. It was an arrow. The cop was shooting *arrows* at him.

Grover said, "Oh, my God . . . !" He was at the top of the stairs on a metal landing. There was a door. He got it open. He opened it into darkness. He was on a wooden floor. It was dusty. He smelled the dust rise and he ran. He was running along a flat dusty wooden floor smelling something cold. At least the cop had stopped riding. He touched something with his foot and then his ankle and then it went around in a circle and it was cold iron or tin and he smelled water.

He stopped, panting.

He stopped and listened.

He heard someone on iron stairs. He heard someone rattling furiously at a door.

Grover, on his hands and knees, feeling along the iron tank, smelling water, feeling its coldness, gasped in a prayer, "Oh, God, for the sake of my seven children—"

"We go together no farther, my dear. The game, for me, is up—but of all the deaths 'tis the best death that I face. Liberty is worn, and brave and ready though he be to sacrifice himself for his old master, he has earned the reward of the ease of an old age in a field of clover somewhere a thousand times more than have I."

In the darkness, in the utter silence and darkness, it was a fine ringing voice. For all the lumps in the throats, there was not even a strangled gasp. The young laced girls had long ago lapsed into happy unconsciousness.

"Professor Quarternight—!"

"No, dear girl, no. I am shot quite full of arrows and I have come at last to the trail that leads only to Heaven. I go now to die—"

"You remind me of my own dear dead Father—!"

"Then I die happy!"

There was a twang.

On his hands and knees groping in the darkness, smelling water, The Master Criminal said, "What the hell's happening?" The voices were above him. Was it the play? He had never stayed to the end of the play. He had heard the end of the play was a girl showing her legs in pink tights.

A voice high above, hit by the very slow arrow, said, *"Uh!"*

A horde of voices shrieked, *"Ay-yi-ya-ya-yi-ya!"*

Quarternight commanded, "Now! Be brave, young woman, and save yourself! Wait for the next bolt of lightning and go! And live long and have many children!"

"The first boy I shall name after—"

The Master Criminal, getting to his feet, shrieked, *"What the hell's happening?"*

"Lightning, Herbie! Give it the big one! Both switches!"

He gave it the big one. He had *three* switches. He gave it three switches.

He had got him. He had caught up. He had heard him in the darkness. Tillman said, grasping him, "I arrest you in the name of the—"

There was light. A lot of it.

Grover looked up. He saw a plywood and papier-mâché and canvas mountain lit by lightning towering above him. It was above a river. Grover, looking dazed, was standing at the edge of the river. It was a river in the floor. It was a lake. It had a bottom of galvanized iron. It was deep. There was a man dressed in Texas cowboy clothes shot full of arrows on a ledge on the mountain starting to draw his guns. There was something else up on the mountain at its very peak. It looked a little like a horse. It could not have been a horse.

"I shall hold them off until death! Now—for the sake of the children you are yet to have and a happy home life, you and Liberty together—*LEAP!*"

The lightning just didn't quit. Maybe it wasn't lightning but the papier-mâché mountain on fire. It could have been. Inside his head, Grover heard his brain pop. Grover said conversationally to Tillman, "A horse with a girl on it just jumped off the mountain up there and they're coming this way." There was a girl on the horse.

Somewhere, far away, someone was shooting Indians and being killed. You could hear the sounds. The girl, on the horse, flying down, her hair blowing, cried, *"Ooohh . . . !"*

"OHHH—!!" In the audience, two thousand people said, "OHHH!" Women revived their unconscious daughters to see it. Men gasped. Boys sat openmouthed.

"OOHHH!!!"

On the stage, from a mountaintop fifty feet at least above the suddenly lit footlights, a girl on a horse, fleeing from Indians, leaped toward an invisible water-tank river to safety with her dress flying back to her pink-tights-encased legs all the way past her knees. It was Art. No one could object. The audience, all gasping, openmouthed, said, *". . . OOHH!!!"*

Tillman saw, in that instant, in the wings, the figures of two men. He saw, in that instant, as Grover twisted from his grasp and, a plumberphile to the end, decided to throw himself into the water tank to escape, two shadows close together in the wings. He saw one of them pull back and then he saw, as a spasm, a jerk, the taller one push back closer and then he saw the gun flashes and then he saw the smaller man fall.

"Save me!" It was Grover. The horse was about to fall on him and he would sink or swim where he was.

In the wings Tillman saw the taller man pull free and turn away and then turn again. He was a shadow, he was a figure, he was—

He saw the smaller man on the ground, his arms thrashing, his heels drumming on the floor. He saw him real, no chimera, no actor— He saw him start to crawl . . .

"Lightning! Footlights! Back lighting, Herbie!"

"Save me—!" Grover, who could not swim, was swimming like a fish in circles in the tank. The Master Criminal, his burst brain for some reason all full of thoughts of cisterns and S bends and the mystery of what happened when you were flushed down Mott's painted porcelain pipes, yelled, "I've got seven children and—"

* * *

He was running. In the sidelights, he could see the stage door to the street and Tillman, chasing after the tall running figure, moving through a storm of water and foam and applause, ran for the door after him drawing his pistol.

"*Ned—!*" Outside the stage door he had stationed Muldoon of the Strong Arm Squad in full uniform in case that had been the way The Master Criminal made his entrances. Tillman yelled in the direction of the door, "Ned! Muldoon! NED!" The stage door was opening, but all the lights were going as the house lights came up and he could see only a shape, a shadow, an outline. Tillman, running, slipping on the water, getting his whistle out and blasting on it, yelled to alert him, "Ned! Your way! *Stop him!*"

He saw the stage door close. In the alleyway outside, there were only gas lamps.

She saved him. The audience, on their feet, hysterical with happiness, saw Little Mary haul something wet and gibbering and very old-looking from the water tank and, joyous in the thought that obviously it was her long dead, semimummified Father making his escape from his collapsed mine in Alaska down a very long river, applauded and roared until their throats hurt.

"Ned!"

Outside, in the alleyway, Muldoon was dead against the wall of the alley with a soft smile on his face.

"Ned—"

People were coming. They were coming out of the side doors of the hotel above the theater in top hats and capes and they were looking down the alley. In the alley, the figure had gone.

"Ned . . ." He was dead. He was dead drunk. In the alley, pulling at him, shaking him, Tillman said, shaking his head, "Ned! Ned . . . !"

Muldoon, opening his eyes for a moment and smiling, said happily, a little surprised, "Ah, Virgil—it's you . . ."

"Ned . . . !"

People were coming.

Back there in the theater, in the darkness of the wings, somewhere there was a shot man.

He had seen, in that instant, in the lightning, the flashes of gunfire. He had seen the outline of the smaller man there in the darkness jerk with the impact of the bullets.

In the alley, people were coming.

"*Ned!*" In the alley, bending over him, Tillman laid him out cold with one blow to the head from the butt of his revolver. It was a clean, glancing blow to the temple.

"Ned . . ."

Turning, holding up his gun and badge to show them who he was, Tillman shouted to the coming crowd, "Help here! A poor police officer has been struck down in the performance of his duty by a fleeing criminal!"

He smelled what it was on Muldoon's breath.

Tillman, sounding desperate, yelled, "Quick! Someone! Brandy to save his life! Lots of it! —*Quick!*"

Back there in the theater, in the darkness of the wings, somewhere there was a shot, dying man, perhaps a man already dead.

Without waiting, Tillman went back up the stairs two at a time to the unlocked stage door, back into the cheering, applauding, thundering theater to find him.

2

Onstage, the vile savage had rubbed off his greasepaint to reveal his white skin and Nordic countenance, and the audience, having cheered and saluted Quarternight, Sweet Mary and Liberty the horse for some twenty minutes, cheered and saluted him too. There were rosettes and roses being given out by girls in calico pioneer dresses and bonnets on the stage and in the audience and the audience on their feet was a sea of red roses clasped in women's and girls' hands at their breasts and red and white and blue rosettes pinned on the lapels of mustachioed, cheering, clapping, thundering men. The entire cast of the show was onstage in a line behind Quarternight: cow-boys, Indians, mountain men, trick shots and knife throwers, horse-handlers and lasso-spinners, the ladies of the Company, midgets who no one knew were midgets dressed as well-behaved, seen but not heard, Western children. They were in the midst of noise, color, life, expectation. Backstage, in the half darkness, in the dust on the wooden planked floor, the dead man lay where he had crawled, his head down over the top iron step of the stairs down to the prop basement. In the sound and splendor all he was was an artifact, something inanimate, and no one cared.

On his knees beside him, Tillman called to Chief Inspector Byrnes at the edge of the wings, looking out, "Sir—" but Byrnes did not turn around.

The dead man was lying on his chest where the blood had come from, his head on the iron step. Tillman said, "Sir, Mr. Byrnes—" but Byrnes was speaking and nodding to the stage manager and making Herbie look up at him with admiring eyes and he did not hear. He had been in the audience. He was the Hawkshaw of the Force, the solver of the three-million-dollar Manhattan Bank Robbery, the head of the Detective Bureau and creator and

16

architect of the Headquarters photographic Rogues' Gallery, the friend of Wall Street and City Hall. He had been in the front row of the audience on an invitation ticket. He was in his second-best tails, his heavy moustaches combed and oiled, with dress miniatures of his medals pinned to his breast. He was, at the Mulberry Street Headquarters Station, the man who would be, after the dithering George Walley either died, retired or became senile, the next Chief of the New York Police.

Tillman, turning the body over, called out in a pause in the tumult, "Mr. Byrnes, he's ready for you." The white shirt was filthy with dust from the floor, caked with blood, and there was the faint smell of burned gunpowder about the wounds. Byrnes knew about clues. Out in the theater where the light was, they were stamping their feet and roaring with approval at something that was happening onstage—perhaps a series of bows. The smell was on the jagged edges of the bullet holes in the shirt where the fabric, ignited at close range, was still smoldering. Tillman, trying to look away, his eyes meeting briefly Muldoon's at the back of the wings, said for the last time, "Mr. Byrnes? Sir?"

He was an old man who had crawled in the darkness twenty feet across the filthy floor and died there in that darkness going down iron stairs to the basement, going nowhere. On his knees, gazing at Byrnes's back, Tillman knew the dead man's eyes would be open. He was nothing—you could tell from his cheap shirt and trousers and boots—he was a nobody. He was not Life.

In the theater, suddenly, as if someone came in from somewhere, someone new, there was a hush.

At the wings, Byrnes stiffened with anticipation.

On the iron stairs, there was a dead old man with his eyes open and pale and watery, staring out through Eternity, his cheap white shirt filthy with dust and crawling and caked with drying blood.

To no one, to everyone, to Herbie the lightning boy who had said nothing at all, Byrnes said sharply, "Shh!"

His hands were trembling. At the top of the iron stairs, Tillman, supporting his right wrist with his left hand, keeping it steady, reached down with his thumb and forefinger to close the dead man's eyes.

They were pale, blue.

The eyelids, as they came down, dead, lifeless skin, offered no resistance to his touch.

* * *

"F. C. Catton of the American Gun Company of Montclair, New Jersey!" On the stage, there was some sort of presentation going on. Entering from the front doors and passing down the aisle to mount the stage, a small, clean-shaven middle-aged man wearing a top hat and tails and carrying in his hands a long brass-bound mahogany case, called to Quarternight, "In recognition of the two-hundredth performance and of your twenty years of exploit and excellence, the American Gun Company, on behalf of the entire nation, honors you!"

The Great Scout must have been seven-foot tall. Either that or Catton was four-foot-six and the Great Scout was merely six-foot-three. Quarternight said, inclining his head to look down and then, having located where the voice was coming from next to him in the spotlight, said to the audience, "I have always used the products of the American Gun Company in my many adventures. They are sturdily made, designed for years of service, do wonderful execution at any range, and are cheaply priced for the person of prudent character."

"Our factory is of the most modern kind with steam- and electricity-driven machinery of the latest design capable of fulfilling the most arduous demands of our customers, whether it be for the humblest game gun for the struggling farmer of the wheat fields, or the most powerful engines of death for the brave soldiers of the great nations of the world who are our friends."

Quarternight said, "It is. I have seen it."

Catton said, "The gun. What a wonderful device it has been through our history. From the first discharge of our ancient forebears that put the savage Red Man to flight, to the glorious blast that set our nation free from our English oppressors, to the Alamo and the late War between the States to the humblest honest man defending the sanctity of his home and loved ones with one of our full nickel-plated rebounding-hammer Everyman line of pocket revolvers, the gun has been the arm of our liberty, the tool of our labors and the sword of our democracy!" Catton said suddenly, overcome by emotion, his practiced lines seemingly forgotten, "This great man here has seen all these things—this—this ornament to our history—has strode across the great plains and on snow-deep mountains in winter. He has fought Indians and rescued eighteen young women from the terror of fates too monstrous and terrible to contemplate, he has killed over eight hundred buffalo, led many of our brave young boys in blue through danger and out of danger, he has fought for law and order and brought peace and respectability to many of our frontier towns and he is, and always will be, the greatest exhibition shot in the world and yet—does he leave no small moment of the day for himself? No, he does not. Yet still he labors even now to entertain, to amuse, to instruct, to inspire and edify us." Catton asked, "In our city, sir, along our dark and sometimes squalid streets, do you not long once more for the great plains and lonely mountains of the golden West?" He tucked the gun box under his arm and patted it, smiling.

His voice rang clear and true. "I do not, Mr. Catton. I long now only for the grace from my dear Creator to finish my work and make of our great cities a New Jerusalem." He waited for the beginnings of the applause and silenced it as soon as it began.

Quarternight said, "I long now only to make our infant country the greatest nation since the birth of recorded history, THE GREATEST NATION the world has ever seen!"

"Sir!" Onstage, Catton touched at his eyes.

He stepped, overcome by the emotion and the applause, for a full half minute, out of the spotlight.

He looked at the face. Tillman said, trying to stop his hands trembling, "The deceased is a white man of about sixty years with regular facial features excepting the eye sockets—which are of greater than average size—with white hair receding over the last few inches of the sides and rear of the head to total baldness, and ears of smaller than mean average size for a person of his cranial classification." In the Detective Bureau, contained in a polished cabinet with a sign-writer's depiction of a cop arresting a thug on its doors, was Byrnes's Rogues' Gallery and Photographic Index. "Length of body about five-foot, eight inches, medium to thin build—not muscular—of a body weight of perhaps one hundred and thirty-five pounds."

On the stage, as the good, modest man composed himself, there was a silence.

He had been shot through the chest. He did not want to look at the wounds. Tillman said, "The body wears pants and suspenders of cheap but serviceable quality and a collarless shirt and sturdy boots of the artisan class." One of the dead man's hands—the right—was outstretched. He moved the thumb back a little with his middle finger, "A smoker. His hands bespeak labor, but not recently, and not of the arduous kind."

In the wings near the stage door, The Master Criminal said, "A horse fell on me." He was wet. He made a puddle on the wooden floor. There were girls in pink tights and black slippers standing about, Indians with hatchets, and ghostly miners with white talcum powder and ash on their faces. The Master Criminal said, "I've been punished. Can I go now?"

A large uniformed patrolman holding him with one hand and his head with the other and smelling strongly of brandy, said, "No." There was a dead old man on the floor with the human bat bending over him. The dead old man wasn't wet; he was covered in blood.

The Master Criminal said to Herbie's back, looking hard at him, "Who are you?"

The Master Criminal had a brilliant thought.

The Master Criminal said to the hair on the back of Herbie's head, which for some reason looked singed, as if it had been hit by lightning, "I have to go home and change. Open the door and let me out, would you? I promise to drop back when I'm dry . . ."

Tillman said, "He has been shot three times in the chest with a small-caliber gun, and there is a rupture wound in the area of the heart and sternum in the very center of the triangle of the three shots—"

It was the dust on the floor and the face. He could not get his breath.

Tillman said, "The man was pinioned with a blade and then, simultaneously, or perhaps a moment later, was riddled with rapid gunfire." Byrnes would not turn around. "The weapon used may have been a knuckle-duster French "Apache" street-gang-style revolver—a barrelless pepperbox-style pistol with a spring blade attached."

"I accept this unsolicited presentation, not for myself, but on behalf of the youth of America who have never known the tribulations and terrors, the joys and freedom of the Frontier!" It was a golden, single-shot, fifty-caliber breech-loading rolling-block buffalo rifle with a full thirty-inch barrel and globe sights, engraved and chiseled full length along the receiver and barrel with cartouches of silver and platinum, the stock of the finest grade walnut root that glittered and caught the light as he held it up above his chest to read the inscription on the back strap: *Presented to Professor C. K. Quarternight, The Western Long-Eye and Hero to Our Youth, by his Admirers at the American Gun Company of Montclair, New Jersey, As an Inadequate Token of the Esteem in Which They and All Who Admire Courage and Fidelity and Honor Hold Him.* He drew a manly breath. Quarternight said bravely, "I am more than a little affected."

He waited again for the applause. Catton said, "Good old Scout!"

Quarternight said, "I accept this award on behalf of the true men whose swords, this night, sleep in their scabbards!" He held the rifle out from his chest. "I accept this award on behalf of the city of New York that allows such sights as the sight I saw this day on one of the great thoroughfares of this metropolis—I accept this award on behalf of the sight of a black man dressed in swell clothes promenading himself in open view of all with a white woman on each of his arms!" His mouth was twisted. Quarternight said, "I accept this award on behalf of that! I call such a sight a coon sandwich! I accept this award on behalf of that!"

Someone in the audience called out, "No—!"

"No? Sir, I promise you, 'Yes'!"

Catton, half turning to the man who had called from the front row, said, raising his hands to ward off the thought, "Oh, no. No, sir, the award is given for the spirit of the young, the spirit of the desire for nature and manliness and self-reliance, the striving for wholesomeness and health and—"

Quarternight said, "I see in this city, in this nation, Jews openly walking the streets and speaking in gibberish tongues and rubbing their hands together as they cheat honest men! I see half-castes and Mexicans and ungodliness eating like a canker into the soul of our nation! I take myself for a perambulation among the trees and avenues of this city of Gotham and I see no happy families hand in hand with the contented smiles of Americans on their faces—I see, skulking in every corner, the Chinese opium seller and debaucher of women and, by him, conspiring in whispers with him, the black-hatted anarchist, the city rat, the mulatto, the Mormon with his many wives and evil ungodliness—I see them on the streets and avenues of this city and on the streets and avenues of all our nation!

I see in all my dreams the lonely graves of true men unmarked in all the corners of our land but for a rough Christian cross and I see lonely women clasping their portraits to their breasts in tears and pride and honor—I hear the sad, gone call of a distant bugle—and I see, in this great metropolis and wherever now—in this great year of 1883—wherever I may roam preaching my message of patriotism and the great deeds of all those gone good men and loyal women, I see Gomorrah! I see—and does no one but I see it?—*a coon sandwich!*"

He lowered the rifle, looking at it. Quarternight said so softly the audience had to strain to hear him, "Perhaps I was wrong. Perhaps I should not have believed in the simple decencies. Perhaps we are not a great nation and all our hopes were illusion." He shrugged. "Perhaps I should not honor this gift. Perhaps I should pawn it to a Jew, or donate it to some son of Ham to complement his garish checked outfit—perhaps I should grant it by deed to a Mormon so he may use it to slaughter one of his unwanted wives; perhaps I should melt it so an anarchist may make a bomb of it—perhaps I should say to the bright eyes of the youth of America, 'Strive not, emulate nothing, do as you will'—perhaps I should vend this symbol of our nation to a Chinaman for opium and dream the dreams that have no end." Quarternight demanded, "Should I do this? Must I do this? *Are there no good men here tonight? Are we come to this?* IS THIS HOW THE BELL OF LIBERTY IS STILLED IN OUR LAND?"

Catton said with sudden emotion, "It is true!"

"IS THERE NO ONE MAN LEFT IN THIS FAIR LAND OF OURS WHO WILL STEM THE TIDE OF THIS DISSOLUTION?"

Catton said, *"You, sir!"*

"OUR POLITICIANS DO NOTHING!" Quarternight said, "The Indian of the West, however mistakenly he may have believed it, at least believed he was defending his own land when he came as a tide against our Pioneers; however pagan, when shown the true light of Creation at least he accepted our Lord as his savior and the true God as his God; however naked, he took to the clothes of respectability to clothe his nakedness at least in winter—" He paused. Quarternight demanded, "Can we say the same of the immigrant Jew, the Mormon, the coon, the anarchist fiend, the enemy within? —The slavering Chinaman? The city *immigrant? The Nemesis?* WHO WILL STEM THEIR TIDE?"

Catton took the rifle and held it for him. Catton said, "The

American Gun Company will undertake to arm every true man fighting for justice—!"

"Honest men fear them. WHO WILL SPEAK FOR HONEST MEN? Women tremble in terror of them. WHO WILL DEFEND WEAK WOMANKIND? Republican politicians, mad for cheap labor, do nothing. WHO WILL SPEAK WITH A POWERFUL VOICE FOR ALL THE SILENT, POWERLESS MEN IN THIS AUDIENCE TONIGHT? Is there a voice that speaks for them? Do I hear that voice? If yes, then WHO—WHO IS THEIR VOICE?"

Herbie said in a gasp, "Isn't he wonderful? *Wonderful!*"

He saw Muldoon rubbing at his head. Tillman asked, "All right, Ned?"

Muldoon said, "Yes. Thanks." He did not, for an instant, relax his grip on The Master Criminal.

Byrnes said in ecstasy to Herbie, to anyone listening, "I knew about this! That's why I was invited! I was consulted about all this! I knew about it . . . !"

Tillman said above the dead man, "I am informed by the employees of the theater that the name of the deceased was Mr. Albert Schweib and that he worked in the capacity of stage-door man, and that he has held this position for a number of years."

Byrnes said, "Ah!" He knew what was coming. He wanted it known. He turned to see if Herbie and the stage manager had heard.

"The deceased wears no pocket watch and evidently had none. Further, no money was kept in the deceased man's trust and, since he had applied unsuccessfully to the stage manager earlier in the evening for an advance of two dollars on his salary due in three days, he was in possession of little or no private funds." He touched at the pockets. Tillman said, "His pockets are not turned out and they are empty." He was trying to think hard. "No one is missing from the staff or company, nor shows any trace of blood, and the stage door is a fire door and is always unlocked during performances or rehearsals or when anyone is in the stage area." Muldoon had been outside the door in the alley all evening. Tillman said, "The murderer must have secreted himself backstage until his crime and then, witnessed by me, made his exit through the door in the darkness." Tillman said, "—assaulting Patrolman Muldoon on his way out." Byrnes would not come. He was craning, watching the stage. He could not breathe so close to death. He did not know if he had said it before.

Tillman said, "His name—I am informed—"

The wounds in the chest horrified him. There was fluid drying on the dead man's lips. The lungs had been shot through and, as he had crawled, they had begun to go into spasms and die.

Tillman said so someone would hear him, "His name was Mr. Albert Schweib."

"WHERE IS GONE OUR AGE OF COURTESY AND CIVIL-ITY? OUR CIVILIZATION? THE MANLY GRACE OF TRUE-BORN AMERICANS MEETING EACH OTHER ON THE STREET? WHO WILL SPEAK FOR THAT? WHERE IS OUR GREAT GOLDEN AGE OF PEACE AND PROS-PERITY AND THE JOYS OF HOME AND FAMILY?"

The man in the front row called with a catch in his voice, "Gone forever! All gone! Gone to nothing! *Gone to dust!*"

Tillman, trying to get his breath, said with difficulty, "Albert . . ."

He held The Master Criminal in a grip of iron. Muldoon said, calling to him, "Virgil—"

"Albert . . . Albert *Schweib.*"

Muldoon said, "Virgil—"

Quarternight said simply, "I intend to seek nomination for public office."

Herbie, at the wings, at one with the audience, shrieked, *"YES!"*

Quarternight said, "At this moment, at this very moment, upstairs in the great paneled meeting room of the Metropolitan Hotel, the caucus of the New York Democratic Party is meeting to discuss this very issue—to halt with one stroke the decay, the corruption, the erosion of everything we hold dear—"

Byrnes said to Herbie, "I knew about this! The Police are not the yelping curs of everyone who may be in power! The Police have a voice in this nation too!" Byrnes, turning his attention to the stage manager, said, shaking his finger, his eyes vague and dreamy, a little unsteady on his feet, "I knew! I was privy to this! I *knew!*"

Quarternight said, "If you will support me—if there be enough good and true, clean-living men who love our nation to support me, I intend to seek nomination for *great* office!"

Herbie, hopping up and down, shrieked, "Yes! Yes! Yes!" He would be nineteen in three months. He was small for his age. Herbie, hopping, jumping, applauding with his hands above his head, his voice lost in the roar of the audience, yelled, "Yes! Yes! YES!"

Byrnes said in ecstasy, "I *knew!* I was consulted! I *knew!*"

"This city—the great city of New York—will be a model for the nation; the Chinaman and the Jew and the Mormon and the anarchist sent back from whence he came and on our great streets only the firm tread of honest, upright Christian American men and women and children, safe and resolute and clear-eyed and free!" Quarternight said, "These things I will do." Quarternight said, "I accept this golden arm as the golden arm of liberty, of justice—and of a new age for all Americans!" He said before the thunderous applause could drown him out, "I accept it as the symbol that rests beneath and beside all the Christian crosses on all the lonesome graves of the Pioneers, of all our brave soldiers, of the settlers and the explorers—of all the hopes and dreams of a nation of heroes!" Quarternight, taking the glittering gun from Catton's outstretched hands as a baton, said, "As Caesar, I ACCEPT!"

He was weeping.

FLEEING FOOTPAD FLUNG INTO FOAM
HUNTED HIGHWAYMAN HIT BY HORSE
Plunged to Punishment!
Door Detective Dunks Diabolical Delinquent
Will It Be Life or Only Twenty Years?

He was weeping. All around, everywhere, everyone was applauding and cheering.

The Master Criminal, wilting in Muldoon's grasp, said desperately, "I'm a professional man, a plumber for the city! *I only did it because I've got seven children and a sick wife!*"

He touched at the dead man's face.

He was shaking.

He had been pinioned like an animal in a slaughterhouse and shot through the lungs and heart.

He had crawled in his own blood.

His shirt was filthy with dirt and grime and death from the floor—

On the stage, the papier-mâché rock began to rise. With it, the footlights dimmed and the spotlight burned bright white with tinges of red and blue in it. The blue caught the brass cartridges in the Great Scout's gun belt and the silver of the massive belt buckle given to him by a grateful Pioneer family of silversmiths he had once saved out in a place that had no name. He was seven-foot tall with long, jet-black hair and a handlebar moustache to make weaker men gasp. His boots were of wonderful soft russet leather with stark white Indian lacing and golden spurs that glittered in the light. He clasped the golden gun across his chest, mountain-man fashion, and his gaze was steely and true.

He rose. He was as straight as a gun barrel, his shoulders held back in perfect posture, and his chin was set and strong.

He remained still as a statue. He was set in bronze. He made the skin at the back of every man's neck in the theater tingle.

His voice was steady, with no quaver. He looked out across the audience to history.

Quarternight said, "I intend—I tell you this night, securing the endorsement of my Party—in the fullness of time, as the New Age dawns, to seek the office—no less—of *PRESIDENT OF THE UNITED STATES OF AMERICA!*"

He could not hear his own voice in the thunder of the acclamation, in the madness.

On his knees, Tillman shrieked at the top of his lungs, "God damn it! *God damn it!* Will no one take a moment to at least say a prayer for the repose of this poor man's *soul?*"

3

"**I**nvestigating officers—?" Muldoon said, "*Us? Why us?*" They were riding on the rear footplate of the Houston Street–Fulton Ferry horsecar going south through a crush of wagons and coaches and handcarts down the Bowery, the two far-from-spirited horses pulling the street railroad car over every broken block and bump and bend in the lifting rails at the same uniform bone-shaking pace and rattling the car and everything in it to bits. Tillman wasn't listening: he was leaning out over the edge of the car standing on the metal step with his hat in his hand feeling the wind on his face and watching something on the street. There wasn't any wind. What there was was noise and people and dust and the stench of horse manure. Muldoon said, "Byrnes is an opium fiend. Didn't you see the look in his eyes? He spends his nights down in Pell Street sucking dream smoke and talking about his triumphs to Chinamen!" He was in plain clothes. He didn't like it. Muldoon said, "Byrnes is—" Muldoon said, "Virgil, are you listening?"

Inside the horsecar, on the right-hand line of wooden seats, the conductor was dozing with his back held absolutely straight against the back of the driver's window. It was the 6:00 A.M. run, the last one of the night shift before he changed over with another driver at the Fulton Street Ferry to Brooklyn. Above him, his metal clock-face fare register was set at two: a heavyset man in his fifties in a tight brown suit and heavy boots reading the morning newspaper about Quarternight and, a little down from him, a young woman, like the conductor, also dozing. Tillman was leaning out enjoying the wind in the street that was not there. He didn't seem to be able to keep still. Tillman, leaning out even farther, gazing up the road, said with the undisguised delight of a collector, "Ned, watch this—this is something rare. You don't see this during

27

the day. They must have a new twist." He was leaning far out looking at a flatbed wagon moving under the new elevated railway tracks by one of the seven-cent boarding houses that lined the place. Tillman said, "This is a new one. They must have a boarded-up door here somewhere—"

"Who must?" All he could see were the black girders and skeleton of the northbound El, thank God, deserted and still and sootless. Muldoon said irritably, "What are you talking about?"

"The flatbed wagon being pulled by the brown horse with the white patch on its face!" Tillman said, "The whole bed's loaded down with boxes and crates and parcels wrapped in oiled paper sealed with red wax." He was leaning out as far as he could go. If a horsecar came out from the south, he was going to end up under the metal wheels as ground meat. Tillman said, "See the two men on the driver's bench—the ones in vests and peaked caps? I'll guarantee you they'll have something about their persons connected with the sea and ships!"

On the wagon, the driver, clipping along, reached into his vest pocket and took out a clay pipe.

Tillman said, "Ah!" The wagon passed out from under the skeleton of the El to skirt the huddles of people setting up their street stalls for the day's business. Tillman said, "Look at the way everyone's looking at their load!" He turned to Muldoon, grinning. Tillman, shaking his head in admiration, said, "Sturgess and Skoler—I've seen those two before! They're masters, geniuses!" Tillman, plucking at Muldoon's sleeve to pull him out over the edge, said, "Watch! Watch!" He glanced quickly into the horsecar to where the sleeping girl and the reading men were. The sleeping girl was about thirty, clean and respectable, with her auburn hair tied in a bun starting to fall down a little around her cheeks. She looked like an honest, good girl riding home from the night shift at a factory. The stout man next to her looked up from his newspaper to her and moved a little closer. Tillman said "Damn!" as, for a moment, he lost sight of the flatbed wagon in the street.

He saw it again. It was moving up the street at a studied, unhurried pace, the pipe smoker starting to have a conversation with his off-sider and, seemingly, asking him something.

Tillman said happily, "And now, out comes the piece of paper." He looked quickly into the horsecar to the conductor. The conductor, as the stout man edged next to the sleeping girl, was out cold with his head down on his chest.

The Bowery, once the great dirt track that led from the sea to

Peter Stuyvesant's first bouweric, or farm, when he had been the Governor of the Dutch colony of New Amsterdam two hundred years before, was packed with stalls and street vendors. The cart went behind one of them, and as a northbound horsecar passed smelling of varnished wood, metal wheels on metal rails and horse manure, he lost it again. Everywhere along the wide street there were tenement buildings and lodging houses and sweatshops throwing shadows. Tillman said as the horsecar moved inexorably on with the wagon going in the other direction, getting away, "Where is it?"

Muldoon said firmly, "Maybe all it is is a domestic. Maybe the doorkeeper—" Muldoon said, "What's his name?"

Tillman said, "Albert Schweib."

"Maybe Schweib was seeing one of those girls in pink tights on the side and his wife got in and dampened his ardor with a little gun and three bullets in the chest." Muldoon said hopefully, "Maybe we'll find her in their room lying dead from poison with a nicely written note we can read asking forgiveness." Maybe then he could go back to the Strong Arm Squad where you knew where you were with a locust-wood club and a head to crack. Muldoon said, having a little dream-smoke dream of his own, "And Mr. Byrnes can come down with his lovely camera and take photographs for his collection and post a reward for information and, at the same time, collect it." Muldoon said, "Did you write down where the doorkeeper lived?"

Tillman said, "Slip Alley off Dover Street in the Fourth Ward by the piers."

Muldoon, because Tillman kept doing it, glanced into the interior of the horsecar. He didn't know what he was supposed to see in there. He saw only the back of the driver's head, a sleeping blue-uniformed and braided conductor, and a well-dressed bull-necked man reading his newspaper supporting his sleeping wife's head on his shoulder. She had nice ankles, the wife. He saw her husband put the side of his shoe gently against the heel of her high-button boot and give it a little affectionate tap.

The stout man had his hair cropped very close. He had a handlebar moustache. He touched at the end of his moustache with the fingers of his right hand and, moving a little behind the open newspaper, out of a sense of propriety, covered his sleeping wife's face a little from the sleeping conductor's gaze.

The girl's head nodded onto the stout man's chest against the dark silk cravat held in place by a little diamond stickpin and, feeling safe and secure and tired, she seemed to settle herself like a cat and, still asleep, drawing a long slow breath, rubbed at his chest with her shoulder to find a soft spot.

Muldoon saw Tillman glance in at the man and look momentarily irritated. Then his eyes went back to the street, found the wagon as it halted outside a boarded-up building, and he seemed happy again.

The horsecar was moving at the pace of a hearse and he was going to be able to see it.

The tabletop wagon stopped outside the boarded-up door and the pipe smoker and his friend—Sturgess and Skoler—consulted their scrap of creased writing paper and had a long conversation.

Tillman, beside himself with joy, said, urging them on, "Read the paper, then look up and down the street and then scratch your head and stand up in the wagon—"

The driver took his pipe out of his mouth, looked up and down the street, scratched his head, and shrugged.

Tillman said in transports of delight, "Look at that, Ned! People pay good money to go to the theater and there are people like that all around them!"

The driver stood up in the wagon and looked up at the boarded-up two-story clapboard building where his paper said the cargo on the back of his wagon—all in from distant lands and wrapped carefully in oiled paper—should be delivered. The horsecar was getting farther away. The driver looked around.

"Come on, Sturgess, you know they're there!" Tillman, craning far out, said in a whisper, "Yes, you know they're there and—" He glanced into the interior of the horsecar where, behind his newspaper, the stout man was moving a little on his seat to get the girl's breasts up against his chest so he could rub himself up against them.

Suddenly, from out of nowhere outside the boarded-up building, there were two men lounging in the street.

Tillman said with pure, undisguised delight, "And there they are! The two helpful local citizens on their way to work who just happen to have half an hour to spare to do their best to assist a fellow Christian and who happen to know when the owner of the boarded-up building is coming back to unboard it."

Her face was against the stout man's chest. He thought no one saw. He moved his cravat a little out of the way and unbuttoned the two top studs of his shirt and let her mouth rest against his naked chest. Tillman, looking back and forth between the street and the car, said softly again, "Damn—!"

The driver of the wagon, standing up, bent down a little to engage the two helpful souls on the street in conversation. They looked like decent fellows in their shirt-sleeves and working boots.

Muldoon, catching Tillman and pulling him back onto the footplate before he leaned so far out he disappeared under the wheels, said, "Virgil, you know I'd do anything for you, but—" He towered over Tillman. He was surprised when he pulled him, how slight he was. Muldoon said, "Virgil, I'm no detective! I'm a—"

The driver's mouth was moving. Tillman, going back out as far as he could lean as if Muldoon had never pulled him in, said in a deep, slow imitation of the driver's voice, "Oh. Good morning. Me friend and me, we's, like, ah, got a valuable consignment—like—for the address here—" The driver looked at the note: "Some swell, rich gent who ordered stuff from London, named, ah—" Tillman said, "Look at the note!" The driver looked at the note. Tillman said portentously, "Ah. A Count von Duke of Baron and we, ah—" He saw the driver shrug: "And we just ain't got da time to wait around—like."

The first respectable, decent Christian on the street said— Tillman saw his mouth form it—"Oh." He said something else. It was probably, "That's too bad, but a man has to keep moving to earn a living."

The driver's off-sider, obviously a man of few words, nodded.

Tillman said, "So—" He was grinning, lapping it up like a cat with cream. Tillman, raising his arms like a conductor with a baton and then rolling his hands like wheels to lead the score word by word, said, "So-would-it-be-all-right-if-we-left-the-stuff-here-in-front-of-the-door-and-you-honest-blokes-tell-the-owner-when-you-see-him?" On the street they were doing it, word for word. Tillman, clenching his fists in triumph, said, "HAHHH!" He was hopping up and down on the footplate. *"Gotcha!"*

He suddenly saw it. Muldoon said in alarm, "Do you mean they're going to steal that stuff the moment the delivery wagon has gone?"

Tillman said, "Absolutely!" On the street, the two good Samaritans were already up on the wagon helping the driver and his partner to unload. Tillman said, "The moment that wagon gets around the corner, those crates and parcels and boxes will be gone from the sight of civilized men forever!"

"Maybe we should get off and—"

"No, *no!*" Tillman, starting to lose sight of the wagon as the horsecar clipped inexorably on, said, shaking his head, "No, no. No!" Tillman said with undisguised admiration, "I've only ever heard of it being done at night and then what it is is that the address is closed for the night." He said, grinning, "Sturgess and Skoler— they must have sat down and thought hard for a long while before they came up with that one." He tried to see them, but they were too far away. Tillman said happily, "Daytime—you have to give them credit."

Muldoon said, "What the hell are they delivering in those boxes?"

Tillman said, "Garbage. They deliver garbage. They clean out basement rooms down by the river below the tideline for landlords and they don't pay the barge carriers to cart it out to sea because they don't want to pay the fee, so they pack it up and seal it and string it and they—" Tillman said in glee, "So they deliver it to a phony address in the street and they let someone steal it!" Tillman said as a connoisseur, "Wonderful! How inventive is our race!" Tillman said, "The Count von Duke of Baron—it must have been! It's too old hat to use John Jacob Astor anymore—" He seemed deliriously happy. Tillman said, urging the two thieving swine in the street on as, no doubt at this very moment, they called their gang of fellow vultures to get the swag in off the street fast, "*Enjoy!*" He said with happy malice, "Ugh! I've seen what Sturgess and his friend take out of those cellars—" He was like a small grinning child at a birthday party. Tillman said joyously, "Ned— . . . *Ugh!*"

They were near the corner of Bowery and Dover, coming to their stop. In the horsecar, Katie the Kisser, her head muzzled hard against the stout man's chest, her breast rubbing at his arm, took a gentle bite and had the little diamond stickpin in her mouth and, at the same time, awoke.

"*Sir!*"

It also woke the conductor.

Katie, a good, respectable girl worn from her honest labors, thinking of what her father and eight six-foot-three-inch brothers would say, said in horror to the fat lecher, "*Sir—!*"

Through the glass of the rear horsecar door, she saw Headquarters City Detective Tillman's face watching her.

Katie said, "Oh!"

She saw him smile at her, for what reason she did not know, a wonderful smile.

She smiled, just for an instant, back. Katie said in horror to the conductor with the stickpin secured firmly between her cheek and upper gums, "Oh, Conductor, you are a uniformed official of this line—please, instantly, protect a poor girl from this man's degenerate urges and see, at Fulton Street, he does not attempt to get on the ferry after me!"

Maybe, maybe with a bit of luck there would be a nice suicide note at Schweib's house. Maybe all it was was a nice little domestic.

Maybe.

Things were starting to heat up a little inside the horsecar and, in order to save time, they got off the footplate where they were and, stepping carefully over the horse manure in the road, began to walk in the direction of Dover Street to Slip Alley where, at the theater, they said Albert Schweib had lived.

4

Below Fourteenth Street, where three-quarters of the entire two-and-a-quarter-million population of New York lived, one-third of all the buildings were tenements and slums. From the outside, many of them looked the same: dark, airless stone and clapboard boxes cut inside into even smaller boxes—tiny rooms where there were no windows and no air and where, everywhere, there was the smell of stale food and garbage and earth-closet privies in the backyards and the smell of goats and clay soil that grew nothing. In Slip Alley, coming in from the waterfront, there was the smell of barnacles and rot and a heavy, cloying stench of the oystermen's catches laid out two streets away and along the foreshore to dry.

On the ground floor of number 16, Slip Alley, Mrs. Meyer, the landlord's agent, looking them up and down outside her door, said, "Flattie and the Elbow."

Muldoon said, "Wrong." She was a slight woman wearing a faded black crepe dress and a clean white muslin apron and a basin-shaped straw hat she had put on quickly before she had opened up. Muldoon said, "Flat elbow and the fly cop." He touched himself on the chest: "Flatfoot dressed up to look like a detective and a flypaper thief catcher." Muldoon said, "Flattie and the fly cop." Slip Alley was in the Fourth Ward of the city. It was where, before they had all begun to make good, the various races of New York—the Irish, the Germans, the Bohemians, the Jews, the Italians, the Spanish and even the few Arabs in the city—had first settled in, living together in some harmony. Now they were all gone, the Irish to the East Side and the Italians north to Harlem and the Jews to Hester and Delancey streets and never come back. Muldoon said to the woman old enough to remember, "Edward Muldoon." He saw Tillman a little down the corridor go out to the

34

front step of the place and look upward at the building itself and back behind him into the alley. Muldoon said, "The key to Albert Schweib's room." Muldoon said with his soft County Meath Irish accent suddenly strong, "D'ye know he's dead?"

Mrs. Meyer said, "The woman who buys the newspaper told me on her way to get goat's milk for her children from next door." She had a handbag clasped in her hand with the fingers down over the closed top to protect whatever was inside. The handbag looked flat. There was nothing inside. She had her fingers clasped so tightly on the bag the whites of her knuckles showed. Mrs. Meyer said, "I'm a respectable person."

Muldoon said firmly, "I can see that."

Mrs. Meyer said, "How can you see that?"

He held her eyes. Muldoon said, "I can see you're a decent, respectable woman because I can see that the floor in this corridor is clean and you don't have to do that. I can see you're a woman who takes pride in yourself." Muldoon said, "I can see that you're a woman who would never open your door to anyone—however high or low—without wearing a clean apron and giving them respect." She had nothing. She looked as if she sometimes barely had food to put on her table. Muldoon said, "I can see you're as fine a Jewish woman as my own mother was a fine Catholic woman." Muldoon said, nodding, "I can see that."

He looked into her eyes and smiled.

He waited politely in the corridor, signaling Tillman to come with his hand, as Mrs. Meyer went back inside her room behind the closed door to get her master key.

It wasn't a domestic. No one but Albert Schweib had ever lived in the little room on the third floor of 16 Slip Alley. It looked as if not even he had lived there. He had been there seven years. If he had had anything the first day he had come to the house, he had had nothing on the last. From the single window in the room, across the roofs of other tenements with their maze of telegraph wires and gray tents set up for the consumptives trying to find clean air for their disease, the new Brooklyn Bridge filled the sky. The bridge—caissons and webs of supports and wires and suspensions stretching across the East River above the masts of ships along the waterfront—was nothing more than a framework, filaments to house the roadway with its twin carriageways and pedestrian roads and twin sets of rails for the steam train in the center. It was a masterpiece, the greatest triumph of nineteenth-century engineering, the longest suspension bridge in the world, due to open in four days.

The room was, as Tillman paced it out, a box ten feet by ten feet. He looked up. The ceiling, once part of a single great pressed-zinc plate for what must have been perhaps the office or living area for one of the late-eighteenth-century merchants when the Fourth Ward had been all of New York there was, was brown with rust and damp and sagging and bulging in the center. Once, there had been some sort of design pressed into the zinc: cherubs and bunches of grapes and flowers. Now, where the floor had been partitioned by a landlord who lived north of Houston Street where there were trees and tranquillity and avenues, the designs and cherubs had been cut by trusses and pierced by nails and screws.

There was a straw-filled mattress on an iron-framed bed and a cracked and burned Niagara portable gas lamp on the floor for light at night and a heavy hasp on the inside of the door and another on that doorjamb and, hanging from the door on the hasp, a good-quality Scandinavian heavy-duty steel padlock with a key.

Schweib had worked at night. The padlock was to keep him safe while he was in the room during the day. The padlock looked new.

Muldoon, standing at the window admiring the bridge, said, "Well . . ." He did not look at the tents for the tuberculosis sufferers on the roofs—he had seen tents before. He looked at the bridge and sucked in his breath in admiration. Muldoon, shrugging, said, "Well, there's an end to it." He looked across the roofs to the masts and the funnels of steamboats in the river waiting to move into the docks along the waterfront to unload. Muldoon said, shaking his head at the great bridge, "Who'd have shares in the Brooklyn ferryboats now?" He reached into his inside coat pocket and took out a hip-flask-size bottle of Old Republic whiskey. Muldoon, taking a swig from it to toast the bridge, said finally, "A mystery until one day some eager young flatfoot on his first patrol pinches someone for spitting on the sidewalk who confesses to it and Mr. Byrnes can be happy saying he suspected him all along and was just biding his time until the arrest." He saw Tillman down on his hands and knees looking under the bed, and, when he could not see anything for the dust and darkness, extending his arm to run his palm along the floor there, Muldoon said, "Maybe the good woman below has got a little something to drink."

There was nothing. Lying down flat and extending his arm under the bed as far as it would go, Tillman, feeling around, felt nothing.

Muldoon said, "Leave it to Byrnes."

He felt nothing on his hands and knees so he turned over onto his back and, staring up at the ceiling for inspiration, pushed hard with his shoulder and got the tips of his fingers against the wall.

There was nothing.

Tillman, turning back over again, began feeling along the iron frames of the bed under the mattress.

Muldoon said, "Byrnes has got an arrangement with the bad elements in this city, Virgil—*quid pro quo*: what they used to say in the old Latin in Ireland: this for that. Byrnes turns a blind eye to every second crime in return for information about every first." He saw Tillman's mouth tighten as, going back down on his back, he stretched hard for a far corner of the bolted-down bed his hand had missed the first time.

Muldoon said, "He lets bad eggs off one out of every two times if they give him information about a crime that will get him into the papers as a detective."

Tillman said, still stretching, "We'll talk to the landlady."

"Landlord's agent."

Tillman said, "We'll talk to her."

"Why?"

"Because it's a mystery."

Muldoon said suddenly, "Cops don't solve mysteries! Not even Byrnes solves mysteries—Byrnes pretends he solves mysteries for the newspapers!" He thought he knew. Muldoon said, "You don't think he solved the Manhattan Bank Robbery, do you—by himself? Like a detective from a book? He solved the Manhattan Bank Robbery because someone a flatfoot arrested for murdering a bloke in a bar told Byrnes who did the bank in return for Byrnes's arranging with Tammany Hall to pick a judge for the trial who would let him off on a charge of accidentally discharging a firearm!" Muldoon said, "All the clues in the newspapers—Byrnes's *clues*— the Masonic symbol on the vault wall, the broken Italian silver stiletto, the scrap of paper with the word '. . . forever . . .' on it, Byrnes invented himself! The robbers agreed the clues were there, in return for not being charged with going armed with a mechanically sound revolver in the commission of a crime!" Muldoon said, "Byrnes gets his clues from Dime Novels—from the Deadwood Dick Western Detective books!" Muldoon said, "He's got a collection of them in his office under lock and key and he goes through them page by page underlining with a red pencil the clues in them he can put in his own cases!" Muldoon said, "Do what everyone else does—send in a basic report written in pencil so he can get you to redo it in ink with the clues in when a flattie catches someone!"

Tillman said, "We'll talk to the landlord's agent."

"*Why?*" He saw the look on Tillman's face. Muldoon said, "*Why?*"

"Because she may know something."

"Virgil—"

Progress. Outside, they were working on the last stages of the great bridge that would link the two cities of New York and Brooklyn. The air was full of telegraph wires linking . . . well, whatever they linked. Progress. In the room there was absolutely nothing, as if Schweib, dead on the floor of the theater, had never lived. In the empty room, one of these days, instead of the table gas lamp with its dull yellow light, there would probably even be the new electricity. Bridges, telegraphs, electrical lighting, elevated railways—some people were even talking about building a railroad under the streets in tubes and shooting people by compressed hydraulic power from one end of the tube to another like olives in glass jars—mysteries . . .

Taking another swig from his bottle, shaking his head sadly at Tillman's set face, Muldoon said with a sigh, "Oh Jesus, Mary and Joseph . . . oh my God, a thinking detective—"

Muldoon, putting his hand to his head, said with the astonishment of a plain, simple man, "Oh my God, *what next?*"

On the wall of the parlor in Mrs. Meyer's three rooms there were framed and tinted daguerreotypes of two children dressed in white, the first about six years old and the second about eight, both little girls, both with a strange angel-like luminescence about them, both with large, shining, too-bright bright brown eyes and both, from the consumption a long time ago, dead.

He didn't ask. He saw her see him glance at the portraits and there was nothing to say. Tillman said, "Did he always pay his rent on time?"

There were little laundered white-lace doilies and antimacassars covering the small cheap tables and backs of chairs in the parlor. From the single window in the room there was a view of the buildings across the alley, clapboard and sinking on their foundations, the windows covered with oil paper to keep in the warmth. The view from the parlor window was through a pair of lace curtains made from something else—perhaps from an old wedding dress—with rust marks and threads of age starting at the corners. Under the window on a doily-covered table there was a very old Jewish nine-candled menorah made of brass polished to gold.

There was nowhere to sit. The chairs were too clean and small and he hadn't been asked. Muldoon, feeling thirsty, running his tongue across his lips, stood at the window and looked out.

Mrs. Meyer said, "Always. Always on the right day he came with the rent." The fly cop was very slight and small with piercing blue eyes. He didn't threaten her, he merely asked.

Tillman said, "He didn't live here. There aren't any clothes in his room. There's nothing in his room."

"He came in every night after his work in the theater."

"You heard him?"

"Yes."

"Did he come alone?"

Mrs. Meyer said a little indignantly, "Yes." She looked at Muldoon. Muldoon turned and nodded to her. He knew what she was. She saw Muldoon look at the fly cop and nod to him too. Mrs. Meyer said, "There was never any trouble with him of that kind."

"What did he do in his room during the day if he worked at night?"

Mrs. Meyer said, "Gentlemen tenants have to go out during the day."

"Where did he go?"

Mrs. Meyer said, "I don't know." Muldoon was craning a little at the window trying to see the Bridge. He did not turn around. All he did was run the palm of his hand across his mouth. Mrs. Meyer said, "He came in after his work about twelve or one in the morning and he—"

Tillman said, "Was he sober?"

Mrs. Meyer said, "Always he paid on time and always, he was respectful and polite and—"

Tillman asked again, "Was he a man of sober habits?" He smiled at her. He seemed to be trying to understand. It seemed like a difficult question for him, some sort of mystery. Tillman said, "The room's empty. There's nothing in there except a bed and a lamp."

"He had things when he came! He had his furniture and his books and his goods—"

"When did he come?"

"Seven years ago." Mrs. Meyer said, "When he came he was a person with belongings and a trade and he—"

Tillman said with no expression on his face, "Has anybody been in his room since you learned that he was dead?"

Mrs. Meyer said, "No." Mrs. Meyer said, "No!" Mrs. Meyer said, "He sold his belongings! He—" Mrs. Meyer said, looking to Muldoon who was not looking at her, "He sold his furniture and his belongings one thing at a time. Before he went out in the mornings he took something with him and he carried it on his back down to the markets and he sold it." Mrs. Meyer said, "A chair, a table, bags of little things in a burlap sack—he took what was his and he sold it—" Mrs. Meyer said, "No one would go into his room, dead or alive!" Mrs. Meyer said, "I have not been in his room since he took it!" Mrs. Meyer said, "I'm a—"

Tillman said patiently, "Was he a man of sober habits?"

Mrs. Meyer said, "No. When he came to me, yes, but lately, no—not for the last six months." Mrs. Meyer said from nowhere, "His character failed him in the last six months—" She fell silent.

"Do you know anything about his past history?"

"No."

"Would you have inquired?"

"No." She looked at Muldoon.

Muldoon said, nodding, encouraging her, "You're a good woman. We know that. If he seemed a good man and he discharged his debts he was a good man. We know that." Muldoon said, "People change through no fault of their own. Life can get hard."

Mrs. Meyer said, "He was a good man until six months ago with always a polite word. He—" Mrs. Meyer said, "People have to live! This is my only income: what I get in commission for collecting the rents! He did no one any harm. Drink was eroding him, but he never, never, once—"

Tillman said politely, "You haven't used his name. Did you call him 'Albert' or 'Bert' or something else, or—"

Mrs. Meyer said, "I called him Mr. Schweib and he called me Mrs. Meyer."

Tillman said, "He's dead. Someone stabbed him to the heart with a pocket knife gun and then shot him three times while he was squirming."

Muldoon said, "*Virgil!*"

Tillman said, "Why do you think someone did that if he was such a polite, good, honest, and respectful man?"

He was a small man in a dark suit and vest with not a single medallion or ornament hanging from his watch chain. He was perhaps thirty-five years old. He was not married, you could tell.

Mrs. Meyer said slowly with an odd thin smile, "The good die all the time. They die young in front of the eyes of the people who love them or they die old, alone . . . of heartbreak."

Tillman said, "Yes." He saw Muldoon glaring at him from the window. He looked away from him. Tillman said, "He died of a secret, didn't he?"

Mrs. Meyer said, "Everyone has secrets."

Muldoon said cheeringly, "Not you. You're a plain, honest woman." He fingered the lace doily on the menorah table and thought to say something complimentary. It was a religious thing. He decided not to say anything. Muldoon said—

Tillman said, "Yes, they do." He kept moving his head slightly from side to side to hold her eyes, to follow them, to see what was there in them. Tillman asked, "What do you think his secret was?"

Mrs. Meyer shook her head. She seemed to be thinking of something else. Her eyes had tears glistening in them.

"Why did he sell his belongings?"

"For money."

"For what?"

"For—" Mrs. Meyer said, "I don't know."

Muldoon, starting to move to go, shrugging to finish, getting ready to leave, said, "Well, it's a mystery, isn't it?"

"Did he have any friends? Did he talk to anyone around here?"

"He worked at night. During the day he went out."

"Where?"

"I don't know." Mrs. Meyer said, "I never saw him during the day and in the evening he went on straight to his work and came back here at either twelve or one and he—"

Tillman said, "And he slept here with nothing in the room except a strong padlock on the inside of his door to keep him safe." Tillman said, "From what? From who? Who would he need to feel safe from in the house?"

Mrs. Meyer said, "No one!"

"What was he afraid of in the night?"

Muldoon said, "Virgil, the poor woman doesn't know!"

"He was afraid of something." Tillman said, "Where are his clothes? His clothes at the theater were clean. Where were they washed? Here?" He said before Mrs. Meyer could answer, "It couldn't be here because his clothes aren't here." Tillman asked, "Where are they? Where is his shaving kit? When he left here in the morning, was he shaven?"

"No."

"At night, if you ever happened to see him come in—" He meant, one late night, when they had both had to use the earth privy in the backyard and both carried their little table lamps to light the way, "—was he shaven then? Had he shaved during the day or the evening?"

Mrs. Meyer said, "Yes." Mrs. Meyer said slowly, comprehending it, "He lived somewhere else. He didn't live here. He lived somewhere else. He didn't go somewhere else during the day. During the day, because I never saw him in the street, he lived at his home and he only came here—"

Tillman said, "Maybe where he lived the rule was different. Maybe where he lived he had to get out, not during the day, but during the night."

There was a sort of gasp. It was Muldoon. Muldoon said in astonishment, looking at them both, "God Almighty—!"

Tillman said quietly, firmly, "I don't believe you ever treated your tenant with anything other than the most strenuous courtesy and politeness and honesty." Tillman said, "I can see you are a woman who has known suffering and tears. I don't believe that someone like you could bring yourself to treat another human being, however down on his fortune he might be or however vulnerable, meanly and thoughtlessly."

"Good man, Virgil!" He sounded like a Catholic priest passing a hardworking family man in the street. Muldoon said in an approving grunt, "Good man."

Tillman asked Mrs. Meyer softly, "Is there anything, anything at all you can tell me that might help us find the person who did this thing to Mr. Schweib?"

She thought hard for him. Mrs. Meyer, putting the joint of her index finger to her mouth, said, "No." She closed her eyes to remember things. "No."

"Do you know *anybody* he might have confided in? Anybody at all?"

Mrs. Meyer said suddenly, "Yes!"

"Who?"

Mrs. Meyer said, trying to remember, "A man . . . Once, about a month ago, a man came for him . . ." Mrs. Meyer said, "A slight man—taller than you—clean-shaven—" She knew about secrets. She said excitedly, "Clean-shaven!"

He waited.

"Clean-shaven and—" She glanced at Muldoon. Mrs. Meyer said, "And smelling of whiskey—"

Tillman said, nodding, "Like Schweib? Like Schweib, in the last six months—"

Mrs. Meyer said, "Yes." She screwed up her face: "I don't know if it was good whiskey or cheap whiskey—"

Father Muldoon, from his six-foot-three-inch-high judgment seat in Heaven, said avuncularly, "Well, of course, how would you . . . ?"

Mrs. Meyer said, "And stale perfume."

Tillman said, "What did he want?"

"He wanted Mr. Schweib. He seemed worried. He said he hadn't seen Mr. Schweib all morning—" Mrs. Meyer said, "—the morning. So he must have known where Mr. Schweib spent his days, mustn't he?"

"Yes."

"—and he—" Mrs. Meyer said, "And I told him I didn't know, but he could rap on Mr. Schweib's door, but I thought—" Mrs. Meyer said, "But he was gone as he should be or he hadn't come back that night and the man—"

Tillman asked, quietly, sliding into her thoughts, "What was his name?"

It came as her own thought. It simply came up from nowhere in her memory and before she could think that she had forgotten it, it was there. Mrs. Meyer said, "Mr. Rufus Carrol." Mrs. Meyer said, "Mr. Rufus Carrol! He told me. I remember it!"

Tillman said tightly, "What message did he give you to give to Mr. Schweib?"

Mrs. Meyer said, "To meet him at the usual place. That was what he asked me to tell Mr. Schweib to meet him at the usual place." Mrs. Meyer said, amazed at it herself, "*At the usual place!*"

Muldoon said in a whisper, "God Almighty . . ."

His voice was a whisper, his mouth tight, his eyes watching her. Tillman said, "And where was that?"

"At his cousin's." Mrs. Meyer said, "They were cousins, Mr. Schweib and Mr. Rufus Carrol—they must have been—because Mr. Rufus Carrol said, "At our cousin's." Mrs. Meyer said, "They didn't look alike at all."

Tillman said in admiration, "What a fine, bright brain you have."

Mrs. Meyer said, going over it, "At our cousin's in Bleecker Street. At our cousin—at our cousin—" It had been a very long time since she had felt needed. Mrs. Meyer, clenching her fist to find it somewhere in her memory too full of dying children and long years of loneliness and weeping, said, "At our cousin . . . *At our cousin Mag's in Bleecker Street!*"

Muldoon said in horror, "Oh my God!"

She saw Tillman's eyes. They were shining. Mrs. Meyer said, nodding, "Yes! Yes! *At our cousin Mag's in Bleecker Street!*"

"Oh my God!" It was Muldoon at the window. He saw Tillman grinning. He saw him take a step forward to Mrs. Meyer and, very gently, as comrades, take her hand and shake it once. He saw him grinning. He saw him look happy. He saw him flex his shoulders a fraction to gain strength for something. He saw him look over and grin.

Mrs. Meyer, for that instant a woman with a husband and children, a somebody again, important, said with joy lighting up her face, "Yes! *Our cousin Mag's on Bleecker Street!* Yes!"

She wished, oh she wished, in that instant following the happiness, she still had someone she loved and who loved her, to share it all with.

5

"**Ach**! Mountain of loveliness lady!" Inside the door of Cousin Mag's Suicide Bar on Bleecker Street, a filthy smoky black hole below ground where the sun never shone, Tillman, offering a lily, said, "Gif me leaf introduce myself: Henrik Harvey Huckenduppler, farmer, of Dutch Pennsylwania, and—" He turned a little and motioned Muldoon forward, "Und mine friend Merle Stoltzfus Zook—also of Dutch Pennsylwania—goot vorker, not married, looking for vife, carrying lilacs for nice vife girl if he find in vicked city." Tillman said in the direction of Cousin Mag by the bar, "Here he. Say goot mornink to lady, Jan."

He was there somewhere behind the lilacs. Muldoon, peering out from behind what looked like every lilac in New York, pressing them hard against his chest like a happy mourner, said, "Hello. Ja." He was standing in sawdust on the filthy floor. On the bar top there was what looked like a dead dog. Muldoon, the hopeful swain, said firmly, "Goot sawdust dis, und goot dog dat." He had said his piece. He stepped back into the gloom.

Tillman said, "Ja." He was just a happy clam from the corn belt. He looked at Cousin Mag. She was just a mountain of flesh with a face like a plate of mortal sins carrying a bludgeon in her left hand and an ancient Colt Walker Dragoon .44 revolver the size of a ham hock in her leather belt. Tillman said, "Haf heard many stories about bad city of New York, but not true, we discover, as haf today sold mine goot Lancaster county corn in bad city for much goot money." He patted his chest where the money was. Tillman said politely, "Mine friend Merle Stoltzfus Zook who ve call Jan because so many Stoltzfuses in Pennsylwania, no judge of animals and joost a plougher—think maybe your dog on bar is dead, lady."

45

At the bar, Cousin Mag breathed out. She breathed through both nostrils at once.

He, like Muldoon, had his pants cuffs rolled up above the top of his boots and his hat set back on his head. Tillman, turning to Muldoon, said chidingly, "Dock not det, dock asleep." He touched at his hat with his lily. Tillman said, "Jan gentle soul, but knows nothing about docks."

All he was above the lilacs were eyes and hair and a hat. Muldoon said with a trace of irritation in his voice, "Know about ears. Haf two of dem myself." A hand came out from behind the lilacs and stabbed a finger in the direction of the bar top, "Dat is boddle of ears."

What could you do? It was so hard to find good bright help in Pennsylvania where everybody had the same name. Tillman said, "No. Not ears. Boddle of pickles."

Muldoon said, "Ears." Along the walls of the place in the darkness he could see the forms of people at benches and trestle tables. He could smell them. Muldoon said, "Peeple." He pointed at the dog, "Dock." He pointed at Tillman, "Henrik Harvey Huckenduppler." He pointed at the sealed bottle of human ears floating in alcohol on the bar, *"Ears!"*

Tillman said, "Joke! Is not real ears." They were. After Cousin Mag bludgeoned you or shot you or butted you with her head like a goat or throttled you with her belt—or simply decided she didn't like you—she bit ears off. She looked, standing there, watching them in utter silence, like the Boulder of Doom. Tillman, taking a careful step forward, said, "Forgive, lady, is thought that wif so much money ve make today, Jan can buy new room for house—is making him proud." Tillman, turning, taking in the men at the trestles who would kill to replenish their tin mugs of beer—the muggers—said disapprovingly, "Alvays remember do to udders as udders should do to you." He heard Cousin Mag breathe. She was deciding whether after she had killed them their bodies should go in the quicklime out the back, or into the river, or merely be thrown out onto the street. Tillman said, "Enough now of lighthearted happiness at making so much money—am on business here to find dear lost brudder-in-law of mine, Rufus Carrol, and am ready to pay fellow—or lady—who help." He was just a happy, rich, country clam. He put his hand in his pocket.

Tillman said to the room, grinning into the gloom, "Haf a nice, honest-earned silver dime for person who tells me vere mine brudder-in-law Rufus is—"

He heard, not only Cousin Mag, but everyone in the room, draw a breath.

Tillman said warningly, "But, no, no, not lily flower—nein, lily flower is for lady here."

He looked at the two hundred and fifty pounds of tender womanhood reaching for her club.

Tillman, grinning, beckoning anyone in the room who might want to do a Christian charity, "Ja? Ja? —Anyone?"

The train now leaving the back of the bar was the on-time Cousin Mag special nonstop express to Eternity. There were a few, smaller tank engines starting to work up steam along the trestles and the benches, but hearing the rising steam, they decided to give the special the road and sat down again.

Jan Zook, the flower-carrying ploughman, said in triumph, "See, dose men haf only vun ear each. Vat is in dat boddle is ears!" The lilacs against his chest seemed very heavy. He staggered a little with their weight. Zook Muldoon said, nodding, "Vill tell at prayers day you vas wrong, Brudder Huckenduppler, and Merle vas right." Muldoon said, "Girls in Soudersburg say no to mine courting approaches because you say Merle Stoltzfus Zook is moron." He was getting a few little hits in. Muldoon said, "Und dat dock on bar is *dead!*"

The train drew in its shoulders. Somewhere in those shoulders, by the lantern light, there were two little burning coals. They were eyes. The eyes caught sight of a shadow moving at one of the trestles and turned on it and the shadow moving at one of the trestles sat down again.

Tillman said to Cousin Mag a moment before her head disappeared into her neck, "Lily, lady?"

"Und den—"

Cousin Mag said, ". . . aaahhhAAAHHH . . . !"

Tillman said, "No lily." He dropped it on the floor and got between Muldoon and Mag. Tillman said—

Tillman shouted an instant before she came at him with her head down like a goat and her skirts flying, "Ned, *get behind me with the lilacs!*" He saw, like an express from Hell, what had the marginal appearance of a woman coming at him with her head down to butt the breath out of him and break him in half. She was roaring, breathing, covering the twenty feet between them in seconds. She came. He weaved. He sidestepped. She missed.

She missed him completely, looked up, blazed the little coal-black eyes, and, missing the gold, went for the silver. The dog on the bar didn't wake up. That dog was dead. Tillman, ducking down, almost losing his footing, turning like a baseballist to follow a fast ball that had gone right by him, yelled, "Ned, lilacs—" He tensed for the sound of the head hitting the lilacs, Tillman, in ecstasy, yelled, "*Lilacs!*"

She hit the chestful of lilacs. There was a strange sound.

It was a sort of hollow whoosh-donging sound. It was the sound of an enraged bull hitting lilacs. It was the sound of a head hitting lilacs—that was the whoosh—and turning them into mulch in an explosion of petals and stalks and color and then it was the sound of a head hitting a street manhole cover behind the lilacs.

THE NEW YORK–ILLINOIS MANHOLE COVER COMPANY
Guaranteed Finest Cast-Iron Quality
Warranted Good

That was the *dong*.

Well, if the New York–Illinois Manhole Cover Company wanted a testimonial from Muldoon, they could always get it. And, if they ever diversified, for poleaxes.

It poleaxed her. One moment she was there, and then she was in the lilacs and then there was a dong and then she wasn't there. She was on the floor. She was a big one. She was being gently rained upon by falling lilacs.

Muldoon said, "Ach!"

He thought he might lean down and place the manhole cover from the street outside gently by her head.

Nah.

He dropped the manhole cover from his chest and, missing Mag's head by an inch as it covered her in sawdust, reaching under his coat for his gun, yelled at the muggers as they rose as one man, "Muldoon of the Strong Arm Squad—one click of the hammer of a pistol and I'll shoot the nearest man to tripes!"

He was at the bar. Tillman, his own Colt Lightning in his hand, pointing muzzle-down into the jar of ears, yelled, "City Detective Virgil J. Tillman! Move a muscle and I'll fire into the jar and burn your ears to charcoal!"

They were looking not at him or Muldoon but at Mag.

Tillman said, "And no one kills her while she's unconscious!"
Tillman said, "Rufus Carrol—we want him! Where is he?" They
were looking, not at Muldoon, not at Mag, not at him, but at the jar
of ears.

Tillman said, "The first man who tells me gets his ear back for
decent disposal and everybody else's back for sale!"

Tillman demanded, "Rufus Carrol! We want him! Where is he?"
Tillman, cocking the hammer on the Colt to send a blast of fire and
smoke and destruction into the vile urn, shouted, "Tell me now or
I'll blast your severed hearers into cinders!" Tillman said with no
tremor in his voice, resolved to do it, "Going . . . going . . ."

"Vun!" In the babble of voices, Muldoon, waving his hands like
a conductor, giving Cousin Mag a kick in the ribs as he stepped over
her, shouted, "One!" They were mobbing him. "Vun!"

Muldoon said politely, "Please, please, joost vun at a time . . ."

She came out shooting. She came from nowhere. There was a long
corridor at the end of the room that neither Tillman nor Muldoon
had seen and the flash from the big eight-shot nine-millimeter
pin-fire revolver lit it up and she was there dressed all in black,
shooting at them. In the bar everyone scattered—they were going
for the stairs to the street.

Muldoon said, *"What the hell's happening?"*

There was a door at the end of the corridor; she was shooting
from the door. The door was wide open and there was light behind
her from a window somewhere and she was starting back into the
room, going backwards, and the shots and the light of the room lit
her up and she was a tall, thin woman dressed in black with long
blonde hair and she—

"Virgil!" Muldoon, ducking, going for the ground as the bottle of
ears exploded in a shower of flying glass, shrieked, *"Get down!"* The
gun at the end of the corridor was blasting explosions of flame and
smoke: he heard the detonation as she fired at Tillman moving
across the doorway. Muldoon, scrabbling on the filthy floor like a
crab in a storm of sawdust and glass, trying to get his gun out in
front of him to get a shot in, yelled, "Virgil! Get out of the line of
fire!" A bullet ripped into the floor beside him and blinded him
with splinters and he had his Smith and Wesson out, trying to cock
the hammer, but he could see nothing for the splinters and the
smoke.

"Albert!" He heard her shriek. At the end of the corridor, firing

wildly, she was shrieking Schweib's name over and over. Tillman was to one side of the corridor. The smoke from the black gunpowder was filling the corridor, coming out in thick acrid belches that bit at his nose. A flame came from the muzzle of the gun thirty feet away and stabbed out through the smoke and was a fireball on the bar as it hit the smashed ear jar for a second time in an instant and set the alcohol running on the bar on fire.

There were people running. The room was filling up with smoke and there were people running and she was shooting in the smoke over and over and the gun was never going to run out of cartridges.

"*Albert!*" She was shrieking, shrieking. He ducked across the entrance to the corridor with his Lightning in his hand and, in a flash from the gun, saw her and she was rocking up and down and screaming and shooting in the doorway. A bullet tore into the brick of the corridor and, hitting something metal in the wall—a support or a strengthening frame or a girder of some sort—whined off and ploughed into the ceiling and brought plaster down, and Tillman was going backwards over something hard and wooden onto his back.

"*Albert—!*" She was sobbing, weeping, rocking up and down, going back into the room and then out again. The thing he had fallen over was a wooden bench about four feet long and Tillman was on the floor with the leg of the thing in his hand and there was a click as she must have reloaded or gotten another gun and a blast of yellow flame and the sound of a long splinter of wood being wrenched upwards by the bullet.

He was tangled up in the bench. He was on his feet with the bench in his hand. There was a shot inches away from him on the floor as Muldoon got a round off from his .32 and Tillman, getting the bench up against his chest, fighting it, holding it by one leg in his free hand, losing it, getting the two top legs across his chest, ordered Muldoon, "Don't shoot, Ned! Ned! Don't fire!" He had the bench hard against his chest like a shield, the top legs over his shoulders. Tillman, starting to run, getting the Lightning out away from the bench and starting off down the corridor like a madman, yelled, "YAAAAH—!"

He saw her. He saw her start. He saw, in the smoke, for a second, her eyes. Tillman, charging down the corridor, shooting all around her, screamed at the top of his voice, "*YAAAAHHHH—!!*"

* * *

She saw him through the smoke. Through the smoke, coming at her, unstoppable, he had his gun out and he was firing—firing at her, near her, at her, all around her, screaming like a murderer, and she fired at him and the bullet tore across the bench as it weaved in his arms and sent a fountain of splinters and sawdust across him and hid him and then he was out of it again, running, screaming, unstoppable, coming, shooting, screaming; and she fired again, and then the gun jammed and she could not get the hammer back as one of the fired cartridges, swollen by firing, must have stuck against the recoil plate of the gun and would not let the cylinder turn and she pulled back hard on the hammer, hauled it free and fired again.

His bullets were all around her. There was brick dust falling from the ceiling and walls and in the brick dust there were bullets smashing, ricocheting, whining out of control all around her and surrounding her like lethal bees. He was coming. She heard him shriek. He was a murderer. He was Nemesis. He was coming, unstoppably, running, screaming, shooting.

The gun jammed. He saw it. It was only thirty feet to the door, but he was running and weaving and screaming, wanting not to stagger as the bullets hit the bench and embedded themselves in the hard wood. It seemed—the corridor—to be forever. He saw her yank back hard on the pistol hammer, look down for an instant in the smoke, and, aiming again to one side of her, he fired into the doorjamb and smashed it to pieces. She looked up and he fired to her other side and made her stagger. He was running out of bullets. He had fired three. He had three left. He saw her look up. He saw her eyes and he fired above her head and made her jerk. He was going to be on top of her. He had two bullets left. He had the bench and the momentum and he fired again to miss and made her wince as the bullet blasted through the smoke and went into the room behind her and smashed something to pieces in an explosion of light and flying glass and he was there. He was almost there. He saw the big gun clear. He saw her look down at it. He saw her eyes and, only eight feet away, he fired his last round straight up into the ceiling and lit himself up in the smoke and the stink of brimstone like a devil, and he saw her eyes for an instant, saw something change, saw her seem to calculate something and then, making the decision in an instant, readying, tensing for the crash as he hit her with the bench, he saw her bring the gun muzzle up and he saw her, with what must have been her last round, put the muzzle against the side of her head.

Tillman screamed, "No!—*DON'T!*"

Tillman shrieked at the top of his voice, "DON'T—!"

She was weeping. It was all happening, suddenly, so slowly. Tillman yelled— His feet were frozen to the floor. He was not moving and he could not move and it seemed to be happening so slowly and he saw that she was weeping and he heard—he actually heard—a thought in her head. He heard Schweib's name. He saw her finger on the trigger and he was opening his mouth to yell, forcing his feet to unglue themselves from the floor and he saw her—

He was an inch, an inch away from her. She was weeping. He saw the tears on her cheeks and he saw that she was old, lined, and he saw— and he never heard the shot, but only saw her face change, become pulp, become blood, become a mask, become something awful and destroyed and wasted and blown to pieces as the disgusting, filthy thing from the gun's muzzle blasted the side of her skull to shards and tore through her brain and destroyed everything worthwhile and human and worth saving and—

Tillman screamed to the bullet, "NO—!" but it was too late and, his face an inch from the exploding, weeping face, the bench falling to one side, he reached out with both hands like a desperate child to hold her together against the bullet, but it was too late, and he was through into the room with her and she was on the floor, jerking and there was nothing to do now, and all the jerking was a reflex and she was gone, too late, dead, and he—

And standing there, looking down, trying to look away, he had nothing he could do, and she had fallen, chopped like a tree, on her back, jerking as she fell, and there was blood and white bone coming out from under the thick blonde hair and she looked shrunken, so much smaller in the long black crepe dress, and he—

He heard Muldoon coming.

He heard Muldoon coming, but he could not turn around to see him.

The stink of gunpowder was everywhere in the room, like brimstone.

In the room there was the sudden silence of death.

In the room, holstering his revolver, his hand black with powder and sawdust and soot, not wanting to see the thing on the floor again, not wanting to see Muldoon, passing by the shattered single window in the room, not seeing out, not looking, in that silence, Tillman, moving slowly, went toward the far empty side of the little clapboard room and there, setting his jaw hard to stop his mouth from trembling, like a small, sad child, stood in the corner with his back to the room and folded his arms.

6

At the doorway, Muldoon demanded, *"Who was she?"* He had dragged Cousin Mag's two hundred and fifty pounds in a chair down the corridor, settled her comfortably in a slump, and now, without rancor, was questioning her professionally with his blackjack.

Muldoon said unrancorously, "You vile, odoriferous tarantula at the throat of all respectable womankind and men, *who the hell was she?"* He gave her a belt across the shoulders with the loaded leather jack that made her flesh quiver. Muldoon said, "You fiendish handmaiden of Hell, *why are you wearing a man's shirt?"* She ceased slumping and sagged. Muldoon, forgetting his gentlemanliness—she was no lady—whacking her a good 'un across the top of the head and getting a sound like a tack hammer on a ninety-pound blacksmith's anvil, yelled, "Who was this poor innocent woman you drove to madness and death?"

Nothing. He whacked her again. Muldoon, spitting it through clenched teeth, said, "You'll swing! They'll take you out to the Tombs courtyard on Centre Street and Monsieur New York will visit you with his little black bag of nooses and knots and—*by God, you'll do a dance before you're jerked to Jesus!"*

In the room at the fire grate, Tillman said, "Leave her, Ned." There were ashes in the cold grate and burned mounds of soft kindling wood, as if someone carefully, methodically, had destroyed every trace of something. He had sifted through the firebox below the grate, but there was only what looked like the thin gray dust of burnt paper and cardboard. Tillman said, "She's out of it for a while."

"She's shamming." Muldoon said, not to be swayed, "I was taught from birth that a man defends and respects women."

Muldoon, taking a swing at her side with the jack and feeling it and his hand sink into the fathoms of flesh, said for sure, "If I can get to anything vital here, I'll wake her up!" He couldn't get to anything vital. Muldoon said tightly, glancing down at the wrecked face of the poor good woman on the floor, "She's led that flower lying dead there into a life of drink and depravity and, by God—" It was like hitting a canvas sack full of molasses. Muldoon, taking a swing at a biceps that had more weight to it than John L. Sullivan's, shouted, "She's—"

"There's no drink here, Ned. She hasn't led her to anything." Tillman, turning to him from the grate, his face changing as he saw the dead woman on the floor, said tightly, "I was within an inch of her. I could smell her breath." Tillman, shaking his head as Muldoon thought he might get another whack in anyway, said as an order, "Leave her, Ned. She's out of it." The dead woman was lying on her back. There was no face. There was only the thick blonde hair, matted with blood. Tillman said, "She wasn't a young woman. She was—"

Muldoon said, "She was someone's mother then!" He had a simple view of right and wrong. Wrong was the blackjack. He reached into his pocket for his brass knuckles. Muldoon said warningly to the disgusting mound of smelly flesh in the chair, "Edward Muldoon of County Meath—I once went thirty-nine rounds bareknuckle with an English gamekeeper—I won't get tired first!" Maybe his locust-wood club. Maybe the butt of his revolver. Maybe a good kicking. Muldoon said, "You're dealing with the New York Police Department here—you're dealing with the world's finest and fairest!" She was a fifty-acre fallow field of adipose tissue. Muldoon, starting to get hopping mad, yelled, "I've got the patience of Job! I'll keep hitting until I find something that hurts!" Muldoon, cracking Mag across the head with as much effect as a fly landing on the face of one of the caissons of the Brooklyn Bridge, yelled, "You led this poor, maddened creature straight to the doors of your bagnio and turned her into a harlot and an adventuress!" Muldoon, putting his face to within an inch of Cousin Mag's face, yelled, *"Who was she? What was her name?"* Muldoon, his face suddenly screwed up tight, said desperately to Tillman, "She shot at us—*what the hell did she do that for?"*

Muldoon said to Tillman moving toward the cupboard near the double bed in the room, *"Who did she think we were?"*

There was a sheet and blanket on the bed and two pillows, both with faded cheap embroidery.

Muldoon said with his strength gone, shaking his head, trying to understand, "Why would a woman, a lady, a gentle creature . . . why would a woman ever set her hand to anything like a gun? Why would someone—why would a gentle female ever find herself shut out of Heaven like that?"

The other gentle female in the room—all the gross lump of her—made a snoring noise; unprofessionally, with rancor, Muldoon, swinging the blackjack, gave her one for luck across the head and said like an angered lion, *"RAGGHH!"*

He had seen her. In that last instant, he had seen her face and heard her thoughts. Or, maybe she had said it or it was an echo, but he had heard Schweib's name.

In the room on Slip Alley there had been nothing of Schweib except the new lock. In the cupboard in the room where the dead woman was, he found Schweib's clothes. He had been there. He lived there. In the cupboard, on hangers, he found his suit and his shirts and his ties and, on a shelf above, two hats: a derby for the winter and an old, repaired straw boater for the summer. He found on top of the chest of drawers in the cupboard, in a little cardboard box, two bow ties for the boater: one dark and proper for the street, another striped and rakish for Sundays.

In the pockets of the suit and the shirts he found nothing but a pair of collar studs and an old, tarnished brass cuff link in the shape of a heart with a single flower engraved on it; a souvenir, or a keepsake, or maybe, maybe something just forgotten.

Everything else had been burned. In the drawers of the chest, as he pulled them out one by one, all Tillman saw were socks and suspenders and handkerchiefs, all laundered, all folded, all like exhibits at an exposition, all bespeaking . . . nothing.

Vests and underwear. Nothing.

In the bottom-most drawer two pairs of boots, both leather, both from somewhere—not on Broadway, but the Bowery—both looked-after and regularly polished, both cracked and soft from walking and age, and both down at the heels and resoled many times.

Tillman said to Muldoon, "Albert Schweib." Standing up from the chest of drawers, he pushed open the door of the cupboard as far as it would go and pulled out the hem of the nearest dress on a hanger in the far end. Tillman said, "He lived here with her. That was where he went in the mornings." He still had the bottom-most drawer open. Along the floor of the cupboard were her shoes and high-button boots, three pairs of them: one low-heeled for walking in long dresses, one pair higher-heeled and prettier for a dress with a higher hemline, and a third soft and blue and pretty with bows for the summer, for walking in the park with the man wearing the boater and the rakish bow tie.

In another, smaller chest of drawers in her end of the cupboard, he pulled open a drawer and saw her unmentionables and closed it again. He smelled the smell of lavender from a potpourri bag.

Tillman said softly, "They lived here together. They were lovers."

Tillman said, "The fire is cold. Long before we got here, she burned everything that might have said who either of them were." Tillman said, "She wasn't a young woman. She was about the same age as Schweib—in her fifties or early sixties . . ." Tillman said simply, "There's only one bed in the room. They were lovers. There's no money. She wouldn't have burned that—she couldn't have if it was in coin. Schweib must have supported her and there was no money left over from one week to the next."

Muldoon said, "Companionship isn't a sin." He looked at Cousin Mag for somewhere vital he had missed. There wasn't anywhere. Muldoon said, "Who was she, Virgil?" It was a direct question. He needed an answer.

Tillman said, "C. R." He had something in his hands from the bottom of the cupboard. Tillman said, "It's a Montgomery Ward mail-order clothing catalog for—" He found the date on the soft cover "—for summer 1883. It's got her initials written on the top corner of it in pencil over and over as if she were thinking what to order." Tillman said, "C. R. It's probably her." He opened the thick publication where one of the pages was turned down. It was the ladies' dress section with a light blue dress circled below the advertiser's puff: *"Ladies' Wash Light Blue Dresses. Garments of Light, Soft Weight for Summer and Early Autumn made by our own seamstresses and in the Latest Styles. Good Value for Money and Serviceable for Years if carefully looked after and altered for the Styles."*

Tillman said, "The order blank in the back of the catalog is gone and the blue dress in the advertisement is on one of the hangers here." He looked down at her. She was dead. Tillman said, "She was C. R. She was Albert Schweib's common-law wife."

When Cousin Mag came to Muldoon was going to beat her to a pulp.

Muldoon said softly to the dead woman on the floor, "God forgive her." He crossed himself.

He was going to club her to cat meat.

In the chair, sagging, Cousin Mag made a groaning sound. It sounded to Muldoon like a sneer.

He was going to punish her to a puddle.

Mangle her to maggot meat.

Mince her. Mash her with his leather blackjack until the thongs creaked and the lead weights ran molten. He saw Tillman, for some reason, take up one of the dead woman's shoes and set it down next to one of Schweib's boots, then another from the second pair, and he asked, a little shocked, "Virgil, what are you doing there?"

He saw Tillman look up and then down at the shoes again, and then start to say something and then change his mind.

Muldoon, starting to come over, said curiously, "Virgil, what are you doing?" He saw Tillman look back to the dead woman on the floor with a look starting on his face that Muldoon could not read at all.

Muldoon said, "Virgil, what is it?" He saw him bend down into the cupboard and feel around at the back of the chest of drawers and then, finding nothing, tap at the floorboards there. He saw him brush dust away with the palm of his hand. He saw him looking hard at the patterns the dust made or, in the cracks in the boards at the bottom of the cupboard, where the dust went.

He heard a cracking noise as one of the boards came up. He saw Tillman reach down into the hole and find something.

Muldoon said, "What is it? What have you found?"

He had found Albert Schweib and he had found the man who had come to Albert Schweib's to tell him one morning to come to Cousin Mag's: Rufus Carrol. He had found a small burlap bag with a Corporal's cloth chevron from the Civil War in it and he knew it was from then because it was wrapped around a stiff, ancient daguerreotype of a group of fifteen men posing stiffly in their uniforms in front of a canvas tent somewhere from that time. They were Federals. Union men in their dark blue uniforms and peaked caps, some of them carrying old single-shot percussion Springfield muskets with fixed bayonets, one of them an officer with a sword and another, a bright, erect man staring straight into the camera's lens with his cap in his hand and a Corporal's chevron on his left sleeve.

Albert Schweib (Cpl.). It was on the back of the mounted picture in ink.

Rufus Carrol (Pvt.). He was the thin, slight, unbearded man standing next to Schweib in the front row smiling, carrying no musket or rifle, his hands grasped in front of him, looking straight ahead.

George Fenney (Pvt.).

Henry Carver (Pvt.).

Unknown

"John"

Colonel P. W. Seward (NYC)—the officer with the sword.

Unknown

Unknown

"Charlie."

Shand.

Warren Cahill.

He read all the nine names and the three listed as "Unknown."

He read the place and the time written in at the bottom of the mount: *Vicksburg, 1862.*

In the bag, also, there was an old, rusty, jammed and empty revolver with the legend *Gilbert and Greer, Atlanta, Ga* stamped into it and the caliber *.36;* a Confederate sidearm taken in battle and let rust.

The picture was a good one, clear, kept carefully out of the damaging sun for over twenty years.

In the room, Tillman looked carefully at all the faces.

He looked down at the three shoes extracted from the pairs in the cupboard and laid out next to each other in a line.

Schweib.

Carrol.

Fenney.

Carver.

Unknown.

"John" . . .

He looked at the shoes.

When she came to in the chair, Muldoon was going to—

He was going to—

He saw Tillman, without a word, go to the smashed window and, looking very small, stand in front of it and look out.

On the floor, the dead blonde woman lay still and dead and gone. Muldoon still had the blackjack in his hand.

For the moment, he could not think what to do with it.

Muldoon said, putting the jack in the pocket of his coat with his right hand and then taking it out again and then putting it back in, "Virgil, what is it?" He glanced at Cousin Mag.

Muldoon, bringing the jack up into his left hand and then taking it away again and then kneading it in with his fists and then letting go of it, finding nowhere to put it, demanded, his mind a total blank, "Virgil? Virgil, Jesus, Joseph and Mary, what the hell have you found there?"

He touched at the window frame. It seemed, sometimes, all his life he had been at windows, looking out. Tillman said softly, "Years. I spent years. Waiting."

He had waited for a face. All his life, it seemed sometimes, when he had been a child, he had stood at a window looking out, scanning the faces of people who went by, waiting for someone to come.

He touched at his face with his hand and felt a man's face. The boy's face had gone, disappeared, been turned into a man's face.

It was there, the awful, terrible loneliness. The place, his window at the Home where he had grown up, where they had taken him in, that was still there too—in this city.

He had spent all his life, when he had had the face of a child, standing there at that window, scanning faces, looking into them, waiting for someone to come.

He looked out the window now and saw nothing, only the bricks of the building next door, little light—nothing.

Tillman said, not to Ned, but to the window—to the window the dead woman had looked from, waiting for Schweib, waiting for them, waiting for someone—"I was taken in from the streets, Ned. I was left there—at the Home"—he looked at Muldoon's face for an instant—"With the good Sisters . . ." He touched at his face, "So I know about windows and faces and waiting and—" Tillman said, "I know about that."

He could not bring himself to turn and look at the dead woman on the floor, nor the shoes in the cupboard, nor the stiff picture he still held in his hand.

Tillman said, "I was an inch from her face. I felt the bullet go in. I felt everything torn to pieces and destroyed and I felt—" He had a good, kind face, Muldoon. Tillman said, "I felt the desperation, the finality, the soul fleeing from the body—and the end of hoping and changing and wondering and wanting and—" He touched at his eyes. His mouth was dry and he could not get the words out properly: "I saw her die. I saw her cease and die and end and everything she ever was or—" Tillman said, "Ned, I saw her face and I saw—" Tillman said violently, "I know about windows and small rooms and waiting and—I know about hoping. I know about being eaten up by hoping and waiting and looking and—*I know about faces!*"

She groaned. On the chair, Cousin Mag, coming around, groaned.

He could have ripped her head from her shoulders. Muldoon roared, "SHUT UP, YOU FILTHY HAG!"

Tillman said, "Ned, cover her face with a handkerchief." He meant the dead woman on the floor. He said, as Muldoon went to do it, "Look at the shoes."

There were three from the pairs in the cupboard, one women's and two men's shoes.

The men's shoes were different sizes. One of them was smaller, like the women's shoes.

Tillman said tightly, handing the photograph to Muldoon, "Look at the face. Look at Rufus Carrol's face." He was standing above the dead woman's body, looking down at the white handkerchief Muldoon had used to cover her. Tillman said softly, "C. R." He took a jackknife from the pocket of his vest by his watch chain and opened it with a click. Tillman said, "C. R. It was on the catalog she used to get her clothes by mail order."

"*Virgil!*" He saw Tillman kneel down and with the knife held like a dagger in his fist, insert the edge into the neckline of the dead woman's dress.

Tillman said, "*Shut up!*" He was shaking. On the chair, Cousin Mag moaned.

Muldoon shrieked, "YOU VILE VIRAGO, HOLD YOUR PEACE OR I'LL CATAPULT YOU STRAIGHT TO HELL WHERE YOU SIT!"

Tillman said, "C. R."

Tillman, cutting, splitting the dress like the skin of a rabbit, exposing her nakedness, said tightly, knowing it was true, "Carol Rufus."

He cut.

He cut.

He cut until the dress was all cut away and there, on the floor, under the clothes, beneath the blonde wig, he had cut all the clothes away and it was a man.

Tillman said tightly, in a whisper, "Carol Rufus."

Tillman said tightly, in a whisper, "God Almighty, Ned, what awful place have we come to? What depths of loneliness and desperation have we plumbed?"

Tillman said, the man talking to the boy who, all his life at the Home the Sisters ran for children who had no one who cared for them, had waited, hoped for someone who had never come, "God, Ned—God in Heaven—despair, love, loneliness . . ."

For a moment his eyes were wild, frightened, staring.

Tillman, in a fury, demanded, "My God, Ned—does every window, every window in every room in this entire world have nothing on the other side of it but an unchanging, unabating, unrelenting *outlook on Hell?*"

7

A parrot flew in through the window. Its name was Fred. Tillman, at his kitchen table in his rooms in the basement of 23 Van Dam Street, smoking a cigar, said, "Hello, Fred."

It was a white parrot. Coming in from the darkness, it perched on the windowsill, blinked its eyes at him in the gaslight, cocked its head to one side, and jumped onto a stuffed sheep from the bordello upstairs.

He was in his shirt-sleeves, collarless. Tillman, setting the cigar into an ashtray by his glass of brandy on the table, rolled down his cuffs in case Fred decided to hop over and sit on his arm. It was an old bird: it had claws like longshoremen's hooks. The bird lifted up one of its claws and dug it exploratorily into the wool on the sheep's back. It turned its head a full one hundred and eighty degrees and looked up at the ceiling.

Tillman said pleasantly, "Quiet night upstairs?" His plated pocket watch was open on the table by his key ring. It was a little after midnight. The bird looked at him and then down to the sheep and then down again to the wooden rocking horse beside it. Tillman asked, "Or do they want something from down here?" His rooms were where they stored their apparatus. By the sheep and the rocking horse there was a box of jockey's silks complete with gloves and riding crop, what looked like a shepherd girl's outfit complete with crook, and, in the corner, a fireman's helmet, bib and braces, a brass Captain's megaphone speaking trumpet and a pair of heavy leather fireman's boots, five pairs of magician's easy-open handcuffs, and the broken ratchet wheel from a rack.

Tillman said, "Would you like some brandy, Fred?"

It didn't. It turned its head and looked up at the ceiling. It hopped off the sheep and stood on a box of India-rubber masks of

63

President Chester A. Arthur and Governor Grover Cleveland. It must have been between shifts upstairs in Mrs. Lawn's Academy for the Teaching of Social Etiquette, *Seven Refined, Well-Bred Obliging Young Ladies*; normally Fred never deserted his post outside on the front steps where he announced new scholars. Tillman said, "Come and sit over here with me."

It wasn't looking at the ceiling. It was listening. It didn't stand still. It started to rock back and forth.

"What's the matter?"

It was a big, white, ancient bird with claws like gnarled tree roots. On the box of masks it started to rock back and forth, looking up.

Tillman said, "Fred . . . ?" He saw the bird's eyes turn to him and then go up to the ceiling again and then swivel, looking around, listening. Tillman, starting to rise, asked, "Fred? What's wrong?"

It was rocking. It was becoming agitated. It hadn't scratched. It always scratched. It began walking three steps in one direction and then three back again. It began shortening the steps and making them two and then one, and then it was rocking again. It began bobbing.

"Fred—?"

It didn't want to be touched. It weaved away from Tillman's hand and landed on the box of jockey's silks, sinking into them, going down, finding somewhere to hide. Then it came up again out of the silk and scrabbled onto the fireman's helmet and bobbed its head. It was listening. It began bobbing rhythmically, up and down, up and down. It opened its beak to make a sound—its tongue came out—and then, bobbing, weaving, starting to swivel back and forth, it closed its beak and made no sound at all. Its eyes were wide, blinking.

Tillman, listening, said, "What? What?" Except for the tapping of the bird's claws on the helmet, he could hear no sound at all, anywhere. He listened. In his shirt-sleeves, with the cigar burning away on the table, he stood up and looked up at the ceiling and listened. He could hear nothing. Tillman, like the bird, putting his head on his shoulder and looking up, said, straining to hear something, "Fred? What's the matter? What's happening?" Tillman said, "Who is it?"

There was a sound at the open window that led out the back into the garden of the three-story building. It was a quick, scrabbling sound. He saw the bird snap its head around to hear it. Tillman, going to the window, said, "What is it?" Tillman said to the bird,

"Fred, what's—" The bird was on the box of jockey's silks and riding crops and white gloves. It leapt from it and got onto the windowsill. Tillman, reaching for the window to protect the bird, said in the same instant as, out of nowhere, a tortoiseshell cat with a head as big as a watermelon appeared, *What can you hear that I can't?*"

Tillman said to the cat at the window, "Archie? What are you doing here?" It was Flossie's cat from the second floor. The bird was going mad, rocking up and down, scrabbling, jerking back and forth. It was not afraid of the cat. It was looking up at the ceiling, hearing something, starting to go crazy. The cat at the window was Flossie's cat from the second floor. It never left her room. It was at the window, opening its mouth to mew. Tillman said, "Flossie? Is it Flossie?" He heard the cat, in terror, start to mew. Fred, leaping onto the windowsill, screeched in terror, hearing something, "Aaawk! *Aaawkk!*"

Tillman said, *"Flossie? Is it Flossie?"*

"Aaawkk! Aaawk! *Aaawkk!*" The cat was stiff on the windowsill, mewing.

The bird was in flight, flapping, screeching.

It was a little after midnight. It was a quiet night, a slow night at the bordello. Tillman, reaching into the box of silks and grabbing at once, in one hand, a striped colored shirt, white gloves and, sweeping his laden hand past another box in one motion for the Fire Captain's brass megaphonic speaking tube, running for his front door to the stone steps up to street level, said in alarm, "God damn it, Flossie—Flossie, God damn it—!"

Flossie.

In the street there were two empty carriages. Under the gaslight he could see the horses kept in place by iron anvil blocks tied to their bridles. The drivers had been sent home: the driving seats were empty. In the windows of 23 Van Dam Street, all the lights were on.

Flossie. God damn it.

In the center of the street, putting the brass megaphone to his mouth and sucking in a breath of monumental proportions, filling his lungs, Tillman, aiming the tube straight up at the second floor, roaring at the top of his voice with Fred appearing out of nowhere, flapping around him in circles, thundered, "THIS IS THE SOCIETY FOR THE SUPPRESSION OF VICE! WE ARE HERE—FOUR HUNDRED STRONG—TO SEEK YOU

OUT IN YOUR DENS OF SECRET, UNHOLY VICE AND INIQUITY! WE ARE HERE! HERE WE COME!"

He was already running for the front steps to the main entrance of the house. He was already starting to put the striped jockey's silks on over his shirt. He was running, going up the steps two at a time, through the unlocked door and into the yellow, gaslit, deserted, silent lobby. He heard doors opening, slamming. He heard heavy footsteps on floorboards. He heard shouts, calls, whispers. He heard alarm. Tillman, his voice amplified by the brass megaphone to the level of the Last Judgment in the heavy furnishings and carpets of the house, roared at top volume a moment before—stuffing the jockey's white gloves into his pants pockets—he made for the coal box at the back stairs of the place: *"THIS*—GOD HELP ALL YOU EVIL FAMILY MEN UP THERE SINNING—*THIS IS A RAID UPON YOU BY THE RIGHTEOUS!!"*

They were running down the stairs like inept, half-dressed Swiss mountaineers, pulling on their pants, fighting suspenders and belts and braces and bootlaces. There were six of them, all florid big drunken men in shirt-sleeves and vests, looking for their frock coats and top hats, ducking and dodging the whirring white eagle or whatever the Hell it was diving and plunging around them screaming, "Aaawk! Aaawk!"

"Dis way, Massas! Dis way to de back door! Dis way!"

Thank God. There was a good loyal small black man wearing a striped silk shirt, white peaked cap and white gloves at the bottom of the back stairs, holding their coats and hats in a bundle, calling them down. He looked like the Black Prince of Monmouth Park, Hamilton the jockey. Thank God. They came down in a wall, falling and tripping on the stairs, reaching out for their coats.

"Dis way! Ezekial Cleveland Quincy Adams Bodine Washington is here to help you fine gent'men, yassir! Quick! Dis way!"

Thank God a quarter of a century ago they had all voted for Emancipation. Thank God for the Colored Man's gratitude. He was at the back door, working the lock, a small, slight, good and faithful servant with a sooty black complexion—coal black—so coal black and sooty for a moment you could almost swear that— Good and noble son of Ham, fast-witted tar baby; he moved so fast and worked so hard on the door lock the sweat came off his brow like liquid coal dust.

"*Aaaawk!*" The bird or whatever it was—the dove of divine domestic damnation—made a run at them, got in between the first three of them and the second three and took a peck at someone's head and drew blood.

Upstairs, Mrs. Lawn, shrieking like a banshee, running down the landing after them, no doubt armed to the teeth, screamed, "Six! Six of you at once? *Six?*" Hell had no fury like an enraged Madam. Ms. Lawn screeched, "*You gentlemen are not gentlemen!*" The bird screeched, "*Aaawkk!*"

They each had their coats and hats. They each had somebody's coats and hats. They were getting their arms in sleeves, fighting, going deaf with undersized hats, going blind with oversized hats, hopping, running, falling, trying to tie bootlaces with two fingers, crashing into each other.

They reached the end of the corridor. Upstairs there were doors slamming and the heavily armed harpie was thumping down the stairs after them. In the street, the phalanx of fanaticism must have been swirling, gathering, readying itself for the assault that would bring the front door down and them with it.

The little black chap shouted, "Dis ole door—! Dis ole door—! He was having trouble: he was wrenching at it. "Dis ole door stuck! Out dere dere be de Freedom Road!—and dis ole door stuck wid no silver dollar to get it open!"

"*Open the door!*"

"Yassir, ole Zeke Cleveland Quincy Adams Bodine Washington, he try, but dis ole door—" He disappeared in a rain of gold and silver dollars falling from de Heavens. Ole Zeke, he said, "Land sakes a massy, it be de Judgment Day and de good Lawd he paying me back for all dose years pickin' cotton on hot days for de white folks!" He got the door open. Outside the door was wonderful darkness and an open yard to Charlton Street. Tillman chortled in ecstasy as they rushed by him in a wind, "Oh, thank you, Lawd! Now I's a rich man and I can buy grits from de store fo' alla ma family every *day!*" Money. Hard cash. It made a poor man free. It made a poor man so free he changed before your very eyes. It made the blackness of his face fall away like sweat. It made— It made the last man in the posse suddenly turn around and look at him. It made the last man, a huge, heavy-jowled Irishman smelling of whiskey and pomade, demand, "You! Are you really a Colored Man?"

"I's happy! I's rich!" Tillman, looking up from his fortune on the floor, said, grinning in gratitude to the good white folks, "Sure nuff." You didn't look into de White Folks' eyes cause dey just didn't abide dat. Tillman, looking into the man's eyes, asked, "Are you really the Deputy Commissioner of Public Works down at City Hall? First floor?"

"You men are not gentlemen!" She was coming. She had at least, if not a scatter-gun, then a notebook and pencil. The bird, going for the front door as the Hordes of the Holy must have begun to charge it, shrieked, "AAAWKK!"

"Me? The Commissioner?" The man, going wild-eyed, grasping him by the shoulder, emptying his pockets into his hand, yelled, "No! Not me!"

"Right!" The man was down the steps and gone into the backyard catching up with his friends before the loyal African even got the word out.

Tillman, obviously the victim of a simple mistake—it must have bin his simple ole black mind—said, "Right . . ."

He could not see them in the darkness and by now they were probably halfway to Central Park anyway, but old Zeke, he knew his place. Politeness never hurt.

Starting to close the door, calling after them pleasantly into the night, Tillman called out, waving, "Y'ALL COME BACK NOW . . . *hear?"*

She had a face like an angel and a figure like a catalog of temptation. Sitting on the edge of her bed, wiping Tillman's face with a perfumed silken cloth, Flossie said softly, "Virgil, you are my hero." She had breasts like melons. She had on only a thin lace nightdress and a little pearl necklace around her neck. Flossie asked, "Virgil, are all men monsters tryin' to take advantage of a poor girl's tender heart and givin' nature?"

"I fear so, my dear." The cat was back. It rubbed itself up against his groin on the bed and purred.

Flossie said, "A cat can always tell a good, honest man." Flossie, dabbing, purring, said softly, intimately, "The simplest of God's little creatures . . ."

"I am."

Flossie said, "I meant the cat."

"Oh." Tillman said, "Flossie, tell me: what's the Fire Captain's brass speaking trumpet used for?"

"Naughty boy!"

The cat arched and purred. It was content. It was settling in for the night.

Flossie, dabbing, smiling, *breathing*, asked in a soft voice, "Virgil, dear, do you have any money?"

"Ah . . ." He reached down to shake the pockets of his pants to show, sadly, as usual, as a good, honest, simple man, he had none.

Tillman said in surprise, his pockets laden with silver dollars, "Well, yes, Flossie"—he didn't so much jingle as clank—Tillman said in happy amazement, "Well, yes, Flossie, it appears I do . . ." Tillman said pleasantly, "Excuse me, Archie."

Gently, not even waking the sleeping, purring animal, he moved the cat carefully off the bed.

On the so soft lace-edged pillow, Tillman, opening one eye, asked dreamily, "And the jockey's shirt. . . ?"

"*Naughty boy!*"

Flossie was no lady.

Her chestnut hair falling all over his face as she rolled over to him, a paean to pulchritude in her little heavenly room, in, really, a most shameless way, she—

She *giggled*.

It was a little after 3:00 A.M.

Walking on Chrystie Street—like Muldoon, dressed in a gray turtleneck sweater like a pugilist out for night training—Tillman said, pointing up, "That was my window, Ned." It was a dark, fire-shuttered five-story building with a gilt sign SHAND AND SON, IRONMONGERS faintly illuminated by a flickering gas-light above the third floor. "It used to be the Home the nuns ran for orphans." They had both been drinking whiskey at Ottomanelli's Oyster Bar on Spring Street. Tillman said, "That was the window just by my bed in the second-floor dormitory." They were both a little drunk. Tillman said, "The school and the chapel used to be around the corner in Stanton Street, but that's gone too, now."

Muldoon said, "What happened to you there, Virgil?"

"Nothing!" Tillman said, shaking his head and smiling, "Nothing at all. They took me in and fed me and taught me. They were good, kind people, the nuns. Nothing—nothing happened to me at all that I'm not grateful to them for."

Muldoon said, "Irish nuns."

"Yes."

Muldoon said, nodding, "Hmm."

The metal fire doors on all the windows were locked shut. It was modern Fire Department policy so as to contain a blaze inside to a single building. Tillman said, "It was the best bed and the best window in the place. I got it because I was taken in as a baby—not taken off the streets, but left there at their door—so by the time I was twelve I had seniority and I got the best bed and the best window." He was still looking up. Tillman said, "I stood there at the window, at first on a box, a lot. I know every flagstone on the sidewalk here and the color of every Belgian block in the road." Tillman said, "High up. Windows high up are good for looking out of and you can't see into them from the outside." Tillman said, "Like Rufus Carrol's window. For not looking into but out of."

"Sure."

He had his hand in a fist on his chest. He opened it and kneaded it and then tapped at his chin with the knuckle of his index finger. Tillman said as if it was of no importance, "We have to find out who murdered that poor man Albert Schweib, Ned, don't we? We're agreed on that, aren't we?" He glanced at Muldoon for an instant and nodded to him.

Muldoon said, "Byrnes is—"

"No, we have to do it, Ned. It has to be us." Tillman said suddenly, "They took me in as a baby when I was one day old. I suppose now, they had to get a wet nurse for me." He was still kneading his hand on his chin, "And a name: they had to get me a name." Tillman said, "Virgil Tillman—that's a good, holy, trustworthy name, isn't it?"

"It is."

"—that's a name that speaks of an honest Christian, isn't it?" Tillman said, "Virgil was the Christian name of one of the Sisters' fathers and Tillman was the name of—of someone the then Mother Superior must have known when she was a girl—someone special to her. She never said who."

Muldoon said, "God has a special place in Heaven for the women of holy heart who become his servants." He took a swig from his flask and raised it to the night sky. "God bless them each and every one. There's nothing I wouldn't do in this world if a good Sister asked me to do it." He handed over the flask: "We'll drink to that, Virgil."

"We will, Ned." It was Muldoon's Old Republic brand. It burned all the way down.

Tillman said, "One of them, Sister Mary Emmanuel, had medical training."

"Sure, they're great, good, clever girls . . ."

Tillman said, "When they found me—when I was left here—she was the one, I found out later long after she had died—who stopped me dying." He was still looking up, his mouth twisted. He lifted the flask and took a second swig. He would not look at Muldoon. Tillman said quietly, "I never thanked her because they told me nothing until I was old enough to know that however hard and long I looked out of that window no one was coming to get me." Tillman said, "Someone rang their bell one night after prayers and they came down and found me—they thought—on the point of death and they gave me last rites and a name and Sister Mary Emmanuel." Tillman said for the second time, "I never knew that until it was too late to thank her and she was dead." Tillman said suddenly, *"I waited! I waited at the window looking out until they finally told me when I was old enough to understand there was nobody coming!"* Tillman said tightly, "In the nights like this one—in the night when everyone else was asleep I waited for someone to come."

He put his hand gently on Tillman's shoulder, but Virgil, shaking his head, pushed it away.

Tillman said, slowly, one word at a time, looking up, "When they found me, I was dying."

"How?"

"When they found me, I was dying from a wound in the chest." Tillman said, "A long needle or a pick of some sort or a—" He touched at the center of his chest, "Here." Tillman said, shaking his head in spasms, "They said—later . . ." Tillman said, "Someone at my birth—"

"God in—"

Tillman said, "—killed me. They thought. And then—" Tillman said, "And then I was brought here."

"By who?"

His mouth was dry and salty. It was the whiskey. "By whoever it was—the other person present—I was brought here by the other person present wherever it happened who didn't kill me!"

"Then you could—"

"Oh, I could be anything. By birth I could be anything from a good Catholic to a Mormon to a Jew to—" Tillman said, "Maybe even half Chinese—"

"No."

"—if I have children of my own perhaps . . ." Tillman said, "Virgil Tillman: it's a good, strong, honest name."

He tried to think. He touched his hand to his head to help. Muldoon, trying to think, said, "But then if there were two people there when it happened—when one of them tried to—and if the other one brought you here to save you—"

Tillman said, "There was only one thrust. There was no second. There's only one scar."

Muldoon said, "My God, are you saying that the person who brought you here—?" Muldoon said, "How in God's name did that person stop the second thrust? *By murdering the murderer?*"

"I don't know."

"Who brought you here? A man or a woman? The mother or—"

"I don't know."

"God in Heaven, Virgil!" Muldoon said, "*God in Heaven!*" He tried to see Tillman's face, but he could not: he was still looking up.

Muldoon said gently, "Virgil . . ."

He was shaking. He was looking up and shaking. Tillman said, not looking at him, "I hate the nights, Ned, I hate the nights."

He had his hand on his shoulder. He drew him in to him. Muldoon, his eyes wet with tears, said softly, hurting, "Ohh . . ."

Tillman said, trembling, shaking, his voice a terrible whisper, his body stiff, like stone, "Honest to God, Ned—*Oh God, how I hate the nights—*"

*

8

Bridges, tunnels, telegraphs, telephones, steel, wire, pistons, wheels, electricity, steam . . .

The world shook. The streets trembled. Horses shied and bolted. Men looked up and gasped, women fainted, firehouse dogs howled—steam, steam, steam . . .

In the cabin of the 7:10 A.M. Manhattan Railway Company elevated train to the farthermost northern reaches of the city on the Second Avenue Line, railroadman Engineer First Class Geraldus van Meer, waving his arms, shrieked down to the peasantry on the streets, "The age of the leg is dead, *dead*, DEAD!"

A symphony of steel and iron and brass—nine tons of one-man Fornley tank locomotive pulling two carriages of wood and glass and more steel and brass and cast iron—roared above the intersection of Second Avenue and Thirty-third Street in a billow of white steam and black coal smoke, its red wheels striking sparks from the lines shaking and vibrating the elevated bridge girders and framework on which it traveled twenty feet above the cobbled and flagstoned roadways, the roadways taking up the pulse and humming, throbbing, opening up cracks that sent dust and grit up into horses' eyes and discommoded pedestrians.

No. 39 "THOR."

He had it painted in gold on the great brass boiler and on the coal tender and on the black, gilt-detailed acetylene carbide night-light below the jet-black sparking and smoking chimney. On his right as he leaned out of the cabin was the East River full of the coming thing: steamboats and paddlewheelers. On his left—he saw them all as he passed over Thirty-third Street at a shattering, full-speed, throttle full-out twelve miles an hour—all the other lines of the Elevateds, the arteries of locomotion quartering the city on Third,

73

Sixth and Ninth Avenues. Of these, the Second Avenue Line was the greatest, going farther than civilized New York man had previously dared go: all the way past Central Park on Fifty-ninth Street into the dark, almost uncharted regions of the streets numbered in three figures—all the way to One Hundred and Twenty-fifth Street.

"THOR." The god of thunder. Alone in his cab, shoveling in selected coal hobs with a brass hand spade, van Meer, passing by windows, shaking foundations, letting go the whistle, passing above a horsecar, sending its driver and Clydesdale into simultaneous convulsions, yelled down, "Dead! Dead! DEAD!" He fed with the brass hand shovel the Ever-Saddled Horse That Ate Nothing. Van Meer, letting go a blast of steam from the piston valves that steam cleaned all the street with the white brush of Progress, yelled down, "Hay—dead! Blacksmithing—dead! The past—dead as a doornail!" Invest in coal. He had. Van Meer shrieked, "Four days from now this train will be the first to cross on the new East River Bridge to Brooklyn!" People looked up. They looked away. Van Meer shouted, "An island no longer!" At the cab window, he was bobbing up and down, alternately shouting and shoveling. Van Meer, racing toward Thirty-fourth Street in the blinking of an eye, stopping for nothing, unstopped by traffic or policemen, time or horse dung, shrieked, "Number 39! Van Meer, Captain!"

God, he loved the New World. At home, in the Netherlands, in his twenties, he had been in the Army. He still had his sword. He had it in his cab with him. *Qua patet orbis*. It was etched on the blade. *As far as the world extends*. It extended, on the island of Manhattan in the greatest new city since the Renaissance, as far as One Hundred and Twenty-fifth Street. In a week, it would extend across the river to Brooklyn. He was the chosen driver for the first crossing. On that day, at the celebration, he was going to propose a Corps of Locomotionists. He had designed a helmet in brass with wings and, where the wings met in the center of the crown, a silver hammer of Thor and two lightning bolts and a number. His was I. He had it with him in the cab, wrapped in tissue paper in a hat box by the sword in its leather scabbard.

He shoveled in selected, perfectly round hobs of coal with his little polished hand shovel and read his brass and blued gauges and meters. He rested his hand lightly on the full-out throttle.

He felt the cool, clean wind against his face.

He breathed in the fresh, balmy smell of the river.

He dreamed his dreams.

Heaven on Earth.

Roaring, bursting with power, whistling when he felt like it, cutting time and distance in half as it had never been cut in half in two thousand years of man's existence, Number 39, flying twenty feet above the concerns of the Common Man like an angel, flew unstoppably, inevitably on toward the north.

At the rearmost window of the second car, Muldoon, disappearing from view in a swirl of coal dust, burning cinders and what looked like bits of flying shavings from the line itself, yelled, "Judas . . . *PRIEST!*" He was vibrating like a tuning fork, both hands grasped hard around the brass knobs on the frosted window, his feet planted across two leather-covered seats, his voice breaking up like a man drowning in surf, filthy muck from the smokestack on the engine—driven by some lunatic—swirling around his head like ectoplasm from a mad medium, a swinging gaslight an inch from his head on the roof of the car banging and crashing against his shoulder and, lit in the Stygian darkness, threatening at any moment to set him afire.

He got the window closed.

All the soot and cinders and filth and smoke and swinging glass and metal billowed up at him like a trapped genie.

He got it open a fraction and the noise and vibration and more filth and smoke and soot sucked in and went for his throat and sent him coughing and hacking.

Air!

He saw Tillman at the glass and mahogany door of the filthy projectile the Manhattan Railway Company had the nerve to think was fit for the transportation of men, women and children, fighting the hinges to get it closed, and Muldoon, getting the window open a fraction to break the vacuum in the bell jar in which they were trapped like flies, yelled, "Get it closed, Virgil!" (It came out as "*ge-t-c-ed-gil—!*"), got struck a mighty whack by the swinging gas lantern, slipped on a layer of soot an inch deep on the leather seat where his left foot fought for purchase, and, starting to go over, yelled, *Jesus, Mary and Joseph!*"

He was dressed for the trip. He had his straw boater and leather leggings and gray dust coat on. At the far end of the car, Tillman fought the door. There was some scientific method of closing the door and half opening the window, or half opening the door and three-quarters closing the window, like the percentage of soap powder and blue a washerwoman put in her copper, but it eluded him. The door, swinging of its own accord, blown open by the pressure of velocity and pure cussedness, bashed him against a water carafe in a brass bracket on the side wall. What was in the carafe was no longer water, it was soot. It bubbled. It smoked. And, as he crashed against it, it came down and broke. Tillman yelled to Muldoon, "Hang on, Ned, hang on! After Fifty-ninth Street, once we get out of the city, it gets better!"

Ah, it reminded him of home, the Fifty-ninth Street Station. It was a Swiss Chalet–style station designed by Jasper Cropsey, full of glass and cast-iron flowers high up in the clouds above the street and even though he had never been to Switzerland in his life, in his joy it reminded him of home.

Van Meer, craning out of his cabin window in ecstasy, yelled at the station, at The New Age, "*Hurrah!*"

THOR, the 7:10 A.M. newspaper, freight, mail and, maybe sometimes, a few passengers express for the far north, roared past the Station without stopping in a cloud of steam, smoke, soot and cinders like a bullet.

Huddled under a fortress of piled oyster trays, fish boxes and bundles of newspapers, Muldoon, looking at the picture in Tillman's hand by the light of a bull's-eye lantern from his knapsack, said, shaking his head, "No, they're not a unit."

"*What?*" Tillman had his head under a blanket in the swirling mist. He looked like a tramp resting on a crossroads for the night, huddled up. He sounded like a man with a tiny little voice shouting next to two hundred madmen swinging sledgehammers against metal plates. Tillman yelled, "I didn't hear what you said!" He thrust out the photograph for the second time. Tillman, seeing in a break in the cinderstorm what could have been a tree out the window, yelled, "I think we're out past Central Park!" He saw, not Muldoon's face, but merely his straw boater floating in midair on a sea of soot: "Ned? Did you hear what I asked you?"

Muldoon yelled, "They're not a unit! The people in the picture! The soldiers! They're not a unit!"

"Who are they then?"

"WHAT?"

"Who are—"

"They're a ragtag of different units and arms!" He saw, for an instant, the stiff daguerreotype materialize in thin air with what looked like a sooty thumb and finger holding it and he stabbed at it with his own black mitt. Muldoon yelled, "You can see that some of them are carrying infantry Springfield muskets and some of them cavalry carbines—and the officer is carrying a sword that looks like an Engineer's hanger!" Muldoon yelled, "They're just a group of soldiers somewhere!"

"At Vicksburg!"

Muldoon yelled, "Why couldn't Rufus Carrol have killed Schweib?"

"He could have!" Tillman yelled, "All the names on the back of the picture have been written in recently! You can tell by the ink and also by the fact that if it had been done at the time, in Vicksburg twenty years ago, all the writer would have had to do is ask each of them their names! Three of the entries for the people in the picture read "unknown," three are only first names, and—"

"How the hell did you get the Colonel's address?"

Tillman yelled, "What?"

"The Colonel—the one in the picture with the hanger—how did you—"

"The Bureau of Elections at Headquarters! I went to the night man at five this morning and got him to open his alphabetical electoral list—the entry read: Seward, Peter William, Colonel (ret.) USA, and an address up here in the Hundred and Thirty-first Street area!"

"What about the others?"

"What?"

"What about the others?"

"Nothing!" Tillman yelled, "He was listed as having a general store up there! There wasn't any age given, but looking at the picture he must be in his sixties or seventies by now!" Tillman yelled, "I wanted to telegraph, but the lines up here still aren't finished so I—" He lost him in the murk. Tillman said in sudden alarm, "Ned? Are you still there?"

There was a sigh. It could have been the locomotive. Nothing could go on so long and so disgustingly tirelessly without at least taking a breath. Tillman said, "Ned—?"

There was a loud sniff.

There was a crash. It was the lamp on the ceiling crashing onto the ceiling. The train must have rounded a bend. The lamp crashed again.

"*Ned?*"

"In the old days—"

Tillman said, "WHAT?"

"*In the old days—*"

"What old days?"

"Any old goddamned days!" He was not to be stopped. Muldoon, roaring at something—maybe the lamp—said at the end of his tether, "In the old days, I remember my old Sergeant—my first Sergeant in the Strong Arm Squad in the good old days when Clubber Williams ran things—giving someone a good kicking and taking me by the shoulder and telling me in a kindly voice—" Muldoon, his voice rising, shouted, " 'Now let me tell you something, my boy. They may beat you in Court, the complainant may not show up, they may jump their bail, politicians may interfere— there are many, many ways they may beat you, but—' " Muldoon yelled in happy reverie, "It was an old lag who'd done a burglary and wouldn't confess to it, " 'but' "—and he whacked him a hell of a whack across the head with his club—" 'but, by God, give 'em a few bruises, and a few bruises they'll have and there'll be no damned mistake about that!' " Muldoon, going light-headed with the lack of air, yelled, "They were good days, simple days! This progress, all this progress and scientific stuff is just codfish oil!" Muldoon, sounding drunk, swigging at his bottle in the darkness, yelled, "Why the hell don't we just beat it out of someone who killed Schweib?"

"Beat it out of who?"

"Anyone!" There was a crash. It wasn't the lamp, it was Muldoon. Muldoon, coughing, hacking, making strangled noises as he tried to drink, breathe and rail simultaneously, roared through the fug, "Leave it to me—I'll find *someone!*"

THE MAN ON THE WHITE HORSE!
Democrats Embrace Philosophy of the Prairie
At Last a Man for New York with Steadfast Gaze?
This Newspaper Says Yes!
We Receive a Long Interview with Professor Quarternight
WE SAY YES!
All Agree Immigration Must Stop!

Ah, brave new world that had such people in it. His wife read a lot—that was all she did—and she had read it to him from a book and he had written it down.

On the front page of his *New York Tribune*, for which he could get twenty-cents face-value price way out in the One Hundred and Twenty-first far reaches of Manhattan, van Meer, humming to himself, looked at an engraving of a tall, clear-eyed, Stetson-hatted hero on a Western horse gazing out into the horizon of life and, setting his throttle on full, touching at his sword with his free hand, leaned against the cab side to read all about it.

The wind must have changed. In the car, the black muck was being sucked out Muldoon's half-open window and there were trees and earth and fields and wooden houses outside and the smell of manure and grass and even, here and there, flowers and fruit. They were like swimmers come up for air. They were like tar boys come up from the pits. Tillman, picking up bits of the broken water carafe and tossing them out the window down to the gravel beds on which the elevated lines rested, asked Muldoon, swigging at his flask, "In the war, were you at Vicksburg, Ned?"

Muldoon said, "No." He looked out the window at a tree.

"I read that it was one of the crucial battles of the war that cut the Confederacy in half—that it opened the Mississippi for the Federal forces."

Muldoon said, "Right." It was a nice tree, but like everything else to do with progress, anything that happened to be near it, it was gone in the twinkling of an eye. Muldoon, nodding, said, "That's right."

Tillman said, "I read the battles around Vicksburg were fought in bayous and swamps and riverbanks and in—" Tillman said, straightening up, "I was only a child at the beginning of the war and—"

Muldoon said, "So was I."

"You fought in the war." Tillman said, "Where? Where did you fight?"

He got no reply.

Tillman said, "What was it like, Ned?"

He got no reply.

"Where did you fight?"

Muldoon said, "Chancellorsville."

"What was it like?"

Muldoon said, "I was seventeen years old." He looked out the window.

"These people: Schweib, Carrol, the Colonel Seward—it has something to do with the war." Tillman, coming over and sitting down, said, shaking his head, "I don't know what it is. It was so long ago." He saw Muldoon's eyes. Tillman said, "Wasn't it? A long time ago?" He asked urgently, wanting to know, "Ned, it's over twenty years ago. Is that—for someone who was there—is that a long time ago?"

They were up high, passing above One Hundred and Sixteenth Street and its shantytowns and wasteland and desolation, the streets from the great master plan of years before laid out and cobbled and paved, going nowhere, crisscrossing each other in rectangles that enclosed only earth and market gardens and shacks, with, here and there, fields of grass and weeds and wildflowers. At Chancellorsville, Muldoon had lain wounded all one night in a field of flowers and thought he had smelled their fragrance. In that field, smelling the smell of flowers, he had lain surrounded by dead and dying men. All that night—

Muldoon said, looking out the window, "Virgil, I was seventeen years old."

"Is it a long time ago? Will it be to this Colonel? Was it to Schweib and Carrol?"

He looked hard at the window. Muldoon, shaking his head, said, "No." He looked now, as he had looked then, for a tree. He had never worked out why.

Muldoon said in a voice so hard and tight Tillman had to strain to make out the words, "No, it wasn't a long time ago."

Muldoon said, "For Christ's sake, for Christ's sake, to me, it feels like it happened *yesterday!*"

Ah, fellow Knights of the City.

At the One Hundred and Twenty-fifth Street terminus of the Manhattan Railway Elevated Transportation Company, Captain van Meer got down from his cab carrying his winged helmet to formally salute the two Police Officers making their way through the stacks of mailbags, barrels, boxes and sacks and trays of fruit and flowers to be taken back to civilization on the 9:35 Southbound Express Number 39 was to become.

He thought he might give them a *salut* with his sword.

He thought they might walk back at the invitation to admire THOR.

He thought, seeing him standing there putting on his helmet grinning and glittering in the sun, the big one reached for his club.

He thought he did.

He thought the smaller one said something to restrain him.

He thought—

He thought he might get back into the cab and close the door.

He got back into the cab and closed the door.

9

America. On the back porch of a single-story clapboard house on One Hundred and Thirty-first Street, gazing into her garden, Mrs. Seward said, "There is something about the word that still quickens the heart."

She was a tall, angular woman in her late fifties dressed in a gray work dress and white apron, her hair pulled back tight into a bun at the back of her head. She gazed out into the garden where her husband lay under a sheet and mosquito net and parasol in a wheeled invalid's bed in a grove made by fruit trees and roses. Mrs. Seward said, "I am a patriot, Mr. Tillman. I believe I have been forced by God to live in a noble land, a land where no man may make a slave of another or suffer under the yoke of cruel despotism." She was gazing out at the net-covered bed in which there was no movement at all. Mrs. Seward said, *"The mystic chords of memory, stretching from every battlefield, and patriot grave, to every living heart and hearthstone, all over this broad land, will yet swell the chorus of the Union, when again touched, as surely they will be, by the better angels of our nature."* Mrs. Seward said, "That is from the first inaugural address of the late Mr. Lincoln." Across the flat fields to the west there were small market gardens and farms of the Italians who had moved into Harlem to work its good soil. Mrs. Seward said, "One of the angels who gave up that freedom now lies sick and silent and paralyzed from strokes." She pursed her lips: *"The scenes of the great battles, like everything else, must fade upon the memory of the world. The husband, the father, the brother—the living history to be found in every family—a history bearing the indubitable testimonies of its own authenticity in the limbs mangled, the scars of wounds—all that will fade, is fading now."* She drew a breath: *"They were a forest of giant oaks; but the all-restless hurricane has swept over them, and left only, here and there, a lonely trunk, despoiled of its verdure, shorn of its foliage; unshading and unshaded, to murmur in a few more gentle breezes, and then to combat with its mutilated limbs, a few more ruder storms, then to sink and be no more."*

The man in the garden was a shadow under the netting, his face in shadow from the parasol affixed to the iron bed by a metal clamp.

Mrs. Seward said softly, *"They were the pillars of our liberty; and now that they have crumbled away, that temple must fall, unless we, their descendants, support their places with other pillars, hewn from the solid quarry of sober reason. Passion has helped us; but can do so no more."* In the garden the big man, Muldoon, was standing under one of the fruit trees out of the sun, waiting. Mrs. Seward said, "The Colonel raised his own troops and went to war. Some people say that war is glorious, but they have not had to soothe the nightmares of the men who went or bite their tongue out of fear of some romantic notion that slaughter is a brave and noble pursuit." Mrs. Seward said, "The War Between the States was a charnelhouse: a butcher's block of blood and agony and the waste of young, fruitful lives and the shrieks of the wounded. I hold my husband dear, as one of the angels, not because he went to glory and adventure, but because—for the nation, for *America*—he took it upon himself to do such things and to endure their horrors and for all the rest of his life, still serving, to endure them in silence." Mrs. Seward said, "My family asked if he treated me well and kindly in our lives together. He has treated all who presently enjoy the liberty of the Union well and kindly—and perhaps therefore he had given his all and need not give more."

Mrs. Seward said, "I cannot offer you lemonade. I have none."

In the garden Muldoon, standing beneath the tree, looked down at the palms of his hands and wiped them on his dust coat. He looked across at the bed.

Mrs. Seward said, "I have no help to move him from the house into the garden, not to feed and tend him, but I thank God for him. I thank God that I may serve him. I thank God that soon he will be on the other side of the river, in Heaven with the saints, called to his rest. I thank God that soon he will shed no more tears and be happy again, and smile, and—"

She was tall and gaunt and angular with a firm, unwavering voice. She looked out at the bed, watching Muldoon a little at a time moving toward it.

Mrs. Seward said, not looking at Tillman at all, "What we all owe such men . . . What we *owe* . . . !"

* * *

In the bed he was shrunken and gray, like a dead man, the netting and the parasol shade forming lines and shadows on the shrunken face. The face, after the two massive strokes—the second only a week ago—was distorted and fixed; the head slightly to one side; the pale blue eyes watery and without light staring up toward the tops of the trees; the hands, like someone deceased not yet laid out, under the blanket by the sides of the tiny body beneath the single sheet.

At the side of the bed Muldoon said softly, "Hello, sir—" There was a sort of small white cap on the man's head, like a Mennonite girl's or the under-veil head-covering of a nun, with thin, white and silver hair coming out in wisps from its sides, and, about the neck, laundered fresh, the top of a cream-colored nightshirt.

Muldoon touched lightly at the head of the frame of the iron bed. Beneath the slightly bunched-up mosquito netting there, the frame was warm from the sun.

In the garden, he smelled the smell of wildflowers though there were none there.

The eyes through the netting were pale and farsighted, looking up. He saw them blink. The mouth was a little open, frozen in a little half *O*. He saw the pupils of the eyes move to see him, then see him.

He touched again at the head of the bed.

Muldoon, smiling, said gently, "Hello. Hello, old chap . . ."

Before she had been a wife she had been someone's daughter. Tillman saw the wedding band on her finger. It was still bright. She had not been married for more than eight or nine years and, before that, she had been someone's daughter for a very long time and, as either the only or the elder daughter, had tended him through old age, to the grave.

He had told her Schweib and Carrol were dead. She had the daguerreotype in her hand, looking at all the faces. Tillman said, "Is that your husband's handwriting on the back? All the names? Did he write that?"

"No." She was not looking at all the faces but only at the face of her husband. Mrs. Seward said, "No. After his first stroke his right side was paralyzed. He could no longer write."

"Is it Schweib's writing, or Carrol's?" Tillman asked, "Did they come here—Schweib and Carrol?"

"Yes." She turned the stiff card over. Mrs. Seward said, "I think it's Mr. Schweib's writing, but I'm not sure."

"They spoke alone to your husband?"

"Yes."

"When?" Out in the garden Muldoon was standing a little way back from the bed with his hand on the iron frame. He seemed to be saying something.

"About a month ago. My husband has been an invalid, now, for—"

"Why did they come?"

"To speak to my husband in his room."

"About what?"

Muldoon seemed to be smiling. He nodded and patted at the head of the bed. She did not take her eyes off him for a moment. Mrs. Seward, handing back the picture, said, "I don't know. I offered them refreshments. I heard voices when I knocked, but after my husband invited me to enter the voices stopped." Mrs. Seward said, "They were smoking cigars in my husband's room with the windows closed. My husband said no refreshments were required." Muldoon was at the bed, still smiling, saying something to the man in the bed. He shrugged. It looked as if he was telling the man in the bed something secret. Mrs. Seward said, "Mr. Schweib was at my husband's desk with a pen in his hand and something he covered with a sheet of paper. It must have been the picture." Mrs. Seward said, "I was in my kitchen. I heard no more."

"Did they walk in the garden during the afternoon?"

"They came in the morning. They did not stay for lunch. My husband, at that time, could only walk with a stick." She gazed out into the garden: "My husband, when we had the general store here, used to smoke cigars only in the open air." She was explaining. "He sold cigars and tobacco. He could not be seen not to set a good example to his own customers." Mrs. Seward said, "I served the ladies in another department." Mrs. Seward said suddenly, turning to look at him, "My husband was always a gentleman."

He wished she had offered lemonade. For his sake, it would have been something to break the questions with—a ritual parenthesis. For her sake— They had nothing. They had neither lemonade, nor, that day, had they lunch to offer. Tillman asked politely, "Do you still own the store?"

"No."

He waited.

She gazed out into the garden.

Mrs. Seward said, "No." Mrs. Seward said, "When he was well my husband traveled often, by locomotive and by the Elevated. He went often into New York and often—" Mrs. Seward said, "Such things cost money."

"Where did he go exactly and why?"

"He did not choose to tell me and I did not ask." Mrs. Seward said, "And at the store, often, he went to his office and wrote letters and received letters. Often, I was left to tend customers alone."

"Did you ever see any of the letters?"

"The letters he received were delivered directly to him. The letters he wrote he took to the post office himself."

Tillman said directly, "Can your husband communicate at all?"

"No." Mrs. Seward said, "He can no longer speak." She anticipated him. Mrs. Seward said, "And, except for some unpaid bills for the store, his desk in the office was empty as was the desk in this house."

"What unit was your husband in?"

"He raised his own troop."

"The men in the picture are not a troop. They were just a group of men at Vicksburg." Tillman asked, "Did he ever speak of Vicksburg?"

"Not in his waking hours."

"In his nightmares?"

"No."

"What did he speak of?"

"He said merely, in his nightmares, that they were all dead." She had not spoken to anyone about it, about her husband, about her life. She read; she did not often speak. She gazed out into the garden and, briefly, seemed to be listening, like an outsider, to what she herself said. Mrs. Seward said, "I do not know, but from his nightmares, they were all killed by men with swords."

"Cavalry?"

Mrs. Seward said, tight-lipped, "Yes. I think so."

"Who were all killed?"

"I don't know. Perhaps his troop."

"At Vicksburg?"

"In a bayou—a swamp. Could that have been Vicksburg? I read that many of the battles were fought in swamps and on the river."

"Was he himself wounded?"

There was a silence.

Tillman said, "Do you know?"

Mrs. Seward said, "I have had to nurse him these last few weeks."

"That is why I asked."

Mrs. Seward said, "My husband was always a gentleman." They had no children. They had married late. Mrs. Seward said, "There"—she touched at her side a little above the waist—"he has a long scar as if from a sword cut." She looked away. She was embarrassed. She watched Muldoon talking man's talk to the poor, gone creature in the bed and tightened her lips. Mrs. Seward said, "I have never shirked from the duty I owe him." She looked down at the splitting, sun-bleached planks on the porch.

"Yes."

"The third man I would not have in my house and, since he must have once been respectable himself and could remember the sensibilities, he did not ask to enter it." She saw Tillman's face. Mrs. Seward said, "There was a third man that day with Mr. Schweib and Mr. Carrol, a tramp, a rum fiend—or at the very least, a man fallen on hard times without the moral strength to restore himself—he came too. He waited outside in the road by the fence—he came, I imagine, on the train with Mr. Schweib and Mr. Carrol, although I doubt the locomotive company would have allowed him to share a car with—"

"What was his name?"

"I was not introduced to him, nor did I seek to introduce myself."

"Was he one of the men in the photograph?"

In the garden, whatever Muldoon was saying, he was saying it softly. Not a sound came to her on the porch.

"He was filthy."

"Did anyone call him by name?"

"They spoke in my husband's room. I heard nothing of what they said."

"Was he one of the men in the photograph?"

"He was in rags, filthy." Mrs. Seward said, not having needed to say it the day he came, "A person like that does not enter the house of respectable people. Particularly with a sick man. There is the question of disease." Mrs. Seward said, "I don't know who he was. He was unkempt and dirty and whatever he may have been once, however deserving of honor he may have been if he had once served his country, by serving now only his own desires and weaknesses he deserved it no longer." Mrs. Seward said, "I have no notion who he may have been."

"Was his name George Fenney?"

"I don't know."

"Or Henry Carver? Or Warren Cahill?" Tillman said, "There are twelve names on the back of the photograph. Only your husband's name and Schweib's and Carrol's names and the names of Fenney, Carver and Cahill are written out in full. The others are merely first names or nicknames or "Unknown." If the man was a member of the group—"

Mrs. Seward said, "I do not know who he was." Mrs. Seward said, "I know nothing. I know nothing about the man or the letters or the trips. I know nothing about my husband's part in the war. I know nothing about what transpired that day—I know nothing. I know only duty, loyalty and work." She looked out into the garden.

Mrs. Seward said suddenly, angrily, "Duty, loyalty, work. Don't you see? *Don't you see how diligently I do it?*"

He was like one of the wax figures in Barnum's American Museum on Broadway: not a man but a representation of a man; the features, the attitude of the body, the anatomy—*something*—not quite right and true and lifelike—something wrong and off center and . . . and *dead*.

The body was finished, useless. In the bed, it merely supported and held that part of a man that had once been human and alive and, moment by moment—too slowly—it was letting go and releasing the living part, suffocating it, making it alone and unsupported like the roadway of a bridge where all the wires and suspensions had frayed and fallen.

Muldoon looked down at the eyes.

Through the netting they were pale blue and watery, looking up at him with no expression in them, the head slightly to one side—the eyes looking up at him or the sky or the trees or whatever they saw—perhaps nothing—the face shrunken, translucent, with only the paralyzed muscles pulled tight and the mouth open in a little half *O*.

The hand above the sheet was open, unmoving clay.

What if, inside the head, behind the eyes, the brain were still alive? What if in there there were words and—what if it were alive and seething? What if it were—

What if it was shrieking in pain?

In the garden, standing at the head of the bed, Muldoon said softly, gently, ". . . sir . . ."

In the garden, although there were none, he smelled wildflowers.

He touched gently at the head of the iron bed with his hand.

He took off his straw boater hat and held it in his hands across his stomach.

On the porch Tillman and the Colonel's wife were talking, talking, but the voices did not carry and there was nothing to be heard.

"Sir . . ." He leaned a little closer. He looked into the pale, gone eyes. He smelled in the little garden the smell of wildflowers.

Muldoon said softly, "Sir, you must bear up now, like a soldier."

He closed his eyes. He smelled the smell of wildflowers.

He looked hard into the gone, empty eyes.

He looked away.

Briefly, still holding his hat in his hands, he looked away to the trees, to the sky.

He looked down again, hard, into the pale, expressionless, watery, empty eyes.

Through the fly-screened back door, Tillman could see the interior of the house: part of the curtained rear parlor and one of the bedrooms. She could not offer them lemonade. She could not invite them in. There was nothing in the house. Everything had been sold. There were no letters or replies to letters. They had all been given to Schweib and Carrol and, after he had realized that Schweib was dead, they were what Carrol had burned in his fire grate in Bleecker Street before he came out with his gun to die.

Taking the broken, rusted Civil War revolver they had found in the cupboard in Carrol's room from his knapsack and handing it to her, Tillman asked, "Was this your husband's?" It was red with oxidation: he saw her look down at it as she took it by the barrel and wipe the flakes of rust off her fingers. Tillman said, "It's a southern five-shot Gilbert and Greer thirty-six caliber cap-and-ball officer's sidearm made in Atlanta, in Georgia, for the Confederate Army." He asked again, "Was it your husband's?"

Mrs. Seward said, "It could have been."

"He gave it to Schweib or Carrol if it was his. When they left, were they carrying anything?"

"A knapsack, like yours."

"Containing what?"

Mrs. Seward said with a half smile, "Not money." The hammer on the weapon was rusted into the receiver. She touched it with her thumb, but it would not move. Maybe she had read about guns like it. Mrs. Seward, looking down at it, said with the interest of a historian, "What do the letters BST mean on the handle?" They were in a little oval cartouche impressed into the wood with a die stamp. Mrs. Seward asked, "Are they someone's initials?"

"It's an inspector's mark, put on at the armory where it was made."

"Oh, yes." Mrs. Seward said, "No, I've never seen it before. If my husband had it, he had it hidden or one of the people who wrote to him sent it to him in a parcel."

He realized she was appraising it.

Inside the house, there was nothing. He wondered what her life must be like. Out in the garden, Muldoon was standing over the bed, looking down. The netting, the parasol, and what he could see of the sheet that covered the dying man were all, like the apron the woman wore over her dress, stark, laundered white. He looked at her hands. They were worn. Her eyes had neither softness nor hardness in them—they were merely there, watching.

Tillman said, "It must be very hard for you in your present situation."

Mrs. Seward said nothing. The rusted gun was of no value. She handed it back.

"Has your husband long to live?"

She smiled at him.

"Do you have someone to go to afterwards? A family? Relatives?"

She shrugged.

Tillman said, "Why did he choose to live so far out of the city? You said he went there often."

Mrs. Seward said, "Yes."

"Do you know why?"

Mrs. Seward said, "No."

"Do you know what he did in the city? Who he saw?"

Mrs. Seward said quietly, "*'Dear Sir: Your note requesting my signature with a sentiment was received, and should have been answered long since, but it was mislaid. I am not a sentimental man: and the best sentiment I can think of is, that if you collect the signatures of all persons who are no less distinguished than I, you will have a very undistinguished list of names.'*" Mrs. Seward said, "*'Very respectfully, A. LINCOLN.'*" It was a famous letter Lincoln had written to an admirer in Washington in 1849. Mrs. Seward said, "Incandescent. That was what one of them said on the way out to my husband, *incandescent*. I think it was Mr. Schweib. Incandescent. He turned at the door as I held it open for him and he said back to my husband with a grin of triumph, 'He will make it *incandescent!*'" Mrs. Seward said, "And then I heard my husband say, 'Like a pearl! Like a pearl!'" Mrs. Seward said, "That is all I know, all I was permitted to know. An incandescent pearl." Mrs. Seward said, "I know my duty. I did not ask my husband what it meant."

"Do you know what it meant?"

Reaching under the netting, Muldoon, very gently, touched the old man's hand. It felt cold and lifeless, without muscle tone. He looked into the eyes, but they registered nothing.

Muldoon said softly, "I was an old soldier too." He patted the hand. Muldoon said, "Would you like your hand under the sheet?" He looked into the eyes and saw nothing. Muldoon, putting his hat back on his head and reaching into his pocket, said, "Here." He had a silver dollar there. Muldoon, offering it, said, "Here. This is to help a little—from one old comrade to another." He saw the eyes and they moved a little. Muldoon, pulling back the sheet a little to put the man's hand in under it, said, "I'll put it here in the bed beside you." He thought he might press it into the warmer hand already under the sheet. Muldoon, feeling something there under the sheet, said gently, "What have you got there?" He pulled back the sheet and saw what was in the man's hidden hand.

He looked into the eyes. They were weeping.

Muldoon said in a gasp, "Oh."

He looked down at what the still, waxen, dying man had clasped in his fingers.

Mrs. Seward said, "Yes, I know what it meant." She read. It was what, only, solely, all her life she had been allowed to do. Mrs. Seward said, "I think what it meant was an address." Mrs. Seward said, "I think it was the address of Mr. Edison's new Incandescent Electricity Station on Pearl Street." Mrs. Seward said suddenly, "I thought about it a lot. I never asked, but I thought about it a lot."

Mrs. Seward said with a strange look on her face, "It was not something I asked my husband or my husband told me, it was something that fell from his pocket, something accidental. I thought about it a lot, like a cipher, a code"—she smiled thinly at Tillman—"A policeman's *clue*."

Mrs. Seward said, "Edison's Incandescent Electricity Station on Pearl Street—that was what they meant. They were going to see someone there."

Mrs. Seward said, "Edison's Incandescent Electricity Generating Station on Pearl Street in the city, I am certain." It was, from a long, terrible life, all she had.

Mrs. Seward, triumphing, keeping her honor, but for once, for herself, triumphing, said, "Yes, I am absolutely certain. *It can mean nothing else!*"

It was a flag. It was not a battle ensign, but merely a flag. It was a shroud. It was Old Glory. It was an ordinary, bought, Stars and Stripes flag folded neatly into a funeral triangle and it was what he held clutched in his hand. It was what happened behind the eyes. It was what was still working inside the head. It was what—

It was all he had left, all he was: it was his winding sheet that would not be sold, but go into the grave with him.

"Sir . . ." He had the silver dollar in his hand.

He closed his fist on it. Muldoon said in a whisper, "Sir, I . . ." He looked down at the coin. Muldoon said, "I'm sorry. I just thought . . ." The man, with no expression, was weeping. The coin felt dirty, foul; he wanted to put it back in his pocket, but standing there, staring down, he could not get his hand to work. Muldoon said, "Sir, I—" Muldoon said, "I'm an old soldier too! I—" He touched at the thin mattress beside the hand holding the flag to—to—

The bed was wet. In the bed the weeping man was wetting himself.

Muldoon said softly, "Oh—"

Muldoon, turning to the porch, holding up his hand in a signal, called to Mrs. Seward urgently, "Ma'am! *Ma'am!*"

He saw her look up.

Muldoon, sounding desperate, waving his arm to beckon her, calling to her with desperation rising in his voice, "Ma'am! Ma'am! Come quickly! Your husband needs you *now!*"

10

Was it a brass band?

Yessir, it was a brass band. It was two brass bands. It was two brass bands and flags and fire eaters and acrobats and Red Indians from the Wild West Show and decently attired lady actresses from Niblo's Garden Theatre and, at the corner of Houston Street, the bandleader, in red uniform with gold piping and braid, his brass buttons gleaming, marking time, puffed himself up like a toad and put his silver whistle to his lips.

The bandleader's silver whistle went "Peeeee—wa—*wit!*" and tubas, cornets, trombones, all flashing gold in the late afternoon sun, they struck up "The Battle Hymn of the Republic" in the first fourteen-piece band at the head, the Red Indians began their circular rain dances or war dances or just general savage contortings with a whoop, the jugglers—four of them in white tights and athletic singlets—began throwing checkered exercise pins at each other at lightning speed, the two fire eaters breathed fire, the flags of the United States on tasseled poles waved bravely in the air, and, at the rear, the second fourteen-piece band, not only brass but with Prussian snare drums and basses, cymbals and a triangle player, snapped into a German polka and fought the volume of the band in front.

In the center of the band rode Professor Quarternight on his seventeen-hands-high horse Liberty.

Behind him strode city Aldermen and Democrats in their best Sunday suits and derby hats with gold watch chains of alarming weight and carats across their middles.

Quarternight flashed in the sun. His Best Western Saddle, a mass of Mexican-silver engraved conchos and tooled leather on the great white horse, held his presentation rifle, reflecting the sun

93

from the gold and silver and walnut-root wood. His two pistols with their elephant-ivory butts were like great jewels in their buscadero holsters. His hair was combed back down over his neck, his hat in his hand. Liberty pranced. The Professor waved to the crowd. Would he draw a pistol and shoot in the air? He reached for one—he touched it. It came out a little. The crowds forming along the street looked up to see what target he would choose—perhaps the insulator of the telegraph-wire pole—and women cringed a little, boys gritted their teeth and stood ready with their fingers in their ears in a lather of desire—but he didn't shoot. He took his hand from his gun and, above the bands, tossed back his head, laughed gaily to show his fine, perfect teeth, all his own and looked after the way mothers said teeth should always be looked after, and called out, laughing, "MY FRIENDS!"

There was a round of applause from the Aldermen. By them, as if choreographed, black street boys and white street boys, earning money, darted the full length of the procession passing out flyers.

The flyers said, "QUARTERNIGHT GAINS THE EN-DORSEMENT!" The Aldermen's gold glittered, the great white horse pranced, the fire eaters spewed tongues of fire into the air. Even dressed, the actresses took your breath away.

THE NATIONAL POLICE GAZETTE
The Leading Illustrated Sporting Journal in America
Richard K. Fox Editor

At the rear of the procession the *Gazette's* photographic wagon was there, the team driven by no other than Richard K. Fox himself in silk top hat and white spats. They were going to take photographs somewhere. THE *GAZETTE* SUPPORTS QUARTERNIGHT! In that covered wagon were all the great secret wares of railway fiction and photographs of belles of the stage, ten cents for six sent discreetly by plain wrapper on receipt of cash. Men in the streets looked away, women gaped.

How the silken-tasseled flags waved bravely in the breezes! The color, the sound, the fire and gold and silver and red uniforms, the martial music, marching feet, determination, progress, clear complexions, fine teeth and dancing horses—the proud, patriotic, historic . . . pure wonder of it, the . . .

"Peeeee-wa-wa—*WIT!*"

In the street, both bands, all the acrobats, fire eaters, flag wavers, jugglers, wagons, actresses—everyone—did a complete, perfect three-hundred-and-sixty-degree circle, and, and—

BANG! BANG!

Quarternight fired both his pistols at once in the air and gave a whoop and a holla and a yell and—

"Peee-wa-*wit!*"

—bravely, on to glory, on, on Houston Street, glittering with the setting sun at their backs, on, on, on—onward—they marched on—on—on . . . *to glory.*

He was going on, onward—to the Tombs. In the Detective Bureau on the first floor of Police Headquarters at 300 Mulberry Street, Dribbling Donahue, his nose on the floor, his arms held behind his back by City Detective Henry Grafton, looking up at Tillman at his desk like a squid looking up from the ocean floor, yelled, "He shot me! That man Tillman shot me! That man Tillman isn't fit to wear the copper badge of an officer of the law in this town! He shot me! He followed me for three days and when he couldn't plant evidence on me, he put it out that the exertions of the chase had overloaded his heart and he was dead and he put on French chalk makeup and got laid out in a coffin in Grisaldi's Funeral Home and when I went in to pay me respects to him as any Christian man would, he came alive and he shot me!"

His nose was an inch from the floor. It looked from his face like Henry had chased him a long way. He had chased him a long way. Grafton, giving Donahue a kick, got his nose a quarter of an inch from the floor and, with another kick, tried his damndest to get it through the floor.

Tillman said, "It was a blank." He looked up at Grafton readying himself for a boot that would send the horrible, smelly, wizened little creature—who could run like hell and thought nothing of leading a man whose wife worked hard to do his laundry through open sewers—by direct post into the next county, and asked, "What's he here for?"

Grafton said, "Pickpocketing. He's gone down in the world. Mr. Byrnes's Rogues' Gallery had him on file as a bank sneak."

"I've never been the same since he shot me!" Dribbling Donahue, making a pool of dribble on the floor, said, "I was fanning his poor dead face in the coffin on one of the hottest days of last summer to send him on his way to Heaven cool and refreshed and he shot me!"

Tillman said, "You fanned me with a bundle of stolen bank

securities you got from the counter of the Bowery Bank while you distracted the attention of the owner—a poor old lady—by pretending she'd dropped some money and you were too crippled to help her pick it up!"

"Little good it did her! You blasted a hole right through them with the powder charge!" Donahue, sneezing, dust getting up his nose from the floor, wondering for an instant if he was being suffocated as he heard trumpet music calling him to Paradise, yelled, "I'll be out of here on bail in an hour!"

"What do you think I should do with him, Virgil?"

Tillman, going back to his electoral rolls of the Annexed Territory of The Bronx, looking for names, said, "Shoot him."

"My family will be here in an hour with Howe and Hummel, lawyers!"

Tillman said to Grafton, "Shoot them too."

"YOU—" He ate dust.

He was a nice young fellow, Grafton, a man with a fine, good wife and two young children who sat on his knee in the evenings while he read to them from books he could scarcely afford, but had given up little personal pleasures to buy for them each week on payday, a genuinely kindhearted man who always had a smile.

Smiling now, he started Dribbling Donahue on his way to righteous punishment in the cells with a kick that would have sent Jack, happily climbing the Beanstalk, back down to the ground on his behind wondering just what the my-goodness-me Hell had hit him.

From Houston Street the bands, the flags, the fire eaters, the jugglers and the man on the white horse began to turn as one into Mulberry Street.

Glory, glory Hallelujah—

From in front of his big brass-bound desk on the first floor, Station Sergeant Fitzgerald roared throughout the four-story white-marble Headquarters building and into the sub-basement cells where Grafton was kicking Dribbling Donahue, "THEY'RE COMING! MR. BYRNES WANTS EVERYONE OUT IN BEST ARRAY ON STREET PARADE ON THE STEPS— *THEY'RE COMING!*

Glory, glory, hallelujah—

In the basement telegraph office, Harry Roebuck, slipping his black-silk sleeve protectors off his snow-white shirt and shaking his head, removing his eyeshade, looking for his coat, said, "I'll do it later, Virgil—first thing." He had the list of names on a sheet of paper on his desk under the glass fish-tank cover where his keys were, "Fenney, Carver, Shand and Warren Cahill—I'll put it on the wire to all the thirty-two stations—"

Glory, glory—hallelujah!

Roebuck said, "I'll do it first thing, but I want to see this! I'm a registered Democrat and my children would never forgive me if—" He had his coat on.

"ON PARADE, ALL YOU BRAVE POLICEMEN AND OTHERS—NOW!"

Roebuck said, "The Sergeant will have me, Virgil, if I tarry." He leaned into the glass tank and switched a mysterious brass switch. "Current's off for repairs." Roebuck, starting to run up the stairs, said, as a promise, "First thing! First thing! I promise!"

"—and his soul goes marching . . . *ON!!!*"

"*HURRAH!*"

"On parade, you brave bluecoats!" It was Sergeant Fitzgerald. By God, it was. He was already outside in the street. The voice could have knocked down mountains: "Line up in order behind *MR. BYRNES!*"

Outside in the street there was applause.

"MR. CHIEF INSPECTOR THOMAS BYRNES—!" He had teeth like ivory. He had a voice like the voice of Saint Peter at the gate. In the street, on his horse, at the front steps of the Station, Professor Doctor C. K. Quarternight called to the Station, the streets, the city, the voters, "MR. CHIEF INSPECTOR THOMAS BYRNES, GUARDIAN PROTECTOR OF OUR GREAT METROPOLIS—WHERE ARE YOU, SIR, AND YOUR FINE, BRAVE BODY OF MEN? COME, YOU NOBLE MAN—COME AND LET US SEE YOU! COME AND LET US SAY IN OUR HUMBLE WAY TO YOU AND ALL WHO TIRELESSLY HOLD BACK THE TIDES OF UNRULY SCUM THAT DAILY INFEST OUR CITY FROM FOREIGN LANDS, 'Thank you, thank you'—THANK YOU, SIR, AND GOD GIVE STRENGTH TO YOUR TIRELESS, UNSTINTING HEART!"

In the telegraph office, Tillman said in a curse, "Damn it!"

"Mr. Telegrapher Roebuck!" It was Sergeant Fitzgerald at the front door like an ogre.

The ogre roared, "Mr. Telegrapher Roebuck, get that coat on straight, sir, *or I'll eat you!*"

"Here before you all arrayed are the sentinels of your city—the highest of the high: humanity's best!" There was quite a crowd outside Headquarters. Byrnes, a General on the top steps above and behind his little army of officers—the plainclothes Detective Squad; the high-hatted uniformed patrolmen and peaked-capped Sergeants; the Steamboat Squad in naval white and blue; the Sanitation Squad in heavy-duty coveralls for entering cellars and hovels where risks to public health in the form of dead animals, garbage and filthy practices were everywhere a-growing; the Steam Boiler Inspection Squad with their glittering copper badges of an exploding boiler and flying human dismemberment; Matron Webb from the top-floor Lost Children's Shelter, fat, black-bonneted and smiling at her grinning waifs and urchins and foundlings (a public service little known to the public or appreciated by them)—roared, waving his hand, "Today, in this modern world, faced as we are by changes in our society too great and sudden to be oft comprehended by the simple man, in a city rivaling ancient Rome in its greatness, who can the citizen turn to but the truest of the true, the finest of the fine—the praetorian guard of the highest moral character, the most patient of the patient—the men of the *New York City Police?*"

Byrnes said, "Now, rushing toward the new century, lit by electricity, propelled across vast distances by the wonder of steam, talking to each other in the blinking of an eye through the wonders of the telegraph wire, *everywhere the victim of clever and modernistic criminals*—safe-breakers with the new tools of compressed air and dynamite—who may we turn to?" There was a silence. It was a good speech. Byrnes said, "In this great city of ours, there are two hundred and sixty-two telephones—and, fear not, the police have three of them! We are no backward force, we are the forefront of progress, ahead of it, monitoring it, using it to keep our streets safe for decent men and women!" He waved his hand to Matron Webb: "Each night in Stations all over the city, the police give homes to thousands of waifs and poor children. Each night—"

Quarternight called out, "God bless you, Mr. Byrnes!"

"Thank you, sir!"

"God Bless you and all your good men!"

"I thank you."

Quarternight's voice rang out loud and true. "God bless the man who puts on the good and true blue with little thought of recompense! God bless and protect the lonely policeman at work in the dark alleys and byways of our city a-checking the doors and windows of our homes and business! God protect the man who alone takes on the might of the criminal classes and tramps in the nether regions of wickedness, depravity and moral bankruptcy!" Quarternight, standing up on his saddle, drawing an Ahh from the crowd, called to the Heavens, "God protect the good ordinary man who wants nothing more than to work hard all the hours God sent in order to clothe and feed and warm his little family! God protect the honest American from the Jew, the nigger, the Chinaman and the Mormon!" Quarternight said, "Mr. Byrnes, you are not alone! This is Rome, is it? By God, sir, you have it in your pithy way of putting it—this is Rome and we are all good Roman citizens!" He lowered his voice: "The histories tell us that when Roman citizenship was offered to all who asked for it, it became as nothing! We are Romans—let us therefore act as Romans—let us cherish and guard our Rome!" Quarternight said, "Send the Chinee, the Jew, the Mormon, the nigger back to the foul quarters of the Earth that spawned them! To each freeborn man, his own protection! To each freeborn man—to each Minuteman—his own American Gun Company rifle above his humble hearth, loaded and dry and oiled and ready! TO THE NEW CENTURY IN THE NEW CITY WITH, NOT NEW AMERICANS, BUT OLD AMERICANS—those old Americans who tamed our land!"

Byrnes said, "It is not well-known that one of the many duties the police perform—"

Quarternight said, "Strike up the bands!"

Byrnes said, "Is the often unsung duty of—"

Quarternight said, "'The Battle Hymn of the Republic'!" On his horse, turning to the crowd, he asked, "Is there any secret spy here among us who will not sing the hymn of our great nation? SHOW YOURSELF NOW! Look at your neighbor—does he sing with pride in his heart? LOOK AT YOUR NEIGHBOR!" The bands began. Quarternight, with a voice that echoed off the white marble of Headquarters, sang at the top of his lungs, "MINE EYES HAVE SEEN THE GLORY OF THE COMING OF THE LORD—" Quarternight yelled, "MR. BYRNES?"

"HE HAS TRAMPLED OUT THE VINEYARD WHERE THE GRAPES OF WRATH ARE STORED . . ."

Quarternight yelled, "Sing!"

And in the street, they sang.

* * *

In the Detective Room, waiting for him by his desk, F. C. Catton of the American Gun Company, wearing a rosette on his lapel, said, "Mr. Tillman." Catton, inclining his head slightly, said to remind him, "F. C. Catton of the American Gun Company of Montclair, New Jersey. We spoke briefly at Niblo's following the unfortunate murder of poor Mr. Schweib."

"Yes, sir. I remember you." Outside the crowds were singing, full of pride. Closing the door to the back stairs to the telegraph office, Tillman said, "I've nothing to report to you so far, I'm afraid." He went to the window and looked out.

Catton said, "Your friend Mr. Muldoon is down in the street singing. He has a fine, fluid bass voice. He was about to come and get you." Catton said smiling, "But since I have no voice at all, I volunteered to let the dear man exercise his lungs and his love of country." He looked down at Tillman's desk. Catton said, "Mr. Muldoon says you have had a very long day, that you traveled all the way to One Hundred and Thirtieth Street." He looked at Tillman's suit. Catton said, still smiling, "I must say, sir, the fabric of your shirtmaker must be of wonderful design: it shows no sign of such a long grimy expedition at all."

"I have been home to have a shower bath and change."

Catton said, "I peeked at the papers on your desk, I confess it. The work of the detective is—" Catton said, "Who, these days with all the lurid adventures we read of the sleuth in yellow-jacketed popular novels, does not dream of being an exciting detective."

Tillman said, "I keep my notes in my lodgings."

"So you may work on them in your own time." Catton, still smiling, full of admiration said, "Ah, to be a hero of the city . . ." He looked for a moment, sad. He looked away toward the window. Catton said, "Who would not be you? I confess it: I engaged Mr. Muldoon in conversation in order to—"

Tillman said, "Ned does not have such a good bass voice."

"The detective!" Catton, smiling, shaking his head, on the point of gentle laughter, said, "No, but I told him he did so I might, just for an instant, come running self-importantly up the stairs to the Detective Bureau and pretend . . . and pretend that—" Catton said, "Foolish, but—"

Tillman said, "Thank you for bringing me the message."

"Yes." The singing was swelling, coming to the climax. Catton said, "A pleasure." Above the air, above all the voices, there was the fine voice of Quarternight ringing out. It thrilled the heart. For a moment Catton listened.

Catton said, ". . . you know, Mr. Tillman, high or low, whoever we may be in our secret hearts, for the sake of our nation, we must see that man the next President!" He glanced around. He was in the little wooden room of real life and real men and important events and no fragile women. Catton, man to man, swearing freely, said, "By the living God, sir, God damn it, *we must!*"

The three glass balls went high up in the air, thrown by a juggler. There was a triple blast from the great presentation rifle drawn so quickly from its scabbard it was nought but a silver blur, and then the glass balls exploded into a million fragments and, floating down from the heavens, there came feathers.

"Throw!" On his horse—standing up—Quarternight had the lever of the rifle working.

The balls went up—one, two, three—four. The explosions echoed through the street. Men cheered, urchins and children gasped. There was an explosion in the sky and the balls came down in a snowstorm of wedding confetti: multicolored, green, white, yellow, brown.

"Throw *five!*" He was reloading, working the lever, bringing the gleaming, wonderful long gun to his shoulder and firing before the words had stopped echoing, firing, exploding the balls, storming confetti and feathers down in a continuous fall.

"Throw—"

"SIX!" It was the crowd.

"—seven!" The shots came too fast to count. The spirit gun of the West, slayer of Indians— The band had stopped playing, looking up, the confetti falling on their uniforms.

"THROW EIGHT!" The eight went up. He was firing and reloading on the back of the horse.

"THROW NINE!" The explosions, the empty brass shells ejecting into the crowd, came too fast to count. The confetti and the feathers became ribbons. The hollow glass balls were going up and detonating faster than the eye could follow. The feathers and the ribbons were coming down in all the colors of the rainbow, falling on uniforms, blowing in the street.

"TEN! TEN! TEN!" In a space too quick for the mind to count

or the eye to comprehend all the ten glass balls were exploding over the sky like fireworks amid cheering and shouting and children running for the spent empty cases.

"THREE! THREE ONLY!" It was Quarternight.

Up, slowly, so slowly, in a long parabola went only, just, merely, three hollow glass balls, thrown so high by the mighty arm of the juggler that for an instant they went out of sight. They did not go out of sight of the hawkeye—they did not go so high or so far that he did not see them. People were running, moving about: the photographer from Fox's wagon, the street children with their flyers, but he was not going to shoot. The rifle was in his hands, but the Great Man was merely looking at them all, at each soul in the crowd with a steady eye and he was not going to shoot.

The balls were falling, falling.

He raised his rifle.

Someone—not Sergeant Fitzgerald—yelled in a voice of iron, "On parade, you brave policemen, STAND STRAIGHT!" and raising his rifle, still looking at the crowd, Quarternight demanded, "Who? Who will not stand with a good and true man FOR HIS COUNTRY?" and he fired—so fast the three shots were one—and in the sky, hugely, massively, the balls exploded and rained down three colors of ribbons and confetti and feathers.

They rained down the red, white and blue.

They rained down the colors of history, of hope, of progress, the future.

They rained down in a bugle call to arms from a single, sole bandsman at the back of the crowd in civilian clothes, and looking up, gasping, each person thought he heard that call not in the street, but privately, shiveringly, proudly only in his secret heart.

"Vote for FREEDOM!"

From the cells, at his barred window, Dribbling Donahue yelled, "*I'll vote for that!*" He was not alone down there. Dribbling Donahue, taking his face away from the bars, yelled, "*Aaarrghh!*"

"Very still, gentlemen, if you please." The policemen were all lined up on the steps with the Great Man standing at their head in his Stetson hat with his gleaming silver rifle, his arm about the shoulder of Chief Inspector Byrnes. "This one is for an engraving on the front page of the *Police Gazette*—steady, if you please . . ." The photographer, reaching around for the brass lens cap of his camera, a bundle under the black-silk cloth at the image scope, said, "And . . ."

They were all wearing rosettes of red and white and blue. In a line, puffed out, they all looked steadily ahead. By Tillman, Muldoon, towering above him, said with his mouth fixed in a fierce grin, "Isn't this—"

"And . . . gents . . . and . . ." Off came the lens cap. "And . . . and . . ."

They held fast, that noble line of men.

". . . and . . . and . . ." They were all covered in confetti and ribbons and little curling feathers. It was one of the modern cameras with a clockwork lens. Reaching out and touching his checked-suited and capped young assistant on the shoulder from under the cloth, the photographer said, "And . . . and . . ."

The assistant had a pan of flash powder in his hand.

"And . . . and . . . NOW!"

Whoosh!

And, and—

The photographer said, *"Perfect!"* And—

There, caught forever in black and white, staring straight ahead with pale, unblinking eyes blinded by the white light, at 5:15 in the late afternoon outside 300 Mulberry Street, on Monday, May the twenty-first, 1883, they were immortalized.

11

"**V**ir . . . gil . . ."

At midnight with the yellow glow of the gas lamp in the street above her, Flossie said softly at the basement door of 23 Van Dan Street, "*Virgil* . . ." She had her red-painted mouth against the wooden door itself. She wore only a light white chemise. "Virgil honey, I know you're in there 'cause I saw your hand at the curtain before you turned your gaslights off . . . Naughty boy . . . !" Flossie, leaning against the door and whispering through the wood, said, "I know you're in there, you naughty boy . . ."

"Mr. Pol-isman . . ." Flossie said, "Mrs. Lawn's gone out for the evenin', Virgil, and I've got a key to your door . . ." She belched genteelly and put her long, red-nailed fingers to her mouth. She had been drinking gin with her cat. Her cat, on the mat, was laid out flat. Snoring. Flossie, putting her hand to the door to keep it anchored to the building, said softly, "Now, Virgil, ah know you have been wonderin' about that li'l ole box of fine duck-down feathers we keep in your rooms under the sheep. Ah know you have been wonderin' with your polis-man's mind just what a fine lady like myself and the fine gentlemen who favor me with their visits do with such outlandish items—" She was lonely. She needed to be touched. Flossie said, "Now, Virgil, let me in—!"

Flossie said, "Virgil, be kind to me." She put her hand against the door. It was hard and cold.

From behind the door, there was no sound at all and, through the curtained window, no light.

Flossie said, "I know you're in there, you naughty boy." Flossie said, "I've got a key."

It was a joke. He was funnin' her. She touched the door with her fingertips. In the night, in the darkness and stillness, in the silence,

104

she touched at her mouth. Her breasts under the chemise were naked and soft and cold.

All she wanted was a little company.

She had a key.

Flossie, tightening the muscles at her neck and setting her face into a smile, said, "Naughty boy!"

She knew men.

She nodded.

She put the key in the lock and pushed open the door a little into the darkness.

On his chair in the old Volunteer Firehouse on Bedford Street, Humpty Jackson, polishing a fire helmet, said philosophically, "Well, Virgil, you work like a slave all your life and you accumulate a few dollars, you take care of the people who are depending on you to put food on their table, and, I guess, when you reach a certain point you look around for something to leave to posterity." He was four-foot eight-and-a-half inches tall, dressed all in black with a hunchback that had a harness over it and onto his left shoulder for the pistol he carried there in a special holster: "When you come to the final crossroads in life's hard highway, you stop and think and say to yourself, 'Have I passed this way and done nothing for my fellow man except kill him?'" He had another gun, a .45 Single-Action Colt in his belt and, it was generally known, a British Bulldog .44 in a rack inside the black derby on his head. His hands, polishing the white Volunteer Fire Chief's leather hat with a silk cloth, were well away from the artillery. "In your own course through this world's hard furrows don't you sometimes consider your place in this sorry scheme of things?" He was an educated man. It was well known amongst his gang and the other fifty gangs of New York that he could read Shakespeare in the original Greek. Humpty, grinning like a goblin in the light of a coal-oil lamp above his chair like a surmounting crown, asked, "Do such things ever sink their way insidiously into your brain pan and—and—and nigglingly discommode you?"

Tillman said, "Constantly."

"Ah."

Outside, in the street, Muldoon was standing with Spanish Louie and Slungshot Sam, a muzzle-loading brass cannon (which, unfortunately, did not belong to Muldoon), and half the black-clad complement of Jackson's Firehouse Gang. He was probably not having an equally uplifting conversation. Tillman said pleasantly, "I see the collection comes along well."

"Ah, yes." Along the walls of the place there must have been two hundred cast-iron fire marks of various fire-insurance companies stolen from two hundred various walls. There was a full collection of the latest Currier and Ives colored prints of the *Lives of a Fireman* and *The American Fireman*, probably stolen from Currier and Ives. There was a line of leather fire buckets with wonderfully painted crests dating from the Revolution and George Washington's presentation plaque to the fire company in Alexandria, Vermont, dated 1775. There was a fire bucket from Buckingham Palace, in England. There was a rack of rifles and shotguns and pistols against the wall in case George and the Queen complained. Humpty said, "A small diversion in life: that is what the man at the crossroads craves—I intend to leave my collection to posterity." Humpty said, "A lot of this stuff was here when the previous owner decided he had a pressing engagement in Patagonia or Tasmania or wherever the next ship leaving New York was headed." Humpty said, "My little band of brothers outside are good boys—they understand in their own brutal way that a man of my education must have something with which to while away his thoughtful moments. They know I have a soul."

"I believe you have recently added a fire appliance to your collection."

"Ah, the Shanghai Man-Killer." He stopped polishing. Humpty said, "Yes. A gentleman who owed the Gopher Gang a little remuneration from a foolish wager on the naggies. It was the pride of his mansion." Humpty, grinning, said, "The Plug Ugly Gang, against all accepted custom, took over the garnering of said wager much to the annoyance of the Gophers and, rather than disturb the peace of New York's citizenry by committing wholesale slaughter on the streets, the Gophers asked my little band of brothers to arbitrate in the matter." Humpty said, "I got, through the most involved negotiations for my services, the fire appliance. The Plug Uglies got a total of three ears chawed off and the gentleman—" Humpty said suddenly, "It's a Henry Waterman manual fire pump built in 1847 with a double-deck side-stroke engine that eight men work like a haywagon and it can shoot a full three-inch-bore jet of water thirty-five feet in the air, straight up, if the crew can keep up the sixty strokes a minute." Humpty said, "It's painted red and gold, with ladders and a cable winch and a leather hose in perfect condition and three brass hose nozzles." Humpty said, "In the

days, you know, when all the gangs were volunteer firemen—the
Dead Rabbits and the Bowery Boys, the Bloody Tubs and the
Dudes and the Sydney Ducks and the old, famous Hartley Mob
and the Molasses Gang, there used to be wonderful battles at the
scenes of fires for the one or two available hydrants and wonderful
volunteer uniforms and high, painted hats and brass trumpets and
much shouting and alarum—" He was a small, twisted, ugly dwarf
polishing a fire helmet. "But all gone now, all gone." He remem-
bered where he had begun: "The gentleman who owned the engine
got to live."

"You were never a volunteer fireman yourself?"

He was a small, twisted, ugly dwarf polishing a fire helmet.
Humpty said, "No."

Tillman said, "Men of steel, the old volunteers."

"Men of steel and hearts so soft as to bring a smile to a widow's
tears."

Tillman said,

> *The fireman, from his slumbers waking,*
> *At once his quiet home forsaking,*
> *Regardless of both health and life,*
> *Rushes to the deadly strife.*
> *While still the cry of wild despair*
> *Is wafted on the midnight air,*
> *Fire! Fire! Fire!*

"What must they have been like, Virgil? Those old Volunteers?"

"Men of stout heart and backs like ancient oak."

"Untiring, fearless, straight and tall. Men women sighed for and
men envied!"

Tillman said, "The American Fireman!"

"Knights of the Night!" Humpty said, "All gone now. Replaced
by steam-boiler pumps and horses to pull the pumps where once
strong men—"

> *One, two, three, four!*
> *The panting Foreman's trumpet bellows*
> *'Pull her along and jump her, fellows!'*
> *Down through the cobbled avenues roar!*

"What a filthy thing for a man progress is, Virgil!"

"It is."

He was, and had been, the most feared man in the New York gangs for some twenty years; an arbitrator, a contractor. He had formed in the last five years what the other gangs, coming to him for justice and internecine settlement, had begun to call The Organization. He had a price list. He had had it printed. The price list read:

Punching	$2
Both eyes blacked	$4
Nose and jaw broke	$10
Thoroughly blackjacked	$15
Ear chawed off	$15
Leg or arm broke	$19
Shot in leg	$25
Stabbed	$25
Doing the big job	$100 and up.

He was a twisted, tiny hunchback with a face yellow and evil in the light from the coal-oil lamp above his chair. He had never been a volunteer fireman. He polished at the hat. Somewhere in the darkness, like him hidden, there was the great fire pump. Somewhere maybe in the city, there was George Fenney and Henry Carver and Warren Cahill and maybe all the other faded, posed faces from the picture taken at Vicksburg two decades before. Maybe . . .

Maybe, in his philosophic moments, polishing another man's helmet painted with a crest and a laurel leaf to show that once whoever wore the helmet in honor had saved a human life, maybe . . .

"In . . . in . . ." He looked up suddenly from his chair.

"In—" His hands were shaking and the grin on his face looked different, forced, put there. "By God, Virgil . . ."

His eyes looked strange, full of anger.

Humpty, gripping hard at the helmet, his eyes staring straight and unblinkingly bright at Tillman's, said, shaking, "By God, Virgil, the old gangs fighting for the one available fire plug—by God, with the old Shanghai Man-Killer by God, and with me as Chief—*by God, we'd have cleared them out quick smart!*"

"Virgil?" She was inside his rooms in the darkness. The door to the bedroom at the rear was open and through the half-pulled curtains she could see moonlight in a shaft.

"Virgil?" The door behind her to the street clicked closed gently on its spring-loaded hinges.

Flossie said softly, "Virgil? Are you here?"

Flossie said, "Naughty boy . . ."

Flossie said, "Virgil, is that you?"

He was the meanest-looking sonofabitch who had ever drawn breath.

Muldoon was a pretty mean-looking sonofabitch himself.

Outside the firehouse in Bedford Street, standing on the curb with his hands on his hips, Muldoon looked at Spanish Louie, nodding. The rest of the gang didn't count: they were up and down the street and in doorways and alleys, dressed in black, lost in the darkness. Louie stood in the street facing him. He could see Louie's hawk nose and Spanish features and nasty little eyes in the light of the single gas lamp over the side door to the firehouse.

Muldoon, still nodding, sucked at his teeth and grinned. He measured off Louie's height. He was six-foot two-inches tall. And his weight. He was spare and hard and, all muscle, about one hundred and sixty-five pounds. He looked at the shape of his head under the slicked-down black hair. He measured the distance between them and nodded.

Louie's black Spanish foreign eyes had no pupils to them.

Muldoon's index fingers, on his hips, moved in and out under his thumbs as he grinned and nodded. In the top of Louie's hand-tooled black-leather boot on the right leg there was a long-barreled .36-caliber underhammer percussion boot pistol. In his wide black belt about his waist there was a brace of pearl-handled Smith and Wesson Number Three .44s with spur triggers. In the left pocket of his vest there was a four-barrel .22 Sharps derringer with gutta-percha grips, and in the right, the ivory handle of a folded straight razor. There was a lump in the righthand pocket of his black pants. It was a set of brass knuckles, and in the left, the outline of a T-shaped Cajun push dagger.

He held Louie's eyes and did not blink. He nodded his head.

It was a whisper. Louie said in the utter silence of the street, "Are you armed, Muldoon?"

It was a whisper. Muldoon, leaning just a little forward, being kind, working out the English of the foreign jabber, said softly, widening his eyes, "No. Are you?"

* * *

They were funnin' her, the two of them. On the hat rack by the door, she felt both their guns: Virgil's little Colt in its shoulder holster and Muldoon's pistol in its rubber hip-pocket holster for his street clothes, and his club.

They were funnin' her, Virgil and Neddie. They were going to jump out and make her laugh and they were just—

Monkeyshines. The curtains on the window in the bedroom were half open and she could see the linoleum on the floor shining with the silver from the moon.

Flossie said, "Now, you boys . . . now you boys . . ."

She knew they were in there, hidin' from her, funnin' her because she heard there, in the bedroom, someone move.

Tillman said, "The telegraph brought nothing. No one at any of the other Stations knows any of them: Fenney, Carver, Cahill, someone called Shand. One of them is some sort of tramp or vagrant: Fenney, Carver or Cahill. If it was Shand, they would have known the full name for the back of the photograph." Tillman said, "If any of them are still alive, if any of them are in New York—if—then they'll be at least forty-two or -three years old by now or maybe even older." Tillman said, "They were the names they used during the Civil War; I haven't got any reason to think they'd be different now unless some of them have fallen foul of the law or taken street names." Tillman said, "I want them."

Humpty said, "Yes." He was not listening. Maybe he was listening.

Humpty said with no expression on his face, "I wish now, Virgil, I had dedicated my life, at least part-time, to glory and good works." He looked up to the rafters above his hanging light: "I wish now, beginning my long struggle all over again from the cradle to the grave, once, I had stood shoulder to shoulder with those old men of magnificent mustaches and sung my songs and reveled in comradeship." He was twisted in the chair, looking up. He made a sniffing sound. Humpty said, "Other men at the summit of their achievements give their fortunes away to good works and are commemorated in libraries; I, on the other hand—"

Tillman said, "The gangs here know everybody."

Humpty said, "I'll tell you a secret, Virgil, because I know it's safe with you and, because if it isn't, I'll have you killed: I sometimes sit here alone, pondering my responsibilities, calculating, for example, how far I can trust Spanish Louie not to make an alliance with the Greaser Gang on Essex Street which he would like very much because he is a greaser himself, or with Spider Kelly on Delancey Street because Spider feels, from a past dispute, that I still owe him for the loss of one of his eyes and both his ears, and I think, worrying at all these problems as well as the daily concerns of business that now I shall never marry and have the comfort and companionship of a home and a hearth and happy family with smiling children around my knees—what single shining moment—that was not fraught with the day-to-day concerns of commerce and assault?" Humpty said, "People don't even fight back anymore—what victory is there without endurance, what triumph without adversity? One of my employees simply says to his victim, 'You have crossed so-and-so person in such-and-such gang and this is nothing personal but we're going to batter you into unconsciousness,' and the victim, knowing the sense of it all, glad that it is to be nothing more final, merely says okay and asks if he might take off his best shirt or some piece of jewelry or some keepsake of sentimental value and present the harder side of his head to be battered." Humpty said, "For a genuinely wicked man, my trade has become as exciting as an old woman beating carpets on a clothesline. Killing is different, but we don't do a lot of that these days." Humpty said, "I'm getting old."

"You've got your collection."

"I have my failed dreams." Humpty said suddenly,

> *To a Fireman's calling, I mean*
> *To draw a few parallel cases:*
> *In the course of my song t'will be seen*
> *What a number of folks it embraces:*
> *The ladies are firemen by trade,*
> *When we ring all the bells about, sirs,*
> *A coquette often dies an old maid,*
> *Because she puts all the sparks out, sirs!*

He sniffed. Humpty said, "I'm a dwarf! In the back of the firehouse with the engine, with my beautiful, ready Shanghai Man-Killer, I've got a little pair of boots and a fireman's uniform tailor-made for me by Lewenstein on the Bowery and I've got a full-length mirror and the brass nozzle of a hose and I—and I, sometimes, don my outfit and hat and laurel leafs and—" Humpty said, "But I'm a dwarf with a hump and—" He was looking up, sniffing. "And—" Humpty said, without looking at Tillman's face, "I tell you this secret because I know you won't laugh, but—"

In the big room, Tillman said not a word.

"But—" Humpty, suddenly looking back, his helmet gripped hard in his hands, his little eyes shining, said, "The brave American Volunteer Fireman, Virgil, gone! All gone! Gone! *Gone to Glory!*"

She heard a click. From the bedroom, she heard a sort of swift click; the sound of metal moving suddenly through still air.

In the front room, Flossie froze.

She heard a breath: a sigh, a quaver, a tremor of sound, a tensing. She heard something scrape against a wall. Through the window of the bedroom the moonlight was going, getting darker as the moon went behind a cloud, and she heard a rustle, a movement.

Flossie said softly, "Virgil? Neddie, this isn't—" She heard—
Flossie said, "This is—"

She heard a rustle. She saw the moonlight going at the window.

". . . Virgil . . ." She was frozen to the floor, starting to tremble. There was coldness coming in the room as the moon went.

Flossie said, "Hello? Who's there? *Hello . . . ?*"

Spanish Louie, sizing him up, said, "Irish, are you, Muldoon?"

Muldoon said, "Yes. Mongrel of some sort, are you yourself, Louie?"

It was a whisper. "One day, Muldoon . . ."

Muldoon said, "Hmm." Virgil was a long time. Muldoon said, "Hmm? Sorry, Louie, what was that?" Muldoon said, "One day? Well, I hope so for you—"

He smiled an evil smile.

Muldoon said in his Irish Christian way, "Yes, with a bit of luck even you may probably be able to raise it *one day*—"

Tillman said, "I'll get you a fire!"

Humpty said, "What?"

"I'll get you a fire! I'll get you a private fire that no one else gets called to and I'll get you flames and people in the street watching, and I'll get you a fire!"

"And a daring rescue?"

"And a daring rescue of a woman!"

"A helpless woman?"

"A sylph if you want! A maiden in night attire calling plaintively for help with her hair flowing back in the smoke!"

"And cobbles? And cobbles striking sparks off the iron wheels of the great Shanghai Man-Killer as my brave boys race her through the streets with their muscles bulging and the sweat pouring off their brows?" He was drooling, licking his lips to stop the saliva running down his chin, "And—and—and me wearing my uniform and boots and—"

"—and carrying your trumpet and standing on the pump and like a General roaring orders at your—"

"At my brave boys! At my men! At my *Company!*" Humpty said, "Will you do that? Will you do that?"

"I'll do that."

"And, and—" He was off the chair, tiny, like a crab, the helmet still in his hands, all his guns clanking and jangling as he moved. Humpty, beside himself, starting to hop up and down, said, "A fire? A real live fire? Not one I set myself for the insurance—not a business fire—but a real—"

"Yes."

"Flames?"

"Flames."

"Smoke?"

Tillman said, "Darkening the sun!"

"Ladders?"

"Ladders!"

"Ladders and hooks and helmets and boots and smoke and fire and—"

Tillman said, "—and desperation. Terrible desperation!"

"Not in a field somewhere!"

"In a street."

"Crowded?"

Tillman said, "Teeming!"

Humpty said, "Oh . . ."

For a moment Tillman thought he was going to throw himself onto the floor and clasp him by the knees.

Humpty said, "Oh . . ." He had the helmet in both hands. He almost put it on. It wasn't time. He was going to put it on. Not now, but— He almost put it on. He held it out in his hands and then pulled it to his chest. He almost put it on. He didn't put it on. Humpty said, "Oh . . ." Humpty said, "Oh . . ."

One day, soon, once, in his mirror, in his soul, in his dreams, in his pain, he would be tall. Humpty said, "Oh . . ."

Humpty, in the shadowy firehouse filled with all the things of all the great men gone to Glory, said, pressing at the brim of the helmet so hard his hands shook, "Oh . . . *God!!*"

"Oh gentle Jesus!" She heard it coming. She heard whatever it was in the bedroom coming as the moon went into darkness and, turning, running, falling, crashing into the hat stand and upsetting all the guns and the club, hearing them hitting the floor and rolling, she got to the door and pulled it open and, getting to the stairs to the street, ran with her nightdress flying up the stone steps into the main house and slammed the door.

"Company's coming! Company's coming!" Out there at the bottom of the steps on his perch she heard Fred the parrot squawking. She heard the door to the basement slam shut.

She was against the big double doors with her back against the lock, jamming it. She saw her breasts rising and falling in terror.

"Company's coming! Company's coming!"

In the deserted, still, moonless street, with no one else in the house but her unconscious cat, Flossie heard the sound of heavy footsteps on the flagstones outside, running.

12

In the rooms in the basement of 23 Van Dam Street, Muldoon, examining the lock on the half-open front door, said for the second or third time, "Are you completely *crazy? Are you away with the fairies?* People are going to roast while that collection of scalpeens, cockroaches and assorted crustaceans try to get the entire one-half brain they have between them to work putting out a fire and—and what do we do? Hold off the good men from the regular Fire Department with pistols and tell them that it's a private affair between us, The Organization and our God who's going to judge us for it at the Final Trumpet?"

He had picked up his gun and club and he was at the door with his hand on the neck of his bottle in his pocket. Miss Flossie was in the room wearing a dress and a bonnet with flowers on it and he thought it not right to take a drink with her all dressed up and not on business. Muldoon, looking polite but disgusted, said, closing the door, "It's an old single-tumbler Dietz lock. My Aunt Maeve who's eighty-three and bedridden could have opened it with a fruit knife." Upstairs, there was the sound of a three-piece string ensemble playing refined music. Mrs. Lawn must have had a special late caller. That was why Flossie was wearing her bonnet. Muldoon, taking his hand off the neck of his bottle, said with a slight inclination of his head, "Excuse me for the rough language, Miss Flossie."

She smelled very nice—elegant, ladylike. She had very sweet-smelling breath, like an Eau de Cologne mouthwash. Flossie, careful to remain standing, alone in the presence of gentlemen said, listening to the music, "Of course, Mr. Muldoon."

Muldoon said in the direction of the bedroom where Tillman was, "Anything?"

Tillman said, "He was left-handed." On the inside wall of the room, by the door, there was the mark the knife blade had made as it snapped out and scraped against the masonry. There were about three feet between the edge of the bed and the doorjamb and he had stood there facing the door with the knife in one hand and put his other, his right hand, against the wall to support himself. On the wall there were the marks of his finger pads, each of the designs, whorls and loops clearly defined in dark, sweaty smudges on the white wall. They were of no use. Tillman wiped them away with a handkerchief from his coat pocket. Tillman said, "Nothing's been moved in here."

"Do you think it was the person who killed Schweib?" Muldoon, picking up Tillman's Colt Lightning where Tillman had put it on a little writing desk and checking the chambers, asked, "What the Hell did he want in here?"

It could have been the knife blade on the little knuckle-duster gun that had killed the stage doorman. It could have merely been a switchblade knife. Tillman said, "I don't know." Nothing in the bedroom had been disturbed. Apart from clothes on hangers in the single cupboard in the room with drawers of collars and ties and socks and underclothes and boxes of studs and cuff links, there was nothing much to be disturbed. Tillman, turning down the gas and coming out into the parlor, said, looking at Flossie, "Maybe it was just a sneak thief. He probably wouldn't have done you any harm." He looked up to the music and then back to Flossie. Tillman said, "That's a very nice bonnet."

Flossie said, "Thank you, sir. I was wearing it when I came down here earlier to ask your assistance in reviving my poor old cat who suffered, I believe, a slight conniption while Mrs. Lawn was out with the other ladies and I was all alone. It was a gift from my dear mother in Tiptonville which is in the great state of Tennessee and I treasure it as a defenseless girl alone in the city with a sick pet." She was so ladylike it hurt. It had hurt. She had a slap mark on her cheek under her makeup from the not-too-feeble hand of an irate Madam. Flossie said, "Fortunately, solely due to the desperate forced ingestion of three drops of medicinal gin as found in most home pantries for the purposes of cooking, the poor beast appears to be on the road to recovery and is presently sleeping peacefully in my private boudoir." She touched at her face. She did not sit down.

In the desk there was another gun. It was the rusted and pitted Confederate Gilbert and Greer revolver they had found in Carrol's room under the cupboard floorboards. It was wrapped in an oil rag, undisturbed. Muldoon, moving it to one side to put Tillman's Lightning in its shoulder holster beside it, said, "What about the photograph of Vicksburg?" He turned to see Tillman shake his head and pull a corner of the picture out from inside his coat to show he still had it. He moved a few papers and notebooks and Tillman's case ledger in the space below the little pigeonholes in the desk. "What about money?"

"What I have I've got."

"Jewelry?"

Tillman said, "No."

Flossie said, "Perhaps—I believe there are such people in the world—it was some fiend driven to lunacy by self-abuse, who, knowing there were young ladies present in the residence . . ." She touched at her face. It hurt. Flossie said in the heaviest antebellum accent she could manage with one side of her face starting to go numb, "Ah do believe that ma old black nanhy, Mammy Mulcback, once let it escape from her lips that in the nigra population of our area there were men who barely became the title of men and who—" She saw Tillman about to ask her something. Flossie said, looking away, "Ah saw nothing of the person as I rushed quickly to defend the home of mah employer by thrusting mah small body hard against the portal to defend both the house and mah honor to the death." Flossie, her eyes filling with tears, said, "That fat bitch up there hit me!"

There was a small curtained bookcase above the desk. It contained copies of the poets, a *Family Medical Adviser*, a dictionary with a supplement on how to pronounce ten thousand difficult words, General Crook's *Memoirs* in two volumes, Shakespeare, Asbury's *Pictorial History of the United States*, Conklin's *Handy Manual and Atlas of the World*, a set of the Wonders of England, Ireland, Palestine and California, a Bible and, at the far left-hand end, what looked like a presentation copy of *Bible Stories for Children*. If the curtain had been pulled back and the books opened and searched for something, then the thief either cared for literature or was by nature tidy and had put them all back in in line and the right way up. Muldoon, turning to Tillman in the center of the room, seeing him standing there merely thinking, said to Flossie, "Are you sure you caught no sight of him at all?"

Flossie said, "I did not."

"You heard no sound?"

"Ah was here on an errand of mercy for mah poor feline. Mah

brain was racing with fear that he might expire before ah could summon help."

Muldoon said, "How did you get in?"

"Ah have a key to be used in the event of fire or natural disaster—or sudden illness." She saw Tillman smile at her. Flossie said, "It is Mrs. Lawn's key, but pursuant to the police and fire regulations, she hangs it in a conspicuous place in the lobby so that in an emergency—"

Tillman, still smiling, said, "Miss Flossie is the designated alarum-giver of this building."

Flossie said, "I was once! I had a little armband and everything! It was red!" Flossie said suddenly, remembering, "*Naughty boy!*" She glanced up quickly to the violin music. Flossie said, "*Shhh!*" She touched at her bonnet and set it straight on her head. Flossie said, "Naughty boy . . ."

Flossie said, "She hit me, Virgil. That fat slug up there in her finery with her private customers on mah night off, *hit* me!" Muldoon, at the desk, was fidgeting, kneading his fingers, not looking at her, touching at his pocket. She saw Tillman smiling gently at her.

Flossie said suddenly in a gap from the string ensemble between *amore* and *brio*, between the giggling and guzzling, "For God's sake, I was almost killed tonight! In the name of God, Neddie Muldoon, you're an Irishman: *don't you have a drop of anything on your person to save a poor, helpless, hard-used woman from fainting dead away from the vapors?*"

About 3:00 A.M., after Flossie and Muldoon had left, it began to rain.

It was a light, soft cool rain and, in the street outside his rooms, Tillman, hatless, his hand on the cast-iron railing by Fred's post at the bottom of the front steps to 23 Van Dam Street, stood smoking a cigar and gazing down the street.

Fred, his duty done the moment all the lights in the house had gone out, was inside, probably in the pantry on his perch, his head tucked under his wing, asleep.

In the yellow halo of the street gas lamp Tillman watched the rain and the blue smoke from his cigar curling in amongst it.

He had no idea on Earth what he would be looking for at Edison's Pearl Street Electric Generating Station in the morning.

In the city, at night, in the darkness, everywhere, hidden,

hiding, there were the poor, the sorrowing, the vicious and the demented, behind—always behind—windows, looking out. He touched at his chest where the scar from the skewer was. He wondered.

He wondered.

He wondered as men had wondered since the caves just where—just where, where in the name of God, in New York City in the last quarter of the goddamned nineteenth century—he was going to get a fire.

13

It looked like Hell. It was Hell. It was Science. It was Edison's Volcano, the Electric Illuminating Company's generating station at 257 Pearl Street, New York.

It sounded like thunder. It sounded like thunder and steamboats and artillery fire and jackhammers and Judgment. It was raging red hot from the fires in the four riveted-steel Babcock and Wilcox boilers in the basement, throbbing with the six 350-rpm Porter-Allen engines on the first floor, shrieking from the six Edison Jumbo dynamos connected to the six engines on the second floor, and, for all anyone knew, frizzing and frying and making men's hair stand on end with the loose electrical fluid from the circuits and wires and leads on the third.

In his glassed-in basement office, the man who Understood All, Overseer Wilson, screamed, "It'll go until there's an earthquake!" It sounded like one was coming. The whole building shook. In the basement an army of stokers built like oak trees shoveled coal into the open boilers in relays. "It'll go until the Crack of Doom! The match is an object now as primitive to the pursuit of Light as the spear was to the pursuit of the dinosaur!" He had a little brass thumbscrew in his hand. He put it up to an Edison vacuum incandescent light globe and turned it: "Click! And let there be light and there is light! Click! No light." The army of stokers were being supplied by an army of coal carriers. Outside in the street their carts and wagons blocked the sidewalk and road. Wilson screamed, "Not since the beginning of time has the human race moved in such a leap, a bound, to approach the paradise of Plato." The stokers were black with sweat and coal dust, their faces red and glistening with the fires leaping out from the open boiler doors. Like Plato, Wilson was a small, bespectacled man wearing a gray dust coat and

120

tightly knotted dark tie, with gold buttons reading EDISON with a lightning bolt on them: "No longer need commerce and reason cease with the coming of dusk. *Click!* No matches, no flickering, no smell—*daylight!*" He saw Muldoon looking at the state of the walls. They, like the rest of the old building, were clapboard. They were shaking. Wilson, stabbing him in the chest to reassure him about the architecture as well as the coming Republic, said, "Mr. Edison is a genius. Who would have thought anyone could have taken a condemned, dilapidated double tenement building and—without a single strengthening girder put in it—turned it into a monolith capable of supporting the weight of over one hundred and eighty tons on every floor?" He saw the look on Muldoon's face. He gave him the thumbscrew to play with.

Tillman screamed, "How many men do you employ?" There seemed to be people everywhere. He counted, as well as the stokers and coal heavers, at least eight shovelers, three sweepers, two of what looked like general heavers by the open door to the street heaving and shoving what looked like solid blocks of metal and swinging them up to the windlasses, eight or nine blackened, half-naked bodies of inderterminate purpose running back and forth between the stokers, the heavers, the shovelers, the *forts* and the sweepers, and two uniformed men carrying clubs keeping back the crowds from the street who had gathered there every day for the past eighteen months the place had been in operation to await the cascades of lava and sparks that would bury them as surely as Vesuvius had buried Pompeii. It was too early in the morning for the religious maniacs warning with placards about God's punishment on man for Tampering, but there seemed to be at least one old woman standing on something in the crowd screaming wordlessly about something. Tillman said, "George Fenney, Henry Carver, Warren Cahill, Shand: do any of those people work here?"

"None of those people works here!"

"Schweib. Carrol. Seward—do those names mean anything to you?" The coal heavers were phantoms with thick hessian bags covering their heads and shoulders like capes. Tillman, straining to make himself heard, yelled, "What about the contract labor? Could any of them—?"

"Mr. Edison is very strict about his employees!" He had a list of names on his desk. He did not look at it. Wilson, watching Muldoon click the thumbscrew, nodding to him to click it again, yelled, "I know the names of everyone. Everyone here in the boiler room is reliable and illiterate." He saw Tillman glance at him, "—for the patents! Everything is patented. There are rivals everywhere!" Wilson screamed, "Upstairs in the engines and dynamo rooms and, of course, in the electrics . . . but down here where the common herd makes contact with us, we employ no man who can read or write!" Wilson screamed, "We light up one-third of lower Manhattan! Two-thirds are still left! People would do anything to get our secret!" He saw Muldoon start as if the thumbscrew were red hot. Wilson screamed, "The thumbscrew switch is a secret of only minor proportions. The vein of gold is upstairs where the chemistry of our electricity is!" He patted Muldoon on the shoulder to let him click on.

Muldoon said, "I've never seen an electrical lamp close up . . ."

Wilson said, "Soft and mellow and grateful to the eye." Wilson said, "So far they're only in banks and stockbroking establishments and in the *Times* newspaper and selected theaters—people who can afford them." Wilson said, "Three cents every time you turn the light on."

Muldoon said, *"Hell!"*

"It'll get cheaper! Think what matches for gas cost!"

They cost two cents for a dozen packets and in each packet there were fifty matches. He thought about it.

Wilson said, "Think of the cost of spectacles, of headaches, of blindness! Think of the lost business when dusk comes! Think that in two thousand years Man has finally harnessed the invisible power of the Universe!" Wilson said, "We've only been at it eighteen months—give us a little time to bring the cost down." Wilson screamed, "We light up one square mile of the city. If we can stay safe from thieves and saboteurs and spies and Mr. Edison can get a monopoly of supply in the Courts, we can—"

Genius was catching. Muldoon, having given the thumbscrew a good click, yelled, "What if you turn it on and leave it on all the time—does it still only cost three cents?"

Wilson said, "The people you name don't work here."

"Have any of them ever worked here?"

"No." There was a little handwritten sign on the wall above the glass over his desk. It read in printed letters EVERY MAN EMPLOYED IN OR ABOUT MY ESTABLISHMENT WHETHER BY PIECEWORK OR BY DAYS WORK IS EXPECTED TO WORK TEN HOURS DURING THE RUNNING OF THE ENGINES AND NO ONE WHO DOES NOT CHEERFULLY CONSENT TO DO THIS NEED EX-

PECT TO BE EMPLOYED BY ME. It was signed, *Thomas A. Edison*. Wilson, his face tight, yelled, "People here who are lucky enough to find work, *work!*"

The Vicksburg photograph was on Wilson's desk. He looked at it. He had seen no face he knew. Tillman, taking it up, asked for the second time, "Are you sure you recognize no one? They'd be older, but—"

"We employ young, healthy men. Anyone over thirty is too old to work." He had a smooth face, but he himself could not have been a day under thirty-five. Wilson said, "It's going to be the New Way: no more old, wise men who do nothing except say that things cannot be done! New men for a new industry—men with young backs and fresh minds!" Wilson said, "All the minds are on the top floor and none of them is in the picture."

"Someone here knows one of these people!" Tillman said, "Two men are dead because of someone in this picture and the only clue I have to follow is the suggestion made by someone that, somehow, some part of the puzzle leads here!" Tillman said, "It's all I have! I am trying to do my job in a scientific way, but all I have, as Mr. Edison must have had when he first conceived this idea, is a vague notion that, given a little good fortune, I may get something solid to take root on fertile ground!"

Wilson said, "Mr. Edison is an authentic modern genius!"

"I am not comparing myself with Mr. Edison!"

"No one could!"

"Quite." He scanned Wilson's face. Tillman, nodding hard at Muldoon to keep clicking, said, "Mr. Edison is the Leonardo da Vinci of our time."

Wilson said, "I don't suppose a policeman, seeing our secret apparatus, would even know what any of it did—"

Tillman said, "A copper like myself and like him"—he jerked his thumb at the happy clicker—"wouldn't have the foggiest."

"Mr. Edison has said that the forces of Progress must always work hand in glove."

"Perhaps, with the coming of light, I may be investigating the last crime to ever take place in the city. Perhaps, with the coming of Edison's light—"

"Edison's *incandescent* light!"

"Even better." Tillman said, "Two men are dead. One of them at Niblo's Theatre where your vacuum globes are installed." Tillman said, "George Fenney, Henry Carver, Shand, Warren Cahill—perhaps someone upstairs knows them in private life."

"You wish to go up in the elevator to the dynamo and circuit rooms?"

Tillman said, "If it's not too much trouble."

He took off his glasses and thought about it. Wilson said softly in a sudden inexplicable pause in the machines and the building falling to pieces, "Business is slow. We have installed only seven thousand electric bulbs in all of lower Manhattan in eighteen months."

Tillman said consolingly, "We must all feel our way out of the darkness a step at a time."

"Upstairs is secret!"

Tillman said, "We will speak of it to no one."

"It is *secret!*" He looked hard at the sign on the wall. He looked out hard at the sweating, glistening, shoveling men. He looked—

Tillman said, "How do we get upstairs?"

Muldoon said with sudden, wonderful expectation, "An *elevator?* Do you have an electric *elevator?* Do you mean to say you have a real, live—"

Wilson said, "*It works by a horse here in the basement turning a capstan! It is lit by a candle on the wall! It—*" Wilson, alone in the basement day after day, surrounded by illiterates, morons, brutes, said in a sudden burst, putting out his hands and crying to Heaven and Mr. Edison who was too busy in the Courts these days to ever come and talk to him, "The expense of electricity! The expense! We can't afford to install even one light or power outlet in this whole building ourselves!" He was at least thirty-five years old. If Edison was right, forty, soon, would be death. He had a wife and three children. He was the Keeper of Secrets. He had kept the one that exercised his mind nightly too long.

In the noise, the stench, the bustle, the activity—the Hope— Wilson said suddenly, desperately, shouting, "What am I going to do if I've tied my entire fate to something that turns out to be just a *toy?*"

H . . E . . N . . R . . Y . . . . . FL . . Y . . NN . . . Standing by his Clydesdale horse in the far corner of the boiler room, the boy, running his hand over his shaven head, yelled obediently, "Yes, sir!" and waved his hand to show he had heard. He was in a deserted part of the floor, practicing, glancing around to make sure no one saw, writing the letters of his name on the horse's flank in the coal dust and sweat.

He saw Mr. Reynolds, the elevator-room operator, holding up

three fingers and he nodded and held up three fingers of his own above the din, mouthing the words clearly, "Three to go up, sir!" He patted the horse and rubbed off the letters. He saw Mr. Wilson with two men in suits and he nodded at him and saluted him obediently with two fingers touching his forehead, *"Three to go up, sir!"*

Letters. He could now, almost, read all the letters on street signs. A nice man from the Illinois Electric Lamp Company was teaching him his letters every evening after work. One day he would even be able to read all the words on the papers Mr. Wilson left on his desk when he had to go to the privy four or fives times a day to relieve himself.

Three to go up. Yes, sir. He was fourteen years old, naked to the waist, with his head shaven against lice.

He knew where the future lay. He knew no one else on Earth apart from Mr. Wilson and the man from Illinois and now him who could even write his own name.

"Giddyup!" Taking off the brake on the drum of the dual counter-rotating cogs of the capstan and starting the horse off in its never-ending circle with a flick of the great rope and leather harness that tethered it to its work, Henry Flynn—H-E-N-R-Y, new word F-L-Y-N-N—rubbing at his head, smiling faintly to himself, sent the heavy wooden elevator-room, like himself, slowly, jerkingly, an inch at a time, cautiously, on its way *up*.

"HEY!" At the capstan, the boy yelled at the top of his lungs, *"HEY!"* There was one of the coal heavers at the open elevator shaft looking up, his head and body covered by a long sliced-open coal sack. Henry Flynn yelled, "Hey, *you're not supposed to be there!"* It was his little part of the world, his and Mr. Reynolds the elevator-room operator's. Henry, coming out from behind the huge horse and putting his cupped hands to his lips, yelled, "Hey! Get back to your job or you'll lose it—and me mine!" He could not see the man's face as he turned—it was darkness in the hood of the sack cape. Henry, glancing back at the horse to see it was still walking of its own accord in its circle, yelled, *"HEY—!"*

In the elevator, Tillman said, "And you are—?" The elevator operator was a balding, sickly looking man in his fifties wearing the company's gold buttons on his blue uniform coat. He was standing to one side of the slatted wooden doors of the apparatus with his hand on a brake lever, looking straight ahead, the fingers of his other hand touching at a cheap brass watch chain with empty charm and medal spaces across his vest. He smelled slightly of gin. Tillman, touching him on the shoulder, said again, "And you are—?"

Where the Hell was he?

He was gone.

One moment he had been there by the elevator-room shaft and the next . . .

Maybe he had gone back to work.

Maybe he hadn't.

"HEY!" Looking around, Henry yelled, "HEY!" The horse was still moving. The boy was midway between the horse and the shaft; he was too far away from his job.

"HEY!" It could be a trick to test him. Mr. Wilson could have gone a little way up in the elevator room, then clambered out and taken the stairs down and then—

No, he couldn't. The horse had not completed its third revolution and the room must still be between floors and there was no way Mr. Wilson could . . .

It was his job. He was out in the open. He ran his hand over his shaven head.

"HEY!"

He tried to see where the coal heaver had gone.

Wilson said, "Reynolds." Wilson said, "He's deaf. He can't hear a word you say." Wilson said, "The war." Wilson said quickly before Tillman could speak, "No, he's a Southerner, from Georgia or Tennessee or some awful place—the wrong side." Wilson said to the man, "Aren't you? You're one of our late Reb scum, aren't you?" The man was looking hard at him with watery blue eyes. Wilson said, "And you drink too much and you haven't got a brain in your head, have you, or otherwise Mr. Edison wouldn't have employed you, would he?" Wilson said, "A moron." Wilson sang, "*Oh, I wish I was in the land of cotton* . . ." In the flickering candlelight in the dark wooden elevator room the man was looking at him with neutral, expressionless eyes.

Wilson said, "Ethan Reynolds."

Wilson said, looking at the man with disgust, *"Up! Three to go up!"* The man, concentrating on reading Wilson's lips, nodded. He grinned.

Wilson said to Tillman, "God, it's all money, money, money! Even him! Even he has to have a wage!"

Henry said, "What are you doing there?" The caped man was at the emergency brake on the inside of the elevator shaft, pulling at it, "You! There!" He started to run, "What are you doing?" Henry, running to get to him before he pulled the brake and stopped Mr. Wilson and his important visitors to upstairs in mid-floor, shrieked, "Get away from there! Don't touch that!" He was fourteen years old. He felt tears coming to his eyes.

Henry, running, pleading, desperate, yelled, *"Don't touch the brake!"*

The man was reaching into the open shaft with his left hand. He was left-handed. Henry, changing direction, coming up on his right to get him, to push him away, to hold him for Mr. Wilson as proof, yelled, "You'll be gone for this!" Maybe he was one of the crazy people the plant employed on piecework: there were plenty of them—maybe he was. You could talk to them. You could talk to them and tell them that if they waited Mr. Wilson would have a nice present for them, or you could— Henry, running, his eyes filling with tears—everything in his life going in an instant— shrieked above the noise of the boilers, "Please! Please don't—"

He saw the man turn. He had no face in the darkness of the hessian sack.

He saw him reach into his pocket with his left hand. He saw, glancing back, the horse still turning. He saw him take something out of his pocket. He saw his hand. He saw—

Henry, rushing unstoppably toward the man, yelled, "Who are you—?" Maybe he was someone. Maybe he was Edison. "—sir? Sir . . ." He saw the man turn full on to him. He saw what was in his hand. He saw the long blade snap out from the end of the pepperbox knuckle-duster revolver and he saw it glint in the light. He saw the man hesitate, decide. He saw— He saw—

He felt the edge of the blade as it went up in the air and passed by his face in a hairsbreadth. He felt something hard grab him on the shoulder. He thought he turned, saw the horse still moving. He thought he did.

"*NO—!*" He shrieked. He felt nothing. He felt only lightness and nothing.

Touching nothing to save himself on the way down, he fell the full twenty feet onto the hard cement at the bottom of the elevator shaft and, shattering both knees, lay insensible like a doll, breathing shallowly, as the left-handed man, glancing down only briefly to him, leaned into the shaft and threw the brake with a click.

In its little circle the horse, its harness traces snagged by the brake, stopped.

The left-handed man's hands were shaking. At the bottom of the stairs to the upper floors, he put the little gun between them like a crucifix and pressed hard to calm himself.

He waited. He touched at the hessian sack over his back and head and, like some medieval serf, he waited at the bottom of the stairs.

He could hear nothing with the sound of the boilers and the engines and his eyes hurt with the coal dust and cinders, but in the noise and stink and sound he was hidden, cocooned, and he waited.

He looked up and to his left.

He heard him, sensed him. On the stairs, he saw the shadow coming, running.

He heard a desperate man coming, running fast downstairs to save his job.

"This is crazy! Why can't we go on up and—" Muldoon, following Tillman, following Wilson, following Reynolds down the stairs, said, "This is madness! We aren't going to steal anything! We're the goddamned law!" Muldoon said, "I'm going to stop and take a drink!"

Tillman said as an order, "Come on."

"I won't come on! I'm too old to clamber out of little boxes through two-foot spaces like some sort of goddamned crab!" Muldoon, stopping, digging his heels in, said, "Hey! You! Wilson! *Stop!*" He held up the thumbscrew and pointing it at the descending man, Muldoon said, "*Click! Stop!*"

He heard him. He heard him come. He thought, just for an instant, that maybe he could say something, that something was there to be said: a word, a name, something. He thought—

At the bottom of the stairs, the left-handed man let his clasped hands drop. He was a shadow, a phantom in the cape and hood. He brought up the little gun in his left hand and cocked the hammer.

He thought—maybe, like Schweib, in anger, that—

He heard him come, he saw him. He saw him close up, coming. He saw Reynolds. He saw the elevator man open his mouth like a dummy, a deaf man, like a moron. He saw his eyes. He saw them watery and blue and distant and then he saw, suddenly, in an instant, something there in them change and tighten and he saw the wateriness go and, suddenly, he seemed to straighten, to lose something soft about his face, and he saw—

Muldoon, aiming the thumbscrew like a wand, said, "Click! Click! Click!"

Muldoon said, "It doesn't work!" Muldoon said, "Nothing in the modern world works!" Muldoon said, "I *hate* the modern world!"

He saw his face. He saw Ethan Reynolds's face. He had the gun up, an inch from his forehead. He saw Reynolds's eyes grow wide and he saw—

They were coming down the stairs, one flight up from the basement.

He saw—

"*JESUS, HOLY CHRIST!*" He heard Reynolds's shriek. He saw the mouth open and the eyes wide with horror. He saw him see the gun.

The left-handed man's legs and hands were steady, strong, firm, and there was nothing, nothing at all to be said.

At the bottom of the stairs, already half turning to flee and avoid the exploding blood and bone, the left-handed man, jabbing the knife blade hard into the left, staring eye, pulled the trigger of the little gun five times in succession as fast as he could, and, saying nothing, with no emotion at all, killed the elevator man instantly, where he stood.

14

At the bottom of the stairs, Wilson screamed, "God Almighty, they got the wrong man—they were after *me!*" He touched his left eye with his hand, staring down at Reynolds's face, and then pulled it away again as if it were red hot. His hands were flexing, his fingers working, doing nothing, propelling him like little screws as he went toward the elevator shaft and tried to look in. "They were after *me!*"

He looked down. He saw the boy on the ground down there, moving and squirming, trying to call out to him to help. The noise of the boilers and the engines was overwhelming. He tried to call down something to the boy, but he could not make himself heard.

Wilson shrieked, "It's probably all a failure anyway!" He shrieked down to the bleeding boy, "The Illinois Electric Lamp Company—me! They were after *me!*" He sat down on the edge of the elevator shaft with his head in his hands, shaking his head and screaming something no one could hear, and wept.

He heard whistles. He was running hard down Water Street toward the Beekman and Fulton Street markets area near the docks and he heard first a single-tone Develine patrolman's whistle, and then a double-tone detective's whistle. The streets were deserted except for piles of garbage on the sidewalk spilling out onto the cobbled roadway—the fish markets had closed for the day, been hosed down, and all the garbage left out in the streets to rot—and the stink of fish and offal and washed-down flagstones was in his nose. He had the split hessian sack over his head like a mask and he ran with his face in a lather of sweat, gasping for breath with the stink of fish and hessian and fear in his nose, suffocating.

"Think! Think!" He forced a mental picture of the layout of the streets into his mind: blocks like cardboard boxes seen from above, buildings and empty lots and little roadways and alleys—he saw Water Street running wide and parallel to the river and the docks with Beekman Street and Fulton Street at either end of it forming the sides of the square, and then closer in, parallel to the river again, Fulton Street and the higgledy-piggledy alleys and lanes of the great flat-roofed covered fish markets—a street map: a street map where all the buildings were gray and monolithic, warehouses, windowless buildings with nowhere to hide.

The single-toned whistle screamed out from somewhere farther down—he forced the picture: in Front Street—going south, coming from Pearl Street from another direction, cutting him off. It was moving fast, blasting out for help.

He heard the double-toned whistle answer back.

The double-toned whistle, the detective, was behind him. Running, gasping, the left-handed man, slipping on something wet and slimy on the sidewalk and reaching out hard in the semidarkness of the crosshatched sack fabric to see, he felt his hand hit something hard and rough—the side of a decaying building with no windows—and scrape the skin off his knuckles.

Lost, he wanted to stop and get his bearings, find somewhere in his map of the mind to go—an alley or a lane or an open doorway—but there was none. He wanted to get the sack off his face and breathe. He wanted to get his gun out and stand and fight, but they had guns too. He heard them coming. He heard the two-toned whistle blast out twice, then stop, then blast three times more, then the single-tone answer back—a signal—and he had no idea where they were, but they were moving, and then he heard another whistle—a long blast of a pea whistle that seemed to come from everywhere.

The pea whistle was up above him, in the air. He heard the two-toned blast once, and then the single-tone twice and then the pea whistle again.

There was nowhere to go. In the street all there were were windowless, deserted buildings with mounds of garbage everywhere and stink and water and he was running through a deserted city with the whistles blasting out, suffocating.

There was another whistle. And then another. They were up in the air. He looked north and saw the wires and trapezes and glittering cables of the new Brooklyn Bridge. They were on the bridge, the whistles. There were people on the bridge with pea whistles, yelling, running, balancing on the wires and the supports, yelling: he saw them. There were people up there, workmen, with whistles. They could see everything. They didn't see his mental map of the blocks and the boxes, they were part of it, high up, like birds, balancing and shouting and urging the running policemen on, yelling instructions for them to turn, to go left, to go right, to go back the other way, blasting on their whistles.

He couldn't breathe.

The left-handed man couldn't breathe.

Gasping, running, his lungs on fire, sliding and slipping in the filth and water on the streets, reaching out to steady himself or save himself as he ran, the left-handed man heard, all around him, the screaming of the whistles.

It was the bastard who had slugged him at Niblo's. Actually, it had been Tillman who had slugged him at Niblo's, but if it hadn't been for that bastard he wouldn't have been slugged. It was the bastard who had slugged him. This was more like it. This was police work. This was running and chasing and blowing whistles and having your gun out and feeling the weight of the solid locust-wood club in your back pocket as you ran and this was what it was all about.

Tillman's two-tone whistle was off to the right on Fulton Street, moving west; and not stopping, going south to cut the fleeing fiend off, Muldoon, the whistle on a chain in his mouth, blew a blast that stopped even the chawbaccies on the bridge, let them know who was in authority, and turned south on Front Street with the barrel of his gun out hard and steady and ready.

"Virgil!" He heard Tillman's whistle again and he located him in his mind and located the running man—for an instant he thought he heard his footsteps—and, getting the whistle back in his mouth, ready, yelled at the top of his lungs, *"Policeman! Any policeman! Mark my whistle!"*

It was the closest they'd come. He was there, somewhere, running away, caught, trapped, and there were two of them and on the bridge all the workmen were yelling and whistling at the chase and it was the closest they had come or might ever come.

They had him. They had him boxed in between Beekman and Fulton and unless he got into the fish markets and down to the docks they were going to get him there. He was going to be out of breath and shaking; he was not going to be able to hold his little gun straight and even if he did, it was a gut-shooter's gun with no range and they were going to get him.

He thought he heard him. He thought he heard the sound of a crash as he collided with a cart or a wall or something on the sidewalk, and Tillman, forcing himself to stop, holding his breath, gasping, listening hard, tried to work out where he was. On the bridge all the workmen were whistling and shouting like Romans in the Coliseum, roaring, yelling and whistling.

He heard Muldoon yell at the top of his voice to them, "Shut up! Shut up! *SHUT UP!*"

The buildings were all deserted or empty or condemned and falling to pieces, all secured or locked or boarded or without windows. The whole area was condemned. Back from the Fulton Street market the city had plans for all the streets with the new influx of Edison's Science and all the buildings were gray and dark and all the doors and windows were boarded up with the dark wood gone rotten and peeling with age.

He was running under a covered colonnade down a deserted alley, the colonnade nothing but smashed and collapsing corrugated iron, all the doorways to the buildings on either side of it boarded shut, and there was nowhere to go and he could not see through the hessian mask or breathe and the pain in his lungs had turned into a torture that sucked at his brain and covered his face in sweat *and there was nowhere to go.* The buildings all around him were collapsing: there were broken bricks and masonry all along the sidewalk and out onto the road. It was a street, an alley, a lane no one used anymore. All the windows were bricked up or boarded, and there was no light. he was running in darkness and he could not breathe and they had him. He heard the whistles.

"Got him!" At the corner of Fulton Alley, looking down, seeing nothing, knowing there was only one more alley before Fulton Street and Muldoon, Tillman yelled, "Got him!" He could not hear Muldoon. "He has to be in the next alley!" There was no way through from Fulton Alley into the next: there was a building at the end that made it a cul-de-sac and went through into the next alley and cut that one off too.

They had him. He was in the next alley.

Tillman, starting to run, getting the Lightning out from under his coat, steeling himself, holding his whistle in his mouth with his free hand as he ran, yelled, "Ned! We've got him! He's in the next street!" It was the closest they'd come. They had him.

On the bridge all the workmen, yelling and catcalling and shouting, high up, two hundred feet away, were blowing their whistles.

Tillman shouted, "Ned! Ned! *Mark my whistle!*"

"*Oh, God! Oh, dear God!*" In Jasper Ward Alley, the left-handed man, on his knees, scrabbling like an animal at the earth, begged his Maker, "God! God! God!" He was below the street, down three stone stairs at a cellar entrance, working at the boarded-up door to get in, scraping and barking his hands as he worked at the stone and the wood and the nails and fastenings with the blade of his knife and his finger.

He was running sweat under the hessian sack, his eyes blurred and full of salt and the stink of hessian and fish and terror.

There was no way on: the alley was blocked by part of a building and, in the little entranceway to the ancient door and the darkness of the cellar behind it, the left-handed man, his mind shrieking at him to stay calm and work at it, dug and twisted and fought at the fastenings of the door with his knife.

Seconds. He had seconds.

He could not get his breath. He had seconds.

"God! God! *God!*" If they caught him, he was going to hang.

"God! God! GOD!" His face was running sweat like water.

With his hands shaking, digging, clawing, scrabbling, the whistles everywhere blasting, screeching, coming for him, the left-handed man, his fists and knife flailing, blinded and sweating, beseeching God, worked at the door.

He was in the right street.

He was in the wrong street.

He was in the last alley and there was no one there and he had gotten the wrong place, but it was the only place and if he was not there—

"NED!" Halfway down the alley, Tillman, looking around fast, yelled, "Ned, did he come past you?" He saw Muldoon, out of breath, appear at the intersection of Fulton Street, his gun out, and

Tillman, lost, confused, yelled, "Did he come past you?" —He couldn't have. He hadn't. Tillman yelled, *"Where is he?"*

"Where is he?" Muldoon, looking around, looking backwards in case, somehow, he had gotten by Tillman, demanded, "Where is he?"

There was nothing in the alley, not even garbage. It was deserted, dead, condemned, gone, something people had simply forgotten about. All the windows on all the old warehouse buildings were boarded up and all the bricks and plaster and mortar of them all gray and ancient and forgotten, silent, left, falling to pieces.

"Did you—?"

The road itself was all broken, all the Belgian blocks it had been made of fifty years before lifting and powdering and broken and unused, the flagstones of the sidewalk cracked and filthy and without a single trace on them. "Ned, did—"

"He didn't come my way!" Muldoon, his whistle in his fist, looking confused, said, "Where is he?"

It was the closest they had come. Tillman said, *"Where is he?"*

On the bridge, all the whistles had stopped.

"Where is he?" In the center of the broken road, looking up and down the still, empty, broken street, Tillman, his eyes scanning all the windows and doors along the sidewalk as far as he could see, said in a fury, "Where? Where? Where is he?"

It was the closest they had come. No one had seen his face. It was the closest—

In the street, Tillman, shrieking to Heaven, yelled, "God damn it, *where is he?*"

He heard him come. He was in darkness and dust and silence, dying by inches, and he heard Tillman come and he heard his boots on the stone steps from the street to the cellar, and he heard him come. He was up in the ceiling, between the stone ground floor of the old warehouse building and the asbestos-sheet ceiling of the cellar—he had gotten up from a mound of rubble and masonry at the far wall of the place and crawled in between the laths and beams where the ceiling had come down in a section—and he lay full length, holding his breath, not moving, holding his breath, dying by inches.

He saw him. He saw him as a shadow, as part of a shoulder at the doorway through a crack between two of the ceiling sheets. He saw him stop, pause. He heard him breathing hard. He felt the asbestos too fragile to hold his weight. He felt sweat dripping from his face. He felt his face against the hessian sack. He felt his legs and ankles and boots on the thin sheeting. He felt it sag. He had one hand flung out onto one of the wooden beams, his fingers curled around it; he felt tiny rotten sodden flecks of it start to come off like cardboard under his palm.

He held his breath. Stretched full-out up on the broken ceiling, lying on frail, thin asbestos, the stink of hessian and sweat and dirt in his nose, the left-handed man held his breath.

The door to the cellar was long gone, up in the far corner of the filthy dusty room, half protruding from a mound of rubble and masonry, its planks black from age and rot. There were no footprints on the floor of the place. He looked down and saw the stone floor hard and dry and there were no footprints.

He listened.

He heard nothing.

He had his pistol in his hand, cocked, and he uncocked it and, lowering it to his side, listened. Muldoon was at the far end of the lane, checking doors, and he could not hear him.

He could not hear anything.

He listened.

There was nowhere else for the running man to go.

He had not come here. In the doorway, Tillman, squatting down a little, looked at the doorjamb. There was still part of the door attached to it, broken in a long jagged break, black and rotten and old. He touched at it and splinters of it came off like sodden paper.

He looked down at the floor.

There were no footprints, and there were no other doors to the place, or windows.

There was nowhere else the running man could have gone.

He was breathing hard, sweating from the chase.

He listened.

In the doorway, squatting down, the pistol across his knees, Tillman, his eyes narrowed, exhaled hard and then, drawing in air, held his breath and, still like a statue, cocked his head to one side and listened.

* * *

His hands were shaking. Outstretched, his hands were shaking and wet with perspiration. He felt his eyes blur. He felt sweat starting in the sockets of his eyes and he felt— He felt his lungs convulse.

He felt himself running out of air. He heard his heart start to thump. He saw Tillman below him: he saw him as a shadow, as an immovable, unmoving black shadow and he felt his lungs convulse and then jerk and then— He felt his left hand move. By fractions of an inch, he willed it to move without sound. He felt the metal of the gun in it. He willed it to go up from the ceiling and, shaking, pause for a moment, then he willed it to come over in an arc toward his face and then, shaking, trembling, his lungs starting to burn, dying by inches, he willed it to brush his face and, carefully, like a claw, put the gun on the asbestos so softly it made no sound at all, and then, the shadow of Tillman below him turning into a blur, he willed the hand to come up and over and, turning into a pincer, cover his nose and mouth and then . . . then *press hard*.

He willed it. If he made a sound he would hang.

In the ceiling, outstretched, his lungs asphyxiating, the left-handed man, dying, aging, his face and eyes turning black, got his thumb and finger and palm over his nose and mouth and, starting to convulse full length, held his life and breath in like a vise.

Nothing. In Jasper Ward Alley there was nothing. At the far end of the alley where the derelict warehouse building turned the place into a dead end all the doors and windows were intact or boarded up and Muldoon could find nothing. Even the caissons of the bridge were no longer visible above the building, and all he could see were the topmost spans of the suspension and a flag flying high on it to warn that there were men working up there.

Nothing. There was nowhere to hide.

In the alley, there was no sound at all.

He listened.

In the street, there was no movement or sound at all.

Down the full length of his body, all the nerves and muscles were ticking, twitching, starting to shake: he felt them. He felt them starting to twitch and tic and go into spasms and start to dry up, to age, to go gray with death and seeping suffocation.

He was floating. The left-handed man, his hand clamped over his face like an iron glove, was starting to disconnect and float, drift away on a warm, salty sea and he was dying, slipping away, ceasing to exist, all the shadows through the crack in the asbestos turning into blackness and dust and the coldness of cemeteries, and he was aging, dying, going out of existence, passing away into nothingness.

Death. He was on the point of death.

His lungs had stopped hurting, stopped crying out, and they were rotting, turning into old meat and going black and heavy and useless.

In the entire world, there was not one pocket of fresh, clean, cool air left and he was in a dark, blackened, fetid forest, rotting like a leaf fallen from a tree, and he—

He was shaking, his body pulsing, trembling, being murdered.

If he let go his hand he would hang.

He continued dying.

In the ceiling, his hand clamped over his nose and mouth, with a will of iron, the left-handed man continued obstinately to die.

He listened. At the public swimming baths he had once won a bet to hold his breath underwater for a full two minutes.

He listened. Squatting down at the doorway, looking down at the dry stone floor and his Colt Lightning across his knees framing it, Tillman waited and listened.

His shoulders were moving, pumping.

In the ceiling he was counting, not numbers, but something. Something . . .

He counted. His shoulders were moving, pumping, and he was counting in the blackness, in the unspeakable feeling of starting to rock and lose control and moan and—

He counted.

He heard nothing.

He counted past sixty and then seventy and then seventy-five to eighty, eighty-one, until his lungs began to hurt, and then he reached ninety and held on.

He was squatting, listening, with the gun across his knees.

Counting, reaching one hundred, Tillman put his free hand on the barrel of the weapon and, holding it tight in both hands like a baton, held on and counted the moments of his breath.

He thought . . .

He thought at the end . . .

"Virgil?"

Another moment, just one more . . .

"Virgil—"

In the ceiling, he . . . he . . .

"Virgil!"

He . . .

"Here, Ned! In here!" Standing up, turning back to the street and light, Tillman, letting go of his revolver and holstering it with his right hand, said, sucking in fresh, wonderful, sweet air, nodding to Muldoon, "Here!" There was nothing. It was the closest they had come to him, but there was nothing. Tillman, holding his hand up to wave then moving the hand in a cutting motion to show that there was nothing in the cellar either, said, shaking his head, "Here. Here I am."

On the span of the new East River–Brooklyn Bridge the workmen must have seen them again. The air was full of whistling. There was a bang that sounded like a gunshot, but it was only one of them up there in high spirits or happiness shooting off a skyrocket they had stored for night illuminations after the grand opening of the bridge by the President on Thursday.

It was the closest they had come.

Ethan Reynolds, elevator operator at the Edison Illuminating Company's Station Number One at 257 Pearl Street, New York.

In the deserted alley, with the whistles and sounds of exploding skyrockets from the bridge filling the air, they walked back toward Pearl Street in silence to find out who and what he had really been.

15

. . . **F**or a long time, huddled like a bundle in the corner of the cellar, unable to move, the left-handed man sat with his head on his knees.

He had no wife, no children. What he did was for himself alone.

For a long time, he sat with his head on his drawn-up knees.

Breathing slowly at first, then deeper, deeply, he gathered back his strength . . .

In the churchyard garden of Saint Luke's Episcopal Church on Hudson Street the Reverend William Beecher, his long black cassock flapping a little in the breeze, said, shaking his head, "Ethan Reynolds was with the church for a long time before I took over a year ago. My predecessor, the late Reverend Isaac Tuttle, employed him as a handyman and gardener as an act of charity, and I inherited him." It was one of the oldest churches in New York, built early in the century from limestone with a tiny semicircular garden and cemetery large enough in those days to cater to the needs of the faithful. All the gravestones, cut from a softer sandstone, were crumbling and the interment ground had been long ago closed. Mr. Beecher, glancing down at the garden with its carefully planted borders of zinnias and roses, said, "My wife's great love is the garden, and upon my appointment Ethan gave up that part of his duties."

Tillman said, "According to the records, he had been employed at the Pearl Street Station for a little under a year."

Beecher said, "Previously, in return for his labors, he received full room and board. With my wife's taking over his horticultural tasks—and the rather sad state of the church's finances—it was felt that certain economies had to be made." He stopped and clasped his hands in front of his chest, tapping his thumbs together. He was a very tall, angular man with vulpine features. "Fortunately, it was my firm belief, and still is, that one of the most important aspects of the church in an often very violent city is the early training and love of God to be taught in Sunday School—a feature of the church my predecessor, for reasons best known to himself, neglected—and I was able to convince myself that Mr. Ethan Reynolds could continue to be given a room here in return for the painting and restoration of the Sunday School facilities for our children." Mr. Beecher said, "Without stipend." There was a wooden signboard set in the garden listing the times of services. Mr. Beecher said, "He painted that. He had an accomplished hand for calligraphy."

Muldoon said, "I thought he was illiterate."

Mr. Beecher said, "No."

Tillman asked, "Was he deaf?"

"Perhaps in one ear—but then, at times, we are all conveniently, let us say, deaf in one ear." Beecher said, "We owe it to him, of course, as one of our worshippers, to see him decently interred as a Christian." He shook his head. He was used to death. Beecher said, "Some sort of accident with the elevator?"

Tillman said, "Yes."

"Poor man." He looked around the graveyard. There was nowhere left. Beecher said, "It will have to be Potter's Field unless he had some money somewhere, and I fear he did not."

"Did he have a family?"

"Dead in the war." They reached the long stone building that housed the Sunday School classrooms and, behind it, Reynolds's room. Beecher said, "One does not intrude, but I believe he fought with the Rebels and as a consequence of supporting the unchristian values of that late aberrated state, lost everything and drifted North as so many did to find work." Beecher said, "He was quite good with the garden, I believe, and handy with tools so he may have been a good artisan in his youth." Beecher said, "He was an honest, forthright man who looked one directly in the eye when receiving directions, so perhaps he had a little occupation of some dignity when young or even his own small business." There was a thick oak door to the stone building; he put his hand out onto the latch and clicked it open. Mr. Beecher said, "I will say this for Southerners— they have manners. Not once has my wife had concern to complain about the way he spoke to her, nor has any lady parishioner ever been saluted by him with anything less than the most correct politeness. And he was respectful to the children without becoming familiar or descending to their level." He pushed open the door into a dim, musty corridor. "He kept to himself like a decent man and I have never had any cause to regret my generosity in allowing him to stay on."

"Did he ever have any visitors? Other men? Recently?"

Mr. Beecher said, "No. We would hardly allow that." Mr. Beecher said, "His room is at the end of the corridor, but I have no key."

"We do." He had taken it from Reynolds's body. There were closed doors on either side of the plastered dark corridor. Tillman asked, "Do you take in orphans here?"

"Hardly. There are institutions for that sort of thing." There was a series of paintings on the wall, above the wooden picture molding that ran the full length of the place, with little designs of angels and illustrations from the Bible. Beecher said, "That's his work up there." They passed by a half-open door to what looked like a classroom. Beecher said, "The Sunday School and, one hopes, soon to also be the Ladies' Auxiliary and Fund-raising Headquarters. He sniffed and looked in, and sniffed again. Beecher said, "Damp. The curse of ancient edifices. A constant, constant battle."

"How did his wife and children die in the war?"

"No idea." He closed the door, still shaking his head.

"He never mentioned it?"

"One did not ask."

"Do the names Albert Schweib or Rufus Carrol mean anything to you?"

"No." He touched at his chin. Beecher said, "Schweib would be a Lutheran name and Carrol—surely Roman Catholic?"

"What about George Fenney or Henry Carver or Cahill, or Shand?"

"Perhaps you had better ask the monsignor at the church of Rome about names like that!" He smiled. He had very large teeth. Beecher said, "No, not the sort of names on our rolls." He looked at Muldoon and knew what he was. Beecher said, "You assume I had a greater degree of familiarity than decorum would call for with one who, after all, was merely kept on as an act of Christian charity." Mr. Beecher said, "I know nothing about the poor man at all except that now the church, which can sorely afford it, must see to his funeral services and that, as God will no doubt judge him, he was an ordinary, decent, willing man who, through his own choice many years ago, had fallen on hard times and was—to be fair to him—happy to seek work when the charity of the church was discovered not to be without reasonable limits." Beecher said, "He was an ordinary, common man—there was nothing unusual or uncommon about him. The city is full of people who, having found a comfortable billet, are happy enough thereafter to remain at it. I cannot see your interest in it at all." Beecher said, "I fail to comprehend why the police are even interested in some industrial accident caused no doubt by—"

Tillman said, "He was shot."

"By whom? For what reason?"

Muldoon said with an evil, Catholic look, "That's what we're asking you."

"I?" He had his hand on the door handle of Ethan Reynolds's door at the end of the damp, stale corridor, his other hand out to Tillman for the key: "How would I—?" Beecher said, "My wife and I would—" Beecher said, "You said—" He saw Tillman looking up and over him, at the ceiling above the door. Mr. Beecher said, "Excuse me, I asked you—"

"Don't touch the door!"

Beecher said, "What? Excuse me! What?"

He saw him see it too. Tillman said tightly, "Ned?"

Muldoon said, "Holy Mother—"

"Excuse me!" Beecher, the key in the lock, said, going red, going angry, "Excuse me. *What did you say?*"

He had been a good, ordinary, common, decent enough, obliging little man who tended flowers and painted signs and angels. He had a room at the end of the corridor where the Sunday School was. He had a double-barreled 20-gauge Pratt Burglar and Trap gun mounted above the door to his room with a trip wire going down to the hinges. He had concealed it behind a square of cardboard. He had—

In the corridor, the moment the door was opened, the shot would have slaughtered everything living within a range of eight yards.

He looked up. He saw it.

Beecher, his eyes wide, his voice going high, said in a gasp, "Oh my God!" He still had his hand on the key in the lock. Beecher said, *"Oh my God!"*

Beecher, his voice shaking, giving an order, said, "Quick! *Do something!*"

In the corridor, Tillman asked, "Okay?" He looked up at Muldoon standing on one of the chairs from the Sunday School classroom, working at the device with his pocketknife. Tillman asked, "Have you got both the shells out and snipped the trip wire?"

He had the two cartridges in his left hand, holding open the twin breeches on the cast-iron gun with his right. Muldoon said, "Yeah." He made a clicking noise with something metallic at the device. Muldoon, drawing a breath, said, "Yes, it's okay now." He looked at the two short cardboard-cased cartridges and read the description of the loads the United Metallic Cartridge Company had printed on them in red. Muldoon said, "They're both double-oh buckshot loads." He turned the cartridges over in his hand and squeezed them, "Fresh."

"Anything else up there?"

"I can't see anything." There was no transom. It was a solid door hung on oak jambs set tightly into the masonry. He shook his head, trying to peer between the top of the door and the jamb: "I can't see anything else." He saw Beecher twenty feet down the corridor, trying not to look hunched against the wall. "What's in this room?"

"I've never been in there!"

Tillman said cautiously, "Nothing? Nothing else up there?" He got down on his hands and knees to one side of the chair and tried to peer under the door for more wires. He glanced up at the door and stood up, touching at the handle of the cast-iron key Beecher had left in the lock: "Did you feel any resistance when you put the key in the lock?"

Beecher said, *"How would I know?"*

"Virgil?" He got down from the chair and, putting the two cartridges in his pocket, looked at the door. "What do you think?"

He touched again at the key. Tillman said quietly, "I don't know." He put his thumb and forefinger around the handle of the opener and moved it slightly to see if it would rock.

There was a faint click. It could have merely been the metal on the tumblers. *"Is there gaslight in there?"*

"Yes!" Mr. Tuttle used to allow him to leave a low light on to cheer him when he came home alone and I—"

Tillman said, "Windows?"

"There is a window on the west side of the room, but it has been blacked for some time. My wife—" He saw Tillman's face. Beecher said, "I don't know what's in there! He had the only key to the place! I could never find out and, although I asked him a hundred times to give me his key for a regular inspection of his quarters, he never did!" He was starting to salivate with fear, wiping at his mouth with his hand. Beecher said, "The only window is blacked out with paper and is always locked!" Beecher said, "Take the key out and give it to me!"

Muldoon said, "With pleasure. We'll go for a walk in the garden and you let us know when you're inside."

"You popish insolent!" Beecher said, "I mean, when you've gotten inside!"

Muldoon said in a whisper, "Mealymouthed Protestant bastard . . ."

Beecher said, "*What did you say?!*"

Tillman said, "Ned, get out of the way." He had his thumb and forefinger on the key and, in one motion, he turned it with a click. Tillman said, "It's open." He pushed on the key a fraction and got a line of yellow light along the doorjamb: "There's a light on in there."

He pushed on the door a fraction, looking for wires, and saw nothing.

The door stayed open an inch and a half on the thick oak jamb.

He pushed and felt no resistance. He saw the light increasing as the doorway widened a degree of angle at a time.

He pushed. He felt nothing and saw no wires. The light in the doorway was coming, coming, and he saw, he was seeing . . .

Muldoon, beside him, tensed, said in a gasp, "God in Heaven, Virgil—God in bloody—"

He was coming fast back down the corridor, his cassock flying. Beecher, red with anger, said, "What? *What?*" and he saw, as Tillman and Muldoon pushed into the room—

—he saw, in the room at the end of the corridor, lit by the gaslight left on all day and night, the gilt and velvet and marble, the portraits, the pictures, the black and white checkered floor, the columns, the sconces and lights of the drawing room of a southern antebellum mansion from the turn of the century. He saw tapestries and mahogany furniture and bookcases and books and prints and gun cases and, through the window, he saw the rolling hills and trees and gentle streams of Virginia, and he saw—

He saw Tillman in the center of the room with his hand on the back of a gilt-encrusted, red-velvet upholstered Louis Quatorze sofa of wonderful beauty and construction. He saw—

Trompe l'oeil. There were no hills or trees or streams; it was a picture painted on cardboard on the window. He saw— He saw the wonderful, elegant, rich furniture and the— He saw Tillman bring the palm of his hand down on the back of the sofa and crush it.

Tillman said, "Paper."

The marble floor was painted wood.

Muldoon had his hand up to the wonderful crystal chandelier in the center of the room. He touched it and it made no sound. Muldoon said, "Wood. And paint."

The wallpaper was all painted on bare boards, the chairs and the glass-fronted gun case, the rack of shotguns and hunting rifles and the oak tantalus with crystal liquor decanters in it, everything, all of it— Tillman said, "Paper and paint and gilt and silver foil and—" He picked up a fine, silver ramshorn snuffbox on a side table and it crushed to nothingness in his hand. Tillman said, "All paint and paper and—" The silver paper of the snuffbox had been engraved with tiny lines etched in with a sharp instrument like a pen nib. In his hand, crushed, he could still read the name on it in Gothic— *Reynolds. Nr. Richmond. Va.*

In the room, faintly, there was the smell of flowers.

On the painting on the window, faintly, seen as three little rectangles beneath a tree, there was what looked like three gravestones.

It was all chimera, fragile, not real. It was the past.

At the open door, the Reverend Beecher said in a whisper, "My God. My God. My God, who—? Who? *Just who lived here?*"

He had. Reynolds. He had lived here before the war. It was his, him: what he had been, what he was. Only one of the pictures on the wall, the hunting scenes, the rural views, the portraits of ancestors, was real, and that was a framed tintype of a soldier in full uniform holding a sword, staring straight ahead unsmiling, with his hand on the back of a chair that had become, was now one of the paper chairs in the room.

It was him. It was Ethan Reynolds. He had been, not a private or a common man or a decent, obliging soul; he had been a full Major General in the Confederate Army with a gold-encrusted sword and silver scabbard.

It was his house. Off to one side of the wonderful room there was a screened alcove with the iron bed he slept on and the pine cupboard he kept his clothes in and on the bed there was a little stacked sheaf of papers, one a telegraphic wire:

Rec'd: The Sum of Five Hundred Dollars by Telegraph.
Being: Deposit for Property Known as "Kirkland," nr. Rich-

mond, Va. being two hundred acres of arable land and
remains of family mansion situate on it.
Dated This First Day of May, 1883.
MERRICK & SARE, LAND AGENTS, Richmond,
Virginia.

It was the house in one of the pictures on the wall. He had
bought it back.

In the alcove, Tillman turned the paper over.

COPY ONLY.
Full Price to be settled in sixty days Five Thousand Dollars
Exactly,
Inclusive of all Fees and Transfer. With thanks.

It was his house before the war. He had bought it back. He had
waited for it, probably, for almost twenty years. In his room at the
back of the Sunday School, over all the years he had been there
with the Reverend Tuttle and for the year he had been there while
he worked for the Pearl Street Station, piece by piece, bit by bit,
with paper and paint and wood, he had made it back and then,
suddenly, three weeks ago, he had bought it back.

He had been, from the photograph, a full Major General. He had
had a wife and two children who, maybe or maybe not, were
buried near a tree on his land. In the room where Muldoon and
Beecher were, everything was paper and tinsel and memories and
loneliness and then something had happened and he had bought the
land back. In the alcove, Tillman turned up the second paper:

ADVANCE TO: Mr. Ethan Reynolds, Esq. Five Hundred
Dollars on Expectation and Collateral of Items Lodged. Other-
wise, Advance to be repaid in Sixty Days at Principal plus Five
Hundred Dollars, plus twenty percent of Principal plus interest
on and including any days between said Sixty and thereafter to
Settlement of this Agreement.

It was dated two days before the receipt from the Land Agents
had been issued. It was handwritten, local. It was headed up *Cnr.*
Rivington and Clinton Streets, NY. with Reynolds's signature on the
bottom. It was a loan Shylock would have been proud of.

It was a dream. It was the dream of someone not in the

photograph at Vicksburg, who had been a full Major General, not in the Union, but in the Confederate Army.

He thought, in his make-believe room with all his make-believe furniture and pictures, his blacked-out windows and his trap gun on the doorway, that somehow, in sixty days, he would be going home. He thought, somewhere, there were five thousand dollars, six with the interest, that he had. He had been a Major General. He had been a maker of cutouts and memories and loneliness and loss and, somehow, suddenly, the dreams were real and he had been the maker of an expectation of five thousand dollars.

The dream had been brought true by something lodged, pledged with someone three weeks ago on Rivington and Clinton streets called—

In the alcove, Tillman said aloud, "Mandelbaum."

Muldoon, coming to him, said, "What?"

Tillman said, "*Mandelbaum.*" It was the signature at the bottom of the promissory note, the person who held the collateral. Tillman said tightly, "Goddamned *Mandelbaum!*" He saw Beecher looking at him. Tillman said with disgust, "Mrs. Fredericka Mandelbaum of Clinton Street—Marm Mandelbaum."

"A *Hebrew?*"

Tillman said with a sad smile to Muldoon, "Mandelbaum . . ."

"Who else?" In the room, everything they had touched had fallen to pieces, become paper and foil and tinsel and paint and chalk. Muldoon said, nodding, "Who else?"

"A Hebrew married woman? In here? In my church? In my Sunday School building? In here?" Beecher said in sudden, impotent rage, "A Jewess? In my church? *In here?*"

Tillman said to Muldoon, "He pledged an object or objects with her as collateral for the deposit on the house he once owned before the war." Tillman said, "Five thousand dollars' worth."

Beecher said, "What object? From the church? What object? There is no object in the church worth five thousand dollars!" Beecher said, "What object?" Beecher said with vehemence, "You lied! You said when you came that he died in an accident! Then you told me he was murdered! Now this!" Beecher said, "What object?" Beecher said desperately, looking around, clenching and unclenching his fists on his chest, wondering how to explain it all to his wife, wondering who he would have to pay to have the mad, evil, tainted room painted over, "A Jew! A Jew married woman! —what else did he do in here to get money out of her?"

He was a man of God. He understood what was in men's souls.

Beecher, his hands trembling on his chest, red in the face with rage, said in a fury, "Married female Jews! Jezebels! Temptresses! Salomes! Madness!" He turned and flung his hand back into the paper, painted room "—all this is caused, all men's madness is, by young, immoral, auburn-haired, flagrantly dressed *women!*"

16

PROFESSIONAL CRIMINAL INDEX No. 205

MANDELBAUM, MRS. FREDERICKA
"MARM MANDELBAUM"

Sixty-three years old in 1882. Jew. Born in Prussia. Height 5 feet 2 inches. Weight 340 pounds. Widow. Brown hair, brown eyes, sallow complexion.

A professional receiver of stolen goods, Marm Mandelbaum is considered the cleverest woman in her line in America, and has dealings both directly and through intermediaries in all the principal Eastern cities, especially in New York, Brooklyn, and Philadelphia, Pa.

A professional criminal of the worst type, much of the theft and larceny in New York especially can be traced to her influence and readiness to advance money for the commission of an offense that may require financing, and her eagerness to purchase valuables already stolen.

She makes her headquarters in a heavily reinforced two-story building on the corner of Clinton Street, NY, from which she never ventures, and can never be found surrounded by fewer than at least half a dozen of the female harpies and viragos of the criminal type who she pretends in a totally false and sentimental way to "mother."

Marm Mandelbaum is believed to retain lawyers in at least four cities and although she had been the major suspect in over seven hundred and eighty offenses in the past ten years, she has never once been arrested or charged with any of these offenses.

This is a genuinely wicked woman, clever and scheming. There is no photograph of her on file, and it should be stated that her lawyers, in particular the notorious duo of Howe and Hummel of Centre Street, near the Tombs, have destroyed the reputations and careers of a number of young detective officers over the years who have attempted to trap her by posing as thieves anxious to sell their "loot."

At her headquarters in Clinton Street, her "Bureau for the Prevention of Conviction," she has created a "fence" between her nefarious clientele and the unwelcome intrusions of the Police upon them. Mrs. Mandelbaum is a loathsome person and it is hoped that her health may fail her in the near future and rid all honest citizens finally of her influence and career.

CIRCULATE BY TELEGRAPH   T. BYRNES
                          Inspector, Chief of Detectives
                                    Headquarters,
                                 Mulberry Street,
                                          NYC.

He should have added: And suffers from flatulence. He should have added: of monumental proportions. In the window of the second floor of her brick and clapboard establishment on the corner of Rivington and Clinton streets, Marm Mandelbaum yelled at the top of her voice, *"Yarr!"* Framed in her window she was a monster, a whale wearing a black silk hat with an ostrich feather curled on it held by a black ribbon under her chin, a very large black ribbon. Hanging out over her window her bosom looked like two anteaters inside a flowered blue and yellow tent that was too small for two anteaters. The anteaters, however, were stuck there. There was no way in or out of the room except by the windows, a single staircase, and the doorway to the staircase, and neither she nor the anteaters would have fitted through any of them. She was massive, monstrous, room-sized, red-faced. She was an eater of sauerkraut and a drinker of brandy and beer. She had run out of all three. At the window, letting go a massive fart, Marm roared across the street to the beer waiters at the Kleine Deutschland beer hall in Clinton Street, *"YAAR!"*

There were six aproned waiters waiting in the street outside the beer hall. They stiffened. They were all peas from the same pod, white-haired, elderly, and wearing black trousers, white shirts and long white aprons down to their ankles. They carried no beer. In the street, all the traffic had stopped.

Marm Mandelbaum shrieked, "*Yaar!*" Her bevy of viragos were off about their business cheating someone, and the little haberdashery store that served as the front to the place was empty.

Marm roared, "Heinrich! HEINRICH DIETZER! Heinrich! Beer and sauerkraut and BRANDY!" She farted. The glass in the window above her horrible head shook. Marm, leaning out—moving her flablike fluid—shrieked, "ARE YOU DEAF?"

He was the one at the end, Heinrich. He had blue eyes, like the rest, but his was starting to fill with tears. He clapped his hands together and shrugged.

"ARE YOU MUTE?"

Ja. Ja. He was. He nodded. His eyes filled with tears. His eyes started weeping. His life was over. He shrugged. He thought about God.

"BRING ME BEER AND SAUERKRAUT AND BRANDY!!" She farted. the fart went Ker-BOOM! "BRING ME—" Marm Mandelbaum, going purple in the face, her little eyes glittering, roared, "YOU, YOUR WIFE, YOUR CHILDREN, YOUR UNCLES, YOUR COUSINS, YOUR SECOND COUSINS, YOUR SECOND COUSINS TWICE REMOVED—ARE ALL *DEAD!*"

He put his hand to his head. Behind him, inside the door of the beer cellar, Muldoon said cheerfully, "Don't look downcast. Face death with a smile on your face." He leaned forward a little and patted Heinrich affectionately on the back. Muldoon said, "A lot of Irishmen would cheer to have their family so easily disposed of." He had a stein of foaming German beer on a table beside him. Muldoon, taking a quaff, said, "Very good beer, this."

Heinrich said weakly, "Our poor establishment is gratified by your kind words." Heinrich said in a whisper to Rudolph next to him, "*Mein Gott, Rudolph, hier ist das Ende . . .*"

Rudolph said, "*Ja. Heine, bitte fur Alles—*"

Heinrich said, "*Und sie, Rudolph, fur—*"

There was a silence. It was a terrible silence. Heinrich said in a whisper over his shoulder to Muldoon, "She's got guns in there—!"

"Has she now?"

Rudolph said, "And knives and clubs and a huge metal safe

and—" He was shaking with fear, waiting for the firing squad. Rudolph said, "You won't get in there!"

"Maybe she'll come out."

There was another pea from the Prussian pod next to Rudolph. The other one said in a gasp, "She can't! She weighs four hundred pounds. She can't come out of there!" There was a lunatic Irishman standing behind them. The other one said to Rudolph and Heinrich, "*Oh mein Gott—!*"

Heinrich said over his shoulder to Muldoon, "You're *crazy!*" He was out in the open in front of the cellar like a tin soldier in the Franco-Prussian War waiting to be shot to pieces by a needle gun. It was the reason he had come to America, to escape being shot like a tin soldier with a needle gun. He felt Muldoon's steadying hand on his spine: "You're crazy in the head. That woman has jewels and diamonds and silk and a safe in that room! That woman has lawyers! That woman has three female Amazons with teeth that could bite off a man's—"

"HEINRICH!"

Heinrich said, "Oh, God . . ."

"RUDOLPH!"

Rudolph yelled back, "I'm only an employee!"

"OTTO."

Otto—the other one—said, "I never wanted to be your brother!" He was talking to either Rudolph or Heinrich.

It must have been Heinrich. If he had been Rudolph's brother he would also have only been an employee.

There were two more of them in the line of white-aproned sitting ducks. Marm shrieked, "YOU OTHER TWO!" They were nobodies. If they lived, they could move to Minnesota and maybe live. Marm roared, "YOU TWO DUMMIES AT THE END!" She quivered, she trembled. She shook. She broke wind and rattled the window panes over her. At her window, Marm Mandelbaum, going black in the face, thundered out like the voice of Doom, "FOR THIS, EVERYONE—EVERYONE—IS GOING TO DIE!"

God, she was horrible. Muldoon, sipping at his beer, peering with interest at her over Rudolph's shoulder, said softly, "Boys, never forget that the duty of a true man is to show a woman who's boss."

It was a good beer.

He sipped it.

Muldoon said with a trace of annoyance in his voice, "Now, lads, no shivering. Sure, it's a beautiful summer's day with no traffic in the street and some of you at least are being paid by the hour." Not exactly brave Fenian men, the Germans.

Muldoon said to stiffen their backbones a little, "Bear up now, lads, and think of Ireland—"

Standing against the window of the haberdashery shop, he had his badge on the breast pocket of his coat and his Colt Lightning in his hand down by his side.

On the corner of Rivington Street, Tillman looked up.

He looked across to the Kleine Deutschland beer cellar and then down the street a little to the Clinton Street lumber yard and the road block they had made for him out of rough-sawn twelve-by-two by ten-foot-long hardwood planks.

He had, laid out on the sidewalk in front of him, a cigar and a corkscrew and one of the shotgun shells Muldoon had taken from the trap gun above Reynolds's door in the church.

He listened.

Briefly, he looked up.

Holstering his pistol, starting to whistle a merry little tune, he squatted down on the sidewalk to attend to the objects there.

There was an explosion of wind of terrifying proportions. It sounded like "MUL-DOON!"

Muldoon, coming out from behind the line of quivering Krauts, said, holding up his stein to salute her, "Ah, to be sure, it is." Muldoon, catching a whiff of a breeze that must have come straight in through the open rear window of the place on Rivington, caught Marm's essence in all its wonderful odoriferousness, and then fled out the Clifton Street window past her toward the bar for a drink, said with a gasp, "God, woman, but your insides are in a bad way!"

"WHATEVER YOU WANT FROM ME, MULDOON, YOU WILL NOT GET!"

He had got it. His nose went numb. It turned the taste of beer to water. Muldoon said, "Okay. God bless you, Ma'am, for being a straightforward woman and saving me the trouble of trying." Muldoon said, "I'll be off then after I've had my fill of another two or five beers."

"MY GIRLS WILL EAT YOUR BALLS!"

Muldoon said, "Are they just away getting a little air at the moment?"

"MY GIRLS WILL CUT OUT YOUR TRIPES AND SELL THEM TO THE CIRCUS FOR TRAPEZES!"

"God protect you for your direct warning." Muldoon said, "Fine by me." He drank some beer. He saw the line of condemned men start to break and, in a voice of iron, said in a whisper, "*Stand still, you men!*"

"I AM IMPREGNABLE!"

Muldoon said, "God, you are!"

"I'VE EATEN MYSELF IN—ONLY AN EARTHQUAKE GETS ME OUT!" Marm, leaning out the window, reaching for the shutters, roared, "THESE SHUTTERS ARE HALF-INCH-THICK IRON! THE STAIRS ARE DEFENDED BY RIFLES! MY GOODS ARE PROTECTED BY A MARVIN AND COMPANY SPHERICAL SAFE PUT IN HERE BY THE MANUFACTURER WHEN THE ROOM WAS BUILT! NO COPPER GETS INTO THIS ROOM!"

Muldoon said, "I've heard that." Muldoon said, "This is good beer. Perhaps you might force a little drop of it upon yourself one of these days for the taste."

There was a blast of monumental proportions.

Muldoon, nodding, said sagely, "Yes, quite right. Too gassy."

Up there in the room it must have smelled like brimstone-burning day in Hell. On the sidewalk, whistling his little tune, Tillman, the corkscrew in his hand, began boring. He bored into a fine Havana cigar.

He brought it up to his nose and smelled its aroma.

He cracked it between his thumb and index finger next to his ear for the sound of the leaf.

He went on with his careful boring.

"WHO'S DOING THAT WHISTLING?"

Muldoon said, "One of the little people." He ordered Rudolph— or maybe it was Otto—"*Stand still!*" Muldoon said, holding up his finger for attention, "It's not often to be seen these days, but in the fine days of the old Celtic twilight when every Irishman was a king or the son of a king and no woman was given a tongue, the little people would hide their crocks of gold at the end of rainbows for the truehearted lad and his lass to stumble upon and—"

"YOU CORPSE OF AN IRISHMAN!"

Muldoon said, "And God, you're a horrible hag!"

"YOU DRUNKEN PADDY SCUM!"

Muldoon said, "By God, I'll offer no more beer to you this day!"

"WHO'S DOING THAT WHISTLING?" There was a blast of wind. At the window the breeze must have changed again and caught even her full on. She gagged. Marm Mandelbaum, all the flesh on her arms and face shaking like jelly, roared, "WHO'S DOING THAT WHISTLING? I CAN'T SEE WHO'S DOING THAT WHISTLING!"

Muldoon said, "No, I'll do no more sweet-talking with you . . ."

"THE ROAD'S BLOCKED OFF!"

Muldoon said, looking down Clinton Street, "It is."

"WHO'S DOING THAT WHISTLING?"

Muldoon said, "It is, and if you could look in both directions at once, or you could fly like Sweeney the Birdman, you'd know that Rivington Street is blocked off too." Muldoon said, smiling, "Now, Sweeney, he was an interesting man from County Sligo way." He felt Otto or Rudolph or Hienrich start to give way under the pressure of his hand. "Now you German lads would be interested in this: Sweeney, it seems, in the old days, was the friend of one of the great kings of Ireland—" He glanced up. Muldoon said, "You might want to write this down—it's an old story that maybe nobody ever wrote down, but it's a good one, and true—"

"YOU ARE GOING TO DIE, POLICEMAN!"

Muldoon said, "Now, this Sweeney, it seems, ran away from a great battle for his king and took refuge in a tree—onto which, over a thousand years or so—he grew . . ."

On the sidewalk Tillman put the waiter's silver corkscrew back into his pocket and took out his jackknife to cut open the shotshell.

He stopped whistling.

He hummed.

". . . and this Sweeney, after a thousand years, it seems, because he was caught in a tree and, as everybody knows, the only things that get caught in trees are birds, this Sweeney—well, would you credit it?—he grew wings . . ."

"HUMMING!" She was puffing, grunting, sounding like a whale, gushing air.

She ate sauerkraut and drank beer and brandy all the hours that God sent.

". . . now, would you credit that if you weren't an Irishman, which you're not?"

"HUMMING! SOMEONE'S HUMMING!"

"They are. I hear it too." Muldoon said, "Maybe it's one of these lads here." He asked Rudolph, "Is it you, Otto?" Muldoon said. "It isn't."

"—WHERE IS YOUR FRIEND TILLMAN?"

Muldoon said, "My friend . . . ? What was the last name again?" Muldoon said, "My friend—who?"

He got it.

He got the cigar finished and held it in his hands and looked down at it, and then put it carefully into his inside coat pocket and stood up.

Muldoon said, "Tillman." He thought about it. "Now, would that be Seamus O'Kelly Tillman from County Carlow? Or Sean called Paddy Tillman from Meath? Or maybe, could it be, perhaps, the Tillman of the clan Tillman who's a black Protestant from County Tyrone and married the daughter of old—"

"TILLMAN!!"

On Clinton Street, waking toward Heinrich to return his corkscrew to him, Tillman, turning and looking up, said, "Afternoon to you, Mrs. Mandelbaum."

"YOU'LL NEVER GET IN HERE, TILLMAN!" He was a tiny, dark-suited man wearing a derby hat; a fly, a sparrow, a nothing. She farted a terrible ominous fart. "YOU'LL NEVER—" She saw him go to, not Heinrich, not Rudolph, not Otto, but to one of the nameless ones at the end of the line and hand him a folded piece of paper. She saw the nameless one, freed, given a reprieve, nod enthusiastically. "—WHAT ARE YOU GIVING HIM?"

She saw the waiter, suddenly, like a jackrabbit, start to run. "WHERE'S HE GOING?"

She saw him run toward the roadblock and, quivering with the joy of life and purpose, hurdle it in a bound with his white apron flying and head toward the south. She saw— She saw Tillman look up at her. She farted. She exploded. She detonated. She—

At the window, as Tillman began walking back toward her across the street, Marm Mandelbaum, an exploding myriad of methane and sauerkraut, brandy and beer, shrieked, "WHAT ARE YOU DOING DOWN THERE?"

She saw Muldoon, releasing the waiters like a school of frantic mackerel, look up, smile and wave.

She saw Tillman, looking determined, reach into his coat where his gun was. She saw him coming, coming. She had both her hands on the steel shutters, starting to pull them shut. Yelling for her viragos, Marm Mandelbaum shrieked in a voice punctuated by pops, "HELP! MURDER! MURDER! MURDER!"

He was happy. He smiled. He whistled. He hummed. Crossing the street, taking the cigar from his coat and lighting it with a lucifer, Tillman, smiling, waving, looked up.

Tillman said to the closing shutters, smiling, ". . ."

She had her hands on the iron shutters. The iron shutters were creaking, closing, coming shut. She saw him say something, saw him smile. She couldn't hear what he said, but what he said was—

Tillman looking down at the burning cigar, said in a soft voice, ". . . . ." She saw his mouth move.

Muldoon walking across, asked pleasantly, "What? What was that, old son? I didn't quite catch it."

It fizzed, the cigar. She farted. She exploded. She filled up the room with methane and brimstone and gas.

Muldoon said, "Very bad for a lad your age, smoking. *Throw that foul weed away this moment or I'll call a policeman!*"

Tillman said, "Fire."

Muldoon said, "What was that?"

She farted. She exploded. She had the shutters shutting of their own momentum when, in the last two inches of daylight, the fizzing cigar came in in a gentle parabola and landed by her feet, rolled, and stopped a little behind her nether regions.

Tillman said conversationally to the pleasant Celtic gentleman by him in the middle of the street, "Fire."

There was a blast of fart of world-splitting proportions.

There was a little flash and a crack as the gunpowder inside the burning cigar caught fire and flashed in the sealed-up room.

Tillman said, "Fire."

There was a fart and then a boom and then a burst, a fulmination, a thunderclap that blew open both the shutter doors, shook the building and broke the glass in the windows and sent shards showering out onto the sidewalk in the midst of shrieks and screams and curses and falling, flying bits of ostrich feather and flowered print dress.

Tillman said, "Fire."

There was a fire hydrant a little outside and to the south of the Kleine Deutschland Bier Keller in Clinton Street and, awaiting the help he had sent the nameless waiter off to summon, Tillman, always a man who spoke too softly, yelled at the top of his lungs to the hydrant, to the street, to Heaven, "—*FIRE!!*"

17

The summon'd firemen woke at call,
And hied them to their stations all:
Starting from short and broken snooze,
Each sought his pond'rous hobnailed shoes;
But first his worsted hosen plied,
Plush breeches next, in crimson dyed,
Then jacket thick, of red or blue,
Whose massy shoulder gave to view
The badge of each respective crew.
The engine thunder'd through the street,
Fire-hook, pipe, bucket, all complete,
And torches glared, bells, and clattering feet,
The Firemen! The Firemen! Headlong to the hellish heat.

On the prow of the Shanghai Man-Killer, Humpty Jackson, his brass trumpet to his mouth, roared to the Heavens, *"GOD BLESS YOU, CITY DETECTIVE TILLMAN!"*

He glittered. He gleamed. On the wonderful wood and brass and silver engine, bright-eyed, black-booted, behatted, bebadged and besotted, Humpty yelled, "PUMP!" The Shanghai Man-Killer was a wonder of an engine. Twenty-five feet long, on iron-rimmed wagon wheels, it was a symphony of gold paint and gargoyles, carved curicles and chimeras, painted panels of classical battle, rape and cherubs. Its hose reels were cast and carved sea dolphins, its shining brass pumping chamber a dazzle to the eyes, its wires and lines and ropes and warps, all its boxes and axles, its traces, its pumping handles encrusted with ornament and affectation, the brakes against its wheel rims anchoring it to the center of the street cast gilded naked Atlases straining at their charge.

"Heave-ho, my mighty men!" They were at the pumping handles, twin side-mounted ricks of gleaming copper and blued steel, six of them, six of the mightiest pumpers born of women, or maybe not: Baboon Baker, Billy Bones McNee, Red Rocks Farrell on one side of the great beast, all their muscles and sinews popping in their uniforms, their feet taken root in the ground—and on the other side, facing them, lips drawn back in ghastly gritted grins of grunting gargantuanness, Slungshot Sam, Crazy Connelly, Razor Riley.

Humpty yelled, *"Pressure!"* He was on the driver's seat of the great engine, hopping, jumping back and forth, his chief's helmet throwing off blinding reflections from the sun. The Grabber and The Throttler—two good and true lads whose hold on things was proven—were at the nozzle of the hose, running it out to the smoke and female shrieks at the smoldering building. Humpty yelled to The Lobster Kid, ready at the fire hydrant, "Stand by for WATER!"

The Lobster Kid was ready. He was at the hydrant. It was his hydrant. No one was going to take it away from him. He had his two Artillery Model Colts out in his hands, the six-pound valve opening lever in his mouth like a dagger. Humpty yelled, "Stand by, Lobster!" Humpty yelled, "Pressure! Pump! Stand by your hose!" Humpty yelled, "A fireman! A fireman!" Humpty squealed in joy, "Oh God, oh God, oh God!"

The three viragos had come back. They were running down the street shrieking, going for the front door of the haberdashery shop. Spanish Louie was also going for the front door of the haberdashery shop. The front door was not locked. The viragos had keys. Spanish Louie had an axe. Upstairs, in the shattered fort, Marm Mandelbaum had a room full of smoke. It was seeping out the shutters and coming through breaks and cracks in the slate roof. It was an acrid smoke, the smoke of burning silk and carpet and drapes and large amounts of human blubber. Humpty, glancing at his gauges, yelled, "PRESSURE!" He saw Spanish Louie hesitate at the unlocked door to the shop. Humpty yelled, "Be not afeared, my noble man—axe the door down with a single blow!" He was hopping, giggling on the engine. He could not believe it was happening. In dreams, all in dreams. Humpty yelled, *"Water!"* and the hose, hit by the power from the hydrant as The Lobster Kid turned the lever, jumped like an alligator all the way across the street, leapt as its flow hit the waiting, primed vacuum chamber of the pump, roared as it filled the chamber, and then hissed as it reached explosive point. Humpty, at the same point, shrieked, "Smash the door! Brain the viragos! Pump, my lads! Aim your hose! Open your hose"—he had his little hand on the valve that controlled all—"and . . . FIGHT YOUR FIRE!"

The door came down in a single detonation of tearing, smashing wood. Two of the viragos came down in a blast of hose water. The third came down in a backhand from the axe handle. German waiters scattered. The water hit the side of the building and cascaded off it in shards of glittering spray. "PUMP! PUMP FOR YOUR LIVES, LADS!" He had something lethal that looked like a hand cannon in his hand. He meant it. Running, hopping, encouraging the full length of the engine, Humpty, urging them all on, shrieked, *"PUMP! PUMP TILL YOU DROP! AND GOD HELP THE FIRST MAN WHO DROPS!"*

It was very educational watching professionals in action. Interested, sitting at a sidewalk table by the beer cellar, Tillman and Muldoon, sipping their beers, watched.

She was shrieking. Inside the shattered second floor Marm Mandelbaum shrieked through the smoke and sound of her premises being watered to splinters, "I'M ON FIRE! MY GOODS ARE ON FIRE! MY CLOTHES ARE ON FIRE!"

He was in. He had axed the door down and made it to the wooden stairs, axed them because he liked axing things and, taking the steps two at a time, Spanish Louie was in, his boots crashing on floorboards, kicking down doors.

Humpty roared through the trumpet, "The shutters! Get the shutters, Louie!" He saw the whole wooden side of the house seem to vibrate as something inside was reduced by axe or boot to matchwood and he ordered The Throttler and The Grabber, "Play your hose on the jambs to cool them down!" There was a bang and then a shriek and then another bang, what sounded like a brief, one-sided struggle, and then the shutter facing Clinton Street blew open with an axe blow and he had somewhere to pour his water.

Humpty shrieked, "Drown that room! Put out that fire! Extinguish those sparks!" He was in ecstasy, jumping up and down like a jack-in-the-box. Humpty, his eyes rolled back, believing he was in Heaven, cried the cry of the volunteer fireman, "SAVE THAT BUILDING FROM A FIERY FATE!" Humpty, glancing down to the straining, grunting, gasping pumpers on the engine, yelled, "Think not of yourselves, lads—there's a rescue to be done this day!" Humpty said, "Ha, ha, ha—hee, hee, hee . . ." Humpty said, "Oh . . ."

Louie yelled from the window, "YOU'RE DROWNING ME, YOU LITTLE DWARF!"

Humpty ordered Louie, "SHUT UP, YOU OILY GREASE LICK!"

"YOU'RE DROWNING ME!" The water, coming in like Niagara, hit him full in the chest at the open window and propelled him back into the room.

"PUMP!" Humpty ordered The Lobster Kid at the hydrant with his two guns out ready to protect the Alamo, "More pressure!"

Louie yelled, "The fire's OUT!"

"THEN LIGHT IT AGAIN!" He had the hand cannon up. He was going to shoot somebody. Humpty, looking around for anybody close, shrieked—

Tillman yelled, "Firemen! SAVE THAT POOR WOMAN!" He was on his feet, pleading with the noble crew, being careful not to spill his beer, "SHE'S SOMEBODY'S MOTHER, BOYS, YOU KNOW; FOR ALL THAT SHE'S OLD AND GRAY!"

"SAVE THAT WOMAN!" A rescue. Humpty yelled, "A RESCUE!" Humpty yelled, "Louie, get that woman on your back, lad, and we'll bring up the ladder!" He ordered the sinking, gasping, suffocating pumpers, "Rest, lads, for a moment!"

Louie shrieked, "SHE WEIGHS FOUR HUNDRED POUNDS!" Bits of the floor seemed to be falling away under him. She was in the center of the room, smoldering, not a pretty sight. Louie yelled, "SHE WON'T FIT THROUGH THE WINDOW!"

"Yaaa—raggh!" It was one of the hawk-faced, black-skirted, black-eyed horrible viragos. She had a knife. She had a notion to slice everybody's gizzard. She had Baboon Baker to get past to get to Humpty to do him first. She didn't make it. She went back to sleep again on the pavement.

Humpty said, "*What?*" Humpty ordered Louie, "Through the window!" Humpty ordered, "Ladders! Ropes! Blocks and tackle! Human muscle!" He saw something that looked like the rear end of a whale in a flowered dress being forced through the window. Like the camel through the eye of a needle, it wasn't going to go. Humpty ordered, "BAKER! FARRELL! McNEE! SAM! CONNELLY! RILEY!" They were all out flat on the ground gasping for air. Humpty ordered, "LOUIE!" The essence of the volunteer fireman was his preparedness for any situation. Humpty said conversationally to Tillman, to Muldoon, to the waiters, to the horrified hordes back behind the roadblocks in the streets, "If we cannot get the poor woman from the window because of her hourglass figure—because as gentlemen we may not manhandle a respectable female—then we must make the window larger." Humpty, his eyes glittering, said, "LOBSTER!" He looked hard at The Lobster Kid at the hydrant. They had everything they needed. He looked up at the thin clapboard on the western side of the building by the window.

Humpty said, "Lobster—*GATLING GUN!*"

If Custer had had one mounted on his fire engine at Little Big Horn seven years ago, Sitting Bull would have been prime cut. Firing .45/70 with hulls the size of cigar tubes and 500-grain bullets with explosive heads as fast as a man could turn the crank—and Humpty could turn it very fast—the ten-barreled Gatling, wreathed in smoke and flame, with a noise that would have woken the dead, began on the wooden clapboard wall to make the window egress for the poor, worried woman a little larger.

It made the window egress for the poor, worried woman a little larger. Spitting fired cases out behind Humpty in a cascade, it first blew the window out in a roar that sent bits and pieces of wood, glass, metal shutters, nails, dust, ash, matchwood, screws, rivets, battens and dovetail joints flying heavenwards and then, working in an arc, exploded all the clapboard planks from the floor to the ceiling and filled the room with lead and smoke and sparks and flying shrapnel.

It rang off the spherical safe. It set bolts of silk alight. It blew out water pipes and tore four-inch-thick beams apart like paper. It chopped whole squares of the wall out. It hit the room like cannon shot. It hewed the floorboards away and sent them spinning. It missed Louie lying flat on his face by an inch and it missed Marm Mandelbaum, flailing about on the surface of an angry sea by nothing and set her clothes on fire. It drowned out her shrieks. It reached up to the ceiling and brought it all down in a snowstorm of plaster and laths. It let in the sky. It hit the roof supports and launched them. It fired through the building as it went upward in pieces and it fired through the building as it came downward in pieces, in even smaller pieces, and then it shot the Hell out of the smaller pieces and sent them up again like confetti and then, as they came down . . .

It beat on the building.

It hammered it, axed it, hacked it, chopped it, turned it to air, carved it, minced it, whittled it, shaved it, beat it by inches to nothingness; it filled it full of holes, and, when all the holes joined up, turned it to powder. It was a lovely class of a gun. Like its user, it exuded power, reliability and a lot of bullets very fast.

Louie, coming up for air for an instant, screamed, *"STOP!"* There was enough extra room at the window. There was no window. There was no wall. There was a mad dwarf, who one of these days was going to meet with a sudden accident, on the engine in the pall of smoke, shrieking and yelling in ecstasy and firepower and—

Louie yelled, "STOP!"

Marm Mandelbaum yelled, "Oh, YI! YA! YI! YAA-RAGGH— *Oh, my Mother!"* She saw through the haze of smoke and debris, for an instant, her spherical, burglarproof, warranted safe. Marm Mandelbaum shrieked, "Oh, my *SAFE!"*

There was a click. It was the click of a firing pin striking an empty chamber. He had run out of ammunition. Humpty said, "Damn!"

Louie screamed, "IF YOU FIRE ONE MORE ROUND I'LL COME DOWN THERE AND KILL YOU!"

Click.

Humpty said sadly on the engine, "Oh."

"LADDER, HUMPTY!" It was Tillman. He had two or three of the thick planks from the roadblock in his arms, staggering under their weight. Tillman yelled, "LADDER!"

Right. *Click.* Humpty said in a whisper, "Damn." He was in charge. He had his plans set and the city could rest safe in its bed with a man such as he in charge. He hesitated not a moment—well, just a fraction to check if maybe there was one more round in the magazine (there wasn't)— Humpty ordered everyone, "Get a ladder up to the second floor!"

He looked hard for a moment to work out where exactly the second floor was. Humpty ordered Slungshot Sam, The Lobster Kid, The Grabber, The Throttler, Baboon Baker, Red Rocks Farrell, Crazy Connelly, Billy Bones McNee and Razor Riley, all good strong lads and true, "Mr. Tillman's got some planks to slide her down! Are we going to be shown up in our duty by a mere policeman? LADDER!" Humpty, in charge, yelled, "Quick lads, *get a ladder to bring the poor woman down on, now!"*

Marm Mandelbaum shrieked at the top of her lungs, "Me BOTTOM!" The anatomical object in question was perched on the top of the ladder on a plank, the other sections of the human frame attached to it by mounds of blubber and assorted limbs, halfway out and halfway in what was left of her room. There was nothing left of her room. She hung on. There was nothing to hang on to but air. She had a firm grip. There were six men anchoring the ladder on the ground at the angle of forty degrees it made against the splintering, cracking clapboards of the second floor. It wasn't enough of an anchor. The ladder was creaking, breaking, starting to bow in the middle, the thick, wide planks lying along its length sliding, giving way, starting to twist.

On his engine, Humpty yelled, "Push!"

On the second floor Spanish Louie, Baboon Baker and The Lobster Kid pushed.

Humpty yelled, *"Let go whatever's holding you!"*

Air was holding her. She wasn't going to let go. Marm Mandelbaum, a whale beached on a very small beach, shrieked, "I'm going to fall!" She slid one inch along the plank. Marm Mandelbaum howled, "That bastard copper lined the ladder with undressed wood! My bottom is full of splinters!" She felt a shove from behind as The Lobster Kid, hanging on to Baboon Baker, got his booted foot in her back and heaved: "MY ASS WILL BE A SIEVE BEFORE I GET TO THE GROUND!"

Spanish Louie said in a voice that sent chills down the backs of prizefighters, "Move woman, or I'll have your liver for my breakfast—"

"MY BOTTOM IS STUCK!"

Baboon Baker said, *"Toss her off!"*

The Lobster Kid said, *"Put your foot in her back!"*

Humpty yelled, "Are you letting me down here, lads?"

Louie said in protest, "I can't toss her off. She's hanging on to something!" Spanish Louie demanded, "Where's Riley? Get Riley up here with his razor to cut her hands off!"

Marm Mandelbaum shrieked, "NO!" She let go a fraction, slid an inch and roared, *"Oh my God!"*

Humpty said, "I'll get more ammo."

Marm Mandelbaum yelled, "NO!" Marm Mandelbaum yelled, "No! No! No! No!"

On her perch, swaying, perforated, yelling, shrieking, calling on God and the unconscious harpies in the street, Marm Mandelbaum, being rescued, shrieked at the top of her lungs, *"NO—!!"*

* * *

They were in the room at the sprung-open safe. It was there, in a little cardboard envelope folder with the name REYNOLDS on it, the collateral for the five hundred dollars complete with a copy of the loan note and the receipt from the land agent in Richmond.

It was two things, one something heavy and round in a velvet pouch—a watch—and the other thing—

The watch pouch had attached to it a paper label reading, "*Watch. Value $500. E. Reynolds Loan*," and a date, and Marm's signature.

—and the other thing was a small rectangular packet wrapped in brown paper and string and sealed with wax. Whatever that was, it had not been opened. On the wax, graved in it, were the initials E. R.

Muldoon said, "What is it?" He saw Tillman hold the packet up to his ear and shake it.

"I don't know." Whatever it was, it was Reynolds's. Whatever it was, it was the answer or one of the answers. Tillman, glancing at Spanish Louie to check he did not see, putting the packet quickly in his inside coat pocket, said shaking his head, "I don't know."

"YAH! YAH! YAARRGGHH!"

She was going, sliding down the undressed planks.

Marm Mandelbaum, quivering, blubbering, going down like gelatin, her nether regions being perforated, how unkind the Fates were to a poor, honest working girl, screamed as the crowd roared in admiration, "YAAA . . . *RAGGHHH!*"

It was a pocket watch of gold and platinum with all the numerals on its face picked out in diamonds, and all its exquisite workings—each cog and wheel and spring—engraved and skeletonized; the face a single chiseled plate of flawless crystal, the name of the maker, *Fournier-Paris*, laid in on the crystal in jet so small and perfect as to be the faintest tinge of color in the shimmering light of the white quartz; the hands wonders of carved iridescent lapis lazuli; the tiny winding key in its little carved place on top of the watch an apostle carved from solid amethyst and set with little rubies and ornaments of gold and silver; the chain holding it to the watch, tiny diamonds linked together by gold.

It was Reynolds's watch. On his knees by the open safe,

Muldoon touched at a tiny diamond on the side and the watch chimed. It was Reynolds's watch. He touched at another diamond and the back clicked open.

> *Major-Gen. E. J. H. Reynolds CSA*
> *Chief Special Operative*
> *War Department*
> *In Appreciation—*

The inscription was signed in engraving. It was signed in engraving,

> *Jefferson Davis, Richmond*
> *1862*

It was signed by the President of the Confederate States of America.

"YAAHHH!!!"

In the ruined room, squatting down in front of the safe, Muldoon, looking at the watch, said in a terrible whisper, "God Almighty, Virgil, this man Reynolds—" Muldoon said in horror, "God Almighty, this watch is from goddamned Jefferson *Davis*—!"

He saw Tillman's face. He saw him put his hand protectively to the sealed packet inside his coat.

Muldoon said in a whisper, "God Almighty, this man Reynolds—the elevator driver at Pearl Street, the builder of goddamned paper rooms—God Almighty, Virgil, during the Civil War, this man Reynolds was the chief, the head—during the Civil War this man Reynolds was the head of the entire Confederate Secret Service!" Muldoon said, gasping at the thought, "God Almighty, for five years—for five years, this man was the number-one spy in America!"

He looked hard at Tillman's face, but could read no expression there at all.

"YAAHHH . . . !" She was going, going.

* * *

Tillman said urgently, "Come on. Now." He had the unopened wax-sealed packet safe in his pocket. He glanced around quickly, but everyone at the shot-to-pieces wall was steadying the end of the ladder and looking down.

Tillman, standing up, taking Muldoon with him, said as an order, "Now. Quick. Time to get the hell out of here. Now!"

"*HUZZAH!*"

It was the German waiters.

"VICTORY!" It was Humpty.

"A RESCUE!" (Humpty again.)

In the street the crowd behind what was left of the roadblocks shouted, "Hooray for our brave firemen!"

Humpty yelled, "Ever ready! Always true! True unto death!" The building, as Spanish Louie and Baboon Baker and The Lobster Kid ran for their lives, was falling down around him like matchwood. Marm Mandelbaum, sliding like a sea elephant down the splinter-filled planks on the ladder, shrieking, yelled, "YAH! YAH! YAH! *YAH!*"

He was tall. He was the Chief. He was a man.

On the wonderful engine, his face blackened by smoke and gunpowder, Humpty Jackson yelled at the running man, "GOD BLESS YOU AND PROTECT YOU, CITY DETECTIVE TILLMAN, FOR YOU'VE ALWAYS A FRIEND IN EUSTACE CLARENCE JACKSON!"

He grinned.

He laughed.

He hopped.

He wept for joy.

"YAH!" It was a strange sound, not human, like a mad female gorilla in the jungle in heat with her bottom full of splinters, looking for someone to kill.

"YAH! *YAAHH!*"

All the way down.

All the way down.

"YAARRGHH! YAARRGHH! *YAARRGHH!*" She made the noise all the way down.

All the way—a splinter at a time—

Down.

18

In the underground barrel room in the Kleine Deutschland Bier Keller, Tillman, working by candlelight on the flat top of a keg, said, "Got it." He had the blade of his clasp knife under the first of the wax seals, slicing through the knot, keeping Reynolds's initials intact on the linked-up red blobs all along the string of the little brown-paper packet. "Got it." He took the string off in a single length and flicked at the edge of the thick oiled brown paper with the knife and got it open and back in a double-folded rectangle: "It's a little wooden cigar box." He got the knife under the retaining pin of the box and twisted and the lid of the box came free.

Inside the box there was a wadding of cotton wool with the object inside resting on it.

He looked at it.

At the doorway to the stairs leading up, Muldoon, keeping watch, said urgently, "What is it? What's inside?" Dead men, Vicksburg, killer doors, paper rooms, gold watches, spies, Rebel revolvers, houses in Richmond— Muldoon said urgently, "*What is it?*"

He looked at it. Standing over the barrel head, by the light of the candle, Tillman looked at it.

Gently, with the tips of his fingers, he touched it to make sure that what he saw was what was really there.

He looked at it. It was the secret, the mystery, the answer to the deaths of Schweib and the man-woman in Bleecker Street, to Reynolds, to— He touched it gently with his fingertips and brought it out in his hand into the light.

171

* * *

It was a glass bottle stopper. It was a glass bottle stopper with a diamond cut of no more than three-quarters of an inch in diameter with a hook set into it and, swirling inside its facets, paint and specks of color making a pattern. It was not a diamond; it was a glass bottle stopper—a pretty one—a pretty one made pretty so that after a man had drunk the contents of the bottle or rubbed it on his aching limbs, or made a restorative elixir from its essence *or whatever the Hell a man did with whatever trash the bottle contained* he might take the pretty, pretty stopper and, with the hook set into it, hook it onto his watch chain as an ornament.

It was an ornament. It was a bauble. It was a geegaw, a bijou. It was trash.

It was—

It was all there was in the box.

Object to be appraised.

It was rubbish, trash, garbage. It was—

It was—

Tillman said in a gasp, "For this? Everything that we did—it was for *this?*" He had the stopper in his hand. He was trembling, fighting the urge to dash it on the ground. It was nothing, a joke. It was—

Tillman said in a fury, "Ned, everything, everything we did— WAS IT ALL—WAS IT ALL JUST FOR *THIS?*"

Tillman said, "God in Heaven! God in Heaven, Ned"—he could not believe at last, it was what they had come to. They had come to nothing. Tillman said, "God in Heaven, Ned—nothing! *Nothing!*" Upstairs, he could hear Inspector Byrnes and the regular Fire Brigade shouting and stamping through the rooms looking for them. Tillman said, "Nothing! *Nothing!* Everything we did—*it was all for nothing!*"

Tillman said suddenly sadly, like a child disappointed at his Christmas box, shaking his head, "Ned—God, Ned, this isn't what I hoped for at all—"

19

Way uptown on Lexington, where the rich people were building their mansions, above the soft glow of the gaslights in the streets, there was in the night sky a ruby glass sign—letters in Heaven twelve feet high—that welcomed, warmed, beckoned, revived, that sighed with soft, soothing promise.

BATHS

The ruby sign was above a glass-topped cupola on the sunbath roof of Doctor Emerson C. Angell's Turkish and Roman Baths on the northeast corner of Lexington Avenue and Twenty-fifth Street. Six stories above the street, on the mansard roof, it glowed above the tallest buildings in the city, could be seen out on the river on the lightest moonlit night, red, green and the deepest shade of velvet blue around the borders of the letters, it shone as an oasis of refreshment and revivification in a desert of urban toil, as a celestial hymn to the kinship between cleanliness and a clear conscience.

Open twenty-four hours a day for the rough and careworn derm, the tired limb, the aching muscle, the throbbing sinew, its three hot-air rooms and cooling plunge baths making soap a needless impertinence, it was a temple of sanitary soothing, a paean of restfulness and relief, the acme, the fullest development—complete with ventilation and sewage—of the genius of the Roman and the Turk of two thousand years ago.

Of new red brick, darkened at all its manly frosted and stained-glass windows in intimate, soft, welcoming light, it called, it beckoned, it occupied an ever-constant place in respectable men's thoughts (and ladies', with warranted dignity and privacy between the daylight hours of noon and three on the second floor), and it sang, softly, liltingly of manliness and rare, anointing, perfumed oils.

BATHS

In the night sky, like a beacon on the craggy, storm-lashed cliffs of life, the ruby glass sign was a shining, homeward, happy light.

We'll go and take a Turkish bath;
'Twill make you supple as a lath,
'Twill set you up from tip to toe,
And put your system in a glow.

GENTLEMEN ARE REQUESTED NOT
TO ENTER BATHS WITH THEIR BOOTS
ON AND TO REFRAIN FROM SPITTING.

They steamed. They soaked. They drenched and sweated and steamed and soaked and exuded all the smell of smoke and gunpowder, streets, soot, cinders, sidewalk and city, and they became clean and blanched, soothed and soft.

They wore only fig leaves made of some material impervious to steam heat tied at the back with draw strings.

They plunged. They swam. They blew bubbles and burbled. They floated. They sank. They sent cooling ice-cold water straining their moustaches and armpits. They got out of the water and steamed and then plunged back in and swam, sank, sailed on their backs and blew waterspouts from their mouths.

They gargled.

They scrubbed.

They sank.

They scoured.

At 1:00 A.M., alone in the two-hundred-degree tiled and stained-glass temple of toil-taking-away, Tillman and Muldoon, sighing, steaming, scouring, *bathed*.

"You don't have to be perfect, Virgil!" At the far end of the plunge bath, Muldoon, treading water, knew what Tillman was doing. He was at the calisthenics corner of the place, testing the heft of three one-pound polished rock-maple India clubs, swinging them in his hands, one in his right, two in his left, humming a little tune.

He hefted them. He tested their balance. He looked up into the air through the steam. He tensed his muscles.

Muldoon said—

He tossed them: the two in his left hand, and they went up and he swung his right hand under them with the single club and sent it up and under the two parabolic arcs and then he—

He caught them. He caught the first from the left hand in his right and, faster than the eye could see, sent it up again and, in the same instant, had the second in his right hand, going up, and *in the same instant*, his left hand had a club flying, wavering a little in the air, and he had another in his left hand, going up, and he was juggling.

He juggled. He caught. He threw. He got the rhythm right and sent the three clubs twirling and spinning and rising and falling in his hands.

He hummed. He whistled. He grinned. Tillman said, "I taught myself this years ago in the orphanage so people would like me!" He juggled. He caught. He smiled broadly. He hummed. He winked.

"Life isn't some sort of goddamned terrible mystery!"

Tillman said, *"It is to me!"*

He juggled. He grinned. He nodded. Still juggling, he took a little bow.

In the steam heat, wearing only the fig leaf and a rough white Turkish towel around his waist, he juggled, juggled unceasingly, standing like a rock on his place on the face of the Earth until, at last, unstoppably, the tears ran, ran down his face.

Tillman said tightly, "It's a terrible thing, Ned, the taking of a human life."

"Yes." They were sitting on the edge of the plunge bath, dabbing at their faces with towels. Muldoon said, "Yes, it is."

"Three lives have been taken: Schweib, Carrol, and now Reynolds." Tillman said, "It's something irretrievable, gone, stolen and then destroyed as if it was of no value—a treasure taken by a thief and then smashed like a bauble and then forgotten." Tillman said, "It's a vile thing—it's not what people should do."

Muldoon said, "You gave it your best try."

"It's done by amateurs, people who turn to murder from a normal life! People who, living a normal life, one day simply become monsters and use killing as a means to an end like a hunter killing an animal in the forest not for its flesh or its fur, but because it simply stands in the way of the track they intend to use!" Tillman said, "To rob a life from someone denies everything that person might go on to be. It fixes him or her in one time or place like the animal on the track and it—it disposes of them merely as a *nuisance!*" Tillman said, "We can't go any further because there's nowhere to go!"

Muldoon said, "You gave it your best try."

"I'm beginning to think there may not be much in this notion of the thinking detective. I'm beginning to think, like Byrnes, that what you do when confronted by a mystery is to go to your tested and reliable Rogues' Gallery of professional criminals, extract a photo, set it in a little wooden frame on the notice board, manufacture evidence to prove he did it and then, when enough evidence is framed along with his picture, bring him in and beat a confession out of him."

Muldoon said, "Sure."

Tillman said, "And then hang him."

Muldoon said, "It's always worked in the past."

Tillman said, "It keeps the politicians and the people happy."

"Everybody likes a good hanging."

Tillman said, "Whoever it is who gets hanged."

"—who deserves it." He was an old Strong Arm Squad man. Muldoon said, "Whoever deserves it if not for one killing then for another, or one he's going to do in the future." Muldoon said, "To be fair, Virgil, we never framed or hanged a man who had a wife and family who needed the support of his labor—unless he really was guilty—and even then the old beat coppers always looked out to see that the family had enough to get by on, guilty or not."

"Maybe we could frame Humpty Jackson."

Muldoon said, "Spanish Louie would be better."

"Or Herbie, the young boy at Niblo's with the electricity."

Muldoon said, "Spanish Louie."

"Or how about Cousin Mag?"

Muldoon said, "Spanish Louie."

"Marm Mandelbaum."

Muldoon said, "Spanish Louie."

"Or how about *you?* Or *me?*"

Muldoon said, "No. Spanish Louie."

"Ned, I have a horrible feeling that all this progress around us—all the electrics and telephonics and bridge building and immigration—I have a horrible feeling that it isn't going to transform us into the new Roman republic or the Greek city-state, but into a jungle full of wild animals killing wantonly for food and a place on the track!"

"You worry too much, Virgil."

"We aren't going to catch the people who did the killings! We aren't even going to come close!" Tillman said, "All there is against them is us and we may not have even asked the right questions!"

"We did all right."

"We collected a boxful of museum exhibits. We collected a photograph and a watch and a bottle stopper and an old rusted gun and a paper room and a man dressed as a woman who was so terrified of us that he killed himself! We collected three bodies! We collected questions with no answers! We collected artifacts for a dusty glass exhibit case and we don't even know how to label them! We could have collected anything! We could have collected dust from the ground, finger smears on my bedroom wall, the pink tights from the girl on the diving horse, one of Edison's incandescent bulbs, a stone from the alley off Fulton Street! We collected *thin air!* The basis of the thinking detective is knowing what to think about before he collects anything! Everything I thought about led nowhere!"

Muldoon said, "There'll always be people like Spanish Louie about if we get desperate."

"We are desperate! We're finished!" Tillman said sadly, "Ned, we're at the end and there isn't anywhere else to go."

"Maybe."

"I thought, this once, just this once—"

Muldoon said, "You did everything a human man could do."

"Just this once . . ."

Muldoon said, "You're physically a small man, Virgil. You worry about other small men."

"Just once, Ned . . ."

Muldoon said, "And you don't drink enough, I've noticed."

"Ned, in Jasper Ward Alley we were a heartbeat away from him!"

"Maybe."

"We were! I could feel him there! I could feel his fear! I could feel him breathing like a cornered animal! We were a heartbeat from him and he eluded us!"

Muldoon said quietly, "Virgil, what happened to you when you were a baby—" Muldoon said tightly, "You have to force yourself to sleep at night, or, if you can't, at least learn to drink yourself into insensibility!" Muldoon said, "Learn to be a good copper: be a model of kindness and respectability to children, protect women and stop the traffic for them to get across the road, be respectful to your superiors, grateful to your politicians, polite to priests and nuns and clergymen and rich people, club people who need it, and—for Christ's sake—learn to sleep at night!"

Tillman said, "Ned, it's a ghastly thing to take a human life: vile, unspeakable, monstrous." He had a strange, sad, faraway look in his eyes. Somewhere inside, he was hurting.

Tillman said with real confusion in his voice, "Ned, I don't know how anybody could ever even contemplate it!"

He could contemplate it. At the doorway to the steam room, Dribbling Donahue, dressed in a towel, wearing boots and carrying the biggest gun he could find in the entire city of New York, yelled, "VIRGIL TILLMAN, YOU SHOT ME WHEN YOU WERE DEAD AND RUINED MY LIFE AND NOW I'M GOING TO SHOOT YOU!" He looked happy. He waved the giant silver gun. He cocked it. He uncocked it. He cocked it again. Dribbling Donahue, slavering with excitement, stopping to wipe the drool from his lips as he stood there sweating, said happily, "I'm Death! —AND I'M KNOCKING ON YOUR DOOR WITH MY GUN!"

He was a killer.

No, he wasn't.

Yes, he was.

Dribbling Donahue said, "Oh, yes, I am!"

Tillman, shaking his head, said, "No."

"I'M A KILLER! I KILL WITHOUT WARNING! I SHOOT FROM COVER AND TAKE MY ENEMIES' LIVERS!" Dribbling Donahue said, "I'M A KILLER ALL RIGHT!" Dribbling Donahue said, "You stay where you are, Muldoon!"

Tillman said, "No, you're not a killer. You haven't killed anyone."

"I'VE KILLED LOTS OF PEOPLE!"

"How many?"

"Today? Or in the last week, or—"

Tillman said, "Altogether. Roughly."

"Twenty-nine."

Tillman said, "No. We would have found some of the bodies."
Tillman said, "No, you don't kill people, you thieve from them."
"HOW MANY PEOPLE HAVE YOU KILLED THEN?"
"None."
"I don't believe you!" Dribbling Donahue said, "You tried to kill me! YOU SHOT ME! YOU WERE LYING IN YOUR COFFIN LOOKING SERENE WITH SKIN LIKE AN APPLE AND WHEN I CAME IN TO PAY MY RESPECTS YOU TRIED TO KILL ME!" Dribbling Donahue said, "You ruined my life."
"That was unintentional."
"Well, you did it." He was shaking his head, then nodding, then shaking his head again, looking upset. Dribbling Donahue said, "A whack over the head I could have understood, but it takes it out of a man to look into the muzzle of a gun and see flame and smoke come out of it." Dribbling Donahue said, "I DIDN'T KNOW IT WAS A BLANK! IF YOU'D TOLD ME IN ADVANCE MAYBE THEN I COULD HAVE PREPARED MYSELF FOR IT, BUT MY EXPERIENCE HAS BEEN THAT WHAT COMES OUT OF THE MUZZLE OF A GUN IS A BULLET!" Donahue said, "My head knows it was a blank, but my chest wakes me up in the middle of the night still cringing and tensing for a bullet in the heart!" Dribbling Donahue said, "That was unfair and cheap of you and you deserve to die for it!" Dribbling Donahue said, "I've killed thirty-nine men already in my life, Muldoon, and if you move you'll be the fortieth!"
Tillman said, "*Twenty*-nine."
Donahue said, "*Whatever!*"
Tillman, starting to come forward, said softly, "You're not a killer."
"I AM! OH, I AM ALL RIGHT!"
Tillman said, "No." He shook his head. Tillman said, "You're like me: you don't kill."
"You tried to kill ME!"
"It was a blank." Tillman said, "I understand that you feel aggrieved, but I ask you, is that any reason to start shooting in a respectable place and have your name known as a murderer?" Tillman said, "You're known as a thief, but not a bad fellow. And you believe in God, don't you?"
Dribbling Donahue said, "Sure."
Tillman said, "I'm sorry I shot you."
It was a huge gun.
Tillman said, "I can't believe that someone like you with a family

would actually threaten two people who have never really done you any harm with a weapon."

Dribbling Donahue said, "I've been pushed to the limit!"

Tillman said again, "I'm sorry my shooting you upset you. I didn't mean it to have any long-term effect."

Donahue said, "Well, it did."

"I'm sorry about that."

Dribbling Donahue said, "I know you've never killed anyone. I know that. And maybe I haven't . . ." Dribbling Donahue said, "I feel aggrieved."

Tillman said, "Give me the gun."

Dribbling Donahue said, "No."

"Give me the gun now."

Muldoon said tightly, "And in return, we'll give you five years for carrying a loaded weapon."

Tillman said, "Just give me the gun."

Donahue said, "Ha! You can't give me five years for carrying a loaded weapon because it isn't loaded! It's only loaded with blanks!" Donahue said, "Ha, ha, dumb flatfoot!" Dribbling Donahue said to Tillman a foot away from him with his hand out, "Apologize for shooting me!"

"I apologize for shooting you." Tillman said, "Give me the gun." Tillman, taking it, breaking it and glancing into the chambers, said, nodding, "Blanks. You're not a killer, Dribbles, and I can see you need to receive an apology for what you consider an unfair trick." Tillman said, "You've had it: I apologized and, furthermore, to prove my contrition, I'm prepared to let this thing go without a charge."

Muldoon said, "WHAT?"

Dribbling Donahue said, "Quite right. I thank you as one man to another."

Tillman said, "Okay."

"—I'm sorry, Virgil, if I frightened you just now."

Tillman said, "That's all right." He looked down at the open gun. Tillman said with a relieved smile, seeing the joke, "Blanks."

Dribbling Donahue said, "Yeah." Dribbling Donahue said, "Tit for tat—right?" Dribbling Donahue said, "Ha! Ha!"

"Ha! Ha!" He was aggrieved. He could see how it was important to get even. Tillman said, "Right. Blanks. Ha, ha!" He closed the gun.

Stepping back, measuring the distance between him and Dribbles for the flash and the burning powder, still smiling . . .

Dribbling Donahue said sadly, "Oh, no . . ."
He shot him.

"Ned! Ned!" In the steam room, looking down at the gun as
Muldoon, using a towel, put the burning hairs on Dribbling
Donahue's chest out, Tillman said, "NED! —NED!"
He had the silver gun in his hands. It was, according to the
legend stamped into its barrel, an American Gun Company .44
Russian Caliber Frontier Double Action Patented Aug. 6, 1881.
Tillman said breathlessly, "Ned. Ned." Tillman said, "NED!"
On the side of the frame there was an inspector's mark.
Tillman, his mouth dry, his heart racing, said with his hands
starting to shake, "Ned—"
BST.
He said in a whisper, "Ned, it's the same mark as the one on the
old Rebel gun in Carrol's room!" Tillman said, "Ned, BST—it
stands for the name of the inspector!" Tillman said, "It's a gun made
by Catton's American Gun Company in New Jersey not a year or
two ago—maybe yesterday—and it's got the same inspector's
initials on it as the old Rebel gun made by Gilbert and Greer in
Atlanta during the Civil War has on it and it's—" Tillman said in a
gasp, "Ned—" His eyes were bright, shining, his hands shaking in
excitement as he held the gun out like an offering for Muldoon to
see. Tillman said, "BST! It's a link, something, something to
follow, a question to ask!"
Tillman said, "God damn it, twenty years later, on an object
made a thousand miles away, it's the same goddamned mark! The
same goddamned man!"
Tillman, shoving the gun hard into Muldoon's chest, stepping
over the moaning, aggrieved Donahue, said in triumph, "Look!
Look!" He was clenching his fists in delight, like a pugilist at the
victory.
Tillman, beside himself with joy and resolution, said fiercely,
"Look! *Look!*"
Tillman said, "At last! At last! Really, truly, honestly, genuinely,
a *clue!*"

20

MEN!!!
ARIZONA!!
Mining In The Small Way In Arizona

In Arizona to those who are disposed to brave the climate, and the often protracted drought, and the isolation from the great centres of life and civilization, there are good opportunities for mining, even on a small scale. The lodes, both of gold and silver, are exceptionally rich, and even the simplest and rudest processes yield large returns. In no other region among civilized nations can a farmer do as GENERAL FREMONT *says many of the Arizona farmers are in the habit of doing—viz.: having found a gold mine upon their farms, which they have not the means of working on a large scale, they pursue their ordinary farm-work, and, when a leisure day comes, dig a quantity of gold ore from the vein, pound it up in a wooden or stone mortar with a log pestle, wash it in an old tin pan, or pick out the gold if it is in large grains, or amalgamate it if it is in small scales or powder after the rude Mexican way, and then expel the mercury by heat. At the next market-day, with their other produce, they bring their bag of gold dust and sell it, repeating the process when spending money runs low. This method of mining is rather wasteful, as much of the gold is lost, but there is more money made by it than in many mines made by more expensive processes.*

The veins and lodes in Arizona are so rich in gold and silver that there is a much better opportunity for men of small means to unite together and reduce the ores in a small way and with inexpensive apparatus, and obtain large profits, than anywhere else.

MEN!!!
ARIZONA!!
GUARANTEED LEGAL TITLES
LEGGET AND TAPPAN
LAND AGENTS
511, BROADWAY, NEW YORK
MEN!!!
ARIZONA!!

It was a wonderfully warm morning, a little after 8:00 A.M., the water behind the rounded stern of the Harlan and Hollingworth steam engine and side-wheel Hudson River steamer placid like a mirror, clear, with silver fishes playing in the wake, the wood of the polished handrails with their brass fittings mellow and gently trembling to the touch with the steady turning of the engines below deck, and Muldoon, standing with his hand on a rail, reading the flyer in its frame by the sliding wooden door to the inside seating, said, thinking about it, "We could do that, Virgil: become partners in it. I could clear the land and learn farming and you could read up on this gold business and in the, say, six months or so before we had a house built maybe do a little Marshaling in one of the towns out there." They were midway across the Hudson on the Vesey Street Pier to Hoboken first ferryboat of the morning, due to pick up the Morris and Essex New Jersey railroad-connection 8:25 A.M. train at the end of the two-and-a-half-mile trip to Montclair. With no jurisdiction outside New York, midway in the river, Muldoon had put his city police badge into his inside coat pocket. Muldoon said, talking over his shoulder to Tillman at the stern, "We could make a go of it, Virgil, retire rich and healthy from hard work, and then maybe look for wives."

Muldoon said, "Pioneers."

Muldoon said, "The Government wants honest men out West. Everybody says so." Muldoon said, "Everybody says the soil out there is so rich in gold that men have stubbed their toes on nuggets the size of cannonballs and gotten so rich already from the gold lying around that they couldn't be bothered to even pick it up and they simply put up a sign on the nugget still in the earth saying *'Mind Your Toes.'*"

Behind him Tillman had his square leather shoulder satchel out on the seat, putting something into it or taking something out.

Muldoon said, "Out there, they say the air is so pure and sharp that a man saves fifty dollars a year by not needing to smoke cigars for the taste or the aroma and, because his body needs no stimulants—that he is so braced by the climate alone—that his expense on alcoholic liquors becomes a thing of the past." Muldoon said, "And that would represent at least another two hundred a year." Muldoon said, "At least."

There was a click as Tillman snapped open the leather satchel and put something into it, probably his gun or his badge or both. Across to the right and south of the ferry there were freight yawls and sloop-rigged skipjack oyster boats under sail on beam reaches in the brisk easterly winds, making their way up the Hudson to the fishing grounds. Muldoon said thoughtfully, "A man has to think of his old age at some stage in his life."

He shook his head. Behind him Tillman was still digging in the bag. To his right, there was, clear in the clear morning, the waterfront of New York, bristling with masts and warehouses and smoke and buildings rising taller every day and people, people seething and bustling.

MEN!!!
ARIZONA!!

It was a rat hole, the whole city. It was a rat hole of filth and stink and people crowded together, hungry and fearful, sometimes hopeless, vicious, lost where all the streets were made of blocks and hurt your feet, where carriages and carts and wagons and hand trolleys ran you down at any opportunity, where trains belching smoke ran not as Nature had intended on the ground, but up in the air, where no man dared go unarmed and where other men would kill you for the arms you carried. New York: in a hundred years it would have collapsed back into the magma of the earth under its own weight, sunk like Atlantis and carried what was left of its brutish humanity with it.

He needed a drink.

New York City.

It was an island called Manhattan twelve miles long and, at its widest span, three miles wide and it held, was holding, intended to hold more every day, more than one and a quarter millions of people by the last census in 1880.

The engines of the ferryboat were throbbing, trembling, warm and mellow and comforting. Muldoon said over his shoulder, sharply, "It's a goddamned rising cesspool of people with nothing!

It confounds me why I can never leave it and not come back, but I can't—"

MEN!!!
ARIZONA!!

Muldoon, turning, said desperately, "Virgil, we have no power in New Jersey. *How the hell are we going to get anything out of anybody at a New Jersey gun company if we can't at least show them a badge?*"

Tillman said, "Ha!"

He had finished at his bag. Wearing spats and a ribboned pince-nez on his nose, a thick leather-bound ledger in the crook of his arm, his eyes bright blue and shining in the clear air, Tillman, leaning back a little to look down his nose at Muldoon, said happily, "*Ha!*"

He took his watch from his vest pocket.

It was Reynolds's watch. He pressed at it and it chimed the hour, a little slow.

"Hmm." Tillman said as beribboned, bespatted, busy, busy bespectacled bureaucrats said everywhere when a watch or a clock was a little slow, "Oh. Oh, dear . . ."

His eyes were bright and shining with anticipation.

Tillman said, "Ah." He set the hands of the watch just aright.

Tillman said, "Hmm."

As the ferry slowed to maneuver for the Hoboken pier where the train to Montclair waited, the air on the water was just so, so bracing.

Tillman said, looking at Muldoon over the glasses with his eyebrows raised and his lips pursed, "Hmm."

Still looking, still grinning, he took off the glasses from his nose and, with a fine, white, laundered handkerchief from his inside coat pocket, carefully, thoughtfully, full of power and pettifoggery, public office and precedent, commenced meticulously, minutely polishing them.

21

His already shining glasses polished anew, the small, tight man in the suit, spats, glancing at the breathtakingly expensive watch, said, opening his leather-bound ledger to check a point, "The Russians want Alaska back."

In the works office of the American Gun Company, Montclair, New Jersey, the works manager said, "What?" There were two of them in there with him: the small man and a large man. They were in the far corner of the barrel-rifling room, in a glassed-in office full of files and orders and custom guns in cabinets lining the walls. It was a little after noon—lunchtime—and the floor of the rifling room was deserted. The works manager, putting his finger in his ear to check he had not gone deaf with the noise during the morning, said, "—What?"

Tillman said impatiently, touching at his chest, "Clarence William Elias Mutewinter, Esquire, on an official matter from your government in Washington. And you are—?"

The works manager said, "Carr." He wore a gray dust coat over a white shirt and tightly knotted tie, "Mr. Carr." He looked into the eyes of officialdom, "Theo Carr. Theodore Joseph Carr." Carr said, "I'm the works—"

Tillman said, "And this is my underling, Mr. Horatio William Hathaway, not an esquire." He nodded at Muldoon to check him off in the ledger, "A coincidence we possess the same given name, but one of no consequence." Tillman said, "The Russians under Tsar Alexander the Second sold your government the territory of Alaska in 1867 for the sum of seven and a quarter millions of dollars. You may not be aware of this, but this was a cause of continuing resentment in all the corridors of power and the café society of Saint Petersburg and, following the assassination of the

186

not-so-good Alexander the Third the same year, the matter has burgeoned out of hand and now the Russians want it back." Tillman said, "For the same price. Obviously, we would rather not give it back."

Muldoon said, "Ah, Alaska, Alaska, verdant heaven of the north."

Carr said, "I always thought it was cold up there."

Tillman said, "When the Russian Bear roamed its hills it was."

Carr said, "And now?"

Tillman said, "As usual, Hathaway, you have said too much."

Muldoon said, "This is Theo Carr, Mr. Mutewinter. He has been fully investigated." Muldoon said enthusiastically, "The snow has been removed by electricity."

Carr said, "God in Heaven!"

"Do you have a family, Mr. Hathaway?" Tillman said, "Indeed you do! Do you care nothing for their continuing prosperity with the security of a government job?"

"Mr. Carr is on our side!"

"That, perhaps, remains to be seen!"

Muldoon said, "Not by me. Both Freddie and I—and I should point out Freddie is the elected representative of this great state of New Jersey—"

Carr said in a gasp, "Do you mean Frederick Frelinghuysen—the Secretary of *State?*"

Muldoon said, "Both Freddie and I—"

Tillman said, "My master is Mr. Arthur, not Mr. Frederick Frelinghuysen—!"

Carr said, "Chester A. Arthur—the—the *President* of—?"

Tillman said to Muldoon, "Go examine machines, Mr. Hathaway. You like cogs and wheels and belts and boilers—although you appear to have no knowledge of the discretion required in the greatest machine of all: the machine of government—go and look at Mr. Carr's machines out on the factory floor!" He turned for a moment to Carr: "What sort of machines are those out there?"

Carr said, "Barrel-rifling machines. They're—"

Tillman said, "Mr. Hathaway, you know the power I have to have you reduced to a crawling insect on the wheel of Washington that crushes, that runs over, that flattens—leave me to speak to this man in peace and perhaps—"

Muldoon said, "I want my opinions heard!"

"You want my job!"

Carr said politely, "Excuse me, but what exactly is your—"

Muldoon said, "I have seen what you have done in your job to destroy so many lives, Mr. Mutewinter, so I do not want your job." Muldoon said to Carr, "We call him, in Washington, The Nightmare Man."

"Go examine some machines, Mr. Hathaway!"

Carr said, "Oh, my God!"

Tillman said, "We have investigated you, Mr. Carr."

Carr said, *"Oh, my God!"*

"And you have been recommended." Tillman said to Muldoon's surly look, "The machines, Mr. Hathaway. *Get thee gone!*"

He went.

He waited. He went to the glass door and closed it. He looked into his ledger as he walked back. He looked into Carr's face. Tillman said, "Mr. Carr, you are perspiring."

"Sorry!"

Tillman said, "Mr. Carr, do you know anything at all about the position of government hangman?"

Carr said, "No!"

"I refer not to some dusty, pathetic, itinerant slayer with a length of hairy hemp recently removed from the tether of his stud bull in some smelly pat-filled field, but to the office of the Federal Executioner for the Government—your Government—of the United States of America."

Carr said, "I'm a works superintendent for a gun factory, a wage earner! I know nothing about where the guns are sent! Any guns that are sent are sent to good, plain Americans or the friends in other nations of good, plain Americans!" Carr said, sweating, "We don't send guns anywhere anymore! Now that Mr. Catton and Professor Quarternight have joined forces, all our guns are sold to supporters!" He wasn't sweating, he was dripping. Carr said, "If the Professor is elected President in a year's time, we will be the official suppliers to all the bands of citizen-protectors against foreigners all over the land!" Carr said, "We send no guns to foreigners! We hate foreigners here!"

Tillman said, "All that is here in my ledger."

Carr said, "Weapons for freeborn Americans!"

"All here."

Carr said, "I hate everybody who isn't a white American!"

"Quite." Tillman said, "The Russians are coming, Mr. Carr, to take Alaska back."

Carr said, "Kill 'em!"

"Ah, that we could . . ." He glanced out to Muldoon. He was

on the floor of the stilled factory, walking down the line of machines, from time to time bending down to examine some feature of them. Tillman said, "But then, out of annoyance, the French would want Louisiana back."

Carr said with a sneer, "The French—!"

Tillman said, "The dreadful French . . ."

Carr said, "They eat frogs!"

"Ah, yes."

"And snails!"

He reached over and touched Carr on the shoulder. It was the Hand Of Doom, like taxation. Tillman said sadly, "Yes. Disgusting. But we cannot kill everybody. We must negotiate. At least with some. We must have the Tsar in all his oily magnificence into our country and we must treat him with all the diplomatic niceties and we must serve his steaming Russian tea—"

Carr said, "Ugh!"

"Quite. And then we must talk back and forth, back and forth, until finally—" Tillman said, "He is like a child, you know."

"You—? You have met—"

"Oh, yes. Many times. A mad, unpredictable child with base desires of the worst kind—"

"A foreigner." He nodded.

"Well, not perhaps in his own country . . ."

"A foreigner is a foreigner! As Professor Quarternight says, if we let one in then we let in—"

Tillman said sadly, "We must let in, in this case, counting all the Tsar's entourage, fifty of them. We must let in his advisers and his priests and his doctors and his brothers and cousins and aunts and nieces and nephews and—" Tillman said, "We must let in"—he dropped his voice to a whisper—"his harem of fallen, loose women."

Carr said—

Business. On to business. Tillman said, "And you, Mr. Carr, you must be present. Discreetly. I might even say secretly. Yes, I would say secretly. You must be there, because the old hangman is too old for the job and—"

"You want me to *hang* the—"

He touched Carr's shoulder again. It was a Government touch. The Government, when it touched, did not smile, it merely acknowledged. "An analogy, my dear man." He glanced out at Muldoon bending down over a machine and peering at something on it. Tillman said, "It pleases me that, as a matter of fact, your alarm at the analogy is so real, because it means that the person, like the old hangman, who recommended you for his place, has told you nothing, analogically or otherwise, about it." He waggled a finger, *"As you must tell nothing about it!"*

"Who has recommended me?"

"BST has recommended you."

"Do you mean—?"

"I mean, BST. Here. At your own place of employment."

"Buford Townes? The old chief inspector?"

"I ask you, has he retired from an active life or not?"

Carr said, "Yes, he retired earlier this year. He—" Carr said, "No, I am discreet. I cannot discuss the secrets of this establishment with anyone without Mr. F. C. Catton's permission, and I—"

"Exactly why you are the man for the job!" Tillman said, "And I have it here from our own investigations that you are a married man of sober habits with children and that your wife is a solid, steady woman of impeccable moral restraint—"

Carr said softly, "Yeah." Carr said, "Yes!"

"—and that, for your country, you would do anything." Tillman said, straightening up, "Mr. Carr, we—your Government—cannot be seen to be offering protection to the concubines of foreign potentates of licentious habits. We could not be seen to do it over the many years previous to this when circumstances forced us to invite into our great moral nation unangelical Arabs or turpitudinous Turks or sinful Slavs or wanton Welsh or bad, mad Bohemians, and we cannot be seen to do it now with the worst of these licentious and evil and immoral and ungodly: the revolting Romanoff." He dropped his voice. Tillman said, "He has twenty fallen women of shattering beauty, long legs, fine, firm breasts and curves to make a man drunk with lust, who know no loyalty even to him, but only to their momentary desires of waywardness and wantonness and unchastity— *We cannot be seen to be protecting such creatures against the bullet, the bomb, the blade because our Government, our nation, founded in virtue, should shun such vileness as the vile themselves shun the light."* Tillman said, "We are prepared to furnish small firearms for their personal protection, but we can go no further."

"We have a complete line of—"

"My dear sir, we cannot furnish *American* firearms!"

Carr said, "No, of course not. Silly of me."

"Untraceable weapons of various pedigrees are collected by trusted diplomats in Europe and secretly shipped." Tillman said,

"But each fallen creature is different—anatomically—and holsters must be fitted on a custom basis for these weapons."

He had stopped sweating. He thought for a moment he might stop breathing. He had a wife like a tree trunk. It was a dead tree. Carr said, "Oh? To what part of the—of the anatomy? Might I ask?"

"Mr. Buford Townes, like the analogy of the hangman I mentioned—"

Carr said, "Oh, yes, yes. Yes. Yes, I remember. Go on."

"—performed this onerous task for us, oh, so many, many times . . ." Tillman said, "The upper leg. The thigh, I believe it is called."

"I know a little about leather work."

"You are too modest."

"You mean, that each of the—of the—" He tried to think of a word.

"—of these foul, immoral, decadent, immorally beautiful women lusting for a man, any man—"

"Requires the personal fitting of a holster to their upper thigh for protection against, against—"

Tillman said, "Yes."

Carr said, "*All twenty of them?*" His mouth had gone dry.

Tillman said, "It is an official position. There is a small stipend."

"Oh." Carr, nodding, sweating, dry, kneading his hands into fists and then unkneading them, said, "Oh." He nodded. He had lost the ability to think, "Oh. Well, a little extra is always handy."

"You do it for Alaska!"

Carr said, "I do. I will!" Carr said, "Good old Buford Townes!" Carr said, "God, I mean, very well." Carr said breathlessly, "Jesus! I mean, of course!"

Tillman said to brave him for the awful opportunity, "It is for your country."

"God bless America!"

Tillman said, "Quite." Tillman, extending his arm to Carr's shoulder, said, humbled, "And God bless you, Mr. Carr."

"Thank you! I mean, yes! Thank you very much! I mean, *yes!*"

"It will be known only to myself, the President, the Secretary of State and Hathaway out there—and of course yourself—that you will henceforth, the commission having been passed to you by your fellow laborer, Mr. Buford Townes or BST as we refer to him—that you, who we henceforth refer to in official communications only as TJC, are appointed the official foreign concubine thigh-holster fitter extraordinary of the United States."

He giggled. He could not help it. He . . . giggled.

Tillman said, nodding, "Yes, there is a certain joy in the security of a government job."

"OH, GOD!!"

Tillman said, raising his finger, nodding for Muldoon to come back in from the factory floor, "Mr. Carr, please. Control yourself. You are a bureaucrat now, sir. You must never, never . . . *drool*."

He was slavering. He seemed to have reached some other plane of existence and only his corporeal body shell and glazed eyes remained in the room.

Coming back into the room Muldoon said quietly so as not to disturb him, "I see, Mr. Mutewinter, you have apprised him of his new appointment."

Tillman said, "I have, Mr. Hathaway, yes." He touched Carr lightly on the shoulder: "Mr. Carr—" Tillman said, "Or may I call you Theodore? Would you care to know the remuneration offered for this position?"

Thighs. Carr said dreamily, "Yes."

"Which?"

Carr said, "Both."

Muldoon said tonelessly to Tillman as if it were merely a matter of curiosity, "Mr. Mutewinter, many of the gun-making machines out there are of southern manufacture, prewar, fabricated in Atlanta, Georgia."

Tillman said, "Old machines, Theo?"

Carr said, "Oh. Yes. Old machines." White thighs. Soft thighs. Carr said, "The rifling machines. The revolver-rifling machines. Yes. Old. Still good. Started out with them. Kept them."

Tillman asked politely, "Oh? Where did they come from?"

Something registered. Carr said, astounded, "I get *paid?*"

"A small honorarium plus expenses." Tillman still had his hand on Carr's shoulder. He squeezed. Tillman said, "Hello, Theo, are you still with me?"

Carr said, "Yes!" The eyes came back. He grinned. His eyes went away again. He was still grinning. Carr said warmly, cozily, "Yes . . ."

Tillman said, "What is the history of the American Gun Company, please, Theo?"

He was gone again. Muldoon, an inch from Carr's face, said,
"*Hey!*"

Carr said, "*What—?*"

He opened his ledger and selected a pencil from the inside pocket
of his coat. He took out the wonderful watch from his vest pocket
and consulted it. Tillman asked, for the records, "The history of the
American Gun Company so far as you know it."

"Oh." The what? Oh. Yes. Carr said, "Oh. Yes." Carr said,
"Um." The American Gun Company—

Tillman said, "Of Montclair, New Jersey."

"Oh." Carr said, "Yes." Oh, that. There. Here. Carr said,
coming out of it, glad to have an easy one, "Oh, here. This. Yes! Of
course!" Carr said, "Um—"

"When was it founded?"

"After the war." Which war? The Civil War. Carr said, "After
the Civil War, in 1869 or '70 to coincide with the western expansion
out to the territories. Buffalo guns and shotguns for game." Carr
said, "And a few revolvers and single-shot target pistols." He
sighed. He dreamed. Carr said, "Is that what your records say?"

"BST—"

Carr said, "Buford Samuel Townes." He thought kindly of the
old man. Carr said with a smile, "My benefactor."

"He thought so highly of you."

"I think so highly of him!"

"How long was he the inspector here?"

"From the beginning."

"And before that?"

Muldoon said, "Before that, Mr. Mutewinter, he was the inspector for the gun makers Gilbert and Greer of Atlanta, Georgia. It is
all in our records."

Carr said, "Yes."

Tillman said, "Was he?"

Carr said, "I don't know." Carr said, "He could have been."

"Was he or wasn't he?"

Carr said, "I don't know. He's a Southerner. He could have
been."

"Gilbert and Greer?"

Carr said, "I've never heard of them."

Muldoon said, "Their names are on some of your rifling
machines."

"Bought after the war."

Tillman asked, "By Mr. F. C. Catton?"

Who? Oh, him. Carr said, "Well, yes." Carr said, "Well, maybe. I suppose so."

Tillman said, "Mr. F. C. Catton is a Yankee, isn't he? He sounds like one."

"He's a Yankee all right!" Carr said, coming out of it, "He's a true-blue Yankee! He and the Professor—" Carr said, "The next President of the United States may be the man on the white horse, and I'll be puffed up enough by it to tell any man who asks and even those who don't that he stood here in my office and shook my hand!" The eyes were losing their glaze, sharpening. Carr said, "Washington, eh? They say the population of that place is made up of one-third *niggers!*"

Tillman said tightly, "What is this?" Reaching into his bag, he brought out the glass bottle stopper.

Carr said, "It's a bottle stopper."

"What color is it?"

Carr said, "Blue."

He held his eyes. It was a test. "What is it made of?"

Carr said, "Glass."

"And what is its current use, Theo, do you know?"

There was a little brass hook on it. Carr said with relief, "A watch-chain ornament!"

He put it back into the bag.

Carr asked, "Did I pass?"

Muldoon said, "Hmm."

He was just the underling. "Sir? Mr. Mutewinter?" Tugging at his sleeve as he bent down to close the bag, Carr said just to make sure, "Um . . . sir? Mr. Mutewinter? Um, Clarence? Was that the right answer?" Carr said in sudden alarm, "Do I still get the job?"

"Do you know anything about Gilbert and Greer at all?"

"No, nothing!"

"Or Vicksburg?"

"Where?"

"Vicksburg in Mississippi! About the battle of Vicksburg in 1862?"

"Only what I read at school! Only that we gave the Rebs a whipping and cut the Confederacy in two and—"

"Does the name Albert Schweib mean anything to you? Or Rufus Carrol, or Ethan Reynolds?"

"Nothing!" Carr said, "Do I get the job? I can do a good job!" He looked hard into Muldoon's face. Carr said with his tree-trunk wife surfacing out of the pool of his thoughts like a whale, "Don't say I don't get the job!"

Tillman said, "Is Buford Townes still alive, Theo?"

It was another test. "Call me TJC! You have to ask, 'TJC, is BST still alive?'"

"Is he?"

Carr said, "Yes!"

"Where?"

"About two miles up the road!" Carr said sympathetically, "Good man that he is, he resides humbly only two miles away from the site of his labors all the last twelve years or so." Carr said, "Think of what he must have done for his country in all that time and I knew nothing about it!" He said, the idea suddenly hitting home, "Old Townes, the official thigh-holster fitter for the United States government—" Carr said, slapping his head, "Well, I'll be!"

Tillman said warningly, "Not a word to—"

He slapped his head. Carr said, "He's blind! The poor old boy's blind!" He had the job. The whale had sunk. He was starting to drool again. He was happy. He was—

Carr said in a lather of joy and salvation, "All those thighs! *Blind!*" Carr said, slapping Tillman hard on the back and almost knocking him over with the force of a new-made man, "My God, my God—*I'm not surprised!*"

22

He could hear the tones in voices. In his open-fronted shooting-supplies stall behind the shooting line of the two-hundred-acre Montclair and New Jersey International Rifle Range, Buford Samuel Townes, wearing no dark glasses to disguise his total blindness from cataracts on his eyes, said as a warning, "Don't lie to me." He was a thin, tight, balding man in his early seventies, his drooping full moustaches completely white, wearing a long chest-to-toe dark gunsmith's apron above stout boots. He had strong, callused hands.

Across the firing line, at the very edge of the range there was a knot of men wearing top hats shooting at a thousand yards and calling scores calmly as their spotters peered through long brass telescopes at the targets. They were using the full back position, firing lying down with the barrels of their Remington-Hepburns and Sharps Creedmore rifles resting on their ankles, the stocks over their shoulders held in place by their left hands twisted behind their necks.

The booming of the shots was slow-rhythmed, regular, deep. White smoke drifted back in the slight easterly wind and hung in the air behind them. They were the American Creedmore team of Gildersleeve and Bodine, Yale, Fulton and Hepburn. What they needed from the supply stall they took and described exactly and paid for. Once, Townes had been one of them. Behind him, framed above the cans of Laflin and Rand Orange Sporting Powder, the boxes of Sharps and Remington cartridges, the patent bullet lubricants, devices, chemicals, preservatives, spare parts, sights and publications for the rifles, there was a framed, faded photograph of all of them seated in canvas shooting chairs awaiting their turn at the first, the fabled Irish-American Creedmore long-range

196

challenge match of 1874. Townes said, "You are a small man. I can hear it in your voice like a tightened violin string." He turned the milky eyes to Muldoon, "And you, you are a large, slow man."

Muldoon said, "A cello."

Tillman said, "I am New York City Detective Virgil John Tillman. My friend is Plainclothes Patrolman Edward Patrick Muldoon." There was a heavy boom as one of the company on the firing line let go his shot. The long dark coats of the shooters and spotters were covered in badges and medals that glinted in the sun. Tillman said, "Are you originally a Southerner, Mr. Townes?"

He listened. They did not. Townes said quietly, "It is in my voice for anyone to hear."

"*Center.*" It was the spotter's voice. It was not a cause for rejoicing. It was a statement of fact.

"You were employed from 1872 to recently with the American Gun Company as an inspector of arms, and before that in the same capacity with the firm of Gilbert and Greer of Atlanta, Georgia, during the war, is that correct?" The eyes were blank: he could read nothing in them. The man stood straight and still like a ramrod, with no sign of emotion, merely listening. Tillman said, "The mark BST on the Gilbert and Greer revolvers from the war and the mark on recent weapons made by the American Gun Company of Montclair, New Jersey, here in the north are both yours, are they not?"

Townes said, "They are."

Muldoon, glancing at the firing line, said, "Do your friends Judge Gildersleeve and Colonel Bodine out there know that?" Muldoon said, "Mr. Gildersleeve, I know for a fact, was at Gettysburg and was Provost Marshal of the 20th Corps when they marched with Sherman to the sea."

Townes said with interest, "I believe they now have the new incandescent electrical lighting in New York." He turned his face to Muldoon: "Is it of great assistance in reading?"

"Yes."

On the range there was a deep boom as one of the party, having held his aim for an eternity of concentration, let off his shot.

Townes said, "Is it of great assistance in reading men's characters?"

Muldoon said, "*We are investigating the murders or deaths of three innocent men!*"

Tillman said, "Albert Schweib of Slip Alley, New York, and Niblo's Theatre, Broadway—"

"The name means nothing to me."

"Rufus Carrol, Bleecker Street—"

"No."

Muldoon said tartly, "The incandescent electrical lighting, by the way, I have it on the authority of the man who runs the company, is not going to last."

Townes said, "I hear you moving back and forth on the ground in annoyance."

Muldoon said, "You are a very irritating man!"

"I am a blind man."

"Blind or not, you are a very irritating man!" Muldoon said, "Sighted, you would have been a very irksome superior man, and, blind, you are still a very irksome superior man!" Muldoon said, "You irk me!"

He showed no expression on his face at all. He merely stood there, straight, listening. He was listening to the team at their business. He heard the snick of the long-range .50-caliber Remington cartridge as the next shooter in turn, Colonel Bodine, late Commanding Officer of the 19th New York Militia, slipped it carefully into the breech of his Sharps Number One rifle and closed the action. Townes said quietly, "Perhaps you should take up rifle shooting, Mr. Muldoon. It is a soothing exercise, which, if properly followed, leaves no lurking desire in the man who follows it to seek amusement and associations that are only tolerated because partially concealed from the gaze of the world by darkness of night. It is conducive to good habits, keeps the mind clear and the body sound and strong, and it contributes to the moral growth and worth, while at the same time cooling the brain and calming it in order to strengthen it against evil temptations and the vices of rashness, temper and injudicious speech." Townes said, "I quote from Judge Gildersleeve's celebrated book on the subject. Perhaps you should read it."

Muldoon, starting to waggle his finger, glancing at Tillman, said tightly, "Virgil, this man is starting to make me hopping mad . . ."

Townes said, "The American Gun Company paid me for the work I did, and fairly, and when I could no longer do the work, fairly, terminated my employment—"

Tillman said, knowing the answer, "Do they pay you a pension?"

"They do not. They are not obliged to. I work. I will work until I die."

Muldoon said as an accusation, "Like guns, do you, Townes?"

Townes said, "Yes, I do."

"Inspect a lot, did you, during the war?"

"I did my work."

"So did your damnable guns!"

Townes said, "The Irish challenge team at the 1874 matches were fine men, good men, straight men, but they were not cool men. Silent men are apt to be cool men, and nervous men are apt to talk a great deal, and the Irish talked a great deal and, trained though they were, shot by talent, by intuition, by a pious and sincere belief that, past their training, there is a justice in the world that gives the race to the God-fearing and the true." Townes said, "The American team believed that the narrowing down of the margin of error by industrious, daily, unstinting practice was the new way, and that practice, practice, practice, and practice only calms a man, concentrates him, raises his level of excellence and his character, and gives him success." Townes said with a trace of sadness in his voice, "Good men, the Irish team, the finest, truest fellows one would be honored to know, but they aimed at the two-thousand-yard mark at a target their intuition and their talent and their good fellowship saw only as a blur."

Tillman said, "The true target is inside you, is it not?"

Townes said firmly, "Yes!"

Muldoon said, "*It wasn't at Chancellorsville!*"

Townes said suddenly, "I am a blind man! All my life I have worked! I work now! A man works until he dies!" Townes said above the blast of Bodine's shot, "Practice, practice, practice—that is all there is to a life! Practice! Practice! *Practice!*" Townes said, "I am an accurate man! The finest expression of that accuracy is the bullet's flight to its target!"

Muldoon said, "All you are is drunk on goddamned gunpowder and pious, persnickety prattle!"

"—I am drunk on the fulfillment of a man's character to be, like the long-range bullet, straight, unerring, unbending to a casual wind, and *true!*"

On the range, Hepburn was shooting offhand. A tall, bearded man wearing a top hat and a floppy silk bow at the neck of his shirt, holding the Remington-Hepburn rifle of his own design carefully across his chest, he stood looking down the range in silence, moving his head slightly back and forth to find the moving tufts of grass that would tell him of an unfelt, vagabond, vagrant breeze moving between him and the target a thousand yards away.

Muldoon said in a snarl, "*Virgil—?*"

He was looking hard at Townes. He said nothing. On the firing line, Hepburn, his shoulders rising and falling as he breathed slowly and regularly to fill his lungs for the long steady hold, brought the thirty-inch barrel of the ten-and-a-half-pound custom Remington-Hepburn Number 3 Long-Range Creedmore rifle up to his shoulder to take aim. The steel octagonal barrel was a full two inches across the flats. It moved up and sat in his grasp like a feather.

"*Virgil—!*"

By the iron gate to the entrance of the place, the horse on their hired carriage had its head down eating the grass that grew along the fence.

Muldoon said, "Virgil, all this damned gunfire is disturbing the horse!" The horse, head down, happily munched as if it didn't have a care in the world.

Poor, helpless, persecuted, dumb beast.

Muldoon said, "Some of us, like the Irish Creedmore team, have *souls!*" The horse probably did, for one. Muldoon said, "You, if you must, *you* talk to this bloody man!"

Muldoon, starting to move, said back over his shoulder, "I, on the other hand, being just a bloody Irishman, I'm going to go and talk to the *horse!*"

Tillman said, "The target is inside yourself. Is it not?"

Townes said quietly, nodding, "Yes."

Tillman said, "Steels, irons, wind directions, ballistics, powder weights, trajectories, primers, patching, percussive forces, tooling, testing, rifling—your mind is full of technicalities. As is mine." He stood rock still with his hands by his sides facing the man, looking into his face, not lying to him.

Tillman said, "Your mind is full of loss, as is mine. My mind is full of the loss of not knowing what my loss is. I cannot sleep because my mind is full of things that I fill it with because to contemplate my loss would be to contemplate nothing and I would sink and drown. So I fill it. I do not sleep. I fill my life and my mind with thought and movement and doing, because, as you know, there is a worm in the night, in sleep, that slithers and infiltrates through any pore left unguarded and, once inside—"

Townes said, "I have led a rich and full life! My blindness is nothing! My blindness gives me peace to contemplate my life!" There was a boom from the range. Townes said, "I am afraid of nothing!"

Tillman said, "I am afraid."

"I am not afraid!" Townes said, "That God has seen fit to punish me with blindness is His doing! It is not for me to question God's will!"

"No."

Townes said, "Loyalty, honor! That is also something else that should not be questioned! I have a loyalty to my employers! That they gave me nothing is right and fair! I want no pity for my blindness and they gave me none!"

Tillman said, "In the city, three people have been killed."

"In the war, thousands of people were killed."

"Yes."

Townes said, "I fear nothing! The silent man is the cool man. I fear nothing." He was kneading his hands. Townes said, "Accuracy. That is what a man strives for."

"To what end?"

"To its own end!" Townes said suddenly triumphantly, "I hear you! I know what you are! You are a small man, like a taut string!" Townes said, "I hear you! I know what you are! Blindness is nothing! It is not a refuge!"

"Accuracy is a refuge." Tillman said, "Walking, looking, watching, seeking for people in the night is a refuge."

"That is *your* refuge."

Tillman said, "People are dead. They were killed like dogs. Everything they were or might be was severed. They were turned, like the young men in the war on both sides, into rotting meat."

Townes said, "I hear it in your voice! *I know what you are!*"

Tillman said softly, "At night, maybe, I am you."

Townes said, "The Irish Team—those Celts—they believed in laughter and God and good times and fellowship and—" His mouth was twisted. Townes said, "I touch a gun and I hear . . ." Townes said, "I hear—I see the blast from the muzzle and the shock of the recoil and I hear—" Townes said, "I hear the screams. The war. I hear the screams of women and I see the flash and then the bayonet at the muzzle and I see . . ." Townes said, "I see the letters of my name through the blood on the receiver and the human flesh on the cylinder and I see . . . BST." Townes said, "I see the letters of my name engraven in light on the dark, dull eyes of women at the moment of their deaths, and I see, at nights, God—God looking at the poor, dead, soft faces and taking them in his arms and looking . . . looking down at my name, and I—" Townes said suddenly desperately, "What if, in Heaven, the souls my weapons slaughtered forgive me? What if they are there awaiting me, to smile upon me and I, I am still blind? What if that is my true punishment not on Earth, but through all Eternity?" Townes said, "Accuracy! All there is in the world is accuracy *and I cannot tell what God has planned for me so I can train myself to be ready for it!*"

Tillman said, "I must know things. It is my punishment. I must *know!*"

Townes said, "I think every man I meet whose face I cannot see has been sent by God to punish me!"

Tillman said, "Please, without it, I cannot fill the nights!"

Townes said, "I hear it! I hear it in your voice!"

Tillman said, "Please! Help me! Tell me what you know about the firm of Gilbert and Greer of Atlanta, Georgia, and about Albert Schweib and Rufus Carrol and a Southerner like you, a Major General in the war named Ethan Reynolds—"

Muldoon was by the carriage offering the horse a drink from his hip flask, or, if he preferred grass, a little conversation.

In his stall Townes said softly, "In the early part of the war, Reynolds was the head, I believe, of some secret organization formed by President Davis; the other names, Schweib and Carrol, mean nothing to me at all."

"Did you ever meet him? Reynolds?"

"No. I saw him once."

"In the Gilbert and Greer Arms Company?"

"Yes. With Mr. Greer in his office. He was in civilian clothes. Someone told me later who he was. He was a rich man with a large plantation somewhere in Virginia and there was some talk that he might invest in the company." Townes said, "Whether he did or not, I don't know. Someone in the factory told me that they had a cousin on the President's staff and that Major General Reynolds did secret work for Davis and was very well thought of." Townes said, "It was early in the war—people talked more then." He listened. All the shooting had stopped and the guns put back in their boxes. Halfway down the range area, the shooters were walking toward the targets to check their scores.

Tillman said, "Some of the rifling machines in the American Gun Company were either made by or for Gilbert and Greer."

"The first American Gun Company revolver was a copy of the old Gilbert and Greer .36-caliber Confederate Army pistol converted to modern cartridge." Townes said, "And they still use a lot of the old tools and dies for the Number One sporting rifle Gilbert and Greer used for theirs." Townes said, "But they're being replaced now that sales are better." Townes said, "Thanks to Professor Quarternight's endorsement."

"Who owns the American Gun Company?"

Townes said, "Mr. F. C. Catton."

"Has he always owned it?"

"Yes. From the beginning." Townes said, "In the beginning it was just him and me and a few casual laborers who came into a shed to work the machines." Townes said, "After the war there wasn't much call for firearms. It took until 1872 or '73 for us to get enough orders to employ a real work force."

"Where did the Gilbert and Greer machines come from after the war?"

"Mr. Catton and I went down south and brought them up here by train."

"To Atlanta?"

"To Virginia." Townes said, "Toward the end of the war everything that could be moved before the Union troops got to it was shipped out to warehouses or hidden. The machines were shipped to Virginia and Mr. Catton and I got them from there."

"From Gilbert and Greer?"

"Both Gilbert and Greer were dead by the war's end." Townes said, "No, we got them from a warehouse a few miles from Richmond—more a sort of barn on an abandoned farm. We had some local boys load them into wagons and put them on the train north."

Tillman asked softly, "Who did he buy the machines from?"

"I don't know."

"Did he have a paper?"

"He must have."

Tillman said easily, "Well, he must have before the railroad agreed to ship them, mustn't he?"

"Ownership papers?"

"Yes."

There was a silence as he thought about it. Townes said, "Yes, I suppose he did. I don't know." Townes said, "Yes. Yes, he did. He carried the papers in a rubber pouch." Townes, shrugging, said, "Why? Do you think he stole the machines?"

"Do you?"

Townes said, "No!"

Tillman asked, "Is he a Southerner: Catton?"

"No! He's a Yankee from—" Townes said, "From—from all over. I don't know."

"What did he do before the war?"

"He was a drummer, a salesman. He was a traveling man with a wagon. He bought cheap in cities and sold dear in the country."

"Did he sell guns?"

"Sure. Of course!"

"Gilbert and Greer guns?"

"He may have. We shipped to wholesalers and drummers all the time." Townes said irritably, "He always treated me fairly. Before the war he may have sold Gilbert and Greer guns from his wagon, but I don't know." Townes said, "Maybe he knew someone who wholesaled guns to him before the war and then, after the war, contacted that person and bought any equipment or stocks from him that were still intact." Townes said, "I don't know."

"After the war, when there was a glut of guns, why would someone want to buy equipment to make more guns? Equipment that required expensive shipping?"

Townes said, "I don't know."

What the person in the basement of 23 Van Dam Street had been searching for was Tillman's police ledger.

What the person in the Pearl Street Electric Generating Company had been following him there for was Ethan Reynolds. In the Detective Bureau at Headquarters, when he came to get him for the group photograph, Catton had asked about the ledger. Tillman said, "Did you know Mr. F. C. Catton during the war?"

"No."

"Then how did he contact you after the war?"

Townes said, "He wrote to me in Atlanta. He knew I had been the Chief Inspector and—"

"How did he get your address if the whole factory had been stripped and shipped to Virginia?"

Townes said, "I—"

"How did he know you had been the Chief Inspector?"

"My initials on the guns: BST."

"How the hell did he know who BST was?"

"What are you trying to suggest?" Townes said, "I—" Townes said, "I loved the Old South and I would have fought as any true Southerner would have fought—did fight—but I have respect for a man on any other side who truly holds his patriotism dear and Mr. Catton—" Townes said, "Mr. Catton is supporting Professor Quarternight's nomination for the Presidency and the Professor, as any schoolchild knows, is an authentic northern hero, a man who unstintingly rallied the troops in the most desolate billets and, heedless of his own safety—" Townes said angrily, "You are slandering the name of a man who is not here to defend himself!"

He had the glass bottle stopper in his hand. Taking Townes's fingers and turning them over, Tillman put the colored object in his palm. The hues and colors in the glass caught the light and glittered. He closed Townes's fingers on it. Tillman said quickly, "What is this? Do you know?"

Townes said, "A bottle stopper." He felt the hook set into the glass. "A watch-chain ornament." Townes said, "Is it?"

Tillman said, "During the war, where was Mr. Catton?"

"I don't know." Townes said, "He was a young man then—in the Northern Army." Townes said, "I think, Mr. Tillman, you have taken advantage of me."

"No."

Townes said, "I think you have!"

"No."

"I think you have taken advantage of a blind man by disguising the tones in your voice, and I think—" Townes said, "*I think maybe you have lied to me!*"

There was a silence. He could no longer hear his friends at the firing line or downrange. A thousand yards away, as tiny silhouettes, they had sat down on the target butts to smoke cigars. Townes said, "I don't think I will say any more."

There was a silence.

Tillman said softly, "One last question. Mr. Catton: is he right- or left-handed?" Tillman said firmly, "No, I haven't lied to you."

He listened. He wondered. He listened to the man in front of him breathing. He wondered. He listened. He wondered if he too, sometimes, was afraid of the nights.

Townes said, "Left." Townes said softly, unsure of what he heard, "Left." He nodded. It was nothing. It was merely a fact. He listened to Tillman's breathing and could not be sure what he thought.

Drawing a breath, saying nothing he should not say, accurate to the end, Townes said, "Mr. Catton, unless he has changed since my affliction, is a left-handed man."

On the ferry back to New York the sun was setting behind the stern, the light going in shadows and blurs behind the shoreline of New Jersey.

On the ferry, at the stern, in the fading light, the faces from the photograph looked out at him with some of their names written in carefully in ink on the back.

Albert Schweib (Cpl.).

Rufus Carrol (Pvt.).

George Fenney (Pvt.).

Henry Carver (Pvt.).

Unknown.

"John."

Colonel P. W. Seward (NYC).

Unknown.

Unknown.

"Charlie."

Shand.

Warren Cahill.

. . . *VICKSBURG, 1862*.

The light was fading, going, turning into night.

At the stern, watching the water, he wanted to put the photograph back into his bag and watch the water and the sunset.

He saw Muldoon, his elbows on the railing, watching him. He could not keep his eyes from the faces.

Albert Schweib.

Rufus Carrol.

George Fenney.

Henry Carver.

Unknown.

"John."

Colonel P. W. Seward (NYC).

Unknown.

Unknown.

"Charlie."

Shand.

Warren Cahill.

. . . *VICKSBURG, 1862*.

The sun to the west was going, fading. "Ned . . ."

They were not a unit.

In the last moments of the day, Tillman said desperately, "Ned, in the name of God—in the name of God—*who are these people?*"

23

In the Detective Bureau at 10:15 at night, examining himself under the gaslight, Detective Henry Grafton said, near tears, "Look at me! This job is turning me into a ragbag!" His suit was covered from head to foot in molasses. It was dry, caked hard. Grafton said, "This is my wedding suit!" He touched the left lapel where, on his wedding day, he had worn a boutonniere. The lapel fell off. Grafton, starting to hop, said, "Oh dear, oh dear, oh dear, what's my poor girl going to make of this?" He had the Klonski Brothers in handcuffs by Tillman's desk. The Klonski Brothers were not covered in molasses. They covered other people in molasses. They were the Molasses Gang. They went into stores that sold molasses to settle a gentlemen's bet about which of their hats would hold the most molasses, offered to purchase both the molasses and two new hats from the storekeeper and then, when the first hat was full, upended it over the storekeeper's head and while he was drowning in the stuff and otherwise engaged, robbed his money till. The storekeeper from the Klonski Brothers' latest little gentleman's wager was Stickney from Stickney's Splendid Store on Canal Street. He was not covered in molasses either. Grafton, as one of his coat cuffs fell off, said, "I can't afford this job! This job is turning me into a tattered wretch!" Grafton said, "I go home at night and my children run screaming from me because they think their mother is about to be attacked by a tramp!" Grafton said in desperation to Stickney, "Mr. Stickney, I saved your cash box and your own clothing—won't you at least give me the price of a new suit?"

He was a nasty, bald, thin little man. Stickney said, "I will not." He looked at the Klonski Brothers, Dutch Herman Klonski built

207

like a barn door, and Little Willie Klonski built like the tiny hinge of a barn door. Stickney said, "All you did was your duty."

Grafton said, "I saved you in the nick of time!" He saw Detective Schwenk unloading Dutch Herman. He unloaded from his inside coat pocket a .22-caliber brass Reid's "My Friend" knuckle-duster revolver. Grafton said, "See!"

Stickney said, "Gracious!" Schwenk put the gun on Tillman's desk by the spread-out photos of Schweib, Carrol, and Reynolds the Mortuary at Bellevue Hospital had sent over. Tillman moved them to one side. Stickney said, "Good God!"

Dutch Herman said with a grin, "Herrr, herrr . . ."

Grafton said, "At least the laundry . . ."

Schwenk got from Herman's coat pocket a "Little All-Right" palm pistol with ivory grips.

Stickney said, "Oh my Lord!"

From his other coat pocket an unmarked French 7mm pinfire revolver.

Stickney said, "Oh my Mother!"

Grafton said, "I've already lost one suit chasing people through the sewers! I have to attend the Brooklyn Bridge opening tomorrow and all I've got to wear if my wife can even get it ready in time is my old policeman's uniform!" Grafton said, "I worked so hard to become a detective! My children will think I've been lying to them if I parade like an ordinary copper!"

An Otis Smith .38 rim-fire revolver.

Stickney said, "Christ in Heaven!" Stickney said, "Weapons of destruction everywhere!"

Dutch Herman said happily, "Huh, huh!"

From Herman's hip pocket, a German 9mm Velo Dog bicyclist's revolver for dogs. Or storekeepers.

Stickney said, "Oh my hat!"

From his desk, Tillman said as a matter of fact, "Willie, you and Herman are going to get twenty years for being armed in public."

A small-frame pinfire revolver from under Herman's left armpit.

A large pinfire revolver from under Herman's right armpit. Obviously, when he walked one of his knuckles dragged along the ground. Probably, considering the balance question, the right.

Little Willie said, "It isn't against the law to carry a gun!"

Schwenk said, patting Herman down around the ankle area as Herman, chatting away happily in his own way said, "Huh, huh," "It's against the law to assault policemen with substances that can be classified as dangerous vitriols." He found a Remington two-shot

derringer and put it on Tillman's desk. Schwenk said with a shrug,
"I've only got this one suit myself, Henry, or I'd offer to loan you
something."

Grafton said, sadly, "Thanks, Franz."

A hundred-year-old flintlock lady's muff pistol in a sock sus-
pended in case he came across a hundred-year-old lady with a muff.

Stickney said, "This is appalling! Do you let these people run
about the streets with impunity with more weapons than a United
States ship of the line?"

Grafton said, "No, what we do is see people like this in the act
of upturning molasses over the heads of honest shopkeepers and we
rush in from the street and save them by thrusting our bodies
between victims, perpetrator, and molasses!" Grafton said, "Heedless of the fact that we have wives and children and devil-
may-caring of the effect it will have on our last good suit and our
little ones' terror at our appearance when, at the end of a long,
ruinous day, we finally go home!"

Dutch Herman said, "Herrr, herrr."

Schwenk said, "Shut up, you disgrace to the entire European
continent."

Little Willie said to Tillman, "All you can do is confiscate the
weapons until our lawyers, Messrs. Howe and Hummel, have us
out of here on the basis that this man here—" He meant Grafton.
"This disreputable-looking street urchin—makes his disgusting
appearance in Court and answers the accusation that he upturned
my hat full of molasses on purpose." He looked Grafton up and
down with distaste. Little Willie said, "This wild-eyed man
frightened us, Herman, didn't he?"

Herman said, "Herrr, herrr."

Grafton said, "I will appear in Court in uniform!"

Little Willie said, "I shall inform the Court that you are in
disguise!"

Schwenk said to Stickney, "Sir, as your savior, won't you give
this man the price of a new suit?"

He looked at the guns. He looked at Dutch Herman. He was a
big one. He had arms hanging down to the floor like pile drivers.
He shrugged. Stickney said reasonably, "Neither of them did
anything to me."

"True." Tillman said from his desk, "Nine guns." He looked up
at Stickney.

He had eyes like tunnels. Stickney said, taking a step back,
"After all, everyone has the right to protect themselves." ·

Grafton said in a mutter, "I'm going to protect myself! What I'm going to do is protect myself by getting a shotgun and—"

Tillman asked Stickney, "Where can such things be bought?"

Stickney said, "Well . . ."

"Do you sell such things?" Tillman, glancing at Grafton said soothingly, "People do have the right to carry guns, Henry, and, after all—"

Grafton said in a lather of self-pity, "My poor wife will be understanding and concerned only about me, and that's the worst part. She is my best friend, the loyalest ally a man could ever hope to find this side of Heaven, and—"

Tillman said, "I seem to remember from somewhere that a little gun like this pinfire retails in the best stores for about a dollar five." He looked up at Stickney for confirmation.

Stickney said proudly, "In Stickney's Splendid Store, ninety-five cents with a discount of five-percent more for cash." Stickney said, "And a box of twenty-five shells thrown in for good will."

Little Willie said, "Good Lord!" Obviously, he shopped in the wrong places.

He picked up the Remington. Tillman asked, "And this one?"

"Two dollars ten in Montgomery Ward's catalog for 1883; one dollar ninety-three in Stickney's!"

"What would Montgomery Ward have charged these poor men for all this weaponry if they had been foolish enough to purchase it from that establishment?" Tillman asked Little Willie with concern, "Did you purchase them from that obviously usurious firm?"

"From Kirkland's on Broadway."

Tillman said, "Mr. Stickney?"

Stickney said, "Ha, ha! Worse even than Montgomery Ward!"

Grafton, looking up at the gaslight as if it were the lamp of his wife's unflickering, shining goodness of heart, said, "Nobody cares for me but my Mary . . ."

Tillman said, "Retail total—what? Twelve dollars?"

"More like fifteen dollars!"

Little Willie, offended, said, "Thirteen dollars fifty cents!"

Schwenk, patting Grafton on the shoulder to console him, patting not him, but molasses, said, "Yerk!"

Dutch Herman said, "Herrr, herrr!"

Tillman, starting to make calculations with his pencil on a sheet of paper, said, "Sold by you in your store on Canal Street, Mr. Stickney—for what? A total of what?"

Stickney said, "No more than nine dollars and seventy-three

cents! Approximately!" Stickney said to Little Willie, "Ha! As I always say, 'The Sage Citizen Constantly Seeks Out Stickney's Splendid Store for Stunning Savings.'"

Tillman asked, "Wholesale?"

Stickney said, "No more to me than any of the other establishments—big or small—a mere total of six dollars!"

"What's a suit cost in your wonderful emporium?"

Stickney said proudly, "A man's round-cornered sack-style suit in the latest fashion, black background with small blue pin check, domestic worsted: a mere three dollars, *with any necessary alterations included!*"

Tillman said, "Want to buy a few guns cheap?"

A friend. Grafton said in his joy, "Virgil!"

Little Willie said, "Christ, Herman, we're in the wrong business!"

Grafton said tearfully, "Virgil . . ."

Schwenk said, "I haven't even searched the little one yet. Anything else would be by way of a discount—"

Tillman said, "Flowers. The discount taken out in flowers for the wife of this brave man." He shrugged at Stickney and smiled. He winked at him. Tillman said, "A small enough gesture."

Stickney said, "Oh, yes." His eyes were glazed as his brain calculated. Stickney said, "Carnations."

"Roses."

Grafton said firmly, "Virgil, on Sunday you will come to my house and my wife will give you a home-cooked meal."

"Thank you, Henry."

Little Willie said, "We're on the wrong side of the law, Herman!"

Herman said, "Herrr."

Stickney, his eyes bright, said, "Done!"

Tillman, looking back down to his desk, said, "Good."

Tillman, nodding, looking down, said, "Good." He looked down to the photographs of the three dead, ruined faces from the Bellevue Hospital Mortuary, gone, gone forever. "Fine."

Schweib, Carrol, Reynolds. He looked down at the pictures of their cold, faded dead eyes. He nodded.

He did not look up into the room. In the yellow gaslight, he looked down to his desk to the faces, nodding.

At his desk, he touched his hand lightly to his forehead and looked down at the faces.

* * *

"Virgil!" Wrenching open the door to the Detective Bureau on the first floor Muldoon called, "Virgil, where are you?"

The lights were still on in the deserted room, the clock on the wall showing a few minutes after 2:00 A.M. There was nothing on Tillman's desk; it had been cleared. Muldoon called anyway, "Virgil—?"

Nothing. Down the corridor, at that time of night, all the doors to the other offices were closed: in room seven the Bureau of Records and Complaints, in room nine the Property Clerk's Office and, as he turned and retraced his steps for the stairs, the Police Board Commissioners' rooms number three and four.

There was no one. The whole place was deserted. He had come from the basement Telegraph Office, and down there, on that floor, all the other rooms, three, four and five for the Steamboat Squad and the Police Sanitary Company had also been unlit and locked.

The last door before the stairs was the Police Architect's Office in room six.

It was locked.

"Virgil . . . ?"

At the bottom of the stairs, calling up, Muldoon yelled, "Virgil! Virgil Tillman! Virgil, *where the Hell are you?*"

He looked at the faces. In the faint glow from the turned-down gas lamps on the walls of room five on the fourth floor, Tillman looked at the faces sleeping on the fifty or sixty wooden pallets that made up Matron Webb's dormitory for lost or abandoned children. Through the barred windows, moonlight came in and illuminated the floor in a faint, washed light.

He had left his shoes outside the door with the Matron's husband, Janitor Webb, and as he walked, looking at the faces of the children, he made no sound.

He heard their breathing. He heard, saw, here and there, one of the children toss or cry out in his sleep. He was in the boys' section, the girls' at the other end of the room screened off by a wooden partition.

He smelled the smell of carbolic soap. It was on the scrubbed floors and scrubbed bodies. He smelled the smell of cheap, serviceable clothing and socks drying somewhere in the airing cupboard.

In the silent, darkened room, making no sound at all, he walked on stockinged feet, looking through shadows and the moonlight, at the faces.

On the second floor all the clerks' doors were locked, and the door to the Bureau of Elections and the Police Supplies storerooms.

He had a piece of paper in his hand like an invitation.

Muldoon, shaking his head in frustration, yelled down the empty, silent corridor on the second floor before moving on up the stairs to the next, "Virgil! Virgil; if you can hear me, *answer me!*"

They were the strays of the city. They were the lost, the hopeless. They were children who were found wandering or stealing or surviving in rat holes or under piers or in sewers. They were the washed, scrubbed, disinfected, deloused. In their sleep, they tossed and sometimes moaned. They were all below thirteen years old because, after that, they did not come to Matron Webb but to Sergeant Fitzgerald at the front desk on the ground floor and they went to prison or were turned out again into the streets.

He looked at all the faces: Irish, German, Jew, Russian, Greek, Italian—Matron Webb took no Africans or Chinese because their habits could not be trusted and the Lysol and carbolic could not cleanse their souls, and perhaps they did not even believe in a Christian God and His charity—he looked, and by one of the barred windows, by all of them, there were upturned boxes, bundles of clothes, objects, shoes that had been placed there as step-ups from which to look out.

Schweib, Carrol, Reynolds.

Boxes from which to look out of windows.

Windows.

In the big room, he heard the faint, steady hissing of the gas.

He touched at his chest.

At the window, he waited.

Touching at his chest with his fingertips like a man praying, at the window he looked out and waited.

In the room, at the window on Chrystie Street, standing on a box, he waited.

Schweib, Carrol, Reynolds.

He had waited at that window all his life, waiting for someone to come.

He had waited so he could say to someone that he was sorry for what he had done.

He had waited, waited.

He had waited to be forgiven.

He had heard—heard now, the only sound in the city, in the darkness, in his heart—only the steady, unabating hissing of the turned-down gas.

"Virgil?" The door to the Police Trial Room and School of Instruction on the third floor was open and he thought maybe he was in there at the books checking something.

The room was empty, the key left in the door by Janitor Webb preparatory to being mopped and polished; the two other doors on the floor, the entrances to the Police Stenographer's Office and the Stationery Clerk's Room, were locked up tight.

"*God damn it!*"

He had his single piece of paper in his hand.

Moving, looking back down the corridor as he went toward the stairs to the top floor, Muldoon said, thinking he had missed him, "Damn it! All the saints and— *God damn it!*"

"*VIRGIL!*"

He had missed him. While he had been downstairs in the cells with Grafton and Schwenk and then later at the front desk talking to Sergeant Fitzgerald, he had gone out the back way through the Mott Street entrance and he had missed him.

There were children sleeping upstairs, and Matron Webb.

"Virgil—"

It was Mrs. Webb with the countenance of a gargoyle and the soul of an angel he feared disturbing most.

"Virgil . . ."

At the bottom of the stairs, calling up into the darkness, Muldoon called out in a whisper, "Virgil, are you up there by any chance . . . ?"

At the window, he touched at his face.

At the window, he could go no farther.

At the window . . .

* * *

"Virgil Tillman, are you up there?" The light was on in Matron Webb's rooms numbers one through four where she lived with Janitor Webb, where, probably at this moment she had stopped drinking her nightly tea and listened.

There was nothing else on the fourth floor but a storage cupboard and the rooms where the children were.

On the landing, Muldoon listened. He looked at the door to the children's room.

He thought he heard a sound.

Going forward, reaching for the brass knob on the paneled, heavy door, clutching at his sheet of paper, Muldoon, tiptoeing so he would not awaken anyone, pushing open the door silently on oiled hinges, called in a whisper, "Virgil, are you up here . . . ?"

He had wanted, all his life, to say he was sorry to someone for what he had done wrong and for that person to forgive him and love him.

From the window, in the darkness across the city, there were only lights and silence.

He watched.

He waited.

They were dead, gone, and nothing now would bring them back to life.

He heard the children tossing.

"Virgil?" He saw him standing there as a shadow.

Tillman said to no one but himself, "I am so, so desperately sorry . . ."

He touched at his face.

Schweib, Carrol, Reynolds. He had nothing, nothing at all. He had done nothing, succeeded at nothing.

"I am so . . ."

Tillman said aloud, "I am so, so . . ."

* * *

Muldoon said in a whisper, "Cahill, Virgil."

Tillman said, "What?" Tillman said in a whisper, "What are you doing here, Ned?"

Ned said, "Cahill, Virgil. Warren Cahill. One of them in the Vicksburg picture, Warren Cahill." He had the sheet of paper in his hand from the Telegraph Office in the basement. Muldoon said, "Harry Roebuck got it in on his machine about half an hour ago. It's a wire. Harry is spitting chips because it was somehow sent on a police telegraph key without authorization or spliced in on a wire on the street." Muldoon said, "It's Warren Cahill." Muldoon said without having to look down at the paper, but holding it up anyway, "TO: TILLMAN, DETECTIVE BUREAU, HEAD-QUARTERS, MULBERRY STREET. WARREN CAHILL YOUR LIST RAT-CATCHER $101\frac{1}{2}$ CHERRY STREET THIS CITY STOP YOUR FRIEND EUSTACE C. JACKSON CHIEF VFB STOP." Muldoon said, "Chief VFB—" He had Tillman by the shoulder. In the moonlight, his eyes were shining, the bearer of good news.

Muldoon said in triumph, "Humpty Jackson, Chief, Volunteer Fire Brigade—"

Muldoon said, "God bless his evil little deformed black heart, *he's found one of them for you who's still alive!*"

24

On Cherry Street lights glowed from the windows of a thousand tenement rooms, yellow, like fires in cave mouths in a mountain.

They were the lights and candles and lamps of the home workers, the piecework laborers—women, men, children—sewing, assembling, crocheting, knitting, blocking and dyeing hats with mercury, painting tiny whatnot decorative objects with lead paint, sewing gas mantles with asbestos string sucked at the tip to enter the eyes of needles, rag picking for threads, working with uncurtained windows closed, their single rooms crowded with relatives and children and mattresses, the garbage in the alleys and lanes below their windows rotting and redolent and putrefying in pools and puddles of urine, the garbage rustling with rats yellow in the gaslights affixed, all broken or splintered or cracked, to walls and posts in the street.

On all the walls of the ground floor of Gotham Court, the first of the great New York tenement houses built on the Lower East Side of the city in 1839, now in darkness, unsafe, all the internal walls, floors and staircases inside it collapsing, the bill posters had had their way.

> ## Dr. MORSE'S INDIAN ROOT PILLS
> ### The Best Family Medicine
> ### IN USE

The Star of Hope . . .
S A V E D !
By Dr. WM. HALL'S BALSAM
—For the Lungs—

PARKER'S CELEBRATED STOMACH BITTERS!
STAND ALONE AS A VEGETABLE MEDICINE
That Is a CURE for DYSPEPSIA,
Loss of APPETITE, General DEBILITY
And all Forms of MALARIA FEVERS
TRY IT NOW. DON'T WAIT!

MALT BITTERS
The Purest and Best Medicine in the World for
Nourishing and Strengthening and for Overcoming
Debility and Wasting Diseases.
The Perfect Blood, Brain and Nerve Food.
STIMULATION WITHOUT INTOXICATION
It Is Marvelous.
BEWARE OF IMITATIONS

THE TEN REASONS

Following will prove why no family in America should
be without Dalley's Magical Pain Extractor
constantly in the house.

BECAUSE *it cures Burns and Scalds, and leaves No
Scar.*

BECAUSE *it will cure a Felon quicker than anything
else known.*

BECAUSE *it gives relief at once, and always cures the
Piles.*

BECAUSE *by it the agony of Corns and Bunions is
relieved immediately.*

BECAUSE *it will make Chapped Hands smooth in a
night.*

BECAUSE *it draws from Ulcers and old Sores their
poison, healing without Scar.*

BECAUSE *Erysipelas and Skin Diseases have found in
it a master.*

BECAUSE *Inflammation in every form gives way to it
as if by magic.*

BECAUSE *since 1840 it has never failed to give satis-
faction.*

BECAUSE *the dealers who sell it will tell you the same
story.*

DALLEY'S MAGICAL PAIN EXTRACTOR
IS SOLD BY ALL DRUGGISTS.
25 Cents THE BOX.

PROFESSOR C. K. QUARTERNIGHT'S GREAT WILD WEST ROUND-UP AND EDUCATIONAL ENTERTAINMENT
Niblo's Gard—

Someone had ripped away the chromolithograph of the Professor on his white horse firing his guns at Indians at full gallop on the Plains, taken it away to a room somewhere, and where the portrait had been there was only a blob of paste and backing paper and the crumbling mortar and bricks behind it.

Facing the postered wall, no longer reading the words, a shadow in an unbuttoned light topcoat and hat, with a dark silk scarf across his nose and mouth against the foul air, the left-handed man turned his head slightly to number 101½ Cherry Street a little down the sidewalk and watched the lights.

He waited.

He had left his rented phaeton carriage tethered to a ring post two streets away, and, watching the lights in the windows of 101½, he waited with his hands in his pockets, standing straight, silently, like a soldier.

She's been work-ing in a broth-el!
We'll tell!
Broth-el!

There were five of them, ragged guttersnipes from one of the alleys or doorways. They were boys aged between fourteen and seventeen, one of the Vampire gangs who extorted money from the housewives doing part-time work at bordellos. Sometimes, depending on the physique, they followed men through the streets to their homes chanting, but generally local women working for the bordellos were easier. They came out with money.

She's been working in a broth-el!
We'll tell!
Broth-el!

They were halfway down the street under a gas lamp, in a circle, the woman in the center of the circle touching at her hat and trying to find an opening.

She's been working in a broth-el!

We'll tell!

Broth-el!

There were pools of light on the flagstone sidewalk and dark shadows of earth where the flagstones had given way, collapsed, subsided, or been stolen for some purpose, the roadway out from the sidewalk glistening dark with broken bricks from the setts, all up and down the sidewalk and out onto the roadway garbage that had been thrown from windows.

"Give us some of your money!"

The woman must have said something, but there was no sound. In the center of the circle she had stopped trying to push her way through. Some of the younger boys were looking up at her.

"She's been working—" They were the voices of young children.

"Shut up!" It was an older voice, someone on the brink of leaving child's play and joining a real gang with guns. The older voice said as an order, "Give us some of your money, lady!"

The left-handed man watched the lights in the three-story building at 101½. Through the curtainless windows and the windows with no glass where the stairs and air ducts were, the left-handed man watched the beams of light from the flashing, changing hand-held bull's-eye lanterns as Tillman and Muldoon moved through the rooms.

She must have said something, or got through. The circle had become a line with her at the head hurrying to the corner on heeled leather boots, and the line was turning like a snake, going in front of her and then breaking away.

"She's been working . . ."

"Give us some of your money, lady!"

She was at the corner, starting to turn.

"Give us—!"

The lights in the building were high up, flickering and moving on the third floor, brighter than candles, passing out of windows into the darkness in beams, moving, changing, crisscrossing, hunting.

"BITCH! GIVE US—GIVE US EVERYTHING NOW, YOU BITCH!" There was a thump.

"She's been work-ing . . ."

"Shut up!"

Whispers. There was a thump. The woman, alive or dead, made no sound at all. The circle had formed again, moving around the corner out of sight.

"BITCH! *BITCH!"*

She's been working in a broth-el!
We'll tell!
Broth-el!
On the street, in the pools of light and darkness, there was no sound at all, nothing.

He waited.

By the postered wall with his back to the roadway, the left-handed man waited straight and still with his gloved hands in his topcoat pockets, watching the lights.

. . . You've been in a broth-el!
I'll tell!
Broth-el!
It was a thirteen- or fourteen-year-old boy, one of the gang maybe left out of the split.

"You're a *gent!*" He saw the scarf. Gents had noses too delicate for the smell.

This gent's been in a broth-el!
I'll tell!
Broth-el!
He watched the lights. At the wall, standing straight, he had his head inclined slightly on his shoulder and, up there, as the beams moved and crossed and searched, he watched the lights.

In his pockets, his hands were locked into fists.

You've been in a brothel . . ."
The boy, in rags, barefooted, was dancing back and forth behind him.

"I'll tell . . ."
The man's left hand was coming out of his pocket, moving in front of him by the wall, out of sight, bringing out money.

I'll tell . . .
Broth-el!
There was a sudden sound: a shhh-CLICK! and the man in the darkness turned with only his eyes showing above the dark silk scarf and the steel of the switchblade knife at the end of his revolver glittered in the light.

The eyes looked through him into Hell.

Shh-CLICK!

There was a flash of light as the razor edge jumped back into the body of the gun and the man's hand twitched with the force.

The left-handed man turned back to the wall and watched the lights.

He heard, behind him, running for his life, the sound of the barefooted boy.

His gloved hand holding the gun going back into the pocket of his topcoat in a fist he could not open, the left-handed man, his body rigid like oak, trembling, shaking with the tautness, inclined his head slightly on his shoulder and watched the lights.

He waited.

On Cherry Street, in the glow and shadows of the gas lamps and all the windows in all the buildings above and behind and around him, he waited like stone, watching the lights.

25

In 101½ Cherry Street they were on the wooden steps on the first floor, shining their lanterns down through the doorless brick entrance to the basement.

The beams crossed on the floor and lit up broken bricks subsiding into the soft clay of the building's foundations. There was a fug in the room: a sort of blue haze moving in fingers across the bare floor. Tillman lifted up the beam of his lantern to the walls. The walls were ancient, cracked and broken gray plaster over bricks and mortar. There were lines of blackness and slime running down the walls and, above them, where the ceiling had been, broken laths and mounds of gray, soaked powder gone solid in lumps. The smell was pungent, airless. At the entrance to the place, the whale oil in the three-inch bull's-eye-lensed lanterns fizzed and spluttered and began giving off a thick black smoke through their chimneys.

There were rags in bundles in the corner of the deserted, vile room—the coiled and twisted, soaked wet and hardened rags of poverty—things too far deteriorated and caked with God knew what to be of any use to anyone.

Muldoon moved his lantern and lit up a corner of the room. The corner had gone, the bricks and mortar given way with age and moisture, the laths and plaster in the ceiling above broken and hanging down like straw.

There were no windows. There was something in the middle of the room, lying at an angle like the top of a coffin come back to the surface in an ancient graveyard. It was a flagstone stolen from the street. Like a raft, the near corner of it sank down into mire and bled black, evil-smelling ooze out onto the floor.

Muldoon said in a whisper, "Nothing here." He listened. There

224

was the sound of water dripping somewhere and he shone the light around the walls to find it and could not. He had his free hand on the butt of his gun in his hip pocket. He took a step down from the stairs like a cautious spelunker entering a cavern and tested the floor against his weight. Muldoon said, "Nothing." He stood listening to the sound of the dripping.

He looked up. Muldoon said, "This ceiling isn't safe." He moved carefully, throwing the light up into the laths and plaster. Muldoon said, "This whole building is going to come down." He reached up and touched at one of the laths with the gentlest of touches and it cracked, making a shifting sound, and brought plaster down.

"Shh—*listen!*" He heard the dripping. Tillman, raising his hand—a shadow behind the yellow beam of the light—said, "*Listen . . .*"

"There's nothing here."

"Listen. Listen . . ." He had his head cocked to one side, his eyes starting to run and smart from the pungent smell of the rot in the ceiling and on the wall. He listened. He threw the beam down onto the floor and followed it toward the west wall—to the darkness at the far end of the room. Tillman said, "There. It's coming from there." He squinted his eyes as, with the beam—coming back along it on the light—there was a sharper smell. Tillman said, "There's a sewer somewhere. There's a—" He raised the light and lit up the far wall at chest height. Bricks and slime. Tillman said, "There—" The circle of light on the wall was moving through the darkness. Tillman said, "There . . ." He lowered the light and illuminated caked hard rags and more slime on the floor.

The light, without warning, passed through the wall and went a long way away and then faded out, out of range. Tillman said, "*There!*" There was a hole on the wall like a cavern hole, big enough for a man to pass through on hands and knees. Beyond the cavern, the hole, there was darkness. He heard the dripping.

Tillman said, "There! It's a sub-basement, an old vault under the street." The floor through it was clean, rubbed smooth by the knees of someone crawling through. The smell. It was coming from there.

The smell was palpable, terrible, poisonous.

Sucking in a last breath of air from the basement room, getting down on his hands and knees, shining the beam of the lantern ahead of him like a probe, Tillman, not hesitating, crawled in. .

* * *

Muldoon said, *"Sweet Jesus!"* It was like lattice, like broken and torn latticework on a gazebo or plant house, or like one of the old, ruined, centuries-old gardener's ferneries on the grounds of the old, overgrown and deserted castles from County Meath in Ireland.

The roof of the place was the sidewalk of Cherry Street, supported by ancient cracking oak beams and bricks beneath the flagstones, all the joints and mortar gaps—the flagstones themselves—cracked and holed and open to let in the light from the street lamps above like an upside-down forest of light, the branches and vines and shafts of light perforating the dank, vile little room like some sort of magic, fading, dead forest.

It was the rat-catcher's room. Everywhere, in piles, in bundles, ordered and disordered, there were wire rat-traps meant to catch rats alive. Muldoon said, *"Jesus!"* There were rat pelts on the floor, rolled in salt to cure them, rat bones in one corner by the far wall where the dripping came from—where a sewer channel ran behind the wall—and everywhere the smell of ancient death and squirming and the convulsions of small animals caught in traps, long dead, drowned in a cauldron against the wall.

Tillman moved the beam from his light and lit up a wooden pallet with black rags on it. It lit up, on a nail on a wooden beam, a tin cup and, by it, on another nail, a cracked and blackened enamel jug. It lit up a shelf on a splintering black beam holding up part of the sidewalk. On the shelf, it lit up a pair of filthy, broken black boots. In the far corner it lit up a bundle of rags, and then another, and then another, bagged in ticking.

The smell was awful. The beam lit up a wooden vat in the center of the place with a lid on it, the staves and rings stained and disgusting, white with oxidation and decay, full of human and animal urine for rat-pelt tanning. Muldoon said, "God—" Muldoon said as Tillman's light moved away to behind his back, searching along the walls, "God in Heaven!"

Tillman said, "Goods!" He was at the wall by the hole, his light tight and hard and bright at point-blank range on a pile of rags and traps. He was pushing them with his shoe, moving them aside, making them make metallic sounds as the traps fell away. Tillman said, "A tin box. A clay pipe. Bottles." He was down on his haunches, waving the rags aside with his fingers. Tillman said, "Goods. Valuables." There was the sound of a bottle breaking on the brick floor: "This is where he stores his—" There was an alcove behind one of the great beams. Tillman, lighting it a fraction, said, "And here there's—" The alcove was closed off by a sheet of blackened, corrugated roofing iron. He pulled at it. Tillman said, "Behind this there's—" Tillman said, "It's stuck." He was on his knees, pulling at it. Tillman said, "Ned."

"Let me have it." He had his light on the floor, the beam lighting up the heavy wooden beam holding up part of the sidewalk. Muldoon, wrenching at it, said, "Here. Pull here." It was stuck, held fast by something. Muldoon, shaking his head, getting close to the jammed sheet of iron, trying to get his fingers around it, said, "No, *there!*" He nodded as Tillman got his fingers around a bulged section of the sheet. Muldoon said, getting down to his work, "Yeah, *there*— Muldoon, straining, said, "On three: one . . . two . . . *three!*"

Muldoon, using all his strength, said, "*Yaaahhh!*"

It stuck.

"*Yaahh!*"

It stuck.

Muldoon, flexing his back, getting his face up against the iron, hauling like a Hercules, said, "YAAHHH!"

Muldoon, falling over, going backwards with the iron as the light on the floor lit up the face of a man behind the iron, said, "Oh!" It lit up the face of a man gone to white powder sitting on a stone, half hunched against the corner of the alcove. Muldoon, going over, reaching for his gun, said, "Oh . . . !"

It was a face gone stark white and powdery, a face a thousand years old. It was the face of a nightmare.

It moved.

It was sitting hunched up on the stone with its hands dropped between its drawn up legs and the face, half hidden by a scarf over the head and ears, moved.

Muldoon, on the floor, scrabbling for his gun, flailing on the floor, all the tendrils of light from the ceiling seizing at him, shouted in terror, "*AAAHHHGGHH!*"

"*Cahill!*" He had him out from his rat hole in the alcove, from his hiding place. He had him on his knees in front of him, slapping at him. He was alive, like pieces of broken china dug up from a garden covered in white dust and filth. His eyes would not open; they were shut tight, without muscles, coverings for his eyes, dust, all dust.

The coat he wore was made from a hessian sack, caked hard with powder and blood. Tillman, slapping at him, said, "Cahill!" Everywhere in the alcove there were bottles thick with dust. There was the stink of human urine. It was on his coat and the rags he wore to cover his limbs. His body was rubber. The eyes would not open. He slapped at him, but there was no resistance and it was like slapping putty. Tillman, shaking him, shouted, "Cahill! Warren Cahill! *Are you Warren Cahill?*" Muldoon was on his feet behind him, shaking himself like a dog. Tillman, yanking hard at the hessian coat around the man's neck to keep him from falling over backwards on his knees, said in disgust, "He's a drunk! He's a hopeless drunk! He's a goddamned *drunk!*"

Muldoon said, "I slipped, that was all. I just slipped."

Tillman said, "He's a drunk. His brain's rotted." He could have strangled the man. "He's a hopeless shell! His brain has rotted out of his head with alcohol and he's just a—" The beam from the lantern Muldoon set on a pile of rags lit up the face. The face was dead. Tillman, shaking at the man, said, "He can't even open his eyes!" Tillman said, at the end, in a fury, "After everything! After everything, he's destroyed himself and there isn't a goddamned thing we can do to change it!" Tillman said in a fury of frustration, "After so long, after coming so close . . ." Tillman said, "*God damn it!*"

The neck was like rubber. The head, like a baby's, fell back with no resistance.

Tillman said to anyone who might listen, "*God damn it!*"

The lights from the sidewalk filled the awful place with tendrils, like seaweed. They filled the place with yellow light like a tomb underwater. They filled the place . . .

"*God damn it to Hell!*"

He was a boneless body. He was a sack of rags.

"God damn it, Ned . . . !"

He was gone, drifted away. Behind the closed eyes there was no human being, no voice, no sight, no life there.

"God damn it, Ned . . ." Letting him down, putting the limpness, the dust, the dead, empty face, the stench gently onto the stone step where, like a dog, like an insect, he must have crawled days, maybe weeks before, Tillman, shaking his head, trying to get his breath in the foul air, his eyes running from the acrid pungency of the sewer, said to anyone who might listen, "God damn it! God damn this man and this goddamned detective business—God damn them! God damn both—both of them—to Hell!"

* * *

He waited.

On the street, listening, hearing the sounds of voices through the broken sidewalk, the left-handed man, as he had in the shadows outside Headquarters all through the night, uncaring of time, unmoving, unblinking—rigid—waited.

"Ned . . . !"

He felt it. As he put the man down he felt it around his neck under the filthy garment he wore under his coat.

"Ned—!" He felt its shape. He had his hand on it in a fist. Tillman, grasping at it, feeling it against his palm, said, shaking, "Ned . . ."

He had his hand around it. Squeezing, he felt its shape. "Ned . . ." He was rigid, a cold tremor moving up his arms and his neck like electricity.

"*Ned . . . !*"

He touched it. He put his fingers in under the garment uncaring of lice or sores and touched it and it was hard and sharp and it was glass, and he put his hand around it and it was on a piece of string or cord, tied to a little brass hook embedded in it, and it was—

It was a colored, glass bottle stopper.

"Ned . . ." In a jerk he wrenched it free from the cord and there, there he had it in his open palm and all the lights in the pretty thing glittered, and he had it, there, in his palm.

It was a whisper. Still holding the man in the alcove, but gently, with no force to it, Tillman said so softly Muldoon had to strain to hear him, smiling, "Ned, you're a drinking man . . ."

Muldoon said softly, "Yes."

Tillman said, not listening, the smile on his face thin and coming and going in the light, "You're a drinking man, Ned . . ."

Tillman said softly, a muscle at the side of his mouth working, his eyes cold, "You and I, Ned . . . if it takes all night or the rest of our lives . . . you and I—"

He was shaking, trembling.

Tillman said in a whisper, "You and I, Ned, here, now—whatever it takes—you and I are going, now, *to sober this drunken bastard up!*"

He had the glass bauble.

It glittered, glittered in his hand.

26

Muldoon said in disgust, "You unlovely man—!" He had Cahill held around the knees in a bear hug up in the air above the open vat of urine, head-down. Muldoon said, raising him up a fraction, "You smelly, unlovely, disgraceful man—"

"Put him in!" He had the cover for the twenty-gallon vat of slime and urine up in his hands like a shield. The urine was seething, bubbling with a stench that drew all the breath from him. It was hissing with nitrates, lava-like, thick with ancient rat pelts. Tillman said, "Drown him in it!"

He drowned him in it. He lowered him in head-first to the shoulders and drowned him in it. He felt the knees twitch, jerk. He felt a kick of galvanism as all the muscles in the hips and chest jumped as the lungs filled with it, fought for air, turned to fists with the shock, tried to expel it, and then, not expelling, sucking it in, sent a throe of horror through all the muscles and kicked.

He held him down. He was kicking, trying to get out. Muldoon, staggering, gripping the knees, held him under.

There was a bubble, an explosion under the liquid. There was a shock through Cahill's entire body, a convulsion.

"Pull him out!" The lights from the lanterns set on the floor lit the wooden vat like a torture instrument, like something black and staved and diabolical in a castle cellar pierced by shafts of yellow light from the broken ceiling.

He came out. The eyes were still closed, the arms limp, hanging down. He was like a slaughtered carcass.

"Again!" and Muldoon set him into the foaming liquid to his shoulders.

There was a bubble, an explosion, a sound, an explosion of bubbles.

"Pull him out!"

Muldoon pulled him out and he came out gagging, the scarf gone from his head, his hair falling out in tufts from some disease, his face with the dust washed off blotched and red and scabified, his arms waving like a frog's.

The mouth was running with vomit, the eyes still, forever, closed.

"Put him back in!"

"—Virgil—!" He had his arms around the man's knees, the feet inches from his face. He was staggering. The feet had been bound in rags. The rags had come loose. Muldoon, getting his breath, staggering through the beams of light trained on the vat, said in alarm, "Virgil, he's got no toes on his left foot!"

"Put him back in and hold him there!"

"There's a wound on his ankle—a war wound!"

Tillman said, "Put him in!"

"Virgil . . . !"

"Put him in!"

He came alive. In that instant, he came alive in a single spasm and convulsed, kicked, fought, all his muscles in a seizure, a paroxysm, epitasis.

Muldoon shouted, "Virgil!"

"Put him on the ground!" He was vomiting, gagging, coughing, his lungs full of poison jerking and contracting, inflating, pushing like pistons. "Get his mouth open!" There was a broken lath from the ceiling on the ground. The man on the ground was thrashing, kicking. Tillman yelled, "Get his mouth open so I can get the lath in to stop him biting through his tongue!" Muldoon was wrenching at the mouth, forcing the jaws open. The mouth was foaming, bubbling. There were no teeth. They all had rotted out. Tillman, dropping the lath and hunching over the man's back with the flailing arms locked in hammering at him, ordered Muldoon, "Get over the legs! Don't let him kick!"

"Virgil, the toes have been chewed off by rats!"

"Hold him loosely!" He was kicking, pushing, jerking. The eyes were open. They saw nothing. Tillman shouted into the face, into the eyes, "Cahill! *Warren Cahill!*"

He stopped jerking. He was momentarily still, wrung out, fluid bubbling from his mouth, and they got him over onto his back.

"*Cahill!*"

The eyes moved, contracted, went from pale to dark, then back again, but they moved.

"Cahill—Warren Cahill—Cahill, we're the *Police!*"

He was an inch from Cahill's face, exploring the eyes.

In the underground, stinking room, in that awful place, in Hell, Tillman shrieked at the eyes, "Close your eyes again, Cahill—close your goddamned eyes again and, by God, this time, *you'll sink!*"

Tillman shouted, "Vicksburg!" He was on his knees with a card in his hand, twisting it and turning it to read the words written on it in the light from the lanterns. It was a papragraph copied out from Ashbury's *Pictorial History of the United States.* Tillman shouted, "The first battle of Vicksburg, October to December 1862: *the first battle of Vicksburg was a siege fought by the Confederacy as a desperate attempt to stop the Federal forces under Grant and Sherman cutting the Confederacy in two by controlling the Mississippi River.*"

The creature was propped up against the side of the seething vat, his head fallen down onto his shoulders, his eyes blinking and open.

"*The first advance by two Union columns was made at the end of November 1862, and the Rebel forces, outnumbered, fell back! However, Grant's supply line to these columns was badly conceived, consisting of only one single-line railway, and the Rebels were able to cut it and give themselves time to regroup. This was achieved by Van Dorn's Confederate cavalry breaking through the lines and destroying an important Union magazine at Holly Springs!*"

Tillman shouted, "*The advance by the Union in disarray, Grant then sent a flotilla of ships and thirty thousand men to attack Vicksburg by water, but again Van Dorn cut the line and gave Rebel General Pemberton time to reinforce the Vicksburg garrison before Sherman could attack!*" Tillman shouted, "*Grant, for his part, had retreated and Sherman's unsupplied forces clashing with the strengthened, resupplied garrison were heavily repulsed with the loss of almost two thousand men!*" Tillman shouted, "Vicksburg! The first battle of Vicksburg!" Tillman shouted, "Vicksburg, 1862: Albert Schweib, Rufus Carrol, George Fenney, Henry Carver, "John," "Charlie," Colonel P. W. Seward, Shand, *Cahill!*"

The voices were coming up through the breaks and cracks and gratings in the sidewalk.

He heard them. The left-handed man, his face to the wall, heard them.

The left-handed man put his forehead to the wall and closed his eyes, his hands in the pockets of his topcoat.

"Oh, God . . ."

The left-handed man, his mouth dry and slightly open, heard the voices.

The left-handed man said in a whisper to the wall, "Oh, God, oh, God, oh, God—" He was sinking to his knees, unable to stop himself, his gloved hands coming out of his pockets to cover his eyes.

"Cahill! *WARREN CAHILL!*"

He heard the voices. He was on his knees covering his eyes, a shadow bent over against the wall, his mouth dry, all the sinews in his neck hurting.

"*—CAHILL!!*"

He heard the voices.

On the street, in the darkness against the wall, the left handed man heard the voices.

"—what was left of the Union ships and boats came down the Yazoo River through the bayous and the swamps in the rain ravaged by insects and sickness . . ." He had the glass stopper in his hand. Tillman shouted, "What is this? Where did you get this—what is it?" The eyes were wandering, out of focus, bubbles and vomit forming on the man's lips and caking on his chin. Tillman shouted, "Reynolds! Major General Ethan Reynolds of the Confederate Secret Service— why did he have one of these and why do you have one?" Tillman shouted, "Reynolds was a spy for the Confederacy at the time of Vicksburg—why did he still have one of these after twenty years and why do you have one? *Why?*"

Muldoon, also on his knees, demanded, "What unit were you and Schweib and Carrol and Seward in? What was your company? Your regiment? Your duties? Your orders?" He reached out and took Cahill by the shoulders and shook him. Muldoon yelled, *"What sort of soldiers were you people?"*

"What's the connection with the gun?" Tillman said an inch from Cahill's face, "A Gilbert and Greer Rebel revolver with the inspector's mark of Buford Samuel Townes on it!" Tillman said, "Townes worked after the war for the American Gun Company— why did Rufus Carrol have the gun?" Tillman yelled, "You were the tramp Mrs. Seward made wait at the fence when Schweib and Carrol went to see her husband!" Tillman shouted, "What happened that day? Did you locate Reynolds, Ethan Reynolds? Between the four of you did you discover he worked for the Edison Electric Company? Reynolds was the head of the Confederate Secret Service when you—all of you—were in the Union Army having your picture taken at Vicksburg! Twenty years after the war why did you have to locate him? What did he know?"

The eyes were going, fading. Muldoon, slapping him across the face with all the force he could muster, shrieked at him, "Wake up, you damned man!"

"Cahill! Warren Cahill—!" He was drifting away. Tillman, taking him hard in both hands by the shirt, shook him. He had the glass stopper held between his palm and thumb muscle. In the yellow light, all the colors in it glittered. The eyes were out of focus, the brain behind them wandering and ruined. Tillman said, "What is this? What does it *mean?*"

He was jerking, gagging, starting to go over onto the floor, gagging, something inside his chest coming up, the bubbles forming fast at his mouth. He was falling from the vat, collapsing, rolling away to the side like rubber, the bubbles everywhere at his mouth. He was falling over like a dead man, not vomiting—all the muscles in his chest and throat soft and sagging, the bile merely dribbling, emptying itself from him because it had nowhere else to go.

He fell on his side, his neck at an impossible angle, the bubbles forming.

Muldoon said, "Useless! Useless, useless man!"

On his knees, the left-handed man said in a whisper, "I'm a Southerner. I can choose! My mother was a Southerner and I can choose and that is what I chose." He had something hard in the watch pocket of his waistcoat and he reached in through the buttons of his topcoat and got it out and held it hard in his hand for strength.

On his knees on the street, the left-handed man said in a whisper to God, *"I'm a Southerner!"*

The object in his hand was a watch. He gripped at it hard. It was gold. Through his fingers, it caught the light from the street lamps and flashed.

On the street, on his knees, he heard the voices.

He heard God not at all.

He heard the voices.

* * *

"Give him a drink!" The creature was on the ground, finished, empty, washed out, the eyes open and blank staring at the stone floor, seeing nothing, all the bubbles and foam and vomit gone from his mouth, his tongue thick and lolling. Tillman asked, "Have you got your bottle with you? If you have, give him a drink!"

Muldoon was on his feet patting at his coat. Muldoon, shaking his head, said, "I haven't got a bottle. I left it at—" Muldoon said, "All I've got is my old patrolman's flute in the watch pocket of my pants here, and I'm not even sure there's anything—" It was the glass, revolver-shaped bottle the old-time patrolmen had used to put in their holsters instead of their guns on winter nights. Muldoon said, "All I had in it was a bit of rum and I think—"

"Give it to him!" Muldoon was towering above him in the yellow light, reaching into his clothing, pulling the glass bottle free, careful not to dislodge the cork: "Even if there's just a smell—"

Muldoon said, "—of the Creature as they used to say in—" Muldoon said, pulling it out, "Got it." He looked down at it and shook the glass bottle, "A drop left. Just a drop."

"Give it to him."

The face was pale, blotched, not human. The eyes were gone. It was nothing but—

Muldoon, the glass gun up in his hand, reaching for the cork, coming closer as Tillman bent to take Cahill in his arms to turn his face toward the light, said softly, advancing, "Here. You poor, bloody ruined man . . . here—"

"*KILL ME!!*" Before Tillman could grasp him he jerked, kicked, pulled away, squirming, scrabbling, digging in the ground with his hands. On the stone floor Cahill shrieked to the shadow above him with the gun, "In the name of God, kill me cleanly! Shoot for the head!" He was scrambling, squirming, turning, trying to get up, reaching out for Muldoon's legs, grasping them, trying to force his head up to the glass gun, "Don't cripple me! Don't leave me for the rats— KILL ME LIKE A MAN!" His leg was jerking, going under his body. He was hiding the ankle where he had once been wounded. Cahill shrieked, his hands together in prayer, "For the love of God! For the sake of my mother—don't shoot me in the foot and leave me a cripple for the rats!"

Tillman, reaching for him, yelled, "CAHILL!"

Cahill shrieked, "Please! Please! Everyone's dead! Don't shoot me in the ankle and leave me for the rats and the corpses!" He had Muldoon by the legs, gripping them, squeezing, holding him fast, his eyes up into the light and the shadows where the glass gun was. Cahill, his eyes bright and wide, pleading, yelled, *"Don't leave me here at night in the swamp with the corpses and the rats!"*

He was at Vicksburg. He was back at Vicksburg, in the bayous, in the swamps.

Tillman yelled in an instant, *"You blue-belly bastard!"*

"Don't cripple me!"

Muldoon said, trying to shake him loose, "I'm not—"

Tillman yelled above the squirming man, *"We're Van Dorn's cavalry!"*

Muldoon said, "What the hell's going on?" He started to put the glass gun back in his pocket out of sight.

Tillman shouted as an order, *"Trooper, shoot that man in the ankle and let him stay here with the rats and the dead men of—"*

"Virgil—!?"

"We're Van Dorn's cavalry and we—"

Cahill screamed, "They're all dead! Everyone around me is dead! They're all dead!"

Tillman shouted, *"Schweib! Albert Schweib!"*

"He's gone! He's safe! He's crawled away and he's—"

Tillman demanded, *"Rufus Carrol! Where is Rufus Carrol?"*

"Run away!"

"And Fenney! Where is George Fenney!"

He was whimpering, sobbing, howling like a dog. Cahill said, "He's dead! Poor Georgie—poor, beautiful George is dead!"

"Where's your Colonel? Where's Seward?"

"Sick!" Cahill said, "All sick! Everyone sick and—" He saw the gun in the Reb trooper's hand. He saw the issue Gilbert and Greer revolver. He saw the cylinder revolve to a fresh charge as the dismounted Johnny Reb saw him and, out of pity, lowered his aim from his face to his ankle. Cahill screamed, "You condemned me to the rats!" Cahill shrieked, "We're all sick! We can't fight! Pretty Georgie's dead from it and Seward's crawled into the swamp to die and Carrol and Albert and—" Cahill howled. "Oh please—in the name of compassion, *kill me clean!*"

Muldoon said, unable to understand, "Pretty Georgie . . . ?" He understood. He gagged at the thought. Muldoon, trying to kick the man away, roared, "What unit are you? WHAT UNIT ARE YOU?"

Tillman said, "Lovers! They're a unit of lovers!" Tillman, down beside Cahill, said with his face twisted, *"Where is this place?"*

"Browne's Bayou magazine! Holly Springs!"

Tillman said softly to Muldoon, "Where Van Dorn made his breakthrough to cut Sherman's supply line."

Muldoon said in horror, "Lovers? The Sods' Unit? The sodomites? The—" Muldoon said with his eyes wide with horror, "They were all—? This man was part of—" Muldoon said, aghast, "My God, they had no unit marking, they had all sorts of weapons and badges and—they had—" Muldoon said, looking down at the crawling, howling creature about his legs, "They were the Sods' Unit? The buggers, the homosexuals removed from—" Muldoon said, "My God, I heard about them in the war!" Muldoon said, "They were a unit of men-fuckers thrown out of regiments and companies all through the Army and they—" Muldoon said in disgust and abhorrence, trying to shake the grip loose from his legs, "All of them, Virgil, all of them: Schweib, that creature Carrol in his woman's clothing, the Colonel with the dried out wife, this one—all of them— *They were the Sods' Unit sent off into nowhere out of sight of the fighting men!"*

Tillman said tightly, "Give me an army of lovers and I shall conquer the world—Julius Caesar."

"These men were sexually insane! These men were criminals against Nature!"

"Cahill . . . !"

He had gone weak. He was weeping. He was at Browne's Bayou. He was in a hideous dark hole underground in Cherry Street, locked into an alcove like a spider. He was a drowner of rats. He was gone, finished, all his teeth rotted out, dressed in rags. Once, he had been a—

Once, he had been—

"Georgie!" He was weeping. "Georgie . . . pretty, pretty Georgie . . ."

He sobbed, holding Muldoon's legs, looking up, rocking back and froth.

Cahill, softly, in the voice of a mourning lover, said sadly, "Georgie, oh, Georgie, everyone's so, so sick . . ."

The watch had been a gift from President Jeff Davis. Inside, on the case, it was inscribed. On the street the left-handed man did not open it. It was merely a heavy object he held in his hand. It was his. He had had it hidden a long time and, now, on the first occasion he had wanted to carry it with him, he did not open it.

He had gotten up from his knees. Standing still, upright, his back against the postered wall, he touched at something hard under his topcoat, along his right side. The street was deserted, silent, lit in pools of yellow light by the hissing gas lamps.

He looked at the lamps.

He held the closed watch hard in his hand, in his closed fist.

He waited.

"What made you sick?" He knew the answer. Tillman, holding the man's shoulder, pressing the warmth into it, said again, insisting, "What made you sick?"

"The rats chewed off my toes in the swamp! The Reb shot for the ankle to spare me, but—" Cahill said, howling, "They came down on us screaming and shooting! We were sick! We all crawled into the swamp to die! Poor Georgie was with me and a Reb—"

"What made you all sick?"

He sang. Half propped up against the vat as if it were a tree and he were dreaming against it, as if he were still young, Cahill sang tremblingly, softly in a voice that had once been sweet,

> *It will buoy you up,*
> *Hip, hip hooray!*
> *And keep you fit*
> *And ready for it.*
> *Bonny brave soldiers in blue,*
> *This is the free fortification for you.*
> *Hip, hip hooray!*
> *We'll eat up those Rebels for sup!*

He had it in his hand. Tillman said, "It's the glass bottle stopper, isn't it? It's the stopper from a bottle of medicine of some sort, isn't it?"

> *Glug, glug, glug,*
> *In your hopper . . .*
> *And keep the stopper.*

He reached out and touched it in Tillman's palm. Cahill said softly, sadly, "Pretty, pretty . . ." Cahill said suddenly, somewhere else, talking to someone else, "Van Dorn came through at Browne's Bayou! No one expected— We were just a rear guard and no one—" His eyes were wide, staring. Cahill, shaking his head back and forth, shouted, *"No one expected the Rebs to break through there!"*

Muldoon said, "And you ran away and let them break through and destroy the magazine at Holly Springs!" Muldoon said, "When Sherman attacked Vicksburg, because of you, his lines of supply were cut and he lost two thousand men!"

"We were sick! We couldn't fight!"

"You were cowards! You were sodomites!"

Cahill said, "We were *poisoned!*"

Tillman said in a steady voice, "By who?"

"By the medicine wagon!"

Tillman said, "What medicine wagon?" He had the bottle stopper in his hand. He kept turning it over and over in his hand, looking straight at Cahill, trying to keep control. Tillman said again in a whisper, "What medicine wagon?"

"Rally, rally, rally, boys!" Cahill said, "They poisoned us so we couldn't fight!"

He found it hard to catch his breath. Tillman said again, evenly, patiently, "What medicine wagon?"

"They knew! They knew Van Dorn was forming to break through and they poisoned us before he came and we crawled away and—" Cahill said in the horror that had brought him to what he was, *"We weren't cowards!* THEY POISONED US! The wagon came by in the morning with free tonic in bottles with pretty stoppers to wear on your uniform for luck and then—" Cahill said, "And then they poisoned us! They " Cahill said, "Schweib, the Colonel, Rufus Carrol, me—we all came to New York to hide in a city and we—" Cahill said, "But we worked it out! At the Colonel's house, Albert and us, we—" His eyes were hard, narrowed, his mouth tight and twisted. "And they poisoned us that morning so we couldn't fight!"

Tillman said, "You were all discharged from the Army as cowards, weren't you?"

"They were going to shoot us! They didn't believe us! *They were going to stand us up against a wall and shoot us!"*

Tillman said in a whisper, "What medicine wagon? You know who was on it, don't you? You know because you found him here in New York, now, twenty years later, didn't you? And you found Reynolds, didn't you? You found the man from the Rebel Secret

Service who had conceived the idea, didn't you? And he told you who was on the wagon, *didn't he?*"

Muldoon said in a gasp, "My God, the watch from Jeff Davis!" Muldoon said, "We could have lost the war!"

"Who was on the wagon?"

Cahill said sadly, dreamily, "It was all painted with pictures of battles and flags and bonny, brave soldiers and . . ." Cahill said smiling, "It was all painted, like the stoppers all pretty and clean and pretty and . . ."

Tillman said with a patience that would last through eternity, "Who was on the wagon?"

"I saw the name!" He was weeping, but there was no sound, and he was talking not to them, but to Schweib and Carrol and Seward. It was his contribution, his last worth, his salvation, "I did. I saw the name under all the pictures . . ."

"What was the name?"

He was nodding, nodding. Cahill said, insisting like a child, "I saw what the wagon had been before it was a wagon to bring cheer to the soldiers. I saw the name. I did—I did!"

Tillman said, trying to hold his voice steady, "It had been a drummer's wagon, hadn't it?"

"I saw the name . . ."

"Before the war, it had been a wagon owned by a traveling drummer, a salesman, hadn't it?"

"I saw the name." Cahill, nodding, trying like a child to offer something to stay in the game, as he had offered it when Schweib and Carrol and the Colonel had found him, said happily, "I saw the name—I did!"

Cahill said in a shriek, "*We were all poisoned!* We weren't cowards!" Cahill said, "*We were all poisoned!*"

Cahill, shaking his head, shouting it to the Heavens, shrieked to explain after all those years, "That day, before Van Dorn hit, *we were poisoned by a traitor!*"

On the street, he had the gold watch from Davis in his open palm.

On the street, he heard the hissing of the gas lamps.

In the sky, dawn was coming in a spreading grayness and the glow from the lamps was fading as the morning came and there were slight fingers of cold with it.

The left-handed man, standing by the wall in the growing light, had his head bowed, listening.

He had no expression on his face.

He touched gently at a button on the watch and the case snapped open under the pressure of a spring and, tinkling, melodically there in the light and the stillness and the coming dawn, it chimed; it played a little tune.

He had his head bowed looking down at it.

It played, in that lonely, gray place, a little tune.

Tillman said, "Catton! It was Catton! F. C. Catton! *Wasn't it?* Painted on the side of the wagon under the pictures: "Catton." It was F. C. Catton—*wasn't it?*"

Cahill said like a child explaining an injustice, "By the time the cavalry hit us at dusk we were all sick. We were dying. Charlie was dead, and Shand, and—" Cahill said, "We crawled away into the swamp to die with our guts on fire, and we—"

"It was Catton—*wasn't it?*" He was trembling. He could not control himself. Reaching for the man's shirtfront and taking it in his fists, Tillman said into his face, "Catton! It was his wagon before the war—WASN'T IT?"

"We would have fought! We would have been brave!" Cahill said, "They cut through us like wheat! They came out of nowhere across the bayou and they cut through us like wheat!" He was rocking, humming, his eyes starting to go, "Rally, rally, rally, boys . . ."

"It was Catton—*wasn't it?*" He shook him like a rat, shouting. His face an inch from Cahill's, at the end, on the brink, there, Tillman shrieked, "F. C. Catton—he was a traitor! He pretended to be a Union sympathizer giving heart to the troops with his tonics and his free medicines—the medicines with the pretty tops you got if you drank the stuff straight down—and he poisoned you to cut a clear way for the Reb cavalry to break through to the river and the supply line at your strong point—*didn't he?*"

Muldoon said in a whisper, "God Almighty—" He looked down into Cahill's ruined face. Muldoon said in a whisper, "My God, man, to be branded all these years as a coward . . ." He had a picture of Colonel Seward in his garden, mute and weeping, wetting himself, all his war stories shameful secrets and— Muldoon said tenderly, going to the lost man against the vat, "Oh my God . . ."

"Catton! Say 'Catton'! Say it! Say *'Catton'!*"

"We . . ." Cahill said, drifting, smiling, weeping, "Rally, rally, rally . . . Rally, my brave boys. Boys, rally, rally, *rally* . . ."

"CATTON! SAY *'CATTON'!*"

Cahill said sadly, quietly, "On the wagon, under all the pictures and . . ."

Tillman said tightly, "Yes."

". . . all the . . ."

He waited, trembling.

Cahill said, "A salesman's wagon, a drummer's— For . . ." Cahill said like a child, happily, "I saw the name—"

He waited, his fists still gripping Cahill's shirt. He could not open his eyes. He waited through an eternity of darkness.

Cahill said, "F. C. . . . *Catton.*"

Tillman said, "Got him! *Got him!*"

In the awful room with the dawn turning all the yellow light gray and cold and full of dust, Tillman, at the end, yelled in final, total victory, "*—GOT HIM!*"

He had put the watch back carefully into his pocket.

On Cherry Street, the left-handed man waited with his coat open and his left hand crossed over his vest out of sight against his side.

He waited.

Catton waited.

It was dawn.

Under his coat he had a shortened and sawed-off American Gun Company single-shot .45–70 Plains buffalo rifle attached by a sling hook to a specially made swivel on his belt.

He waited.

He waited until the moment Cahill appeared at the end of the lane to Cherry Street with Tillman and Muldoon on either side of him, and then, drawing the weapon in a single arc and cocking the hammer and pulling the trigger in a single motion, all the buildings and windows in the place shaking and echoing with the roar, shooting for the head, killed him where he stood blinking at the light.

They were on either side of him: Tillman and Muldoon.

The blast, tearing at their ears, ripping the air around them apart like a burst boiler, knocked them both instantly off their feet.

27

He was blind from the blast, knocked back into the alley, covered in brains and blood. Cahill was on the ground kicking, in spasms, his head blown away, his arms flailing galvanically against Tillman's head and shoulders. The sound of the gunshot was still echoing, rolling against the tenements and buildings in the street. There was another roar and the sound of something being torn loose from a wall—mortar and bricks—and then the popping of Muldoon's .32 as he must have gotten himself upright and fired back. Tillman, pushing, rolling away from Cahill, wiping at his eyes with the back of his hand, yelled in the instant before the huge gun went off in the streets and sent a five-hundred-grain bullet tearing and whining off the corner of the alley, "Don't let him run! Stop him! *Don't let him run!*" He was on his feet, staggering with the third shock wave, reaching under his coat for his Lightning. Tillman seeing Muldoon on his knees at the end of the alley recovering from the shot, yelled again, *"Don't let him run!"*

"He isn't running!" Muldoon, chancing a glance around the corner, shouted, "He's in the middle of the street, reloading!" He had his little Smith and Wesson up, thumbing back the hammer for a quick shot around the alley.

"Relay! Shoot in relay!" They had to get out of the alley. Tillman, drawing a breath, getting to the corner of the alley, brought his Lightning up and, aiming for the street itself to keep the bullets from flying into the buildings, shot four times as fast as he could pull the trigger. Tillman ducking back to reload, yelled, "Fire on him!" He was on his knees pulling the fired cases out of the cylinder of the gun with his thumbnail. It was Catton. In the street, it was Catton. There were two quick shots as Muldoon emptied his Smith and Wesson and then, all six chambers of the Lightning

243

reloaded, Tillman was back at the corner of the alley shooting again.

He had the Smith reloaded in an instant. Muldoon yelled, "Loaded!" There was white smoke everywhere from the shots. Muldoon, pushing Tillman aside as Tillman bent down to the loading gate of the Lightning again, still holding back two shots, yelled, "I'm going to let him have them all!" He saw Catton standing there, closing the breechblock of the buffalo rifle. He saw it come up.

There was a blast from the street that hit a loose flagstone on the sidewalk and exploded it into dust. There was a click and then a ringing sound as Catton pulled open the action of the buffalo gun and sent the empty brass case bounding and ringing onto the roadway over his shoulder.

They were both fully loaded: Tillman with six shots in the Lightning and Muldoon five in the Smith and Wesson. On the roadway Catton had a huge hull of a shell in his hand, ramming it into the open breech of the rifle.

Tillman yelled, "Go!" and together he and Muldoon were out of the alley heading for the other side of the street, firing as fast as they could pull the triggers of the guns that waved, moved, jerked as they made for a doorway on the other side of the street.

Tillman yelled at Muldoon, "Load!" He had two shots left in his own gun. He saw Catton, working at the gun, look up and slam the breech shut and he put a shot so close to him that it actually hit the shoulder pad of his long coat and ripped away the lining. He had one round left. Muldoon was behind him in the doorway working at the catch on the little Smith to close it, dropping live rounds either from his hand or the cylinder. He saw Catton get the action closed. He saw the big gun come up, actually for an instant saw the black hole of the muzzle looking for him, and then, in the moment of firing, Muldoon laid down a fusillade of shots and the buffalo gun of its own volition, its own terror, went off and blasted into the air.

"Empty!" He was reloading, reaching into his pocket for what was left of his limited supply of cartridges. Muldoon dropping to one knee, trying to load with his eyes on Catton, yelled, "Empty, Virgil!"

They couldn't charge him. Catton had the breech open again, and the fired brass case flying out with the spring on the extractor and he was twenty-five yards away and both their guns were empty but for one round. The air was full of drifting white smoke.

"Load! Load, Ned!" He saw Catton get the shell in and then jerk as it stuck in the fouled breech. He saw him shove at it. He saw him look up in sudden terror, and Tillman, getting the loading gate of his Colt open and thumbnailing all the fired shells out, yelled, "He's jammed! Load! Load and we'll—"

The big shell made it into the breech of the buffalo gun, but the lever stuck and the breechblock would not close.

The were both loaded. Tillman yelled, *"Catton!"* and then the obstruction cleared and the gun came out closed and loaded and the muzzle was searching for them, found Muldoon on his knees, and in the instant Tillman, leaping at Muldoon like a cat to knock him aside, shrieked, *"Ned!"* detonated and blasted a track of dust and stone and pumice along the flagstone and step in front of them like an express train.

He was running. He had the fired shell flying out behind him and he was running, trying to reload. It had failed him, the gun, and he was running toward the stone doorway to Gotham Court fighting at it, wrenching something on it to clear it.

"Don't let him get into the buildings!" He fired, but at that range no one could hit anything with a revolver. Tillman, on his knees, trying to take aim at the man's legs, shooting off his entire load of six rounds and straddling the man's feet in dust and flying stone, yelled to Muldoon, "Wound him! Drop him!" The little Smith and Wesson went off five times in rapid succession beside him, but the bullets were too weak and they whanged off the ground with no more force than corks. They had fired thirty-eight rounds in less than the minute and a half since Cahill had been killed and hit nothing. Everywhere in the street there were people coming to their windows. In the gray, slate-sharp dawn, Tillman, running, trying to run the man down before he got into the tenement with his gun, yelled, loading the gun, dropping cartridges as he ran, *"Don't let him get into the buildings where the people are!"*

He was in the courtyard of Gotham Court, in the shadows of the five-story rotting buildings on three sides, running across broken cobbles and blocks and flagstones through rags and garbage and filth toward the main block of tenements.

Behind him, on the street, he heard them coming, their shoes ringing on the stones as they ran reloading.

The big gun was jammed shut with the fouling of the gunpowder from the shells as tightly as if it had been brazed and he could not get it open however hard he pulled down on the cocking lever. It was useless, a club, a length of useless wood and steel and he could not get it open to get a shell in and kill the first man through from the street.

He had a gun tool in his vest pocket on the end of his watch chain: a round extractor tool, a giveaway to shooters from the gun company with little sharpened edges for use as a turnscrew and he got it out, but there was nowhere to get the honed edge in against the frozen breechblock and as he pulled the tool the gold watch fell free and opened and began chiming at the end of the chain.

He heard them coming. Something in his shoulder hurt and he winced and saw that all the padding in his coat had been shot away and that there was blood running down the coat, and then, where the bullet had burned and ripped away the skin there was a sudden sharp pain and he reeled, still trying to work at the breech with the tool and, somehow, got the lever of the gun down and cleared the jam.

He had the gun loaded in an instant, the muzzle searching down the darkness of the tunnel to the street where they would come, and he saw a shadow and fired and filled the tunnel with an orb of violent yellow light that lit up Tillman's head and shoulders and seemed, in that moment, to blast his face away.

Muldoon yelled, *"JESUS!"* as the shockwave in the confined space hit him like a wall of water, then seemed to set him on fire, and then he was going backwards, reaching out for Tillman, falling, being knocked down and reaching with his flailing hand for Virgil, then there was a recoil in the tunnel—the wall of water coming back—as Tillman, standing like a rock, his hair flying in the hurricane of the buffalo gun's bullet, fired back his entire cylinder of six shots and the tunnel was full of smoke and stink and pungency and Muldoon could see nothing.

The shots were all going off the bricks in the tunnel.

The air was full of smoke and stink and powdered bricks.

Catton was turning, working the gun and running toward the doorway to the eastern block of the building, going for the stairs and the darkness.

He did not know whether he had been shot or not. Tillman, wrenching Muldoon up to his feet, deafened by the gunfire, yelled, "Ned! Ned! *Are you hit?*"

There was no light on the stairs except for a shaftway at the end of each of the corridors on each of the floors and he was running up inside a mountain, an extinct volcano, his shoes crashing at the rotting, rising planks and shaking them, weakening them, making them creak and groan as they started to give way.

He was saturated with sweat, his neck wet with it, his hands holding the gun slimy and slippery, his clothes thick and filthy and starting to stink under his armpits—his armpits burning.

He was running up the stairs through garbage, through filth and effluvia and trash, through bundles of rags in ticking bags and rags themselves and the droppings of rats and roaches and the roaches themselves, scurrying in hard-shelled whispers under his shoes.

The stairs were steep. He was running, pushing, taking the steps two at a time, his knees and calves starting to cramp with the effort. He was filthy, covered in burned powder, his hands slippery and slimy, black with the stuff becoming liquid with sweat.

He was breathing hard. He heard his own breath. It sounded like breath through consumptive lungs, through holed organ pipes, and he heard the flying watch broken, smashed, out of control, chiming, chiming at the end of its chain.

The gun action was clear. Dropping cartridges from his pocket as he tried to get them out with his hands wet and slippery, he heard them falling behind him as he ran, banging and ringing off the stairs. The walls of the stairway were thick with dirt and filth.

In the darkness, hearing Tillman and Muldoon on the stairs behind him, hearing clickings, snappings, sounds as they reloaded their guns, he got a shell into the breech of the sawed-off custom rifle and, shooting down into the darkness, tearing a thunderball of light and fire down at them, and, going up, going nowhere, *ran.*

He saw him. He was at a right angle to the stairs, going for the next flight, and in the fireball of light he saw him. He saw his eyes. He saw his face, blackened with powder like a china doll's, and he saw him there running, with the recoil of the huge gun pushing it up and to the right in his two hands. On the stairs, with Muldoon behind him, Tillman saw him.

The light from the shot was going. It was holding. It was gone. It was a retina image and it was still there, and bringing up the Lightning, trying to hold a sight picture as the light or the shadow of the light or the image of the light faded faster than he could think, Tillman, aiming hard, fighting to keep his hands steady, shot the image once in the upper leg.

He had hit him.

He had missed and the bullet had gone into a room somewhere where there was a family, or—

"*Aaah—!*"

He heard him scream.

Somewhere up there, in the darkness, he had hit him.

In the darkness, up there, he heard Catton scream with the pain.

There were doors opening and slamming. In the tenements they slept twelve or thirteen to a room: men, women, children, their rooms nothing but stables with straw on the floors and wooden pallets around wooden tables and trestles and workbenches where they all worked at their labors in shifts.

He saw faces at the doors, pinched, white—the faces of children in rags framed by faint lights of candles or lamps or the coming day from the windows behind them, their eyes wide and brown like rats' eyes.

He saw them see him. He was climbing, going higher, his leg hard-shot and bleeding, his face and hands black with the slime from the gun, his coat where the first bullet had hit him in rags, losing padding like a scarecrow, his breath coming like a consumptive's, the watch at the end of the chain, turning and spinning, glittering in the faint light, chiming, chiming . . .

He had nowhere to go. He was crippled, shot hard, starting to flag, covered in sweat and slime, ceasing to be who he was, going up, going nowhere. He was foaming bubbles at the mouth.

He was bleeding, hurting, sinking into slime, being pursued, run down.

He heard them coming.

He was screaming with the pain.

He was becoming a rabid dog.

On the landing of the fourth floor Catton, gasping, failing, dropping the gun on the floor by his feet, his lips drawn back over his teeth, drew his little knuckle-duster knife pistol from his pocket and, hearing them coming, turned to stop and fight.

"*Police! Shammes! Politzei! Carabinieri! Garda!*" He had no idea who they were. They were the faces of the poor. They were coming out of their rooms staring, their faces white, blanched with no sun, their eyes blinking. They were the tenement dwellers, women, men, children, grandparents. At the doors, they were coming out. He was on the third floor, heading for the landing for the fourth, the second-to-last level. They saw him and Muldoon with their guns out, blackened like Africans.

"*Get inside!*" Tillman, waving them in with his gun, gasping for breath, running fast for the stairs to get Catton while he was still screaming with the pain from the wound, yelled in English, Yiddish, German, Italian and what he thought was Irish, "*Police! Shammes! Politzei! Carabinieri! Garda!*"

They understood not one of the words. They were something else, from somewhere else.

Tillman screamed in English, "*Get inside your rooms!*"

He reached the riser at the stairs to the next floor and, not stopping, with Muldoon only inches away behind him, took the stairs two at a time without pausing, up into the darkness.

He was gasping, panting, puffing, trying to form words. He was hurting, bleeding. At the top of the stairs, looking down, his eyes wide and staring, Catton said over and over, "Shoot for the navel. Shoot a man in the navel and you may not kill him, but you'll put his nervous system out and paralyze his brain, and then—" He had been told that by a shootist, by a Westerner, "Shoot for the navel and . . . shoot for the navel of a man and . . ." He was losing strength, then gaining it, then losing it again, the little gun held out stiff in his hand: "*Shoot for the navel and . . .*"

"*NED—!*"

"*JESUS IN* "

They were caught on the stairs. Catton, on the landing above them, his hand stiff, outstretched, fired everything in the gun down the stairs and tore the wall to pieces and splintered the banisters and lit up everything in a single volley of shots fired too quickly to be distinguishable as separate, and in the same instant was devoured by the flashes from Tillman's and Muldoon's guns as they shot back and tore all the floor and stairway newels around him to shreds.

At the top of the stairs he was screaming, hit, staggering, running blood in rivulets down the risers.

Muldoon said, "Virgil, I'm hit!" and he was gone, rolling back, falling over and over.

"*CATTON—!*" He saw the man as a shadow, a form, and he brought the Lightning up, but there was only a click and Catton was reloading his own gun, pulling at something on the cylinder, sending empty cases flying in the air, and Muldoon was rolling away, going over and over calling for him.

"*Ned—!*" He had the Lightning in both hands, pulling at the loading gate, wrenching at the fired case heads with his thumbnail, but they were jammed in tight and would not come and he could only get one out. Tillman yelled, "Ned— HOLD ON!" He tried to see Muldoon's pistol but it was gone with him, and Muldoon was at the bottom of the stairs, rolling with the pain.

He heard a clicking and he got a single round in his own Lightning and slammed the loading gate shut not knowing where the live round was in the cylinder.

Tillman yelled, "Ned! Are you—"

Muldoon yelled up, "In the hip! I'm hit in the hip! There's no blood— I'm just knocked down!" He was rolling, moving away, reaching for his revolver beside him.

Muldoon, not finding it, hearing Catton on the landing, yelled, "Get him! Get him! *Get him!*"

"*CATTON!*"

He was finished. The little gun was empty. There were no more shells in his pocket, and even if there were his left arm had ceased to work with the first wound and he could not work the loading mechanism, and he was finished.

"CATTON—!"

On the landing, shot through, Catton, his shoulders bent, trying to catch his breath, covered in filth, waited.

He was coming, coming cautiously. Tillman said carefully, "Catton—"

Tillman taking the steps one at a time, moving up with the gun out in his hand, thumbing back the hammer to feel for the faint resistance of the single shell against the recoil shield, said evenly, slowly, "Catton, this is City Detective Tillman . . . Catton, you won't get down the stairs again . . ."

He waited, looking down.

Tillman said, "Catton . . ." He felt the loaded shell, looser in the cylinder than the fired ones, touch the recoil shield of the revolver. He felt it as a slight, minute pressure. "Catton . . . the other man isn't dead. The other man's at the bottom of the stairs waiting for you and you won't . . ." He heard no sound at all. Tillman said with his heart in his mouth, "Catton . . . This is

City Detective Tillman. You know me. We've spoken as fellow men to each other . . ."

Tillman, six steps from the landing in the darkness, said in a whisper, "Catton?"

He saw him at the top of the landing. Tillman said in warning, "*Catton!*"

"*Catton!*"

He was walking, shuffling, looking down at the blood on the floor, looking down at its shadow, feeling it flow. The watch was still chiming, running down but chiming, and he smiled a little at that.

"*Catton!*"

There was someone calling. Catton, lifting the hand with the useless gun in it and waving it back over his shoulder, said pleasantly, "Yes, in a minute." He was a little preoccupied at the moment. He was walking home. He had something he wanted to tell his parents and he was walking slowly home in Atlanta and . . .

"Catton! *Stand still, Catton!*"

Catton said, "In a minute." There was no harm in him; he was simply walking home.

He didn't think the gun in Catton's hand was loaded.

Catton, turning, a shadow on the landing, said, drifting, going, said in a sudden soft southern accent, "There's just some small little thing I have to—" He was at the door to his parents' house. His head was cocked slightly to one side as if he were smiling to himself. Catton said, "In a minute, Beau—first I just have to . . ."

"You're dying. You're bleeding to death." Tillman, rooted to the spot, said warningly, "Catton, just turn around and—"

> *Rally, rally, rally—*
> *Glug, glug, glug,*
> *In your hopper . . .*
> *And keep the stopper!*

He was giggling. He had gotten a watch for it. Like his mother, he was a true Southerner. He knocked on the door.

"*CATTON!*"

"Madam." The door opened and there was a woman there holding a baby in her arms. She looked a little like his mother.

Catton, taking her hand and starting to bow, said gently, graciously, "Madam . . ."

"CATTON—!" He had the gun up. A light from a lamp on a trestle table in the room was shining through the open doorway. It illuminated the woman's face and the face of the child. As he bent to kiss the woman's hand it illuminated the knuckle-duster knife-pistol in his hand.

"Catton! Turn around here and—"

He saw the woman's eyes grow wide. He saw her jerk with fear. The baby against her breast was awake, staring. He saw the woman see Catton's face as he straightened up.

Catton said, weeping, sniffing, "Madam, oh Madam . . ."

He let go her hand.

Tillman shrieked, "CATTON—!"

Catton said suddenly, *"We'll eat those Rebels for sup!!* Rally, boys, *rally!"*

Her eyes were terrified. She could not understand a word. Tillman saw her jerk back with the child in her arms.

"Boys, rally, rally . . . !" Catton said, "God damn it, *I did it for you!"*

He saw the hand jerk and there was a snap and a flash of bright steel as the switchblade knife came out from the end of the revolver, and he heard the woman scream, and he heard—

He saw the knife come back.

"CATTON!"

He saw the knife come back. He saw the skewer.

With the last round in the Lightning, aiming for the head, he shot him instantly, stone cold dead, where he stood.

. . . he heard there, in the half-light, in the doorway of the room, the baby, safe in its mother's arms, suck in its breath, fill its lungs with air, and—wonderfully, new and fresh with life—wail.

28

He drew a breath. On Cherry Street standing by his carriage watching the two bodies being loaded into the backs of the horse-drawn ambulances from Bellevue, Chief Inspector Byrnes said, shaking his head, "So they were all sodomites?" He had the Vicksburg daguerreotype in his hand together with Catton's gold watch and the colored glass bottle stopper from Cahill's body: "All of them."

Across the street at the entrance to Gotham Court Muldoon was being helped to a police carriage by Sergeant Fitzgerald and an ambulanceman. He had not been shot, but pierced by the glass flute in his waistband when he had been thrown against the stairway wall by Catton's rifle shot. He had his tunic open to his waist, Fitzgerald a step behind him inconspicuously shuffling bits and pieces of the broken flask into the gutter with his foot as they fell out of Muldoon's pants. Muldoon's great hairy barrel chest was circled by a bandage. It was a huge, hairy barrel chest. In the street, respectable women in the crowds from the tenements looked away. Tillman said, "Yes, sir." Muldoon looked across at him and winked.

It was a little after 8:00 A.M. on a dull, slate-gray morning when the crowds of men and women and children should have been at their honest work. There were uniformed men from the Broadway Squad, all over six foot two inches in height, Byrnes had brought with him to move the crowds along, and he beckoned with his finger for them standing in a knot to spread out and move the crowds along. He looked down at the photograph. Byrnes said, "This one, Carrol, he dressed as a woman?" Byrnes said, to make sure, "He's dead, isn't he?"

"Yes, sir. He was Schweib's lover." He saw Byrnes's face. "After

253

his friend Albert Schweib was murdered at Niblo's he assumed he was going to be next. He assumed Muldoon and I were his murderers. He killed himself out of fear and grief."

"And Fenney, and Carver, this 'John,' and this other one 'Charlie'?"

"We never found them. Nor, apparently, did Colonel Seward or any of the others." Tillman said, "It was a ragtag unit of sodomites quickly transferred from other units and put together to keep them away from married men and young boys."

"Commanded by this man Seward."

"Yes, sir."

"Who was another one."

"Yes, sir." Tillman said, "The unit such as it was was sent to guard a bayou on the approach to an important Union supply dump during the attack on Vicksburg by Sherman. Sherman's supplies came down a single line and could be cut by a single cavalry action at exactly that point." Tillman said softly, watching Catton's body covered by a bloody sheet being loaded into the back of the first ambulance, "Van Dorn's cavalry hit their position at dusk and cut them to pieces in minutes because that morning the defenders had all been poisoned, and when the attack came they were all either dead or crawling away sick into the swamps. Van Dorn's force was therefore completely intact when it hit the magazine at Holly Springs and was able to destroy it completely and, single-handed, change the course of the war for almost three months." Tillman said, "I don't know it for a fact, but I think the survivors were all court-martialed for cowardice and cashiered out of the Army." Tillman said, "I think the Colonel, Seward, has been trying to prove for almost twenty years that they were not cowards."

Byrnes said, "Catton?"

"Schweib recognized him at the theater as the man who had driven a comfort wagon into the bayou and dispensed free tonics to the troops to keep their spirit up. The tonics were poison of some sort. He and Carrol and Cahill went to Seward with the news that they actually had the man they believed had done it to them and they—"

Byrnes said, "Set out on a course of blackmail."

"I've no evidence of that." Tillman said, "I'm not even certain at first Schweib recognized him. In 1862 Catton must have been only twenty-two or twenty-three years old. What Schweib or Carrol may have realized was that the inspector-mark on a Confederate pistol one of them kept from the battle was the same as the mark on some of the guns Catton's company made in the north after the war. Schweib may have confronted him the night he was due to make a presentation to Professor Quarternight, or just spoken to him and suddenly recognized him, and Catton killed him."

Byrnes said, "Catton was in the audience that night I was."

"At one stage he must have had to go out to get the rifle he was to present at the end of the show. It would have been sensible for him to have left it with the stage-door man, Schweib, for safekeeping." Tillman said, "The rifle was a custom-made engraved weapon that would have taken months to manufacture and engrave. It may well have been the last gun the inspector at Catton's factory, Townes, inspected. It may have been that exact gun that had the marks on it Schweib recognized." Tillman said, "It was a fine gun. Any man having it in his safekeeping would have looked at it. He may have caught Schweib looking at it and Schweib—" Tillman said, "After Catton killed Schweib, he simply ran out at the stage door around to the front entrance of the theater and came in with the rifle." Tillman said, "Schweib's death was in the newspapers. When Muldoon and I went to Bleecker Street to Carrol's room, he—"

Byrnes said with his mouth twisted, "She. It—"

Tillman said, "—committed suicide."

Byrnes said, "God Almighty!" The crowds were being pushed back by the Broadway Squad. They were fine examples of what police should be. Tall, straight, firm, towering with authority, they moved the crowd back by the simple fact of their presence.

"You look disgusting, Tillman. Look at you: your clothes are torn and your shoes scuffed and you stink of gunpowder and dust and dirt and God only knows what else!" He reached out to take the lapel of the man's coat between his thumb and forefinger, then changed his mind. Byrnes said, "You look like a chimney sweep!" Byrnes said, "You've got blood all over your shirt!" He didn't want to hear any more. Byrnes said, shaking his head to get it over quickly, "What about this man Reynolds—the one killed at Edison's? He wasn't another—"

"He was the head of the Confederate Secret Service."

"Married? With children? A normal man?"

"His wife and children were killed during the war. He was the one who conceived the idea of sending Catton in with his wagon in advance of the cavalry. He had his own plan to blackmail Catton. He paid a deposit on what had been his lost family home on the expectation that when Seward and the others confronted Catton with their evidence of what he had done, he would have been in a position to extort payment—" Tillman said, "He had no charge of cowardice to lay to rest. Like the others, he was a ruined man, but all he had need of to restore his position in society was money."

Byrnes said, "Your friend Humpty Jackson destroyed a building on Clinton Street by Gatling gunfire."

Tillman said, "Reynolds knew for a fact that Catton was the wagon driver because he himself had recruited him."

Byrnes said, "For money."

"Catton may have lived some time in the South when he was a boy." Tillman said, "After the killing of Schweib and the suicide of Carrol, he tried to question me in Mulberry Street about the investigation. When I told him nothing he broke into my lodgings in order to read my casebook notes. He followed me and Muldoon to the Pearl Street generating station not knowing who we were looking for—as we had no idea who we were looking for— recognized Reynolds, and killed him on the spot." Tillman said, "He followed us here for Cahill."

In the ambulance wagon Muldoon must have felt faint. The ambulanceman was giving him a tot of medicinal brandy to force down. Byrnes said, as Sergeant Fitzgerald must have also had a touch of vapors and got a drop himself, "Poison!"

Tillman said quietly, "Yes, sir. It was in the tonic bottles. Somehow Catton must have been given permission to pass through the Union lines with his wagon, and somehow—"

Byrnes said with a snarl, "People will drink anything if they believe it will do them good." He wished to God he could have men who kept themselves clean. "Dress something with a pretty label or a colored stopper and people of little intelligence will believe every claim it makes for itself and rot their innards with it." He took a step forward to scream at Fitzgerald before he took another swig, but Fitzgerald, seeing him, did not take another swig and went through an elaborate charade of grimacing at the filthy, unfamiliar taste of the spirit. Byrnes said, "I assume, Tillman, that your fingernails are not normally in that filthy, broken condition?"

Tillman said, "No, sir."

He wondered, sometimes, what the world was coming to. Byrnes said with sudden feeling, "Poor Professor Quarternight! How hard is the row he must hoe to see his vision of a proud, honorable society come to fruit with such people everywhere around us!"

Tillman said, "Yes, sir."

Byrnes said, without force, "Your hands look like a sewerman's." There was a silence. "Your clothing is totally ruined, you know." He sighed. He looked down, "And those boots can never be worn on official duty again, if ever. Detective Grafton, I note this morning, is in a brand-new suit for the opening ceremony at the new bridge—perhaps you should consult him privately for the source of his dress sense." Byrnes said, "Or perhaps invest in material of a more durable kind." Byrnes said with disgust, "Sodomites. Cowards. Spies. Men dressed as women . . . sexual insanity and alcoholic ruin: it is hardly suitable material for one's memoirs, is it?" He glanced at the crowd drooling over the two bodies in the ambulances covered in bloody sheets, "And as for the public exposition in the newspapers—"

"Yes, sir."

"Yes." In the alley where Cahill had been killed one of the Broadway Squad, ever mindful of decent behavior, had found a pail of water and was carefully washing away the blood and other matter from where Cahill had been killed. Byrnes, to himself, said, "Yes." He looked away and down at Tillman and the blood and gunpowder and ruined clothing and scuffed boots and filthy hands. Byrnes said quietly, "People don't think much of a fellow who's killed someone, you appreciate." He saw Tillman, for an instant, look away. He looked him up and down. "Perhaps—" Byrnes said, deciding, "The official bridge opening with the President in attendance is to be at 2:00 P.M. this afternoon." He reached into the pocket of his coat: "I happen to have several spare tickets for the spectator area." Byrnes, handing them over gingerly, avoiding the filthy claw that took them, said, "Perhaps, City Detective, in view of the—the situation—perhaps, perhaps rather than being part of the official police contingent on the bridge—"

He looked hard at him. It was an order.

Byrnes said, nodding, trying to force a smile, "I think perhaps—um, Virgil—all things considered, perhaps, instead, you should stand privately. . . . With friends."

29

He stood with Flossie and her cat.

"This greatest achievement of mankind!" It was the President, Chester A. Arthur. Flossie was dressed in her best finery and her new hat. She squeezed Tillman's arm. Flossie said, "Oh, isn't this wonderful!" The President in his shining top hat stood on a dais out in the open air of the bridge footway with the great cast-iron edifice of the Manhattan terminal behind him. *"This most magnificent expression of the genius of man!"* There were soldiers of the 7th Regiment in full parade uniform surrounding the dais, looking outward, the wood and steel of their polished rifles gleaming in the sun. There were policemen in dress uniform with epaulets and glittering silver badges with plumes in their helmets, Overseer Wilson from the Edison Electric Company looking up at the incandescent lamps that would light the mile-long bridge at night, firemen in brass helmets, on the dais with President Arthur, Grover Cleveland the Governor of New York State and his lady, the Mayor of New York Franklin Edson nodding and smiling, bareheaded, his black hair pomaded until it shone like ebony, bishops, vicars and rectors smiling blessings, and—everywhere—stretching back as far as the eye could see, people in their best suits and dresses, the women a garden of silk parasols and exclusive hats.

There were bands waiting, photographers waiting. At night there would be the turning on of the lights and a display of five hundred monster exploding rockets.

She wore a silver souvenir medal Virgil had bought for her. It was on her breast. *"Two Cities As One! New York and Brooklyn!"* She was a little flushed. She fanned herself and Archie the cat and Virgil with a souvenir fan.

Dimensions of the Great East River Suspension Bridge

It was printed on the fan with a chromolithograph of the great structure linking the two cities across the river.

The Bridge crosses the river by a single span of	—1,595 feet.
It is suspended by four cables each in diameter of	—15½ inches.
The width of the Bridge with tracks for carriages, steam trains and walks for foot passengers is	—85 feet.
The approach to the Bridge on the New York side is	—2,492½ feet.
The approach to the Bridge on the Brooklyn side is	—1,901 feet.
The height of the Bridge from the center of the span to the water is	—120 feet.
The estimated cost of the Bridge is	—$15,000,000.

It was too good to use. She folded it and slipped it into her satin purse. Flossie said, "Look! It's Mrs. Roebling!"

He was a beautiful, courtly man with kind eyes and wonderful, luxuriant side-whiskers. He was the twenty-first President of the United States, a New York man himself. President Arthur, bowing to Mrs. Roebling as she mounted the dais to stand beside him and Mrs. Arthur, said, *"This triumph of the genius of the Roebling family!"* Like ants, down all of the 2,492½ feet of the approach to the bridge on the New York side, inside the cast-iron terminal and spilling out of it, there were over seven thousand invited guests. Unlike the police and politicians and firemen and Tillman and Flossie by the ceremonial ribbon thirty feet in front of the dais, they could hear nothing. Men in the crowd relayed the voices, *"Engineer John A. Roebling! Engineer Washington A. Roebling! Mrs. Emily Roebling!"*

FIRST TRAIN ACROSS THE BRIDGE, THURSDAY,
MAY 24, 1883.
PUBLIC SERVICE WILL COMMENCE
SEPTEMBER—FARE 5¢.

It was the Second Avenue Elevated driver in his winged helmet. The painted banner hung from the cabin of Number 39, "THOR." THOR was waiting carriageless a little outside the terminal in the midst of the crowd, puffing steam on the center rail track, polished like a jewel. There was applause at the mention of Emily Roebling's name, then a cheer. THOR blasted out steam like a dragon.

Flossie said, "Oh, Virgil!" He smiled at her. Flossie said, "You look lovely." He was bareheaded in his new suit. Flossie said, squeezing, patting him on the arm, stroking Archie against her breast, looking down at her medal, smelling of attar of roses, "Oh, Virgil—" She giggled.

He saw Byrnes, Grafton, Fitzgerald and wincing Muldoon in the police contingent. He saw Chief of Police Walley in a uniform befitting a French Field Marshal. He saw bankers, backers, businessmen, judicial bench sitters, nabobs, aldermen in great gold chains. He saw the Press, like hawks, scribbling and sketching. He saw, behind them, big-wheel cyclists with ribbons and pillbox velvet caps, behind them again, in the crowd, sandwich sellers and fan and medal vendors, hot-potato wagons with black-peaked chimneys puffing smoke.

The President said, "You all know how, so many years ago, the patriarch of the Roebling family, Mr. John A. Roebling, the builder of the Monongahela Bridge in Pittsburgh, the Niagara Bridge, the Allegheny Bridge and the Cincinnati–Covington Bridge of 1867, conceived of a single great link between the two cities of this our premier state and how, only his preliminary drawings done, he was accidentally cut down by cruel fate in 1869. You all know how his son took up the fallen flame and then himself was crippled while on the construction of the great caisson on which we stand while working below the waterline at a depth of one hundred and twenty feet in pressurized air, his body crazed beyond repair by the awful curse of the bends and how, e'en then, with the *spunk* of the Roeblings not dimming with each generation, Mrs. Emily Roebling who is here today took over the reins of the great task herself—a mere woman—oversaw the construction of this great project for . . . *for fourteen years!*"

There was a cheer. It began close to the dais and was relayed back and swelled.

"—but there may be those among you who do not know that for each of those fourteen years—in all this long five thousand one hundred days, Washington A. Roebling, crippled, in steady, unabating pain and torture from his destroyed mortal shell, sat at his window in his house on Columbia Heights and watched, oversaw, checked, followed every step of the construction however minute it might be through the glass of a telescope!" Chester Arthur said turning to the north, *"He is there now!* He watches us at this exact moment, at the pinnacle of his triumph, unbeaten, unbowed, his vision strong and unwavering, his—" He was overcome with emotion. He laid his hand on Mrs. Roebling's shoulder. "After the ceremonies, at 3:30 P.M., I go to pay my homage to him. I go to—" He wiped away a tear, "I go to—I call to him from his creation, yea, on the very brink of declaring his victory full—I call to him and all the twenty thousand men who labored on it, to Mrs. Roebling, to the immortal spirits of John Roebling—to those Americans!—Huzzah, Mr. Roebling! Huzzah! Huzzah! HUZZAH!" The President shouted, *"He can hear you! He heard you!"*

The President, waving his hat, shouted to the north, "Huzzah! *HUZZAH!"*

It relayed. It grew. It swelled. It sang on the roadway and on the approaches and in the terminal and far back toward the roads and streets of the city, into the city itself. It raised itself past all the wires and cables and flags and bunting into the Heavens.

"HUZZAH!" It was the roar of ten thousand voices.

She gripped her cat hard against her breast.

Flossie, all flushed, her eyes shining, said in ecstasy, "Oh, Virgil, Virgil, Virgil—!" He was her beau; she was his lady.

"HUZZAH! *HUZZAH!"*

Flossie, joyous beyond words, her eyes full of emotion, said, shining, "Oh, Virgil—*it's all just so wonderful!"*

In the river below the bridge, all the piers along the shoreline were packed with people.

In the river there waited at anchor six Navy battleships from the North Atlantic Squadron, their turrets trained up to the skies, their decks lined with sailors in their dress whites, their masts and wires flapping with bunting. Around them all the ships and boats of New York and Brooklyn were there: the black, iron-hulled screw-prop three-masted steam-and-sail New York to Havana *Crescent City*, its decks lined with day-trippers, its bow like a light attracting moths a-buzz with yawls and skipjack oystermen sloops and cutters; the 408-foot Pacific Maid steamer *The City of Peking* off a little astern of her, riding at anchor, people crowding her railings looking up; the Hudson River Steam Company's ferry *Swamp Robin*, listing with humanity, white and shining and puffing smoke; the ferry *Columbia*; the 400-foot-long sidewheeler *Thomas P. Way*, the Jersey ferry come around from the Hudson River with a thousand passengers dressed for a picnic; the *America*, dressed in bunting, the last of the Fulton Street ferries, laden with celebrants, celebrating a final trip before the breakers' yard; the excursion steamer, *The President Polk*, its paddlewheels slapping spray; the river itself churning and white-foamed with turning screws and scurrying pleasure boats.

The bridge above them in the afternoon light was a shadow, a cloud, a cobweb, a symphony of wire and cable and stone.

President Arthur thundered, "The wire wedding of New York and Brooklyn! The joining together of Athens and Rome! The link, the pathway, the steam-train track from the darkness of the caves to the light of a new age!" The crowd was applauding him, cheering. "From this day, no man—"

There were whistles in the river, sirens, steam horns.

In the river, all the sailors lined up on all the decks of the monster gray battleships shouted, "HUZZAH!"

There were hydrogen balloons breaking loose on the roofs of all the buildings along the waterfront piers; picnics, parties in progress with top-hatted and straw-boatered men with glasses of champagne, ladies in silk dresses and wide hats with fruit juices. According to their respective stations in life, they were in circles and groups and knots along the roof of the Police Gazette building, on ships' chandlers' porches, warehouses, bank establishments, on the streets looking up, in the alleys and lanes applauding and smoking cigars and gaping with admiration, in the deserted and ruined places like Jasper Ward Alley with their children in rags, remembering the day.

They were color, life, humanity.

Above them towered the Triumph of the Age.

"—no longer—"

Everywhere the voice of the President, his clothes and face and whiskers glowing like a monument, his stance like a statue's in a holy place of the nation, was relayed to his people.

"—no longer can any man say, 'The tyranny of distance exileth me from my brother's side.'" He glanced at Overseer Wilson in the crowd. "Tonight, this web shall shine with the lights of a thousand artificial stars. This day, at either end of the span that links two cities, telegraph offices have been set up and any man may send a message across singing wires to any other man in the country. This day steam trains shall give terror to Time and cross a great river—cross a hundred and twenty feet above a river in the sky itself—in the twinkling of an eye! This day—"

In his cabin Engineer First Class Geraldus van Meer let go a piercing shriek of delight from THOR's whistle.

"—this day, our Republic comes of age!"

On all the ships, all the sailors led by bearded, clench-fisted officers brimming with pride, cheered. On all the boats and all the ships, Old Glory flew.

On the dais President Arthur's cabinet of Republicans, nodding, smiling to constituents, puffed with pride.

"*Soon telephone wires will link us!* A statue of the goddess of Liberty out there"—he threw out his hand toward the ocean— "A Colossus like Rhodes—a modern wonder of the world—will stand welcoming humanity to our shores!" He dropped his voice: "There are men of genius at this very moment inventing machines that will cut distance itself into fractions!" It was a secret known only to him. "But I can say no more about that. There are men on the brink of creating perpetual-motion machines that will slave uncomplainingly for the betterment of humanity without ceasing!" The President said, "American genius! Freed from the constraints, the chains, of the Old World we Americans are not serfs to history, but we have become the lords of it!" The President roared, "Today we link two great cities into one! *What nation on Earth has ever done such a thing before?*"

She glowed with pride. She was a lady, he her gentleman.

She held her cat hard in her arms. Her hands were trembling. Flossie said, "Oh, Virgil, Virgil . . ."

He smiled at her.

Flossie said, "You lovely man. You handsome, lovely man . . ."

Thor was nine tons of Firnley tank locomotive. It was the New Age. In his cabin van Meer touched at his golden winged helmet and blasted at Thor's whistle.

Flossie said, "Oh, Virgil, I—"

"*SHUN!!*" In a single clatter, all the soldiers slammed their boots onto the ground and came to attention. On the bridge, high up, done by an invisible hand, a giant silk flag of the Union, a star-spangled banner, snapped out and stood proud in the breeze.

"*I go now to declare this triumph open and, on behalf of the Government, give it as a gift to the people!*" The President put his top hat on. It was a wonderful hat, gleaming black and perfect with the labors of the finest hatters in the land. "Where are the golden scissors that will cut the tape and the bonds of the past?" The scissors were on a velvet pillow held by a colored man wearing a white, powdered wig and cutaway coat. Arthur said, *"No man in our nation is this day the slave of another."* Arthur said, beckoning him over, "I go arm-in-arm onto the footway of the bridge with Mayor Edson to snip once at the bonds and shackles that bind every man and show him the way into the light of liberty and transport and into, a child advancing at last on firm feet, into the New Age!"

He walked, he passed not like any other man, through the crowd. On the river and on the waterfront, all the commotion and bustle was stilled. On the bridge, the crowd opened and stood back and tried to see his face which was the face of a President and was not like the face of an ordinary man as it glowed, groomed, clear-eyed. Men and women stood back as his shoes fell with the soft tread of a man who did not smell as other men did, who did not perspire or become disheveled. Each of his whiskers was set exactly where it should be.

Flossie said in a whisper as he advanced, not toward her, but to one side where a yellow ribbon across the bridge, on orders, in awe, had stopped flapping in the breeze and stayed still like a painting, "Oh, Virgil. Oh, Virgil, I may faint away—!"

The President's eyes looked kindly into every eye that eyed him. There was a hush.

"Oh, Virgil—" He saw her. She looked into the President's face. Flossie said quickly, "Archie, look—!" She had Tillman's arm in a grip of iron. She held Archie the cat against her breast with her other arm so tight he jerked. Flossie said, "Oh—oh—" She thought, as he glanced at her, as she saw his kindly, good face, that the President might speak to her. "Oh, sir—" She was going to say, "Oh, sir—" Or—"Mr. Arthur, sir—" or, "Sir, Mr. Arthur" or—

Flossie said, "Oh, Virgil—!"

She squeezed her cat.

"God bless you good people one and all!"

In his cabin, van Meer rested his hand on Thor's whistle cable.

In the river, with no order, in all the gun turrets of all the batteries of guns on all the battleships, gun layers loaded six- and eight-inch blank charges into chambers and slammed shut the breeches.

Everywhere in the river and along the waterfront and on the bridge itself flags flew in the rising breeze in glory.

In all the city, at 2:00 P.M. and one minute exactly, there was a hush.

On the bridge, loosing himself gently from Mayor Edson's arm, President Chester A. Arthur took up the golden scissors and held them on high for the good, godly people to gaze upon in glory.

Flossie said in a whisper, "Oh, Virgil . . ."

He smiled and, without looking at her, patted her hand like a husband.

She squeezed her cat until Archie's eyes began to pop. He squirmed. She did not feel him. Flossie said in a prayer, an orison to her corsets, "Oh, please, please, Flossie, don't faint . . . !"

Archie's eyes went bulbous.

In his cabin, Engineer van Meer's hand trembled on his whistle.

The flags on all the ships flew bravely in the breeze.

He was not a mortal man. He was the twenty-first President of the United States. His hat gleamed like polished jet.

He touched at the ribbon and drew it in toward him with his smooth, beautiful hand, his manicured fingernails gleaming like little perfect shells: "At this historic moment, at this cutting, this severance—this *linking*—"

Archie's body, from ears to tail, jumped like a spring.

"*This, this*—"

It convulsed. Running out of air, it convulsed from one end to the other.

" YOU USURPER OF THE DREAMS OF ALL FREE MEN!"

Arthur said, "What—?" He turned.

It leapt. In Flossie's arms, going for the air, Archie leapt.

"YOU FALSE LEADER! YOU STEALING MAN! YOU THIEF OF THE NATION! YOU—*JUDAS!*"

Archie was up in the air, turning over, somersaulting, six feet off the ground, falling fast toward it, turning over, its tail stiff, flying, landing.

Arthur, looking back, said, "What—?"

There was gunfire. There were the twin booms of revolvers fired fast into the air. There was a cheer. There was a roar. There were signs, placards appearing in the air. At the far end of the crowd on the approaches there was a commotion. Arthur said, "What?" He looked around for someone to tell him. Arthur, the scissors in his hand, his eyes wide with fear, said to anyone who might listen, "What? *What the Hell's happening?*"

He saw Democrats! Democrats! Everywhere there were signs and placards and yells going up. They were the yells, not of good, grateful Republicans, but of Democrats!

"JUDAS!!" He heard a deep voice ring out down the length of the approach. He saw, for an instant, a cat hit the footway of the bridge by the ribbon and begin running. He saw—

"HUZZAH!" He heard a cheer. It was not for him. He saw, coming, the commotion. He saw the crowds part. He saw—

"Virgil! *Save my cat!*" He saw a small black-suited, bareheaded man with a loose woman duck under the ribbon for the running animal. They thought it was part of the ceremony, the people by the ribbon. They yelled, "HUZZAH!" The crowd on the approach was parting, opening. There was a commotion there. The bridge was full of Democrats. Chester Arthur, looking for somebody, anybody to tell him what was happening, yelled, "What? What? What's happening here?"

He saw, in that instant coming at him at the gallop, the Spirit Tumbleweed of the Prairie, the Undisputed Champion Shot of the World, Professor C. K. Quarternight, the New York Democratic Party Presidential Candidate, coming at him in his full buckskin dress, whooping and yelling, his ivory-handled pistols in their holsters on his beaded belt, a glittering, razor-sharp silver saber in hand high above his head ready for the kill.

"*JUDAS!*"

On Liberty, unstoppably, he was covering the last fifty feet between them like a steam train.

There were whistles, sirens, yells, cheers.

The bridge was salted everywhere with Democrats.

On the bridge, riding for the President and the yellow tape, Quarternight shrieked like a madman, "Judas! —*JUDAS!*"

30

People were running, fleeing. On the wooden roadway he was riding over rolling parasols, smashing them, splitting them into shreds of bamboo and silk and wires, sending the shreds up into flurries with fans and rolling hats, ribbons and the effluvia of the fleeing. Women were running, screaming, running and weaving to get away with their husbands' hands on their shoulders pushing them. On the roadway, Liberty's hooves clattered like musketry. There were placards, posters appearing in the crowd, then disappearing, being pushed down as the fleers collided with the salted Democrats and knocked them down.

Thor's whistle was screaming nonstop, the engine panting, blowing, sending out gushes of live steam as van Meer, overwhelmed in his cabin by Republican supporters or men afraid for their children, his helmet knocked from his head, hung on to the whistle cable like a mountaineer being pummeled by rock falls.

"JUDAS!" He hit a spinning parasol full stride and tore it to shreds. He was covering the last fifty feet to the ribbon like a steam train. He was whooping, yelling, his silver saddle and silver pistols and beads and boots flashing in the light, all of Liberty's leather and silver and nickeled buckles shining like the charger of a knight. Quarternight shrieked, "Republican *Judas!*"

Against the railing of the bridge Flossie was cowering, her eyes wide with terror, her eyes flitting back and forth to Archie on the bridge with Tillman. She heard the hooves bear down on her and the man on the white horse was coming for her with punishment in his eyes, the horse's nostrils wide and flaring, and then there were running men in the way—a black man wearing a white wig and a soldier—and then as Quarternight slashed at them and sent them

267

cringing, he was pointed in another direction and she looked around for somewhere to go.

There was nowhere to go. At the dais, Byrnes roared to his policemen, "Do *nothing!* This is a political matter! Look to your jobs and do *nothing!*" He was rushing back and forth in the uniformed mass gathering his charges up like chickens. He saw the Captain of the 7th Regiment knocked down on the roadway screaming orders at his troops—in the chaos he heard nothing of what he said—and the honor guard were breaking and covering the President and Mayor Edson and Mrs. Roebling, pulling them back, surrounding them, getting them back to the dais in a phalanx.

He was on his back like a turtle, being run over, his bandaged side where the glass had been on fire with the kicks and blows of the running, shrieking people. Muldoon, trying to fight his way up, looking for Flossie and Tillman, catching a blow from a shoe in the side of the head that sent him spinning, yelled, "Virgil—" and then Quarternight was above him. He looked up and above him he saw the huge white horse in midair leaping over something, coming down like death, all its flanks white with foam and sweat, and then he saw the silver sword, butt-end down, club someone hard against the temple and Overseer Wilson from the Pearl Street Station was beside him on the ground rolling and bleeding, and the hooves came down in a shower of sparks struck from the iron nails in the wooden roadway and he saw, for an instant, Quarternight's face, and rolled away.

"JUDAS ARTHUR!" The voice was a bellow. He was reining back on the horse, turning it, wheeling it, making it prance. He could not see President Arthur for the soldiers.

Quarternight roared, "*Judas! Betrayer!*" Quarternight screamed at the troops, at the bridge, "No more immigration! No more *infestation!* A land made for *white men!* A land fit for the men who tamed it!" He saw Arthur being propelled up the dais steps, ducking, keeping down. Quarternight, wheeling, striking sparks from the nails, roared at him, "*A land fit for freeborn men!*"

Someone hit her. People were always hitting her. Against the iron railing, Flossie felt someone drive a fist hard into her ribs and she was caught in the web of rails and uprights and cast-iron dolphins and acanthus leaves being pushed through, and then, as the fleeing crowd tried to force by her, she was being lifted up and over and she saw the river below the bridge and she was being forced over.

"*Exclusion! Exclusion!* A land for Americans! Exclusion! *Exclu-*

sion!" He was turning, swinging the sword, screaming at the top of his lungs. There were people coming toward him, running, placards held over their heads with pictures of heathen Chinese devouring white women painted on them in crude colors, great Negros with watermelon mouths grinning over the burning pyre of a map of the nation ripped in half, caricatures of sail and steam ships laden with the moronic faces of foreigners pus-filled and running with plague and cholera and insanity, Quarternight himself on his white horse, and everywhere, everywhere portraits of Arthur conspiring with all the degenerate races of the world at a table stacked head-high with gold.

On the bridge Quarternight shrieked, "Alarm! *Jews!* Mormons! Africans! Chinese!" He had the sword held high. He swung it in an arc about his head, his face flushed and running sweat, his eyes wild: "Alarm! Alarm!" He was shrieking to the heavens, "Alarm! Alarm! I sound the *alarm!*"

She was going. He had her. She was going over and Virgil had her, but it was not Virgil, and she saw Virgil for an instant on the bridge with Archie in his arms fighting the crowd to get through to her and it was Neddy Muldoon and she felt his arm like a tree trunk take her around the waist and lift her up and then a groan as someone pushing, shoving behind her tried to push her over and was felled like an ox and she was in his arms, against his chest, and she was safe, saying, "Neddy . . . Neddy . . ." as he took her away.

"I SOUND THE ALARM AS PAUL REVERE ONE HUNDRED AND EIGHT YEARS AGO SOUNDED THE ALARM!" It was his famous ride. It was to be his famous ride. On the roadway, kicking at Liberty with his silver spurs, Quarternight, the silver sword flashing in the air above his head, turning, wheeling, thundered to the city, "THE MAN OF THE PLAINS SOUNDS TO YOU—THE ALARM!" and he was riding hard for the ribbon across the bridge scattering men fleeing in that direction, sending them back, knocking them off their feet, clearing the way.

"I SOUND—" and he was at the ribbon with the sword held high above his head—the way to the other side clear, the way to freedom and honor for freeborn men clear—and he was at his moment in history.

"I SOUND—"

He was at his moment of glory.

"—I SOUND THE ALARM!" and the sword, glittering in the

light, all the strength in his arm welled up into one single blow, slashed through the ribbon as he passed by it and turning, in a frozen instant that no man might ever repeat—a moment to be engraved on every newspaper in the land and every history book ever to be written—he lifted Liberty's head up and he was an icon.

They were frozen, stilled, become background. They were his people. He was henceforth, forever, immutably, theirs. He was the man on the white horse. It was the crowning pinnacle of his life and the life of his nation, and he said, in that moment, not the words that he had practiced, but the words that in that moment, in that instant, came out wild and joyous and triumphant and unguarded and glorious.

He was in his enshrinement. He was on the brink, at last, of grandeur.

On the bridge, the words chilled Tillman to the bone.

On the bridge, there, then, his eyes wild and staring, Quarternight, exhorting, putting backbone and courage into men, shouted, prancing his horse, "Rally, boys, *rally!* Boys, rally! Rally! *Rally!*"

31

. . . **A**nd it was him.

And it was *him!* He was the one. It was not Catton, it was him. The name F. C. Catton on the wagon at Vicksburg had been painted over to be replaced by something else, something that would get the wagon through the lines. It had been painted over by the name QUARTERNIGHT. Catton had only been in his early twenties at Vicksburg; Schweib hadn't recognized him at Niblo's Theatre twenty years later, and he hadn't suddenly recognized Quarternight because he already knew it had been them—Reynolds had already told. What had happened was that he had seen the presentation rifle with Townes's inspector's mark on it which was the same as the mark on the old rusted gun one of Van Dorn's cavalrymen must have dropped at the bayou—and he had found his last piece of evidence linking them.

It had all taken too long for it to have been Catton—Seward and Schweib and Carrol and Cahill had met at the house up on One Hundred and Thirty-first Street weeks before the killing.

Schweib and Seward and Carrol had been gathering evidence. They had found Cahill, told him nothing because he was a drunk, but taken him to Seward's as another one, another survivor, another piece of evidence. It was him. It was Quarternight. Like President Arthur on the bridge, he had passed through the crowd—the crowd, because of who he was—had opened for him like a river and, like Vicksburg, because of who he was, what he had been, what he meant—*beyond suspicion*—he had passed through unchallenged.

He had been the reason the medicine wagon had passed through the Union lines without challenge.

On the bridge, Tillman, transfixed, stared at him.

It was him. He was the one.

It was *him*.

It was Quarternight.

It was him.

He was a hero of the West, a pioneer. He was a man the Dime Novels wrote about, an Indian-tamer, the man of the prairies, the plains. In his buckskins and silver, six-foot four-inches tall with his great moustaches and flowing hair, he was a legend. He was the savior of women and children, the undisputed champion shot of the world. On Liberty, the curved silver sword above his head, he was every man's secret heart—*and it was him!*

On the bridge, turning the horse, wheeling it, making it prance, a glittering giant holding back the crowds by the slashed and flapping ribbon, Quarternight roared, "I recall to your minds—"

He wheeled. He controlled the great white horse as if it were part of him. He turned it, made it obey his wishes, touched it not at all with the shimmering Mexican spurs on his buckskin boots: "I recall to your minds—"

People were still running. They were coming up from the rear where the fighting at the train was. By the dais, the Captain of the 7th Regiment honor guard, drawing his pistol from its holster, ordered his disorganized troops, "Two cordons! First squad form a cordon where the ribbon was! Second squad on me!" He was a West Pointer. His President was behind him at the steps of the dais, down low with his lady and the Mayor of New York and his lady and Mrs. Roebling. They were safe. The first squad and the Captain's pistol protected them. The crowds were not violent, they were merely swirling and running, the placards and posters held not as weapons, but as placards and posters. Between the dais and the spot where the ribbon had been there was a space. The crowd had not yet made it there. Beyond that spot there was the man on the great horse and, farther away down the bridge and a little man holding a maddened, fighting cat in his arms. The Captain glanced back to see President Arthur and could not see him for the height of his squad.

The Captain, holding the pistol by his side, taking charge, a hero before the gaze of his Commander-in-Chief, ordered the first squad, "*Cordon—line!* First squad cordon line across the bridge, arms at port!" They were running, forming the line. At the dais, the crowd was coming, swirling.

"Second squad—fix . . ."
And he stopped them, he halted the crowd.
". . . *bayonets!*"
He stilled them where they ran with the sight of the cold steel.
"First squad . . ." They had the cordon line formed across the bridge.
". . . one round ball ammunition . . ."
The man on the white horse, like a knight, was wheeling, maneuvering, like a knight, magnificent, martial, all his weapons and armor glittering in the light, the great white horse, foaming with sweat, its nostrils flared like a charger's, striking sparks off the roadway with its shoes.
". . . LOAD!"
And he stopped them. He stopped the crowd.

"—I recall to your minds the hour of peril one hundred and eight years ago! I recall to your minds *another* rider, *another* clarion call!"
And it was him. It could have been no one else. He was the one who had taken the wagon through the bayous at Vicksburg. Catton had been twenty-two or -three years old—he was only a companion, a lackey, a hander-out of medicine bottles, a gun salesman.
"I recall to your minds the night of April the eighteenth, seventeen hundred and seventy-five when *another* man carrying a sword rode the length of our nation crying a warning to all the humble homes of America—"
His voice was rich, deep, histrionic. He was the spirit, the chalice of all that had gone before. He was a mountain man, a scout, an Indian slayer. He was the West.
"I recall to your minds *Paul Revere!* I recall to your minds the infestation of our shores, not this time by the British, but, this time, by the subhuman effluvia of the world! I recall to your minds the Chinaman and the Jew and the Slav and the heathen and the sweating, oily Arab! I recall to your minds the terror in the eyes of the wives and daughters and maids in your households! I recall to your minds President Arthur who will not sign the Chinese Exclusion Bill! I recall to your minds—"
Tillman screamed at the top of his voice, "It was you! *You* were the one!"
"I recall to your minds—"
"You!" In his arms, Archie, held fast, was howling and slashing with its claws. Tillman, starting to move forward, yelled, "There!

At Vicksburg! At the swamp before Van Dorn's assault—it was *you!*"

"I recall to your minds—"

Tillman screamed, "It was YOU!"

He turned on his horse and saw him, saw a fly, a sparrow, a nothing. "I recall to your minds—"

Tillman shrieked, "Schweib! Carrol! Reynolds! Murphy! Catton, one way or another, killed them all—*for you!*" He was alone on the bridge, moving forward, moving backwards, the cat in his arms frantic with fear. Tillman shrieked, *"It will buoy you up, Hip, hip hooray! And keep you fit—"*

From the crowd, Byrnes screamed, "TILLMAN—"

"and ready for it—"

"TILLMAN—!"

"Bonny brave soldiers in blue, This is the free fortification for you!"

"TILLMAN!"

His face was drained of color. He held the cat in his arms in a grip of iron *"Glug, glug . . . In your hopper . . . And keep the stopper!* Rally, rally, rally . . . !"

"Tillman, I order you to—" It was Byrnes. He was on the dais, his fist clenched, shouting.

"You go to *Hell!*" He was advancing on Quarternight, pressing Archie hard against his chest with his left arm, freeing his right hand, reaching inside his coat, his breath coming in gasps.

Advancing, Tillman yelled—

At the dais, the Captain, his voice ringing out with no hesitation in it ordered his squad at the cordon, "SHOOT ANY MAN WHO DRAWS A GUN!"

Tillman screamed— He took his hand out of his coat. He saw the glittering sword in Quarternight's hand. He saw Quarternight's eyes. Tillman, on the bridge, alone, holding the cat, trembling, full of strength, shrieked, "You had Catton kill people for you—ruined people, people with nothing! You killed them twice over! You killed them at Vicksburg and then here again, and you did all of it, here and at Vicksburg . . . you did it all for *money—!*"

He saw Quarternight's eyes. He saw what was in them.

Tillman roared, "You *scum—!* You *filth—!*"

Tillman roared, "You *scum—*you *filth . . . !*"

He had from his inside pocket not his gun, but Reynolds's glittering glass bottle stopper flashing with light in the sun.

It was a talisman, an amulet, shining with light like a crystal.

Tillman roared at the top of his lungs, "You . . . *TRAITOR!*"

* * *

He was finished if he was wrong.

He was finished if Quarternight disdained him.

He had no evidence. He had only what he had deduced. The Thinking Detective. The Ratiocinator. Like Byrnes's ten-cent Sensational Novels. Like Byrnes's ten-cent Sensational Novels and their *clues*.

On the bridge, Quarternight said, "I recall to your minds—"

Tillman yelled, "Traitor! You worked for the South in the Civil War and you killed men and you were a *traitor!*"

"I recall to your minds the midnight ride of Paul Revere when . . . when in all the humble houses of America, he . . ." He was looking back, losing his thoughts, letting the sword drop to his side and then bringing it up again. Quarternight said, stronger, "That epic moment in our history when *one man—one man alone—*"

"You poisoned men! You came under false colors like a thief and you poisoned men at Browne's Bayou so Van Dorn's Southern cavalry could cut Sherman's supply line in half! They promised you no survivors, but there were men—boys—there on both sides who could not deliver the final killing shots and the degenerates and sodomites, men less than human who survived to crawl away, were tainted with dishonor and cowardice and sentenced to rot, to hide after the war wherever they could find refuge!"

He saw the crowd stilled. They were not stilled by the soldiers' guns and bayonets. They were stilled to listen. Quarternight shrieked, *"This is not true!"*

"—but they tracked you, they followed you! They followed you, tracked your every move for twenty years! They tracked the hero of the West, piece by piece, bit by bit, writing letters, gathering evidence, locating survivors—and they found Buford Townes's name on the Gilbert and Greer pistols that had slaughtered them and they found the same name on your pistols and on the rifle Catton gave you at the theater!" He was moving forward, back. Tillman yelled as Quarternight made the horse trot, stop, hold its ground, then trot again in circles, "The sickness and death in the swamp wasn't God-sent! The sickness and death was sent by you!" Tillman shrieked, "You poisoned them with something concocted by you and by Catton and by Major General Reynolds of the Confederate Secret Service!"

"I know nothing of such things!" He could not control the horse. It

was jerking and pulling its head around against the slackened reins. Quarternight, jerking hard at the beast, pulling it up, jabbing it hard with the rowels of the Mexican spurs and then, as it tried to rear, pulling the bit hard into the mouth, roared to the crowd behind the cordon of armed men, "I know nothing of such things! In the war I was a hero to the troops! I put courage and backbone into boys not old enough to be away from their mothers' aprons! Boys fighting for the flag that this day flies proudly from the bridge, the same flag that flies proudly in every hamlet and village and town in our nation!"

"You fought—you slinked like a thief in the night—for the *South!*"

He touched at his ivory-handled revolver. He saw the rifles of the troops.

"You did it not for loyalty, but for money!" Tillman screamed before the man could answer, "You were a nothing! You were nothing but a reputation! All you had was your name and stories about what you had done before!" Tillman demanded, "Gilbert and Greer—did you have shares in the company? Did you part-own it—was that what you protected that day at Browne's Bayou—or did Major General Reynolds—"

"I owned nothing in the villainous South!"

"—or did Reynolds offer you something else as a reward?" Tillman, holding the stopper up like a beacon, yelled, "You got no watch! What did you get?" Tillman, turning to the cordon of soldiers, watching their guns, keeping his own hands out in the open locked on Archie and the stopper, yelled, "What he got, whether the South won or lost, was the machinery and the factory!" Tillman yelled to Quarternight, "Catton owns nothing of the American Gun Company—it is your company, it was your machinery he got from the farmhouse in Virginia! He had no bill of sale, his removal of the equipment onto the train up here to the North was not questioned, because it was all in your name!" Tillman said with disgust, "Your name! Doctor C. K. Quarternight, the Western Long-Eye, the Spirit Tumbleweed of the Prairie, Champion Shot of the World—" Tillman screamed, "And *TRAITOR!*"

"I—" He tried to turn to the crowd.

Tillman yelled, "All I have to do is check the ownership records of the company in New Jersey!"

"The company in New Jersey was set up to manufacture the rifles that

each free man must own to protect his home from the infestation of immigration!"

"Catton killed Schweib because Schweib knew! He killed Schweib because that night at the theater Schweib had all his evidence in place and he wanted—" Tillman said, "What? What did he want?" Tillman said, "He wanted his name cleared, did he? He wanted his name and the name of all the others cleared from the charge of cowardice, from the belief each of them had lived with for twenty years that their own fear and terror killed them and made them ill—" Tillman screamed at the man, "If it had been money—if all they had wanted was money you could have bought them off—but they didn't want money, they wanted reputation!" Tillman, moving toward him, said with eyes full of hatred, "They wanted *your* reputation!"

"I know nothing of such things!" Quarternight, turning back to the cordon, the crowd, called out, "Paul Revere! I recall to you—Paul Revere—"

"Rufus Carrol killed himself because he thought he was next! He fought until he had only one bullet left and then he put his gun to his head and killed himself!" He was facing the man, twenty feet away, looking up at him like a sparrow shouting at a lion, "At Mulberry Street Catton tried to see my case ledger—to see who else there was—he broke into my home to find it and he followed me to the Pearl Street Station to see who was there—and he found Reynolds there! Reynolds could have been bought off with money! For money Reynolds would have denied everything and kept you safe! Reynolds was waiting for you to be given the Democratic nomination—waiting for you to be someone—and then you could have bought him off with money!" Tillman said, "Reynolds—for money—probably would have helped Catton kill people for you!"

"You are a Republican sent here to slander me by my enemies!" Turning, fighting the horse, Quarternight said to anyone who might listen, *"He's a Republican sent here to slander me!"*

"How many more were there? After Cahill? Or were Catton's final orders simply to kill me and Patrolman Muldoon and put a stop to it there and then?" Tillman, seething with an urge to get to his pistol, yelled, "He blew Cahill's head off like an overripe watermelon!"

"*You* are a watermelon! A nigger! You are a nigger in disguise and— Mr. F. C. Catton, I learned recently quite by accident, was a Southerner on his mother's side." He was facing the crowd. He was talking to faces, the troops, he was talking to no one.

Quarternight said, "I was going to break cleanly with him, because although he may have fought bravely and well as a gentleman for a cause he believed in at the time, this great Union of ours is yet not fully healed from—"

Tillman shrieked, *"He was a spy and so were you!"*

"I know not what he may have done during the war, but the mere fact that once he faced our bonny boys in blue in arms—" He wrenched at the horse which no longer felt his power: "The fact that he may have—"

"He was a spy for the Confederate Secret Service under Reynolds and you, you were a *mercenary!*"

"These are lies!" Quarternight, wheeling, his face twisted, his sword pointing at Tillman's heart, yelled, "This man is a *Jew!*"

"And you are a *traitor!*"

"A Jew and a foreigner!" Quarternight, wrenching the horse back to face his supporters, demanded, "Look at him! He is small like a European—like a rat, or a bird or some evil black thing that scuttles in the slums and Casbahs of an Arab shit-pot!" He shrieked, "Look at him! He wears no hat! His suit is new! He has been dressed and tricked up and made to look like one of us—to sound like us—by conspirators against the United States, by foreign potentates and sultans and international Jews and niggers and he has—"

His voice carried. Tillman said with his voice strong and firm, "You are nothing. All your exploits are lies. All you have is your name and your name is a lie." Tillman said softly, "You even lied to Reynolds. At the battle of Vicksburg, like him, did you really think the South could still *win?*" He was scum. He was filth. He was a man on a white horse dressed in tailor-made buckskins and glittering carnival geegaws. *"Did you even care?"*

"This man—this man—"

Tillman said so his voice carried to the crowd, "Did you ever really rescue a maiden from the savages and mortgage her life with your own? Did you ever really do that? Did you ever blaze a trail in the mountains? Did you ever? Really? Did you ever really live on the prairies or the plains? Or did you only ever live in the theaters and the tent shows of the cities? *Did you ever serve your country?* Any country? *Anyone?"* Tillman screamed, "Did you ever do anything in your life that was noble and good and pure? *Or did you live your entire life as a lie, as a sneak, as a poisoner—as a coward!"*

"I will be President of these United States!"

Tillman said, "You will hang."

"I will be President of the United States!"

Tillman said, "You will hang in the courtyard of the Tombs prison on Centre Street and then your body will be buried in quicklime with no marker."

"I WILL BE PRESIDENT!"

"Virgil—" It came from the crowd. It was Muldoon.

Tillman said, "You will be dead." Quarternight had his back to him and he could not see his face.

Somewhere up near the troops, Muldoon, caught, unable to get through, could see his face. Muldoon yelled, "Virgil—!"

Tillman, his hands trembling as he held the cat, walking forward, said, "I arrest you for the murders of—"

"*Virgil*—!" Muldoon screamed, "Virgil, LOOK OUT!"

Quarternight screamed, "Jew! Dago! Nigger!" He was turning, slewing the horse around, the strength in all his body in his spurs against the horse's flanks, overwhelming, mastering it, the sword in his right hand coming up and glittering in the light. On the bridge, Quarternight screamed, "All my life—! All my life I have been purer and better than other men!" Quarternight yelled, "Nigger! Jew! Mormon!" The spurs ripped deep into flesh and drew blood in spouts from Liberty's flanks. Quarternight, his face mad and wild, his features a death's-head under the flowing black hair, maddening the horse, screamed, "Now! Now—!"

Quarternight, slewing the horse, making it skid as it turned, screamed into the crowd, "You! You scribblers! You chroniclers of great deeds! See a Dago *die!*"

He was a giant on a great white horse with the silver sword held high in his hand for the death cut.

On the bridge, Liberty's hooves striking sparks from the nails in the wooden roadway, he came at Tillman like a banshee, screaming and swirling the silver, glittering, razor-sharp sword above his head.

He was screaming, whooping, gone mad, the great sword slicing through the air above his head, the horse's nostrils flaring, the eyes wild and maddened from the spurs, out of control, bolting, the air rent by the thunder of the hooves on the roadway.

His life was being expressed out in seconds. He was frozen, alone. In his arms Archie was snarling, scratching, hissing, eyes wide and bulbous, claws out and ripping at Tillman's coat, fighting to get free.

"Virgil—!" He heard Muldoon roar. He saw, vaguely, away, down there, the soldiers pushing and being pushed, being shoved aside. He saw blue uniforms. He felt the roadway trembling under his feet and Archie was against his chest fighting and convulsing and he could not get to his gun under his coat, could hit nothing with it if he did, would be shot dead by the soldiers if he tried, and the horse, its hooves like the thundering of a pile driver was huge, beating down on him, filling the sky and the bridge, the sword above the mad, wild face, glittering, flashing, going up for the blow.

Tillman said, "Oh, my—God!" He saw it come down. He saw the sword come down. He saw the skewer. He saw the point come down and aim for his heart and he felt his chest convulse and his heart stop. He saw it come. This time, he saw it come. His hands were over his heart, holding Archie. He felt the ice cold of the blade in his chest: he felt his chest take it and accept it and all the steel pierce through him and kill him before it pierced him and killed him and he felt his life still and freeze, and he felt Archie in his arms kicking and clawing, hissing and snarling.

On the bridge, a moment before the clash, he was an insect. He saw the horse's great chest ten feet from him, all its muscles and sinews working. He saw the mad, screaming face behind it. He saw the sword come up. He saw it point at his heart for the death blow. He felt everything, everything he had done in his life had been for nothing.

He felt—

He felt—

He did not die.

He had Archie in both hands at his chest. The cat was roaring like a lion, spitting, hissing, claws out and wicked. He heard, a moment before he struck, Quarternight scream with triumph, and in that moment, this time, he did not die.

In that moment, with all the force he had, he threw the cat with all its claws out and stiffened past the horse and, like a panther, into Quarternight's face.

And in that moment he did not die. And in that moment as the horse, its mouth torn and wrenched from the bit, went over backwards, he saw the sword falling away from Quarternight's hand as he clawed at the cat embedded in his face like daggers, and he did not die.

And in that moment—

And in that moment—

On the ships' bridges, they saw it. They saw something happen, a commotion, an event, a man doing tricks on a horse and they thought they were too late and missed the signal and the moment was past. On the bridges, bearded men reached for the speaking tubes that connected them with the gun turrets and whistled hard down the tubes to give rapid orders.

"Virgil!" He was running with Fitzgerald and the policemen, dragging at his pistol, pushing the soldiers and their rifles aside. He saw the horse going, rearing. He heard a terrible scream as flesh was torn away.

He saw the horse going up, the sword in Quarternight's hand falling away. He saw the horse skid and fall, collapse. He saw Quarternight's face ripped and torn as Archie held him. He saw him fall, crash, be rolled under and pinned. He saw Archie leap free and snarl in triumph. He saw—

In the river they had ready for the celebration a tremendous salute.

"FIRE!"

In the turrets, simultaneously, all the gun layers touched at the electric triggers of their guns in a single salvo.

And in that moment, he did not die.

On the bridge, shouting, entreating, imploring, Tillman called across the city to anyone, anyone who might hear, "My name is City Detective Virgil J. Tillman, thirty-four years old! Is there anybody—? *Is there anybody out there who knows me?*"

32

In the evening, with the wonder of Electricity, the bridge—a beacon in the city—was lit from end to end with a thousand incandescent lights.

Ablaze from the New York side to Brooklyn, the pyrotechnicians fired off their exploding rockets from it all night, like comets, into the sky.